BREAK

D0665234

In a daring departure from its long established policy of publishing only non-fiction works, **Look** magazine offered Leon Uris' sensational new novel to its readers. What made **Look** break tradition?

TOPAZ

"MR. URIS' LATEST AND MOST EXTRAORDINARY WORK . . . Although it is fiction, many of the incidents are based upon fact. His sources include former members of various diplomatic and intelligence services . . . their revelations [are] presented with the skill of . . . one of the most popular storytellers of the twentieth century."

—Look Magazine

BREAKING RECORDS!

Leon Uris' most explosive novel,

TOPAZ

TOPAZ

A NOVEL BY

LEON URIS

*This low-priced Bantam Book
has been completely reset in a type face
designed for easy reading, and was printed
from new plates. It contains the complete
text of the original hard-cover edition.*
NOT ONE WORD HAS BEEN OMITTED.

RL 8, IL 9-up

TOPAZ
A Bantam Book

PRINTING HISTORY
*McGraw-Hill edition published October 1967
4 printings through February 1968*

This book appeared in 2 issues of LOOK *Magazine in
September 1967*

*Bantam edition | September 1968
22 printings through December 1980*

ISBN 0-553-14845-1

Published simultaneously in the United States and Canada

---

*Bantam Books are published by Bantam Books, Inc. Its trade-
mark, consisting of the words "Bantam Books" and the por-
trayal of a bantam, is Registered in U.S. Patent and Trademark
Office and in other countries. Marca Registrada. Bantam
Books, Inc., 666 Fifth Avenue, New York, New York 10103.*

PRINTED IN THE UNITED STATES OF AMERICA

31 30 29 28 27 26 25 24 23

This book is dedicated
to my friend
Herbert B. Schlosberg

CONTENTS

TOPAZ

PART I

ININ

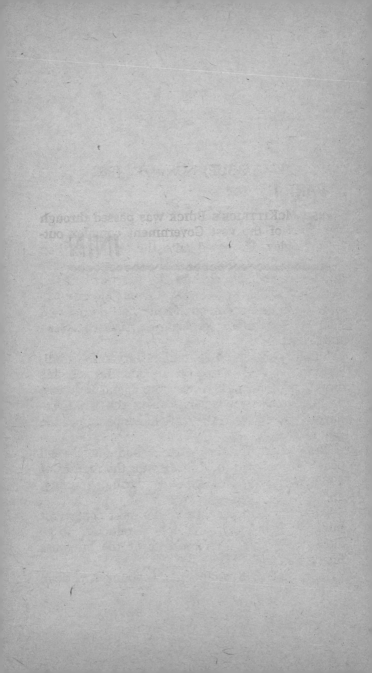

(PROLOGUE) SUMMER, 1962

MARSH MCKITTRICK'S BUICK was passed through the gates of the vast Government complex outside Langley. He eased onto the turnpike, then sped toward Washington, touching his briefcase nervously and looking into the rearview mirror. Two cars filled with heavily armed guards followed closely. Sanderson Hooper beside him and Michael Nordstrom in the rear seat remained speechless.

Marsh McKittrick felt small victory in the vindication that was about to be his. Responsible directly to the President on intelligence matters, he had argued vociferously about the Soviet behavior in Cuba since the terrible happening at the Bay of Pigs.

The Soviet Prime Minister had interlarded peace pledges with bold threats for the months of 1962 and acted with growing daring, cunning, and menace.

Sanderson Hooper, one of the most competent intelligence evaluators, had been reluctant to go along until now. The contents of the briefcase finally convinced him.

In a matter of moments the young American

President would be faced with a terrible decision. And was not this decision too great a judgment for a single mortal? Was it not God's decision if the human race should survive or perish?

For an instant McKittrick disliked his own fleeting thought that the President might back down under the sheer weight of the consequences. Who really knew or had any way of knowing the President's steel? Well . . . we'll all soon find out, McKittrick thought.

His hands became clammy on the wheel of the car. He sighed a half-dozen times to relieve the tension that welled in his chest and he looked again to make sure the guard cars were close at hand.

He opened the side vent to spill in fresh air for relief from the heavy pall of pipe smoke glumly puffed by Sanderson Hooper.

All the clues were there. The sudden increase of shipping from Soviet-bloc nations into a revitalized Cuban port, the influx of thousands of Soviet "technicians." Numerous unidentified trips to Moscow by key Cuban officials. What did the Cuban buildup mean? There was no real proof, only a myriad of speculations. But it was enough to create a growing uneasiness in the American Congress and rumbles for action.

With instant access to the President, McKittrick, Nordstrom, and Hooper were led immediately to the office in the West Wing.

Marshall McKittrick unsnapped his worn briefcase, withdrew a folder of reconnaissance photographs which had been taken by a U-2 aircraft from high altitude. He spread the pictures on the President's desk and handed him a high-powered magnifying glass.

4

"Woods near San Cristóbal, Mr. President. This site has been recently cleared. Blowups and the photo analysts will be here within the hour."

"Spell it out, Mac," the President said tersely.

McKittrick looked to Hooper, then Nordstrom. "It is still speculative but we are all in accord. . . ."

"Spell it out," the President repeated.

"In our opinion, the Soviet Union is introducing missiles into Cuba armed with atomic warheads and aimed at the East Coast and Midwest United States."

The President set the magnifying glass down slowly, resigned that he would have to hear the words he had so long dreaded.

"We are in a state of grave national crisis," Sanderson Hooper blurted as if speaking to himself.

"I'll say we are," the President answered with a tinge of irony in his voice. "Once we walk out of this room . . . . people can start getting killed."

(1)
LATE SUMMER, 1961

THE DAY WAS BALMY. The certain magic of Copenhagen and the Tivoli Gardens had Michael Nordstrom all but tranquilized. From his table on the terrace of the Wivex Restaurant he could see the onion dome of the Nimb, saturated with a million light bulbs, and just across the path came a drift of laughter from the outdoor pantomime theater. The walks of the Tivoli were bordered with meticulous set-in flowers which gave out a riot of color.

Michael luxuriated in detailed observation of the strong, shapely legs of the Copenhagen girls, made so by the major source of transportation, in that flat city, bicycle riding.

He fiddled with the little American flag on the table as the waiters cleared away a few survivors of three dozen open-faced Danish sandwiches.

Per Nosdahl, who sat behind a Norwegian flag, passed out cigars and held a light under Nordstrom's. Michael puffed contentedly. "The boss would frown on us smoking Castro stogies. I miss Havana," he said to his deputy in Denmark, Sid Hendricks.

7

Per imposed a half-dozen cigars on Michael, who gave in then patted his filled breast pocket.

"So, we'll all meet again two weeks from today in Oslo," said H. P. Sorensen, speaking from behind a Danish flag.

The other three nodded. Michael took a last lovely swig of beer from his glass. "I keep telling Liz I'll bring her to Copenhagen some summer. You know, strictly on a vacation . . . whatever the hell that is."

The headwaiter approached. "Is one of you gentlemen Mr. Nordstrom?"

"Yes."

"Telephone, sir."

"Excuse me," he said, folding his napkin and following the headwaiter from the terrace into the enormity and plushness of the Wivex. The orchestra played the "Colonel Bogie" march from *The Bridge on the River Kwai*, and the Danes kept jovial time by clapping in rhythm.

The waiter pointed to a phone booth in the lobby.

"Thank you." Michael closed the door behind him. "Nordstrom," he said.

"My name means nothing to you," a heavily accented Russian voice spoke, "but I know who you are."

"You've got the wrong party."

"You are Michael Nordstrom, the American Chief of ININ, Inter-NATO Intelligence Network. You sign your cables with the code name 'Oscar,' followed by the numerals, six, one, two."

"I said you've got the wrong party."

"I have some papers of extreme interest," the voice on the other end persisted. "NATO papers in the four-hundred series. Your contingency

8

plans for a counterattack if the Soviet Union invades through Scandinavia. I have many other papers."

Nordstrom squelched a deep sigh by placing his hand quickly over the mouth piece. He caught his bearings immediately. "Where are you?"

"I am calling from a phone booth over the Raadhuspladsen."

Nordstrom glanced at his watch. One o'clock. It would take several hours to formulate a plan. "We can set up a meeting for this evening. . . ."

"No," the voice answered sharply. "No. I will be missed. It must be done immediately."

"All right. Glyptoteket Museum in a half-hour. On the third floor there's an exhibit of Degas wire statuettes," Nordstrom instructed.

"I am familiar with it."

"How can you be identified?"

"Under my arm I carry two books, *Laederhalsene* in Danish and *The Rise and Fall of the Third Reich* in English."

"A man named Phil will contact you." Nordstrom hung up.

The first obvious thought that crossed his mind was a rendezvous trap in which the Russians could photograph him contacting a Soviet agent for future blackmail use. He would send his deputy in Denmark, Sid Hendricks, to make the contact, then lead the man to a place which he could cover against being followed or photographed. The pressing time factor annoyed him, but bait or not the Russian's opening gambit was taken.

Michael placed a coin in the phone box and dialed.

"American Embassy."

"Nordstrom. Get the ININ office."

"Mr. Hendricks' office, Miss Cooke speaking."

"Cookie, this is Mike Nordstrom. You're buddies with the manager of the Palace Hotel . . . what's his name?"

"Jens Hansen."

"Get him on the horn and tell him we need a favor. Large suite at the end of a hallway. Something we can block off and cover from all directions."

"How soon?"

"Now. Send four or five of the boys down, tape machine and cameras. I'll meet them there in twenty minutes."

"Got it."

Michael Nordstrom was a bit heftier than he would have liked but he still moved with deftness and grace. He wove his way back to the terrace quickly. A scream shrilled out from the roller coaster. "Sorry, fellows, office wants Sid and me back right away."

The Danish and Norwegian ININ chiefs stood and they all shook hands.

"Have a good trip back to the States," H. P. Sorensen said.

"See you in Oslo, Mike," Per Nosdahl said.

Sid Hendricks reminded Sorensen they had a meeting next day and the two Americans departed.

They got into Sid's car on H. C. Boulevard. "What's up, Mike?"

"Russian. Maybe a defector. Go right away to the Glyptoteket's Degas exhibition on the third floor. He'll be carrying two books, *Laederhalsene*— and, uh, *Rise and Fall*, the Shirer book, in English. Identify yourself as Phil, then have him

10

follow you. Waltz him around the Tivoli a few times to make sure he isn't being tailed by his own people. End up at the Palace Hotel. One of the boys from your office will be waiting and tell you where to take him. If you don't show in an hour, we'll know it was a setup. Check him out carefully as you can."

Sid nodded and got out of the car. Nordstrom watched him cross the avenue. The curtain, a mass of bicycles, closed behind him. Nordstrom emerged from the other side of the car for the short walk to the Palace, then grumbled beneath his breath. This sudden turn of events would force him to cancel a date with a lovely Danish miss.

(2)

FIFTEEN MINUTES had elapsed when Sid Hendricks entered the block-long red brick building housing a conglomeration of art treasures, sponsored by a Danish brewery.

He paid a krone admission, bought a catalogue, then made directly up a long flight of stairs on the right side of the main lobby.

The room was empty. Hendricks studied it for unwanted guests but could spot none. He thumbed through the catalogue, then moved around the dozens of Degas wire studies of horses and ballet dancers, each an experiment to capture phases of motion. He stopped before a glass case and looked long at a particularly magnificent piece, a rearing horse.

"Unfortunately, we do not see much Degas in the Soviet Union."

Hendricks squinted to try to catch in the glass

11

the reflection of the man who had slipped up behind him, but all he could make out was a transparent disfiguration.

"A few pieces in the Pushkin Museum in Moscow," the Russian accent labored, "and somewhat better in the Hermitage, but I do not get to Leningrad often."

Hendricks turned the page in the catalogue. "Never been there," he answered, keeping his eyes straight ahead.

"I have. I'd like to leave."

"I don't think we've met."

"Not formally. You are Sidney Hendricks, in charge of the American ININ Division in Denmark."

"Anyone can get that information out of the Embassy Directory."

"Then, how about this information? Your boss, Michael Nordstrom, is in Copenhagen to meet the Danish and Norwegian ININ counterparts, Nosdahl and Sorensen, to discuss expansion of an espionage ring of Scandinavian students studying in the Soviet Union."

With that, Sid Hendricks turned and faced his adversary.

The two stipulated books nestled tightly under the arm of a man of shorter than average height. Russians look like Russians, Hendricks thought. High forehead, suffering brown eyes of a tortured intellectual, uneven haircut, prominent cheekbones, knobby fingers. His suit showed Western styling but was sloppily worn.

"Follow me and keep a hundred-foot interval."

Hendricks passed from the room through a group of incoming art students and their instructor.

On the street he waited on the corner of Tietgensgade until the Russian emerged from the museum, then crossed to the Tivoli Gardens and paid an admission into the Dansetten.

Cha-cha-cha music favored the midafternoon dancers. Sid sighted in on a pair of unescorted girls sitting hopefully in a corner, and invited one to dance. His cha-cha-cha left much to be desired but it did give him a total vantage. The Russian entered, watched, did not appear to have followers.

Hendricks abruptly left the astonished girl and plunged into the maze of zigzag paths, hawkers, strollers, the labyrinth of glass buildings, the blaze of flowers, the multitude of restaurants, exhibits, fun and amusement booths, the fairyland that made up the wonderment of Tivoli.

Sid Hendricks led the Russian in circles. Along the artificial boat lake he doubled back so that he walked past his pursuer, then made up the steps of the multitiered Chinese pagoda. From here he could look down and study all the activity below. Only the single Russian clung to his trail.

He was now satisfied that the Russian was not being followed, and he passed from the Tivoli, crossing the teeming Raadhuspladsen filled with the usual complement of pigeons that inhabit city-hall squares throughout the world.

His deputy, Dick Stebner, waited in the lobby of the Palace Hotel. Without further word, the three walked the stairs to the third floor. The long corridor was covered by Hendricks' men. Stebner made down the carpeted hall to an end suite, opened the door and the three of them entered.

Harry Bartlett, another deputy, waited by the false fireplace. The Russian stood in the center of room. The lock clicked behind him.

"Who are you? What do you want?" Bartlett asked.

"I want to see Nordstrom," the Russian retorted. "You are not Nordstrom. You are one of the ININ men in Hendricks' office."

The bedroom door opened slowly. Michael Nordstrom entered. His bulk made the Russian seem even smaller. "Yes," the latter whispered, "you are the one I wish to see."

"Shoot."

"Shoot?"

"Who are you? What do you want?"

The Russian studied Stebner and Hendricks at the door and the other one, Bartlett. "My compliments to you, Nordstrom. You are very good. You did this quickly and your Hendricks is clever. Do you have a cigarette?"

Michael cupped his hands to hold the flame and his eyes met the Russian's. The man was frightened despite his professional poise. He sucked deeply on the cigarette as though calling on a friend and he licked his lips in a gesture of fear.

"I am Boris Kuznetov," he said, "chief of a division of KGB. I wish to defect."

"Why?"

"I have reason to suspect I am going to be liquidated."

"What reasons?"

"Two close comrades in KGB who shared my views have been purged recently. I travel in the West often. This time surveillance on me is unusually heavy. And then," he sighed, "a close dear friend told me before I came to Copenhagen that if I have a chance to clear out, I had better make the break."

14

Kuznetov pulled hard again on the cigarette. He knew the men arrayed before him would naturally suspect he was a plant.

"This friend of yours," Hendricks said, "wasn't it dangerous for him to warn you?"

"It makes no difference if you are a Russian or an American, Mr. Hendricks. Our profession is cruel, yet . . . they cannot take from us all that is human. Humans, in the end, are compassionate. Someday you may need a friend. Someday a friend will need you. Do you understand?"

"If you are under such tight watch," Nordstrom challenged, "how did you cut yourself loose just now?"

"I am in Copenhagen with my wife and daughter. I left them at the restaurant. As long as they have guards on my family they know I will return, so it is normal for me to be away for a few hours, perhaps to make an intelligence contact, perhaps to shop, perhaps even to visit a woman. But I am a devoted family man and I always come back."

"How did you know I would be at the Wivex Restaurant?"

"Because of your basic intelligence attitude. We Russians hide our intelligence people and never let it be known who they are. You Americans advertise who is CIA, who is ININ, on the theory that people will come to you with information. In this case, your theory works. It is not secret you are in Copenhagen. You always eat at Wivex or Langelinie near the Little Mermaid. You like Danish seafood. It is not hard to find out. Today I checked your reservation at Wivex and so I ate at Seven Nations just over the square."

"You said you carried documents."

"Yes. They are hidden in Copenhagen. I will tell you where they are when we make our agreement."

"All right, Kuznetov. I'm impressed. We'll get back to you in twenty-four hours."

"No!"

"What do you mean?"

The Russian's breath quickened. Fright, real or played, was in him. "I am afraid now to return to my embassy. We must do it right away . . . today, and my wife and daughter must come with me."

Kuznetov studied the skeptical American eyes. They all glowered in suspicion at the man who called himself Kuznetov, watched him fidget and breathe deeply over and over. The clock from the city hall tolled the hour, massively.

"How long can you stay out now?" Mike Nordstrom asked.

"A few more hours."

"Get back to your wife and daughter, then go shopping or do the Tivoli for a few hours. I'm going to make a try at putting it together. Do you know Den Permanente?"

"Yes. The building that houses the permanent exhibits of Danish arts and crafts."

"It closes at five-thirty. Be there at the counter at the silversmith, Hans Hansen. It's near the main door. Now, take a good look at these three gentlemen. One of them will be standing by to lead you to a waiting car."

"You must not fail!"

"There's a fifty-fifty chance we can do it."

"My guards . . ."

"We'll handle them."

The Russian called Kuznetov walked slowly to

16

Michael Nordstrom and held out his knobby hand. Nordstrom shook it, haltingly. And then Boris Kuznetov walked to a seat, sank into it, held his face in his hands and sobbed.

(3)

NORDSTROM DISPATCHED Stebner and another deputy to tail the Russian, then sped back to the embassy with the rest of his people, locking the ININ offices behind them.

TOP SECRET EYES ONLY TO SAILBOAT 606. CONTACT MADE COPENHAGEN WITH BORIS KUZNETOV. CLAIMS TO BE KGB DIVISION CHIEF. DESIRES TO DEFECT WITH FAMILY. PLANS UNDER WAY. I WILL TAKE FULL RESPONSIBILITY. NEED GREEN LIGHT IMMEDIATELY OR NO GO. OSCAR 612.

Coats off, ties open, sleeves rolled, Michael Nordstrom and his men plunged into formulating a quick but foolproof plan. They set into motion the obtaining of cars without diplomatic plates, finding a hideaway on the northern coast, getting a light plane on stand-by and flying Nordstrom's own plane out of Denmark to a German airfield. Individual assignments were passed out and rehashed. The minutes ticked off too quickly, and as the hour neared five o'clock, ashtrays brimmed and the tension rose to fever pitch.

The phone rang.

"Mr. Hendricks' office. Miss Cooke speaking."

"Cookie, this is Stebner. Boss there?"

She handed the phone to Michael. "Nordstrom."

"Stebner. Do we go?"

"No word back from Washington yet. If I don't hear in ten minutes, we cancel. What's your picture?"

"He just entered Den Permanente with his wife and daughter. We've spotted four guards working in two pairs."

"Did the guards go inside the building?"

"They sure did."

"Beautiful. I'm sending a half-dozen of the fellows down now. Stake them out around the entrance. If we get a cable to go, watch for Bartlett driving a blue, 1960 four-door Ford sedan with German plates. You make the hookup with Kuznetov and get in with him."

"Got it."

Nordstrom set the phone down and sent the men off to cover the Den Permanente entrance. He and Miss Cooke waited alone in the office. They both lit cigarettes. He paced. She tapped her long-nailed fingers on the desk. All around Copenhagen, bells rang out the hour of five.

"I guess we're out of business," Nordstrom mumbled.

Sid Hendricks tore in from the code room and set the cable before his boss.

TOP SECRET TO OSCAR 612. GREEN LIGHT. SAIL-BOAT 606.

Den Permanente houses the works of Danish artisans from crystal and silver to modern teak furniture and wild patterns in fabrics. Like Denmark itself, the place was not large, but its wares were magnificent.

Near the building, Stebner and a half-dozen ININ agents waited for Bartlett and the blue Ford.

18

Stebner took a position so that he could clearly see Boris Kuznetov with his wife and daughter. They came down from the second floor. Mrs. Kuznetov read the time from a lavaliere watch. Stebner wondered why her husband loved her so. She was a drab and dumpy woman. The daughter, he estimated, was about twenty. A fine figure, but it ended right there. Severe hairdo, no make-up, flat shoes.

Stebner glanced over to the first set of guards. He was positive of them because he knew that one was an Assistant Resident of the Soviet Embassy. This pair lolled about a table filled with carved wooden figurines of comic Vikings, those monkeys who hang arm to leg in a chain, and several families of teakwood ducks.

The second set of guards was a pair of women hovering over a fabric counter. They used females, no doubt, to be able to keep tabs on the Kuznetov women, even in the public toilets. The Russian women stuck out like a pair of sore thumbs among the lovely Danish creatures around them.

Boris Kuznetov pointed to the display counter of the silversmith, Hans Hansen, and they walked toward it, containing their tension admirably.

Down the block, a blue Ford turned the corner.

The ININ agents closed in on the entrance as the car moved into the curb lane and inched through the ever-present sea of bicycle riders.

Now it was halfway down the block.

In the building, the five-thirty closing bell rang.

Kuznetov looked desperately toward the door.

Stebner took a step inside and nodded. The Russian offered his arm to his wife and daughter, took the few steps outside quickly.

The guards dropped the merchandise they were fingering and followed.

Stebner slammed the doors of Den Permanente in their faces, shoved Kuznetov and his family into the rear of the blue Ford and got into the front beside Bartlett.

Kuznetov's guards flung the doors of Den Permanente open and rushed to the sidewalk, only to collide with an ININ man on a bicycle who rode into them. Everyone sprawled to the ground, and as they scrambled to their feet the other ININ agents jostled and bumped them creating an instant of confusion, just long enough for the car to turn the corner and go out of sight.

It sped north out of Copenhagen along the coastal road with the Kuznetovs crouched in the back. Beyond the suburb, Bartlett turned the Ford off the highway and onto the pier at Taarbaek to switch cars.

Nordstrom and Hendricks were waiting in the front seat of a Mercedes, Stebner transferred the Kuznetovs and Bartlett returned toward Copenhagen again.

Nordstrom turned to the shaken family. "Everything's going to be all right," he soothed. "Try to keep calm."

Kuznetov nodded that he understood.

"You owe me something. Some documents."

Kuznetov took a baggage claim check from his wallet. "At the luggage storage at the main railroad station."

It was given to Sid Hendricks to follow through and then they continued north. A few minutes before Elsinore stood Kystens-Perle, "The Pearl of the Coast," built like a ship with the superb Hamlet Restaurant on the first floor and hotel rooms above. A most chic place for lovers to rendezvous. Stebner guarded the door of Room 6, while Hendricks and Nordstrom kept the family calm inside. Fear, that most prevalent of Russian products, had consumed them into a stunned whiteness. A torturous hour passed, during which he learned little more than that Mrs. Kuznetov's name was Olga, and the daughter's Tamara.

The sharp ring of the phone startled them all.

"Hello."

"Sam?"

"Speaking."

"This is George. Cessna 310 is at the Elsinore Airport, cleared, warmed up and ready to go."

"We're on the way."

The flight was choppy. The damnable northern European weather moved in and flung them around. Tamara Kuznetov became sick, adding to everyone's discomfort in the small craft.

It turned dark and the weather had fallen nearly to the ground as they approached the British air base at Celle, in northern Germany.

From the Ground Controlled Approach shack on the strip, the voice of a British airman talked them down through the clouds and cross winds.

"Flaps down . . . glide . . ." The lights of the field burst through the fog. A sigh of relief as the little bird touched down. A FOLLOW ME jeep led the Cessna back out to the end of the strip where Nordstrom's plane with Department of the Interior markings was revved up and waiting.

In moments, his Convair was airborne, pushing through the turbulence toward the Atlantic . . . America . . . and Andrews Air Force Base.

THE HIGH-WALLED, long-lawned house in Laurel, Maryland, was guarded by a quartet of Doberman watchdogs and three handlers, on shifts. Two guards were constantly on duty on the grounds, and in the house itself another guard slept within earshot of the terrified Kuznetov family.

Two weeks passed before Michael Nordstrom felt they had calmed sufficiently to send in Wilcox, the chief ININ interrogator, and his team.

Boris Kuznetov toyed with Wilcox, saying nearly nothing. Each session ended with the Russian's daily depression, or he would order them away in a tantrum.

Nordstrom was in no hurry. The suitcase, retrieved by the baggage check in Copenhagen, was filled with tens of dozens of documents. Time would be needed to translate them from Russian, and they would be under study for months to determine whether they were of value or elaborate fakes.

From the first snap readings, W. Smith, the ININ Russian expert, ascertained that most of the papers dealt with NATO matters. This was a hopeful clue, because all NATO documents were numbered as to the copies made and the persons who had read them. It could eventually boil down to a question of finding a common reader of all the papers, in order to dredge up a great traitor inside NATO.

But, in reality, all that Boris Kuznetov had really done was to present them with a gigantic puzzle. Who, indeed, was Boris Kuznetov? How had the NATO documents gotten back to Moscow? As in any intelligence organization, Soviet

KGB chiefs knew few names outside their immediate circle, and what Kuznetov knew he kept locked in his mind. Obviously, his wife and daughter were under orders to remain completely unresponsive.

At the end of a frustrating month, Wilcox complained bitterly to his boss.

"Nothing. Not even his birthplace. Nothing."

"Keep at it."

Wilcox reddened. "If you ask me, Mike, we ought to dump the bastard on the steps of the Russian Embassy."

"Sure, and we'll never get another Russian defector."

"I've never run into one like this."

"You're tired, Wilcox. Take a few days off."

The perplexed interrogator mumbled something derogatory about his chosen line of work, then apologized to Nordstrom for letting his chief down.

"We've been through defectors. They're frightened animals. Alone, wanting to live, wanting to die. In strange waters. Keep loose, Wilcox, he'll come around."

Michael Nordstrom stayed outside the circle of interrogators, making himself available only as a friend to whom Kuznetov could complain and, perhaps, confide. Slowly, the Russian dropped hints that he knew the inside workings of many secret matters.

"Do you want me to tell you why you fired the German, Captain Von Behrmann, from his NATO command? I tell you. He talked too much in bed about how important he was, and of the placement of NATO submarines in Soviet waters."

On every occasion of a visit to the Laurel house by Nordstrom, the Russian would try to startle him with a new piece of information.

"Come on, Boris. You're always feeding me news that's water under the bridge."

"Water under bridge?"

"Day-old news."

"Then, how about this?"

Boris Kuznetov put on a startling display, revealing the depth of his knowledge. For over an hour he recited from memory the structure of the entire American intelligence establishment, the names of department heads, their assistants, special operators, secret posts. It was done with total accuracy.

Sanderson Hooper, the Chief ININ Evaluator, was a disheveled-appearing, white-haired man in his early sixties, who would be better placed as a professor or an obscure poet. He was the one responsible for finding the key to fit into the lock to open the puzzle of the Russian. Nordstrom had always leaned on Hooper heavily, and as the mystery of Kuznetov thickened, he tried to press for an answer.

"As we all know," Sanderson Hooper said calmly, not responding to the pressure, "this Kuznetov is an extremely skilled and highly placed agent, knowledgeable in NATO matters. He has a remarkable mind."

"Is he authentic or the greatest fake and best actor of the decade?"

Sanderson Hooper's bushy brows furled in concern. He fiddled with the tobacco in the omni-present pipe. "What do we have, Mike? A defector who wants sanctuary and protection. He's made no deals with us."

"But he keeps feeding us just enough bait to let us know he's important."

Hooper puffed, folded his wrinkled hands and mulled. "Don't lean on me yet for an official evaluation, Mike, but I will give you a guess. My guess is that Boris Kuznetov doesn't really know what it is he wants. He fled because he thought his life was in danger, and now he can't make up his mind."

"Hoop, I'm not going to hold you to this, but are you saying he's the real article?"

"My hunch is that Boris Kuznetov will turn out to be the most important defector we have ever received."

(5)

"I'M COOPED UP HERE! My wife Olga complains day and night. Tamara is miserable."

"What the hell do you expect?" Nordstrom answered. "You've locked yourself up for three months. You're bound to be on edge."

Kuznetov had grown sallow and morose. Michael knew the family was arguing more heatedly each day. Then Olga and Tamara made a few cautious ventures into the town, and one trip to Baltimore. The revelations whetted their desires.

"Why don't we work out a trip for you to, say, New York?"

"No."

"Then out west."

25

"No! You know I can't leave," he intoned shakily, with the glaze of fear returning to his eyes.

"You'll be protected."

Kuznetov shook his head "no." "Perhaps, if we could move. If we could live in the country so I could at least go out for a walk."

"Let me see what I can arrange."

Boris studied the American with somewhat of a hint of guilt. "You are a fine man. If our positions were reversed, things would not be so easy for you," the Russian said.

Camp Patrick was tucked snugly along the Patuxent River outside of Laurel and midway between Washington and Baltimore in catfish country, tobacco farms, and summer places.

The camp was built of logs and pine. A central complex held one major building that housed the office, kitchen, recreation room, and a number of smaller classrooms and briefing rooms. To one side stood a softball field and a pair of tennis courts, on the other side a riding paddock.

Along the riverfront there were a number of cottages with screened-in porches. The camp had been abandoned when Nordstrom took it over as an ININ training site. It was convenient for special schoolings and particularly for important weekend briefings. On occasion, he had hidden defectors there, as he now hid the Kuznetov family.

During the winter Kuznetov seemed to thrive in the new surroundings. True to his profession as an intelligence man, he read compulsively, devouring a dozen newspapers and periodicals daily, along with three or four books each week in English, French, and German, as well as his native language.

Nordstrom approached the Kuznetov's cottage these days to the sound of Tamara's piano. She played magnificently. Olga now attempted to prepare luncheons and dinners, still baffled by the array of electric kitchen utensils and the unlimited varieties of food.

The American and the Russian took long, unhurried winter walks along the river, during which Boris expounded Communist dialectic, literature, the American technical wonders, music. He was a well-informed buff on Western art and philosophy. Yet his only mention of personal matters was that Tamara had great promise as a musician and it was a pity to keep her from her studies.

As the winter wore on, the confinement of Camp Patrick began to play on the family's nerves. The Kuznetovs had, in fact, traded a small cell in the Laurel house for a larger cell.

Yet Nordstrom sensed a softening. The interrogators, who had accomplished little, were called off at the turn of the year, much to Boris's delight.

Michael Nordstrom's patience paid off.

On a particular night in early spring he stayed over for the running of the weekly film for the family in their living room. A new breed of spy literature was being born. This film had the usual suave British hero lipping sly *double entendres*, being pursued by a bevy of half-naked girls, and using technical gadgetry to challenge the imagination. The dark Russians were depicted as men with dirty fingernails, ill-fitting clothes, sinister, brutal, mysterious, dedicated to false gods. Except for one Russian, a female agent of KGB, portrayed by a large-busted Italian actress whose Russian accent was unbelievable.

There was a bedroom showdown. As the scene flickered on the screen, Boris Kuznetov put his head back and roared with laughter and he laughed till he nearly gagged.

Michael had never heard him laugh before.

After the film, Kuznetov treated himself to a rare drink of liquor. On his walks, he often commented, as an aside, that the Western agents drank too much. He, himself, was virtually a total abstainer. But on this night he felt good.

"The days are long," he said, placing a log on the fire and weighing his words with meticulous care. "I would like some company. Someone from my own part of the world. A fellow European."

Nordstrom raised his eyebrows. "Do you have anyone particular in mind?"

"As a matter of fact, yes."

"Who?"

Boris stirred his drink, took a short sip, looked into the budding fire. "Devereaux. André Devereaux."

"Who?"

"SDECE, the French Secret Service. Your ININ Counterpart in Washington. You know him quite well."

Boris looked at Michael's poker face.

"Why Devereaux?"

"Frenchmen are jolly."

"What else?"

"I need some jolly company."

Nordstrom did not reply. The request was coldly calculated and Kuznetov wanted to speak no more about it.

"I'll think it over," Nordstrom said.

Marshall McKittrick, the President's Intelligence Adviser, appeared to be exactly what he was, a well-groomed, silver-haired, meticulously dressed, dollar-a-year executive, who had served three Presidents without portfolio and was known as a member of the White House inner circle and the President's personal watchdog on intelligence matters. He grimaced as Sanderson Hooper spilled tobacco over his highly polished desk.

"How did Kuznetov know about Devereaux?" McKittrick asked.

Hooper swept up the tobacco like bread crumbs and placed them in the large crystal ashtray, a gift of the President.

"Possibly through one of the British defectors in the last several years. Or he could have been briefed by a Soviet resident back from Paris or Washington."

"I've worked with André Devereaux for twelve years," Nordstrom said. "We set up ININ together, Marsh, and he's the one man in Washington I'd stake my life on."

"Devereaux is not the question, Mike. He's French. He's obligated to report to his own people in Paris. You know as well as I how leaky the SDECE is and how careful we have to be in turning over information to them. Question, is, do we share this secret with the French?"

"On the other hand," Sanderson Hooper intoned, as if debating it out with himself, "Kuznetov made a well-calculated, deliberate request. He wants to see Devereaux for a particular reason. Perhaps the reason is that he's ready to open up."

"What do you think, Mike?" McKittrick asked.

"I've had the feeling he's ready to talk. We have

to take the risk of sharing Kuznetov with the French."

"Whatever," Hooper added, "the Russian holds the cards and he's playing the hand."

"All right," McKittrick said decisively, "take Devereaux to see him."

(6)

"KILL HIM! He is a thief and a robber!"

"André! Will you stop making a spectacle of yourself."

"But my God, woman. Did you see that play? He was safe by a mile!"

Nicole Devereaux tugged at her husband's jacket, and he sat down as the argument raged around the umpire at home plate. "Safe! Safe! He was safe!" yelled Devereaux. And, being French, he made a brandishing gesture at his throat to the umpire and sulked to regain control of his temper. He chomped through the hot-dog bun, then fished around beneath his seat for the paper cup of beer.

He was what one would define as a charming-looking man in his mid-forties, complete with graying temples. Most women thought him sexy. He had a way with his eyes, with his gestures.

As play resumed, Nicole returned to her deliberate mask of boredom.

Mickey Mantle strode to the plate.

André caught her fixed icy glare from the corner of his eye. Oh, well, he thought, she will only have to suffer two more innings.

The drive home was in silence. André took the long way, past the Capitol and along the Mall. The cherry blossoms were ready to burst and the city was bathed in the full breath of early spring. He looked at the Lincoln Memorial, never tiring of it. It was his city, this Washington, in many ways, even more than Paris.

The Georgetown suburb had been the beneficiary of a large restoration program. They had one of the high-ceilinged period houses near Dumbarton Oaks, which, over time of a decade, Nicole had furnished with taste and distinction.

They entered. The truce was over.

Nicole slammed the door and whirled on him. "A hell of a Frenchman you are! You baseball watcher! You . . . you bourbon drinker!"

"Madame Devereaux," he said, oozing cynicism, "I do not consider these pleasures an affront to the honor of France!"

"But you like everything American, my dear. Particularly their women."

"What is that supposed to mean?"

"Nothing, darling, but I do hear Virginia McHenry is quite a piece."

"So that's it. Nicole, when are you going to stop listening to gossip and eating yourself up on rumors?"

"I did not mean to insult you about American women. You'll jump into bed with anyone."

"You're the one who sounds like an American wife! Complaining, jealous, shrewish. No wonder they've got a country of rich widows. And you act just like one of them."

The dogs, Robespierre and Picasso, entered to greet them, but retreated quickly.

"I happen to like baseball," he said, calming, "and the Yankees are in town."

"And it also happens that this is your first night off in three weeks."

31

"So you want to drag me to New York to sit in a theater . . . a drafty theater . . . and watch a rotten play and drag me back to Washington in the middle of the night, and you'll complain about the damned play all the way home. Don't you know you complain about everything, woman? This house, my position, your social duties, the maids, the car, your clothing."

They made it to their separate but equal bedrooms.

André Devereaux had explained to his American friends that separate bedrooms was one of the most civilized contributions of the French bourgeoisie.

Tonight, for example, it served as a safe sanctuary.

And, after all, Nicole was only next door, and no matter how serious the argument, the door was never locked.

He flung off his sport shirt and threw it into the chair untidily, knowing this would gall Nicole. She threw the door open.

"My gratitude for the lovely evening, and particularly the hot dogs . . . with the works."

A deliberate thump of his shoe was followed by a long silent stare from one to the other.

"What is the matter with us?" she said, puzzled. "After twenty years some sort of terrible chasm has opened. We can't even talk to each other anymore. We only seem to want to hurt each other."

"When one is very young," André said, "one is able to give and take a fearful beating. But, even with the strongest, time wears them thin. Scar tissues develop over the continued wounds. You see, we don't have to hit each other very

32

hard anymore. Just a well-directed jab to the scar and the wound breaks open and the blood pours out."

André was able to twist and punish her with his words and suffocate her into silence. Nicole knew that the way of things allowed him to wear his "gallantry" on his sleeve, a walking martyr, and as he grew more weary from the pressures of his work his "martyrdom" became more apparent to her, if to no one else. But what of her? She had to take it all in silence and perhaps suffered even more deeply because of the silence.

"André, can we talk?"

"Honestly or dishonestly? We'll only seek justifications. Neither of us really wants to know the truth about ourselves. One of the great human capacities is to avoid introspection at any price."

"You know you tie me up with your words. It's not fair."

"Please, Nicole, I'm very tired."

She returned to her bedroom without closing the door. André sat on the edge of his bed, looking unseeingly at the patterns on the rug. The telephone rang. He lifted the receiver wearily.

"Devereaux."

"Mike Nordstrom."

After twelve years in Washington, André still could not get used to the idea of speaking to a colleague by his first name. Funny bunch, the Americans. "Oh, hello, Mike," he answered, glancing at his watch. It was past midnight.

"I've been trying to reach you all evening."

"I was at the ball game."

"How did it go?"

"Yankees won. Ford was superb, but it was a

good game. Maybe we'll catch one together next week."

"Sure. Listen, I know it's a hell of an hour to call, but we've got to visit tomorrow."

André understood the intimation. It was obviously something important. "I'll clear my desk early."

"Good. How about lunch? Market Inn at one."

"Fine."

"And, André. Try to keep the weekend clear. We may have to go out of town."

"I'll do that."

André replaced the receiver as though it had suddenly become very weighted. He bent over to unlace the second shoe and his left arm went without feeling. He tried to stand, reeled to his leather chair. His breath quickened and light-headedness engulfed him. His eyes rolled back and he brinked on darkness.

What had Dr. Kaplan said about these attacks? There was an exotic name, narcolepsy. Drowsiness, loss of memory, loss of the use of an arm or leg.

Sometimes it lasted only a minute . . . or it could last a day. Thank God, he was out of his attacks in minutes.

He staggered to the bathroom and gulped down an ephedrine pill, then fell back in the chair waiting for the attack to pass.

Take it easy, Dr. Kaplan had warned. How? Avoid tension. How? Take a rest. How? Perhaps the doctor thinks intelligence men should form a union and strike for better conditions? No country could afford to pay their intelligence people on an hourly basis. They'd run out of money.

In addition to running the SDECE establishment in the Western Hemisphere, he was the French ININ Chief. The situation between Washington and Paris continued to deteriorate, and he had placed himself squarely in the middle. . . .

Nicole stood in the doorway in her nightgown. "You look as white as a sheet. Are you ill?"

"No . . . no . . . I am all right."

"The phone call. Was it bad news?"

"Only Nordstrom."

"Would you care for some tea or a brandy?"

"No. . . . Nicole, I know I promised to go up to New York with you this weekend to see Michele, but . . . I may have to go out of town on business."

For a time she only stood. "Good night, André."

"Nicole."

"It's all right, dear."

"Say it. Another disappointment. Stop making me feel guilty."

"You're making yourself feel guilty. Or is there something you have to be guilty about?"

"No."

"Then you don't have to explain."

(7)

HOUND-DOG RUFFIN was in a spiritual mood. The great blues warbler sat before a rinky-dink piano and sang about cotton fields in the sky.

Hound-Dog animated as his pudgy fingers lit in and out of the ivory and his foot thumped out in rhythm.

> Just a closer walk with thee,
> Credit Jesus is my plea. . . .

André Devereaux entered the Market Inn, squinting to adjust to the sudden loss of daylight. Hound-Dog tipped his dark glass in a gesture of recognition.

Michael Nordstrom waved from the bar and slid off the stool. They made for their usual booth in the rear of the room. The Market Inn was a deliberately ramshackle structure set in an unlikely location under a freeway. It was camp in the land of camp. The two intelligence men studied the faces of the diners as they made for the rear. The room was filled with the usual complement of lunching Congressmen.

André gave passing notice to the nudes that adorned the walls, as Michael ordered steam beer and crab cakes.

"How's Liz?"

"Nagging. She's commenced with the opening shots of a campaign for a new car we can't afford. Just a little hint, now and then. Subtle, that girl. Nicole?"

"We speak less these days but much louder. Nicole wants me to quit the service on the pretext we should grow old gracefully and enjoy each other. Does she ask too much, Mike?"

"Is that really what she's asking for?"

"No, not really. Nicole always looks upon the past as a treasured memory, forgetting how she hated it when she lived it. Like our trips to the Caribbean. She remembers the exotic sunsets and the lovemaking, but she's conveniently forgotten the poverty, the mosquitoes, the hurricanes. But what the hell, Mike. Maybe she's right about this. What do I have to show for twenty years in this profession?"

"Internal hemorrhages," Michael answered,

washing down a couple of pills to coat his ulcer. "It would be hell for us if you left Washington, André. With one of President La Croix's men in your office, relations could break down entirely. You know what I mean."

"May I suggest my ass is getting burned from the griddle you set me on."

The Senate bell rang three times to indicate a vote would take place in the upper chamber in fifteen minutes. The dozen Senators present signed their checks quickly and, outside, the car-parkers had their motors running and doors open to prevent any delay in the return to the Capitol.

The crab cakes arrived. Michael grimaced as André smothered his in a French sauce.

"Nicole is going up to New York to see Michele and do some shopping for the embassy affair next week. I had promised to go up with her before you called. What's so important?"

"Does the name Boris Kuznetov mean anything to you?"

"No. Who is he?"

"He claims he's a division chief in KGB."

"Claims?"

"Defector. We've had him since last fall. He's at Camp Patrick. He asked to see you by name."

"Well, isn't that interesting."

"I'm going to ask a favor of you, André. I know this is a little out of line, but don't cable Paris about this man. At least until after you've spoken to him."

André pondered for a short moment. "Fair enough," he said.

37

8

HENRIETTA TODD, wife of the Senator from Kansas, sat before her committee with her Ben Franklin-style half-glasses attached to a silver chain that encircled her heavy neck and multitude of chins.

The Chairwoman of the Annual Garden Party and Concert for Korean Orphans checked studiously down a roster listing possible candidates to sponsor the forthcoming event.

"Nicole darling," she said, "do you really think we should retain Mollie Spearman as a sponsor this year?"

"Of course we should," Nicole answered coldly. "The affair wouldn't be complete without Mollie's name."

"It's just about impossible to have a function in Washington these days without Mollie Spearman. Perhaps we should be original."

"Or obvious by the omission," Nicole countered.

Henrietta Todd feigned a sigh of disappointment and put an okay after Mollie Spearman's name. "Very well," she said.

The inference was again clear. This was the third subtle mention of Mollie Spearman's name during the afternoon. The good ladies, led by Henrietta Todd, prodded their velvet barbs to convey the latest gossip that André was having an affair with the famous Washington hostess.

Liz Nordstrom watched the scene from the opposite end of the table, wincing inwardly as the bitches clawed. She waited until the moment the meeting had dissolved into tea and gossip and went to Nicole. On closer look Liz saw that Nicole was shaken despite her outward composure.

"I hate to pull you out of here, Nicole," Liz said, "but I have to stand Little League duty. Shall I drop you off?"

Nicole nodded weakly that she'd like to leave and they both intoned good-byes.

"Good-bye, darlings," Henrietta Todd said, smirking over her Ben Franklins.

Liz backed the car out of the driveway and ground it into low gear angrily. "I hate women, particularly Henrietta Todd. If she hadn't grown so grotesque and disgusting, her own husband might still sleep with her . . . if he's ever sober enough. She just can't stand to have younger, beautiful women near her."

"Please Liz, don't say anything."

"I won't, except I don't believe there is a thing between André and Mollie Spearman."

Nicole closed her front door behind her and leaned against it holding her throat until the sound of Liz's motor faded. She walked upstairs listlessly and slumped on the edge of her chaise longue, then reclined slowly . . . and wondered. André and Mollie Spearman? It hardly seemed likely. Why did it strike her so hard?

Her French liberalism notwithstanding, when she was young and vain and proud, she boasted that idle boast of young, vain, proud wives that she would not tolerate affairs by her husband.

But pride is a fool's fortress.

The first time a woman learns what every wife must learn, that pride is forfeited with astonishing ease.

And, once the illusion is shattered, the further acceptances are in silence. But after that first terrible time, no matter how many one learns of or suspects, it never comes without deep hurt.

Once tolerated, there is a choice of looking into yourself and attempting to understand the failing that led to the husband's straying. Or there is the ability to understand it for what it is and pass it off as meaningless. But few women are able to make these choices.

Instead, the path to destruction is followed: To build a store of bitterness and to inflict pain on your partner for his pain to you. To avenge. . . .

Nicole pulled to a halt before the chancellery just as André emerged with his usual bundle of late work in the attaché case she had come to detest. Tonight there were no receptions or social engagements so she knew he would work straight through after dinner until past midnight.

She slid over as André walked around to the driver's side.

"Your car won't be ready until tomorrow," she said as he drove off.

André looked at his attaché case and sighed. "I have an idea," he said impulsively. "Why don't we drive to Baltimore now and catch an early film? There's a western I want to see, and afterward we could have a nice seafood dinner at Miller Brothers."

"It sounds wonderful."

Nicole found herself sitting close to him, which she rarely did anymore, and she rubbed the back of his neck. He looked at her and smiled, and as they stopped for a red light he put his arm about her and kissed her.

And, for the moment, everything was fine.

9

A FEW MOMENTS past Washington brought Nordstrom and Devereaux into the Maryland countryside, now showing off its full springtime glory.

"It's beautiful," André said, "just beautiful. It reminds me of my own little province in France."

Michael smiled to himself. Frenchmen always made modest reference to their home as "little," be it a fifty-room manor.

They turned off the highway onto a secondary road. A lush pastureland broke on both sides of them. "Nicole and I should drive out here. We haven't been to the country for such a long time. It would do us good."

"Promises, promises. Why make them? We can never keep them. And our wives only make us feel guilty when we're called away."

Past Laurel they were among the dirt farms. In a while they drove on a remote, unpaved road that ran parallel to the Patuxent River and led them into the private confines of the ININ camp.

Nordstrom halted briefly before a camp gate marked with a freshly painted sign, long enough for the guard to recognize him and wave them through.

Nordstrom pulled up to the main building and pointed to the largest of the cottages. "I'll wait for you in the office."

As André crossed the assembly ground he was lured by the sound of piano music coming from the cottage. It was Chopin, and the player played it superbly.

As his foot touched the bottom step, making it creak, the music stopped abruptly and he could hear footsteps inside, beating a retreat.

41

"My daughter, Tamara," a thickly accented voice said. "She is very shy."

André turned and sighted down to the far end of the porch where a smallish man was framed in sunlight reflected from the river. He approached, squinting. Boris Kuznetov sat before a palette, dabbing a touch of paint on the canvas. André came up behind him. It was quite a good painting, he thought, of post-Impressionist influence, of the huge willow tree which wept into the river on the opposite bank.

Boris set his brush down, wiped his hand and extended it. "You are Devereaux," he said in passable French. "I recognize you from the descriptions."

"Isn't this kind of art frowned upon?"

"I've traveled too much in the West, I'm afraid. Our social realism makes for quite poor art. Come, let's take a walk."

As they left the porch, André caught a glimpse of the two Kuznetov women staring at him from the shadows of the curtains.

"I've been curious to meet you, Devereaux. You've been a difficult opponent. A number of times we attempted to put you in embarrassing positions so we could force you to deal with us. But no luck. Anyhow, I'm tired of Americans and they're tired of me, so I asked to see you."

"I'll have to accept that until you want to tell me the real reason."

Kuznetov smiled.

"I hope you like Laurent Perrier Grand Siècle 1959," André said.

"Yes, an excellent champagne."

"I brought you a case."

"Wonderful. The French have good taste. The

42

Americans are harsh, particularly in their intellectual outlook. With them, everything is mechanical and everything is business."

"Oh, I don't know. Bourbon is a marvelous drink when you get the hang of it."

They reached a creaky pier, lined with rowboats and small outboards. Kuznetov commented on the beauty of the place. He picked up a flat stone and tried to skim it, but was unsuccessful. They continued on, along a narrow path beside the bank.

"Why were they going to liquidate you?" André asked abruptly.

A pained expression came over Boris Kuznetov's face. He stopped at a large, familiar rock, sat on it and stared moodily out to the river, watching a swift current swirl around an exposed sandbar.

"All my life," he said slowly, "I have been devoted to the Party. But even in these enlightened days of Comrade Khrushchev there are no retirement plans for a KGB chief who falls from favor."

"Why did you fall from favor?"

"Many reasons. No reasons. Mainly because I am too honest. I refuse to distort my reports and my views in order to play politics and please certain ears. I always gave my evaluations precisely as I saw them. In the end, the powers that be could not accept what I had to say. As you know, Devereaux, it is the disease of our profession. Every intelligence service in the world suffers from the same thing. We go to abnormal lengths, expense and danger to obtain information. But then the real battle is to get your own people to believe you. You, Devereaux . . . you have all kinds of trouble with Paris, and the American

43

President doesn't believe half of what CIA and ININ tell him."

"On this we agree," André said.

"But let something go wrong and see who gets the blame."

"What did you tell them?"

"That the West is too strong. With NATO, the Soviet Union and the Warsaw Pact countries are badly outgunned. Moreover, we won't catch up. Because I sat in the inner circles as an adviser, I argued for a sincere *rapprochement* with the West and peace for the Russian people. They have ugly labels for such thinking. It is not what the military wants to hear. But I will not lie, because I don't want the Soviet Union destroyed."

Kuznetov stopped abruptly as though surprised at his own dissertation. André understood it as a need for the Russian to confess to a "neutral" party, to try to purge himself and justify and smother the guilt of his defection.

"I just wanted to meet you and see what kind of man you were," Kuznetov said.

They returned to the cottage in silence. All the way back André watched him thrash out a decision, hesitate, then say, "I warn you, Devereaux. It would be foolish to cable French SDECE of this meeting."

"Why?"

"Because anything that Paris knows, Moscow will know in twenty-four hours. For the good of your own country, don't send a report."

"That's quite an accusation, Kuznetov."

"Your service is very leaky. Just . . . keep quiet."

"I'll think it over for a few days."

"Will you visit again?"

"As you wish," André said.

They shook hands tentatively. Boris opened the screen door.

"Kuznetov."

"Yes?"

"Now let me give you a little advice. You say the Americans are not civilized, but you also knew when you defected they don't play your game of assassination and torture, nor do they use your family as hostages. But don't mistake this as a weakness, because it's strength. You'd better make up your mind to tell them what you know."

"I am not a traitor!" Kuznetov cried. "I fled only for the lives of my family! I love Russia! I love my country!"

"Yes, that's the sad part of our business. I'll have the champagne sent over."

(10)

FROM THE BEGINNING, Nordstrom had ordered the Kuznetov family photographed secretly, as well as complete tapings made of their conversations. The three of them had been recorded profusely by hidden cameras and listening devices.

Dr. Bennett Block, a renowned plastic surgeon from Johns Hopkins, was brought to Camp Patrick under the guise of being a guard in order to study the features of the family firsthand.

On a night several days after Devereaux's fourth unsuccessful visit to Camp Patrick, Nordstrom entered the Kuznetov cottage with six mysterious boxes, which he placed on a bench. He also carried a half-dozen photo albums.

Olga and Tamara, as always, retreated to another part of the cottage.

Boris understood at once something vital was about to take place.

Nordstrom handed him three of the albums. Each contained several dozen pictures of Boris, Tamara, and Olga from every conceivable angle. The Russian thumbed through them without comment.

Michael opened three of the boxes and took out full-scale head models, which were astonishing likenesses of the Kuznetov family. Coloring, eyes, hair, profiles, shape of noses, ears, were in perfect shade and proportion. "I think you'll agree," Michael said, "these are reasonable facsimiles of what you look like now."

Boris nodded. Michael handed him another album, filled with artists' conceptions of how their appearances might be changed. Then Nordstrom opened the second set of three boxes, containing head models of what the Kuznetov family would look like afterward.

"You've been under the observation of one of the best plastic surgeons in America."

"I suspect it was the short fellow with the thinning hair, gray eyes, smoked Lucky Strikes and wore a Genève wristwatch."

"That's him. His name is Bennett Block and he's out of Johns Hopkins."

"One could see he has the hands of a surgeon, and he didn't speak the language of an intelligence man."

Michael smiled at Kuznetov's astute observation, took his pen, and used it as a pointer on the head model. "In plain language, they can do something with surgery on your nose and chin. Dental work here and hair dye, mustache and glasses. Scar will be added to your forehead.

Change of height through special built-up shoes. Your own mother wouldn't recognize you."

The "before" and "after" models presented dramatic evidence.

"It will be easier with Tamara and Olga. Just westernizing them will make a major difference, with a minimum of surgery. Olga can lose between twenty-five and forty pounds. Women's wigs and hairpieces have been so perfected that not even an expert can detect one properly worn. New wardrobe, use of make-up and Western grooming habits would bring about a total change."

Kuznetov studied everything before him, then walked to the mirror and stared into it. He poured himself a rare drink. "Ingenious."

Michael continued in that brisk manner that marked him as an American. "For your wife, a crash course in English. For you and Tamara, a private tutor for as many hours a day as you can absorb. All of you will get elocution lessons to change the pitch and rhythm of your voices. You'll be schooled on being an American. We'll teach you American history from our side, jazz, sports, inside jokes, everything. You'll be taken on a full familiarization tour of the country. We figure that by the end of a year it would be pretty difficult to tell that you hadn't lived here most of your lives."

"You are being very entertaining tonight," Kuznetov answered sharply, as though annoyed.

Michael went on, all business. "We'll prepare a full set of all necessary papers. Birth certificates, college degree, honorable discharge from an American military service. You'll be provided with records to show you've been a member of certain social and benevolent societies and have carried insurance for three decades."

Nordstrom lit up, held the flame for the Russian's cigarette. It was like the first time at the Palace Hotel in Copenhagen. The man's nerves belied his outward calm. Kuznetov was very shaky.

Nordstrom let it all sink in.

"I saved the best for last." He opened a folio containing photographs and specifications of a modern motel. "This is a real-estate listing for a forty-two-room motel in Bakersfield, California. It has a good bar and restaurant business and exchange privileges with a nearby golf course and riding stable. Year-round swimming pool, centrally air-conditioned. A separate and very nice apartment for the owner. The present owner nets over twenty thousand dollars a year in addition to his quarters and board. That's clear after taxes. We will install you in here with sufficient equity to guarantee your income for life. There's a good small college in Bakersfield, and after you're settled, maybe you'd like to teach here. Los Angeles is within spitting distance. Excellent concerts, good museums, beaches, libraries."

"You're very thorough."

"As for Tamara . . ." The mention of his daughter brought on an obvious reaction. "As for Tamara, four years of music at Rochester, at Curtis, Peabody, or Juilliard. She'll graduate with a degree."

Kuznetov shook his head, pinched his brows with his fingers. "I have no answers for you tonight."

"Have one by tomorrow," Nordstrom said tersely.

Boris looked into stern eyes. Yes, Nordstrom

48

was all business now. "I understand that to be an ultimatum."

"You've got the picture," Michael answered. "You've been calling the tune for over six months. From a professional standpoint I'd play for another six months, even a year."

"And from a personal standpoint?"

"I'm sick of you. You've taken deliberate advantage of the fact that we won't terrorize people."

"My alternative?"

"Papers and taxi fare to the nearest airport. Tickets to the city of your choice and one month's allowance. From then on, brother, you're on your own. Go live in the shadows and spend every breath in fear waiting for the KGB to liquidate you. You've got no one to blame but yourself. You asked for Devereaux. Then you conveniently forget why you wanted him. He may be able to keep the information from Paris for a week or even a month, but sooner or later French SDECE has to be advised. The minute this leaks to Moscow, your value to us drops close to zero."

"I understand," Kuznetov said harshly.

"You've planned enough liquidations to know what a filthy bunch of gangsters you slept with in KGB. You don't owe those butchers a goddamned thing."

The screen door slammed behind Nordstrom.

Kuznetov had run out the string. But even so, how much longer would the Americans have played? And how much longer could he bear the unhappiness of Olga and Tamara?

He stood before the models, then suddenly swept them off the bench with a backhand, sending them crashing to the floor.

49

He saw Olga edge into the room, marble-faced. "We heard everything," she said. "Tamara translated to me what Nordstrom offered."

"I don't want to talk about it tonight."

She followed him across the room until the wall stopped him and continued to speak at his back. "You swore to us if we were able to make an escape we would have a decent life. We've never had a decent life, Boris, except those few moments we could steal at a concert or a museum or a restaurant in the West. Look at your daughter! She is a young woman and she wants to live! What kind of life will you give her after tomorrow? Hiding in terror! Can't you see the difference between these people and ours? They were going to kill you!"

"Stop it, Olga!"

"Boris," she said in the first outright defiance of him in her life, "you are going to tell the Americans everything."

"No . . . never . . . never!"

Tamara was in the doorway, her eyes filled with tears. "Papa. I was raised as a good Communist and I loved Russia, too. I loved Russia until I was ordered to spy and report on you. I love you and Mamma more. Since I found out they meant to kill you, I've grown to hate them. Oh, Papa, do you know what it is like outside in this country? I've almost died from wanting it." She knelt beside the fallen model of the woman they could create of her. "I want so much to be her."

Tears streamed down Boris' cheeks.

"Boris," his wife said, "you must talk to the Americans. Tamara and I will not spend our lives running."

He was boxed in. The choices were clear. The great secret within him was being squeezed out.

The secret of Topaz.

(11)

"MICHELE, LITTLE DARLING!"

André embraced his daughter; they exchanged kisses on both cheeks. Robespierre, a scented, rhinestone-collared, silver-gray miniature poodle, bounced and yapped. Picasso, a mournful beagle, planted all four feet firmly and wagged so violently his whole body went into motion.

André held Michele off at arm's length to inspect her and smiled. They moved through the house, upstairs, arms about waists trading the usual amenities. Everything at college was just fine. The New York theater was barely decent, but the Comédie Française would be playing a limited engagement.

"Will you come up for a few shows, Papa?"

"I'd love to, but I hate to promise. The work load . . ."

"Promise. And I promise I won't be disappointed if you can't make it."

"In that case, I promise to try."

She branched off to her own room, to apply the last icing to perfect herself for the Franco-American Legion of Honor dinner at the French Embassy.

Being many years the senior of her daughter, Nicole had started her routine two hours earlier. Nicole's tension was apparent, particularly to Robespierre, who reflected her nervousness in his nonstop prancing. Nicole labored meticulously, plucking each brow, penciling the lines with a Da

51

Vinci-like skill and creaming away the creases.

André grunted a hello and retreated to his sanctuary, donned his smoking jacket, fixed a bourbon, settled in his leather chair, and snapped open his briefcase.

Now came the microscopic search. The unromantic stomach-turning labor necessary to an intelligence man in a day that never really ended, using amounts of stamina that could not be measured.

In the twilight hours, long after offices closed and other breeds of men took pause to reflect, he turned to just another phase of the day's work. Now to pore through the cross section of clippings from some fifty magazines and newspapers of ten countries. There were stacks of memorandums, communiqués, and letters that came in the late transmission to study for possible action.

He set the trash basket at chairside, petted Picasso, and began going through the clippings with the dazzling speed of the highly trained eye. Most of them ended in the basket. A few were marked and kept.

What did he look for? The awarding of a new government contract. A riot in Africa. Ship movements. Transfer of military personnel. Publication of a technical study. Anywhere and nowhere could be that clue to fill in a space of the great, shifting, eternal puzzle.

Nicole's bedroom door opened sharply. Robespierre was shooed in. "Do take him, André. He is being such a bother."

The animal flitted across the room and leaped on André's lap. He flicked the dog off as though it were an unwanted fly. After a second and third rejection, Robespierre bore a destroyed expression and took his place on the floor beside the always serene Picasso. Picasso lifted his sad face, sniffed the perfume on the poodle and moved away, contemptuously.

With a side glance André could see Nicole at the dressing-room table, pondering into the mirror in deep concern over a wrinkle that had not been there yesterday, and astutely applying the bottled and boxed beauty.

Michele came in in her robe and fingered through her mother's cosmetic assortment, and they chatted rapidly as the hour of truth approached.

Matched book ends, André thought. Michele was her mother twenty years ago. He sipped his bourbon and watched them help each other in the hairdo ritual.

That oaf, that clod, that stupid ass Tucker Brown IV would soon be clomping up the steps for his date. What made Tucker palatable was the hundred-million-dollar Brown shipping fortune. Yankee traders or some such. Tucker Brown IV, crewcut yachtsman, Princeton, State Department career man. If he were on my staff, André thought, I wouldn't trust him to zip his own fly.

But . . . Michele loves him. Or rather, finds him decent enough to marry.

If Tucker Brown IV applies himself diligently and the family donates enough money to enough political campaigns, he might make it as ambassador to some island kingdom in ten years or so.

Now my Michele. There's a catch! French! Impeccable taste. Magnificent hostess, multilingual. Chic! When this girl dresses!

Maybe it's not such a bad match. God forbid

53

anyone think me a snob, André acquitted himself. Only, some times I wish Michele would find a boyfriend I could converse with. The terrible thought passed through him that Michele Devereaux would fall in love with a poor intellectual. Maybe I am a snob. A few years with Tucker, a child, a divorce and a good settlement! What the devil am I thinking of! After all, a man only wants what's best for his daughter. What a little charmer.

"André."

"Eh?"

"Start to get ready, darling."

He went to the safe in the closet floor and deposited the contents of his briefcase, then made for the bathroom. A cordless razor, a new gadget, zipped over his face. So damned clever, these Americans, he thought. How in the hell do they manage to produce clods like Tucker Brown IV?

He shaved in meditation of his own hot situation. Words with Ambassador René d'Arcy were becoming more and more acid. D'Arcy belonged to the President, General Pierre La Croix. Once he, André, had been a La Croix man, but he had joined that narrowing circle of independent thinkers in top diplomatic positions. André had stretched his pro-American attitudes to the limit and watched the constant slide of relations with France, helplessly.

Yet André Devereaux held a position of unique strength within the Embassy. His integrity as a Frenchman was beyond question. Conversely, he was held in great esteem by the Americans. For SDECE to tamper with André's office would be to further sour relations with the Americans. He still had great use to Paris as the honest broker.

54

He entered the shower.

The business with Kuznetov was again placing him squarely in the middle of an uneasy situation. How much longer could he go without reporting his knowledge of the defector to headquarters?

Every time he had made the decision to send the cable to French Secret Service he remembered the Russian's warning and he justified another delay.

He emerged from the shower.

His mind suddenly switched to that sound of music he usually heard when he entered the compound of Camp Patrick. Tamara Kuznetov. What a difference between daughters.

The Russian girl was rough-hewn and without an ounce of sophistication. On the other hand, she desperately devoured books and lived deeply in her music and dreamed to be able to teach or to play in a symphony orchestra. Lack of nonsense in that girl. A life of constructive contribution. Perhaps his little Michele had much to learn from her.

In the end, what would Michele's life be? A good marriage to a wealthy man and to continue life in the world of drones. Lord help her if she had to do an honest day's work. But I am to blame. Nicole and I. This is the way we created Michele. What is her sense of values? Where will her iron come from in the crisis?

He grumbled to himself over the lack of assistance as he went through the awkward business of maneuvering into studs, links, black tie, suspenders, cummerbund, and the cumbersome device to keep one's shirt from spilling out.

Without benefit of a final mirror check, André placed on the big horn-rimmed reading glasses he used when his eyes were tired, and began going through the New York and Washington newspapers.

In about an hour, his women were ready and presented themselves at his door simultaneously.

"You are glorious. Both of you. How can I be so lucky?"

He kissed his wife's cheek, and he meant it. The front doorbell rang. That would be the idiot, Tucker Brown IV, in his punctual American way.

André placed his arm through theirs, and they made off to the Legion of Honor dinner to preserve and defend the glory of France.

(12)

IT IS ARGUED that the great mansion housing the Embassy of France on Kalorama Road is even more splendid than the White House. This would be a difficult point to debate on this night of the occasion of the Legion of Honor dinner.

A two-block-long trail of limousines was passed through the police cordons on to the semicircular driveway to deposit the most elegant cargo of the season before the massive iron grille doors.

The most delicate of battles was to ensue in that war called protocol. Sides chosen, five hundred combatants. Two hundred Americans of the highest diplomatic, cultural, military, and political rank to be found in Washington versus two hundred of the cream of the French colonies of New York and Washington. A hundred more top-rank strays of other nations were there, along with the usual clever contingent of crashers whose sole diet consisted of what they could scrounge up at the nightly cocktail parties in Washington.

France, indeed, was at subtle war this night to preserve, defend, and perpetuate the legends of French superiority, its army a few million Parisians, its banners a bit tattered and faded. What was missing in numbers was offset by the zeal and arrogance of the Parisians.

André and Nicole swept into the grand foyer. At the far end of the great room, Ambassador and Madame René d'Arcy anchored the receiving line near a massive Louis XV chest. A string of aides hovered about smartly, plucking the very important from the receiving line and moving them effortlessly and directly to the Ambassador and his wife.

Claire d'Arcy was fluid and French and beamed beneath high smartness. D'Arcy, a small, rotund, and lively person, greeted each guest with the fervor of finding a long-lost brother. They had created a meaningful protocol, far from many of the burdensome, stiff receptions of Washington. Yes, the French could show them a few things about protocol.

Michele and Tucker Brown IV made for the relative quiet of the canopied balcony overlooking the sweeping lawns behind the embassy.

Here, they fell into the first of the subdivisions of bores and snobs. This was the lowest group of the snob order. They were the pseudo sophisticates—the French food and wine snobs (Americans, for the most part).

The duel opened with the ground rules that only French wine could be considered. It was all merely a case of which French wine was superior to which French wine.

But Tucker Brown IV owned appalling bad taste. Unfortunately, he shot the same blanks he generally did in the State Department. Looking and acting much like an eager, uncoordinated Newfoundland puppy who tripped over its own outsized paws, Tucker made a feeble case on behalf of German wine. Then he compounded the blunder by the mention of a California wine! Noses sniffed contemptuously. Michele giggled. An unbearable silence was broken by another of the lowly order, a food snob.

Tucker Brown IV then proceeded to put his other foot in his mouth. "There's some really great French restaurants in New York, and for my dough, the Rive Gauche right here in Washington is tops."

"But, Tucker, it's more than French. It's run by a Corsican!"

Laughter.

Misfortune continued to plague Tucker Brown IV, who a little later found himself standing squarely in the middle of the French-language snobs. French, as spoken by Frenchmen, was the only language. The world standard for diplomacy and culture.

So Tucker tried out a bit of butchered French. They grimaced in pain, then smiled indulgently.

But then everyone corrupted French, the language of poets and of the greatest literature of man.

André stifled his yawns as he drifted from sortie to sortie. The back-hacking this night was but a more elaborate showcasing of the kind of thing that went on endlessly. As usual, the Americans were getting mauled. After all, they were only trying desperately to imitate the French and were forced into playing a game the French had invented and mastered.

Unfortunately for France, André thought, snobbery and conversation were not the things that made for world domination. As American domination became ever more apparent, French words grew ever more acid.

The Americans were swamped in matters of art, literature, perfume. Paris was the hub of the universe, leather goods, materials, and fashions. France was the arbiter of man's good taste, love songs, love-making, crystal, silver, and political aplomb.

The French astutely avoided counterattacks in sports, education, science, production, democracy, and military strength, which indeed was a sore point with Frenchmen.

The French used the word "pedantic" quite often to describe a number of things non-French. The Americans insisted Paris had the rudest, most self-centered, gouging citizenry in the world.

André became hungry.

He mounted the stairs to the grand dining room and pecked away at the banks of caviar, pâté de foie gras, salmon, cheese soufflé, truffles, feuilletée, remindful to him of waste. André, the tired man at the embassy, disdained a civil service in which half the time of a French official was spent at ceremonies and the other half at parties, and they weren't the people's servants, but rather their masters. He wanted to go home. There was a half-night's work undone.

The Ambassador wended his way to the grand foyer, walked up the staircase to the balcony. The orchestra sounded out for attention. Guests drifted in from the music room, the salons, from the terrace and lawns and dining room. Fat little René d'Arcy was framed between a tricolor and an immense portrait of President Pierre La Croix. He raised his glass.

"I offer a toast to the oldest unbroken alliance in the Western world. To the unity of France and the United States."

After his oration he retreated to the Green Room, sanctum of the very special. Empire furnishings, upholstered in green silks, in Egyptian shapes, were topped with Napoleonic crowns. René d'Arcy commanded hushed awe as he went through his famed cigar-lighting ritual.

A cigar was carried in with great pomp on a sterling-silver tray and its end nipped by a sterling-silver cutter. A servant held a candle in a sterling-silver holder. For a full five minutes d'Arcy passed the cigar over the flame from end to end, warming it . . . just so. Without puffing, he darted the tip into the flame until it lit itself. A great "ah" arose around the Green Room for the masterful performance.

Courvoisier Reserve, a hundred and fifty years old, was served, and those in the inner sanctum prevailed on d'Arcy to tell a few spicy French jokes and please them with his imitations of Churchill and Hitler.

André walked out on the balcony with Mollie Spearman, once a crude semiprecious stone who had come from the West fifteen years earlier and acquired the finish of a polished gem. Mollie and André were each other's kind of favorite people. Just a bit away from them Nicole was speaking to a younger military attaché of the Canadian Embassy.

She was no beauty, his Nicole, but she made full use of what she had and any man would find her desirable. Nicole was poised and elegant and she flirted in measured terms.

André wondered, as he always had, if she had lovers. It was part of the hurt inflicted by his own mother, a legacy of being orphaned that his father bore like an unhealed wound.

It would be a small chore for him to really find out about Nicole's fidelity but rather beneath his dignity. But where on God's earth would this precarious road end for them?

Would Nicole be seized by a desperation to prove her desirability, and thus fulfill his fantasy? He had tried so often to let her know she was loved but, somehow, Nicole never really listened or understood. Perhaps, as he told her, he was so obsessed with the ghost of his mother that he loved her and unconsciously rejected her at the same moment. He did not know.

Marsh McKittrick came alongside him. He excused himself to Mollie Spearman.

"Boris Kuznetov has had a heart attack. He's at Bethesda Naval Hospital."

"Oh, dear God," André sighed.

"I'm heading there now with Mike. Follow us in fifteen minutes."

"Right."

In a moment Marsh McKittrick disappeared with Mike Nordstrom. Liz Nordstrom stood emptily by the main door watching them go.

Now he would find Nicole and do the same. He asked Tucker Brown to see his wife home, gave his regrets to René d'Arcy, and followed the Americans to Bethesda.

ANDRÉ ENTERED the hospital room and stood next to Marshall McKittrick and Nordstrom before the oxygen tent covering the body of Boris Kuznetov.

The cragginess of the Russian's face was rendered even more pronounced by his waxen stillness. The sounds were heard of the suffering for breath, the hiss of the respirator, the soft rubber steps of the nurse, and the intermittent weeping of Olga Kuznetov.

Americans grit their teeth. The French wring their hands. Russians weep unabashedly. Olga Kuznetov's flat face was wet with expended tears. She wrung her sopping handkerchief and rocked back and forth. Tamara stood above her mother, weeping too but quietly and glassy-eyed.

"How bad is it?" André asked.

"Bad," Nordstrom answered.

André took a step forward, and as he became fixed upon Kuznetov, he was suddenly consumed by fright. He saw a vision of himself lying on the bed, fighting for his own life. He heard the crying of Nicole and Michele. Yes, it would be like this . . . even with Marsh and Mike in the room.

It's the end for all of us in this business, André thought. Who escapes? Would his end be in a prison in a strange land or in the gutter of an alley with a bullet ripping away the face? Or would it come from the black depression that forced so many of his colleagues to destroy themselves by their own hand? Or a sudden massive pain in the chest?

What did Dr. Kaplan call it? Narcolepsy . . .

"See that Madame Kuznetov and her daughter are comfortable. Get them a room right here in the hospital. Tell her we'll do everything in our power," Nordstrom's voice intoned. "I want six guards on him at all times, and inform me immediately if there are any changes in his condition."

"Yes, sir."

André did not feel Michael tap his shoulder. "We might as well go," Michael said.

André came out of it. They paid respects to the wife and started to leave.

"Wait," McKittrick said.

Boris Kuznetov's eyes fluttered open. He stared at them, raised his hand feebly.

"He's in no condition to speak," the doctor said.

Kuznetov persisted.

"Only a second, please," the doctor warned.

Through exhausting effort Boris made it clear it was André with whom he wanted to talk. André knelt beside the bed. The oxygen tent was lifted from him. He placed his ear close to the Russian's lips.

"Devereaux . . ."

"Yes?"

"You must not tell Paris."

"Why?"

"There is grave danger . . . for France."

"What danger?"

"Topaz . . . Topaz . . ."

Kuznetov's hand fell. He closed his eyes, exhausted by the effort.

They walked the long corridor. "What did he say?" Nordstrom asked.

"It made no sense," André answered. "No sense at all."

NICOLE WAS propped up directly in the middle of André's bed. The gauntlet was down. Robespierre had his chin cradled on his mistress's stomach, and his eyes followed André with fear and suspicion as he undressed.

Nicole had had too much to drink, a habit she was picking up from the American women. American women drink too much, he sputtered under his breath. They have to in order to sweep aside the taboos imposed by Puritanism. Love is bad. Sex is evil. So drown it, in order to do the things a European woman comes to naturally and without all this sense of guilt.

Once when Nicole got high on wine she was passionate. These days she was a bitch. Upper lip narrowed. Upper teeth bared. André undressed with deliberate slowness, letting Nicole stew, giving his teeth an extra long brushing, running the water at full blast.

"Michele took a late plane back to New York tonight," Nicole opened.

"What for?"

"She's cramming for exams."

How logical women are. Michele never crammed for an exam in her life, and if it were necessary, by some odd chance, she could carry a book or two to Washington.

"Any other reasons?" André felt compelled to ask.

"She needed your comfort tonight."

"Are you going to get around to telling me why?"

"She and Tucker had a fight."

64

"I didn't know Tucker fought. And I still don't see why she went back to New York."

"Because she had a fight with Tucker."

"Her logic and your logic are absolutely similar. And if Michele had a fight with Tucker, that is no reason for her to go back to New York or for you to start one with me."

"She needed your comfort."

"Then why the hell didn't she stay?"

"What's the difference? You're never here when anyone needs you. There have been a few times, my dear, when I've needed your comfort, too."

"I admit I am a bad husband and a bad father."

"No one said you were."

"Where in the hell do you think I went to-night?"

Robespierre left the room.

"Isn't it strange that Mollie Spearman left a few minutes after you? Isn't it convenient that I had to remain till every last person was gone."

"Oh, my God, woman. Will you please shut up?"

"Did you meet her for lunch last week or didn't you?"

"Yes, in a secret rendezvous at the center table of the largest dining room in Washington. I needed a favor."

"Yes, yes, yes. I understand Mollie is quite liberal with her favors."

"All right, my dear. You've got me cold. I'm desperately in love with Mollie Spearman and I want a divorce so I can marry her right away."

Nicole spun off the bed, lifted an ashtray and smashed it against the wall. Then she buried her face in her hands and cried.

"Go to bed," he said.

"I had a long talk tonight with Dr. Kaplan. He said you're on dangerous ground and you can't push yourself any further."

"So is that a reason to make a scene? Besides, the good doctor and all the good doctors are alarmists. That is their stock in trade, to alarm, to give advice no one can follow."

"How in the name of God can you ask me to stand by silently and watch you die? André, let's try something else. They don't even appreciate what you're doing here. The Embassy is filled with strangers."

"And how do you intend to live outside of this rarified air?"

"Why don't you stop blaming me for something you can't give up?"

"You're right, of course, Nicole. I am afraid I am committed to a battle from which I cannot withdraw."

"There are men who have left the service who live like decent human beings. We have many friends . . . and opportunities. In Paris, in Washington if you wish, New York, anywhere. Maybe even on an island in the Caribbean."

"An island in the Caribbean," he said.

André stretched on the bed and he patted his knee for her to come beside him and they snuggled together. "Wouldn't it be wonderful if we were as compatible out of bed as we are in? The trouble with us is that the night always ends and there's that day-to-day living."

"As long as we have this," she said.

His mind had strayed to that hospital room in Bethesda and the shadowy word "Topaz." He would never leave, for his commitment was total.

PART II

The Rico Parra Papers

(1)
SUMMER, 1962

In New York City, Rico Parra, high in the Castro regime and leader of the Cuban delegation at the United Nations, strode into a room set up for a press conference. He sat behind a name plate bearing his rank and stared angrily into the television cameras and at the assemblage of reporters. His black eyes bore hatred and his black beard glistened under the lights.

"Negro members of the Cuban delegation have been mistreated and insulted by the staff of the Wharton Hotel. It is typical of the disgusting behavior of the imperialists. This outrage is protested by the Government of Cuba."

Pencils quickened as the Spanish translator intervened.

Rico Parra smashed his fist on the table again and again, spitting venom and denouncing the Yankees with every catchphrase in the Red book.

After twenty minutes he had overrun his translator and become hoarse from the tirade. "The delegation of Cuba is, therefore, moving to the

West Side, where we will be welcome and among our own people. We are leaving directly for the San Martín Hotel."

The bearded revolutionaries and their female staff, some sixty in number, marched on foot across Manhattan to an area largely inhabited by Puerto Ricans and other Spanish-speaking Americans, where they took possession of the fifth, sixth, and seventh floors of the venerable old hotel.

During the 1920's, before the accepted integration of New York's big hotels, the San Martín had won a measure of renown as the hostelry for left-wing political refugees of high rank from the revolution-torn countries of the Caribbean and South America. Legendary were the meetings in smoke-filled rooms following abortive attempts to overthrow various Latin American dictators, meetings attended by Spanish-speaking reporters hard up for news and all sorts of camp followers. Yes, they had all come to the old San Martín Hotel and flooded its shabbily decorated suites.

In addition, it attracted a number of Latin American entertainers and boxers. Among the minor notables had been one Benny García, known and somewhat remembered as the Sugar Cane Kid. Benny García followed the usual format of Cuban fighters of that era in that he was a colorful welterweight with a vicious but wild right uppercut and not enough ability to carry him beyond the No. 4 rating in his division.

Benny García's star also dimmed, as such luminaries always did, a few years after he fought a few too many fights, and his brief hour of glory gave way to younger, stronger, hungrier men.

The Sugar Cane Kid remained on the far West Side, to become part and parcel of the San Martín

Hotel, first as a glorified bouncer, then as a member of the hotel security staff. He and the hotel faded into drabness together.

But Benny García proved far more wily as a hotel dick than he had been in the ring. For a hustler, there was always a buck to be made. Trade was brisk in girls, a room to hide in, a place to play a crap game. Benny passed packages, held bets, passed tips, and asked no questions.

When Rico Parra and the Cuban delegation arrived suddenly and dramatically, the San Martín found itself in an instant of revived glory.

As a fellow Cuban, the Sugar Cane Kid, whom many of them remembered, was in a position to offer a variety of services.

Rico Parra himself was somewhat a purist. He had that dedication and holier-than-thou infection that are the trademark of the revolutionary breed, and did his playing in secret.

This was still in the early days of the Revolution, and the traditional hot Cuban nature of the other delegates had not yet been bludgeoned by such idealism. There were many, many, many favors the Sugar Cane Kid could perform.

High in rank among the delegates was one Luis Uribe, a thin, nervous, chain-smoking translator and a personal secretary to Rico Parra.

The Sugar Cane Kid's appearance on the fifth, sixth, and seventh floors became commonplace in the loosely guarded, undisciplined atmosphere of the Cuban delegation. Uribe made it a special point to befriend the ex-fighter.

Benny García was quick to pick up a signal that Luis Uribe had something to unload. Maybe Uribe, knowing he was coming to the States, had slipped a few gems out of Cuba. A lot of them did. Maybe

71

Uribe was looking for a moment to defect. There could be a good payday in helping to pull it off. Whatever Uribe had in mind, Benny García let him know cautiously that he had found an ally . . . of sorts.

A week after the Cubans arrived, Benny was on his usual rounds, picking up odd jobs, running errands, arranging for girls. Luis Uribe tailed him to the elevator.

"I must speak to you."

"Come down to my room in ten minutes."

Benny locked the door behind him and the tattered window shades were drawn, darkening the dank little apartment. Luis Uribe wore the mask of a man deep in confrontation, on the verge of a terrible decision.

"I must get my family out of Cuba," he sputtered at last. "The country is destroyed. For myself, I do not care. I'll stay and take prison. But I have three sons and they must have a chance for life."

Benny thought it was paternal as hell, but his battle-scarred face showed no further sympathy.

"I've scraped together everything I have. I can arrange a boat, but I need another two thousand dollars."

"Man, that's a lot of bread," Benny said, "a lot of bread."

Luis Uribe shook visibly. His mouth dried, and he asked for water and drew a glass from the leaky faucet. "I've got something worth that much."

"Maybe I can find you a buyer. What you got?"

Uribe could not bring the words out.

"Well, man?"

"As you know, I am personal secretary to Rico Parra and I have access to his suite."

"Yeah . . ."

"What I have to sell are the documents in Rico Parra's attaché case."

(2)

LOTS OF TIMES Benny García did odd jobs if the contacts and the price were right. Maybe a jealous husband wanted the boyfriend worked over. Maybe a guy wanted his business partner roughed up. Odd jobs like that.

He was good pals with Detective Leeman, who was in charge of the territory that included the San Martín Hotel. Sometimes a hood came into Leeman's territory and they didn't have anything exactly legal to move him out of town. So Leeman would clue Benny and he would arrange that the guy cut out, quick.

A year earlier, Detective Leeman had talked to Benny about some strange business. A hit was needed on someone, but not a hood. Someone on the expensive East Side. A foreigner with a lot of respectability. Detective Leeman was his pal so he didn't ask questions, just took the job and did his work.

The job had something to do with "detaining" an Algerian United Nations delegate while some other guys rifled his apartment.

The final instruction had been given by a Frenchman. Benny knew that the Algerians and French didn't like each other so he put two and two together. Orders for the job must have come from some high-placed Frenchman. They paid good, too.

Benny mulled over Luis Uribe's proposition. He figured that the French already knew of his good work; maybe they'd deal with him. Chances were they'd be interested in those papers in Rico Parra's briefcase.

He dropped around to the station to see Detective Leeman.

"Leeman, how do I see someone in French Intelligence?"

"What you up to, Benny?"

"Got a tip that may interest them. Swear, it's got nothing to do with your action. You got my promise on that."

"French Intelligence officer is called Special Labor Representative. Go to their labor office on Madison Avenue. Guy's name is Prévost, Gustave Prévost. Now you sure you're not making a mess for me?"

"You got my word, Leeman, my absolute word."

"I'll call Prévost for you and set up an appointment."

Gustave Prévost rocked back and forth in his chair, tapped his fingertips together, and otherwise appeared to be sniffing constantly in short, darted breaths.

Benny García related the story of Luis Uribe and his offer.

"You say he has complete access to Parra's papers?"

"Yes, sir."

"How about getting other people in and out of the Cuban's rooms?"

"Well, they've been disarmed and them people is always creating such a rumpus . . . hell, I just come and go like I please."

"What is Mr. Uribe asking for the papers?"

"Twenty-five hundred," he answered, tacking his own commission of five C-notes onto the price. Hell, wasn't much for that kind of work.

"Where can you be reached?"

"San Martín Hotel. I got an apartment there. I'm always around."

"I'll pass the information along to someone who may be interested. You'll be contacted."

(3)

WITHIN A FEW HOURS of his meeting with Benny García, Gustave Prévost was aboard the Eastern shuttle flight to Washington and went directly to his boss, André Devereaux at the French Chancellery on Belmont Road.

André Devereaux detested this man. He was of that breed of locusts which had swarmed into and infested the French Secret Service, who took the job for its money, for an easy life, for the parties and ceremonies that went with it, and with none of the deep conviction and love of country of the dedicated intelligence agent.

Gustave Prévost had none of these qualities, nor did the school of sharks he swam with. His talents lay in the sly games necessary to safeguard his mediocrity. André would have fired him long before, but all the Gustave Prévosts secured their flanks by a series of alliances in their mutual survival society. André was faced with the fact of an SDECE riddled with them.

Gustave lit a cigar with his solid-gold lighter, revealing a pair of solid-gold cuff links. Ostentatious for a man of his position. "It smells bad," he said sniffing at the air with blatant cynicism.

"A setup. The Cubans are out to feed us a mouthful of false information."

"No matter if the contents of Rico Parra's attaché case are real or fake. They are being offered. We must take them. We will make a determination of their value later," André said.

This, of course, was what Prévost wanted to hear, for now the decision was Devereaux's, not his. He had no further responsibility in the matter. If it all succeeded, he could take credit. If it failed, he could tell Paris later that he had warned Devereaux of a trick.

For a bastard who wants my job, André thought, what is poor Gustave going to do when he can't pass the buck and must make his own decisions?

"This will be a costly business, Monsieur Devereaux. Can our budget stand it?"

"Good intelligence cannot be run at cut-rate prices. So don't spend so much on foolishness for the next couple of months, Prévost. Perhaps one less present for one less lady."

"Sir, do you accuse . . ."

"Certainly I do. Your accounts at various jewelry stores are getting a bit outrageous."

Gustave Prévost flushed and sputtered.

"Get back up to New York," André said contemptuously. "I'll arrange the entire operation from here. And, Prévost, damn you, don't bungle things at your end."

(4)

BRIGITTE CAMUS knocked and entered André's office in a single motion, and she knew the instant she saw him. André's forehead was beady

76

with sweat. He was having another of his attacks.

He fired a warning glance that she was to say nothing.

Brigitte Camus, his secretary of a decade, understood but deplored the situation. She advanced slowly toward his desk, ready to defy him and call the doctor.

"Well?" André said between labored breaths.

She set rolls of quarters, dimes, and nickels on the desk top. "Pepe's ticket is at the National counter," she said.

André forced his left hand out, grabbed the desk pen and scrawled that unreadable chicken track that represented his signature, and affixed it to a dozen letters, cables, and coded messages. She lifted the papers dutifully and made for the door, then turned. "Monsieur Devereaux!"

"That's all, Madame Camus."

"Perhaps you'd care for a glass of sherry," she blurted, fishing for a reason to remain.

"Make it a bourbon. A stiff one."

The first sip warmed him and the attack waned. His eyes followed her as she moved papers about to consume time in the office. Dear Brigitte. Still a very attractive and desirable woman in her late forties. A widow with a son in college, yet she still had her admirers. Like the good Frenchwoman, she made the most of what she had. It was comforting to watch her come and go and be around him these days. She was concerned and devoted.

"Call Madame Devereaux and tell her I'll be late."

"I already have."

"What's on the damn calendar tonight?"

"Early cocktails, Ghana Embassy. Late cock-

77

tails, Sierra Leone Embassy. Tomorrow a dinner for the outgoing Nigerian Ambassador."

"African week," André grunted. The French were bad enough with protocol and wasted far too much valuable time on it, but the Africans were something else. The Africans imposed their new-found acceptance with an overpowering vigor. Their game of diplomatic musical chairs never ended. André held second rank in the Embassy under René d'Arcy and was in heavy demand to attend the functions, and the functions had increased fivefold in a decade, thanks to the Africans, who were easily offended by an absence.

"Perhaps you could get someone to attend for you," Brigitte said.

"The honor of France requires my presence," André mocked. "You may go, Madame Camus."

She hedged.

"It's quite all right. I'm fine now."

She started for the code room. "Monsieur Devereaux, when will you take a rest?"

"In heaven. I'm looking forward to my first good night's sleep there in twenty-five years."

She was about to sob.

"Don't, please don't," he said.

André departed immediately from the Chancellery and drove down Massachusetts Avenue lined with the embassies, legations, and consulates that made it a political artery of the world.

He parked in the lot near Union Station, entered its cavernous confines, and made for a random phone booth, closed the door behind him, unwrapped the rolls of coins, stacked them like poker chips, and opened shop by depositing a dime and dialing the operator.

"Operator. May I help you?"

"Thank you. I want Miami. Area 305. Person to person with Mr. Pepe Vimont at number 374-1299."

He repeated his instructions indulgently to her questions. She thanked him. A rain of quarters clanged into the coin box with the sound of a muted church bell.

"Pepe's bar."

"I have a long distance call for a Mr. Pepe Vimont."

"This is Pepe Vimont."

"Here is your party, sir."

"Hello, Pepe. This is Joseph. I called to wish you a happy birthday."

Pepe Vimont's pulse quickened upon hearing the voice of the man he knew only as Joseph. "I think we have a bad connection," Pepe said quickly, answering the code. "Can you call me back in ten minutes at Eva's number?"

"Yes, very well."

Pepe set the receiver down, untied his apron and tapped the other bartender on the shoulder.

"I've got to go out for half an hour."

Always when the rush is on, the bartender thought, but said nothing. He wasn't really too unhappy about it because it would give him a chance to pocket a few bucks.

Pepe left his bar on Southwest Eighth Street in the heart of Miami's Cuban refugee district and walked a block and a half up the Tamiami Trail, then crossed to where a violent neon display shouted out "Tropicburger" in four colors. At the outdoor stand of the drive-in, Cubans in gleaming white shirts nipped down *cafecitos* and talked in their loud, quick voices.

79

Over the parking lot stood the phone booth coded as Eva. Pepe entered and waited.

During this time, in Washington André Devereaux left Union Station, crossed the avenue to the Commodore Hotel, where he took up position in a new phone booth and watched the lobby clock tick off. He placed a call to Eva's number.

"Hello."

"Hello. Is this Pepe?"

"Yes."

"Joseph. You will go to the National ticket counter at the airport tomorrow. There will be round-trip tickets to New York in your name. It will be a short trip. No more than overnight at most."

Thank God, Pepe thought.

"Bring your Tessina camera and several rolls of film."

"Yes, go on."

André carefully detailed the movements that Pepe was to make in New York and how his contact would link up with him.

He repeated the instructions to perfection.

"Good luck," André said and hung up. He left the Commodore Hotel and plunged into the endless round of African cocktail parties.

(5)

PEPE VIMONT, born José Lefebvre, was the son of the foreman of the Vimont plantation on Guadeloupe in the French Antilles.

When his parents passed away, the elder Vimont, who was without a son, took young Pepe as his own and gave him his name.

He was a student at the Sorbonne in Paris when

the Second World War fell upon France. Choosing to ignore the safe route and return to Guadeloupe, he retreated first into Vichy France, where he joined the fledgling Resistance. The paths of war took him to North Africa, where remnants of defeated France were reuniting under the directorship of Pierre La Croix into the semblance of a combat force and a quasi government.

Pepe, a light-skinned Negro with sharp features, was able to pass the line easily as a Muslim. He learned Arabic and was soon plunged into the cesspools of Casablanca, the Casbah of Algiers, Cairo, and Dakar as an intelligence agent for the Free French.

As the war progressed and Pierre La Croix reclaimed Vichy French possessions in the Caribbean, Pepe was tranferred as an operator in that arena.

The end of the war found the elder Vimont passed away and the plantation in a hopeless state of financial ruin.

Pepe returned to France and was further trained at an SDECE school at Étampes near Orléans. After a brief mission in Cuba, he resigned from the service and decided to remain in that country and obtained citizenship.

Pepe Vimont was among the first to flee Castro, emigrating to Miami, where he purchased a small bar in the southwest section among the refugees.

When his record and whereabouts came to the attention of French Intelligence, André Devereaux sent an agent down to contact him. Pepe agreed to take on special missions for the French to augment his income.

Pepe liked Miami. It was the first time he had been able to settle long enough to marry and begin a family. His wife was a lovely Cuban girl, and they had a son and another child on the way.

Only the mysterious voice of Joseph broke the otherwise pastoral existence of family life. Where did the voice come from? He did not know, nor did he inquire. But it was the man coded as Joseph who could trigger him down to Argentina or to the islands.

It was so strange this time, so very strange, the first call for a mission inside the United States.

(6)

NATIONAL'S DC-7 afternoon flight touched down at Idlewild International at four in the afternoon. Pepe Vimont skimmed through a copy of *Ebony* as the airport bus passed through the tunnel to the East Side terminal in mid-Manhattan.

He proceeded to play out the instructions that Joseph had given him over the phone the day before, going by foot to the Doubleday bookstore at Fifty-second Street.

"Do you have a double album called 'Roger Williams' Songs of the Fabulous Forties'?"

"Yes, sir."

He asked the clerk to play side one, band five, on the demonstrator and listened to a minute of the Warsaw Concerto. Pepe studied the vibrant sounds of Roger Williams seriously, purchased the record and left the store.

The hookup was made.

An agent whom he would know as Maurice trailed him as he continued up Fifth Avenue and crossed over to Central Park opposite the Plaza Hotel. He took up a bench not far from the waiting line of hansom cabs, lit up, puffed and watched the admixture of New York sophisticates enter the Plaza for after-work cocktails and tourists and romanticists clip-clop off through the park in the aged carriages. A big red sun fell suddenly into the Hudson River, immersing the park in evening shadow.

A nondescript man sat at the opposite end of the bench, also carrying a bag from the Doubleday store.

"Excuse me," he said. "I believe you left this on the counter."

Pepe stared at him blankly, accepted the bag, opened it. It contained a volume, Irving Wallace's *Chapman Report*.

"Yes, this is mine. Thank you."

"You are Leonard."

"Yes," Pepe answered, "and you are Maurice."

The man nodded. "Follow me at a distance."

Pepe kept a trained interval of several hundred feet as Maurice walked toward the East Side all the way across to Second Avenue. After doubling back to check for possible tails he entered an opening, "RITE WAY GARAGE . . . PARKING BY THE MONTH."

Pepe made up the narrow walk alongside the ramp to the second, third, and, finally, the top level and scanned the field of shiny car hoods. A headlight in the rear of the garage flicked off and on quickly. Pepe wove in and out of the tightly packed vehicles to where Maurice waited and took a seat alongside him.

Maurice unlocked the glove compartment and withdrew two packets of money and gave clipped, precise instructions, which Pepe repeated.

"You are working with a Tessina?"

"Yes," he answered, showing the camera strapped on his wrist like a watch.

"If all goes well, you should be out of New York by eight o'clock."

"Fine with me."

"As soon as you have finished the job, take a taxi to La Guardia Airport. Purchase a TWA flight bag and put the film in it. I'll be waiting near the main newsstand and will also have a TWA bag. We'll switch by the paperback book racks."

Pepe pocketed the bills and shoved the door open.

"Good luck," Maurice said.

"Thanks."

(7)

ANDRÉ GLANCED at his watch as Nicole applied her never-ending finishing touches.

As in any plan in this state of motion, he wondered if and when and how he had left loopholes. Perhaps it was a mistake to put the "dead-letter drop" on a flying aircraft, but he had to move Pepe in and out of New York quickly. If the Americans got wind, they might accuse him of espionage or, at best, be very angry he had not advised them in advance. Furthermore, he wanted the film out of New York because he did not trust it to that jackass, Gustave Prévost.

The sitting in the dark, the not knowing, this brought on the tension. Pepe is a good man, André thought. Why the hell am I reviewing him now? At any rate, nothing to do but sweat it out.

Nicole made her entrance. He admired her,

kissed her cheek, and they left the house and drove off.

His thoughts were on the centents of Rico Parra's attaché case. It would be a windfall if they were not deliberate fakes. Rico Parra had recently returned from a conference in Moscow in which a number of new pacts had been negotiated. Certainly Rico Parra carried papers to discuss with the Soviet leaders while they were all in New York at the United Nations.

"Michele phoned today. She's terribly unhappy about this fight with Tucker."

"Eh?"

Michele . . . fight . . . Tucker . . . Sarah Lawrence . . . blah . . . blah.

Damn him! Nicole thought. Nothing is important. Not me. Not his daughter. Look at him, detached, in another world. And I've always been shut out from it.

"What did you say, dear?"

"I said the New York Yankees lost to the Washington Redskins."

He stopped at Wisconsin and M streets, where the car parker greeted him familiarly and Blaise, the owner of the Rive Gauche, ushered them in.

Tonight it was an intimate dinner of six. All ININ people. His Italian and German counterparts and their wives. The Italians were palatable. A dull old married pair with flocks of children. The Baron and his wife were something else. In a word, André detested most Germans, and the Baron was no exception. Only an overdue social obligation compelled him to share a table with a German.

It was the Baron's wife who annoyed Nicole. A little dumpling, not yet thirty, with a figure unmarred by childbearing. She displayed her bosom to the nth degree. Well, Nicole thought, she was keeping more than one bed warm in Washington, and small wonder. The Baron was an utter, total washout. She wondered if André had gotten around to sleeping with German women, or this one in particular.

They approached the table. The Baron and the Italian stood, smiling. Nicole's hand was kissed, and André kissed the hands of the ININ wives.

Damn her, Nicole thought through smiles, look at the way her dress hangs open.

André looked at his watch again. Pepe Vimont should be in a taxi now, he thought, heading for the San Martín Hotel.

(8)

"OH, JESUS," Benny García moaned. He crossed himself. He hadn't crossed himself for many years. When he entered the ring he used to do that. Suppose something goes wrong, he thought. I should have never got mixed up in this. These Intelligence guys are dangerous.

He twisted his neck, trying to break loose the kinks. Benny García was queasy in the guts and perspiration popped out over his lip. It was like the night he fought Lupe López. He was stiff and could find no way to break loose. If he could have gotten past Lupe López, it might have meant a title shot. At least, every old pug thinks he once had that chance. But Lupe López caught him cold and worked him over something fearful for five rounds until the referee stopped it. Most of his bad cuts came from that fight.

The Sugar Cane Kid felt the same stiffness now. He pivoted on the swivel stool at the lunch counter of the coffee shop across the street from the San Martín Hotel.

That's him! Benny thought as Pepe Vimont entered. Yeah, that's him all right. Doubleday book bag and a green necktie.

Pepe found an empty booth, ordered a milk shake and waited.

Benny slipped in opposite him, set down a pack of British Players cigarettes. Pepe opened the box and saw the folded two-dollar bill in it and closed it and handed it back.

"Benny García?"

"Look, man," Benny said rapidly, grabbing Pepe's sleeve. "Something's gone wrong. Jesus."

"Cool it. Get your hands off me. Talk softer and slower."

Benny sucked in a half-dozen deep breaths. "Rico Parra was supposed to go to a party uptown at the Russian's hotel. That's why we figured on tonight. Luis Uribe could get in and out easier. But Rico's sick. He's in his room screaming and hollering and throwing up. People are running in and out like crazy."

"Shouldn't Uribe be able to get the papers out during the commotion?"

"Suppose he gets caught?"

The milk shake came. It was watery. Pepe fished around for the blob of ice cream with a long spoon.

"What did you and Uribe work out?"

"He needs the bread so he says he's gonna try to get the papers down to my apartment come hell or high water."

"Good. Let's get over there and wait for him."

Benny García's leather-scarred face contorted with fear.

Rico Parra stood by the telephone in a faded robe, slapped his forehead and screamed at the man on the other end of the line. The floor was littered with newspapers, empty bottles, and unreclaimed dishes. Rico slammed the phone down, paced, puffed his cigar, and went into a coughing spasm.

"I want to see the doctor!"

"Get a doctor" was aped by a half-dozen flunkies, one of whom scurried out.

A waiter was passed into the room by the outer guards. He rolled a table up to the great man. Rico Parra plopped before it. The waiter lifted the lid of the soup tureen and ladled the contents into a bowl. Rico surveyed the table. "I asked for Coca-Cola! Where the hell is my Coca-Cola?"

Luis Uribe had entered the room quietly and went to Rico's desk, a familiar place to him, and began to gather up the papers on it.

"I'll bring your Coke right away, sir," the waiter said.

"You speak Spanish!"

"Yes, sir. I am Puerto Rican."

Rico arose, coughed, spat, missed the wastebasket, then put his hand on the waiter's shoulder. "Don't call me 'sir.' There are no servants in Cuba. Only servants of the Revolution. You are my *compañero*, and one day you will be liberated. Make that a large Coke."

"Yes, sir."

Luis Uribe moved toward the door.

"Uribe!" Rico shouted.

"Yes?"

"Where are you going with those papers?"

"You asked for translations and notes for tomorrow's meeting with the Soviet delegates."

"I told you to work on them here and not take them from the room."

"You were supposed to go out for dinner, but you're sick. How do you expect me to work with all this noise? I can't get them done in time."

"Well . . . all right . . . you can do it in your room, but be careful. Hernández, you go and stay with him."

Luis Uribe crossed the hall, trying desperately to think out what to do as the hulking Hernández lumbered after him and closed the door behind them.

Uribe stacked the papers on his own desk and flicked on the lamp. Perhaps he should call down to Benny García. No, that would be too risky.

He scratched a halfhearted note on the foolscap pad. God! He needed the money. He had been utterly determined to go through with it when he knew he was coming to America.

Maybe try to deal with Hernández. To guess wrong on him would mean his life. Hernández was oversized for a Cuban. A thug who could destroy with either hand and a devoted bodyguard of Rico Parra.

Minutes ticked off as he played listlessly with the translation. How long would Benny García wait?

Hernández sprawled on the couch across the room, thumbing through a Spanish edition of *Life*. He suddenly threw down the magazine, came to his feet heavily, stretched and grumbled.

"Goddamnit!"

"Eh? What's the matter, Hernández?"

89

"Nothing."

"Then be quiet while I work."

"Rico is my *compañero*. I do anything for him, but sometimes I wonder. He never gives nobody a night off. He doesn't even think about it. Anyhow, I thought he would be at the Russian dinner tonight. So I asked Benny García to get me a woman. She's waiting in my room. I haven't had a woman since I've been in New York. How long you be working on that stuff?"

"Till after midnight."

"Goddamn."

Hernández cracked his knuckles, then phoned to his room. The woman was still there. He hung up, buried his face in his hands and sobbed. "She won't wait. She's got to go home to her husband in an hour. Son of a bitch."

Luis Uribe, a man who had lived his life on nerve's edge, suddenly showed a magnificent moment of calm he never knew he owned. He took off his glasses, shoved his papers aside and folded his hands, looking much like a stern schoolmaster at the sobbing Hernández.

"Hernández, I am going to do you a favor. I will let you go to your room if you promise to do your business and be back in forty-five minutes."

Hernández looked up in disbelief.

"You are a man. You need a girl."

"You really mean it?"

"Of course."

He threw his arms around Uribe in a bear hug. "What a friend! I thought you were an old woman."

"For God's sake be careful," Uribe said. "We will both get into serious trouble if Rico finds out."

Hernández put his finger to his lips in a to-the-

90

death vow, flattened against the wall, opened the door a crack, blew a kiss to Uribe and sneaked out to keep his rendezvous.

Uribe began to shake. The papers rattled as he gathered them and shoved them into folds of the day's *New York Times*.

Benny García bolted the door of his apartment behind Uribe. "God, man, thought you'd never get here. I was about to give it up."

"We do not have long to work," Uribe said. "Just half an hour."

"The papers," Pepe Vimont commanded tersely.

"Here . . . in here . . ."

"Spread them out on the floor, quickly."

Pepe unsnapped the Tessina camera from his wrist, knelt, focused and shot film after film with the calm and precision of an expert marksman.

"Gather them up."

He handed the roll of money to Benny García and beat a hasty retreat from the San Martín Hotel.

The TWA bags were switched at La Guardia Airport. Maurice caught the eight o'clock shuttle to Washington. As soon as the seat-belt sign was turned off, Maurice went to the men's room and placed the film in a small plastic bag and shoved it down the used towel disposal unit.

Twenty minutes outside Washington an agent named Michôt entered the men's room and retrieved the bag of film.

A banana flambée sent up a pillar of fire. As the plates were delicately served, the performance was interrupted by Jeannine, the hostess, who led

André into the owner's office and shut the door after him.

"Devereaux," André said into the phone.

"This is Madame Camus. The letter you were waiting for has arrived safely."

(9)

THE FINCA SAN JOSÉ lay midway between Havana and San Julián and not far from Pinar del Río. It had been a massive estate which belonged to a single family and was broken up by the Cuban Revolution and turned over to the hundreds of small farmers who had toiled there in feudalism for generations.

With the old masters out of the place, the Revolution turned the land back to the people with great, great fanfare. Dignitaries from Havana, Castro district leaders, new agricultural commissioners, and dream-makers all descended on the Finca San José.

Impressive documents filled with seals, government stamps, and flourishing signatures were handed over to the peasants to certify that the land was now theirs, forever.

Speeches and a week-long celebration praised the Revolution.

And the speechmakers departed. In their place, the Finca was swarmed over by the new breed of bureaucrats.

A model house was built. It was the forerunner of an entire new village that would come . . . someday.

A school was built. The first in the history of the Finca. Others would follow . . . someday.

A communal was established where a man

could air his complaints. Heaven had been promised on earth.

But when the full heat of the summer struck, the peasants came to realize that the new bureaucrats had merely replaced the foremen of the old days. In the beginning, for a time, the hoax worked, for the illusion of the small landholders was so great and so desperate that they were unwilling to believe that things could really be worse than before the Revolution. They were worse. The always increasing quotas imposed a toil beyond capacity.

They spoke among themselves at great length about the documents of ownership and even went to someone outside the Finca who could read and write.

The documents said that no farmer could sell or rent his land. How could he own it if he could not sell it?

The documents said the land had to be worked diligently and the quotas had to be met or the owner could face imprisonment.

The documents said that the land had to be farmed by the oldest son after the death of the father. This eternal bondage was the Revolution's definition of "ownership."

It was clear they were deeper in serfdom than ever. Finca San José and hundreds of other "liberated" villages about Cuba dried up listlessly and reverted to ramshackle pestholes.

One day a large convoy of Czech-made trucks showed up at the Finca gate. Most of the trucks were empty. Others were filled with soldiers of the Revolution.

The village alarm bell was rung and the men ran in from the canebrakes with machetes in

93

hand, the women from the hovels and the sugar mill, and the children from the new school which taught little but Revolution. They were herded to the village square, now called Liberation Plaza, and addressed by a Castro official from the back of one of the trucks. He read from a document equally as impressive as their own "ownership" documents.

His document said that for the betterment of the Revolution the Finca San José was to be evacuated. He did not explain how this would be better.

The families were given an hour to gather together their belongings of not more than two suitcases or packs and to load aboard the trucks for resettlement. They were dispersed with the Revolution's slogan, "Fatherland or Death," ringing in their ears.

It was not much of a place, this Finca San José, but it was the only home that any of them had ever known.

No time for weeping or sentimentality! Onto the trucks and away! Long live the Revolution!

Among the Rico Parra papers was an involved document spelling out the terms of a Cuban-Soviet pact which had been negotiated earlier in Moscow. Rico Parra was to turn over certain details to the Soviets in New York during the United Nations meeting.

André Devereaux found most enticing the sudden evacuation of Finca San José and its reassignment to the Soviet armed forces.

Another portion of the pact pertained to the port of Viriel, which lay fifty miles due east of Havana. It was an old port and all but rotted with disuse. Now Viriel was to be reactivated and become the recipient of a sudden large influx of Soviet shipping. Elaborate security measures were to be taken to cloak the port in secrecy. With Havana more than adequate, it appeared obvious to André that the Russians were hauling in secret cargo.

Other articles of the pact detailed the arrival of heavy construction equipment and materials specifically for storage tanks and the building of barracks and highway and rail spurs in the Pinar del Río and Remedios regions.

With this windfall in his hands, André Devereaux was now compelled to reach a crucial decision. If it were a correct decision, he would have to reach it alone and it did not necessarily mean a popular decision.

According to the bylaws of Inter-NATO Intelligence Network, if the security of a sister country was threatened, a person in Devereaux's position could report directly to the threatened country without prior clearance from Paris.

André knew the Americans had Cuba under surveillance by U-2 flights.

He also knew that the American espionage ring in Cuba was broken and that in large measure America depended upon her allies, who still had relations with Cuba.

Further, the Americans had become disillusioned with the data they got from refugees and generally considered it unreliable.

While André had the authority to turn over a copy of the Rico Parra papers to the Americans without the permission of Paris, it was not so simple. Relations between France and America had deteriorated to such an extent that the exchange of intelligence had all but dried up. Any action by him which favored the Americans would be gravely frowned upon by Paris.

But suppose he sent the film to Paris and did not advise the Americans? There was an equal chance he would receive orders not to divulge the Rico Parra papers. The Americans might well be kept in the dark about events that threatened the entire hemisphere.

For André it was a familiar position. He was once again squarely on the griddle.

After two sleepless nights he came to his desk haggard and close to exhaustion. Two copies of the film were made to be kept in Washington. The original negatives were to be dispatched by courier to SDECE in Paris.

When his decision had been made, André scribbled a cable to headquarters:

I HAVE OBTAINED FILMS OF DOCUMENTS CARRIED BY RICO PARRA. ORIGINAL NEGATIVES EN ROUTE BY COURIER. BECAUSE OF URGENT NATURE OF IN-FORMATION, I AM USING MY PREROGATIVE AND SUPPLYING AMERICAN ININ CHIEF WITH A SET OF FILM OF ALL DOCUMENTS.

DEVEREAUX

(10)

AMERICAN ININ headquarters stood in an unmarked old red brick building in the Foggy Bottom section of Washington.

Marshall McKittrick received an urgent call from ININ while en route to a concert at the White House.

Nordstrom, Hooper, and the ININ chiefs, without the luxury of procrastination, had pored over the Rico Parra papers. Sanderson Hooper briefed McKittrick and ventured the opinion that the papers were authentic.

The green phone to the White House was rung.

And aide tapped the President's shoulder as he listened attentively to a world-renowned cellist in the East Room. At the end of the number, the President excused himself.

"McKittrick, Mr. President. I'm afraid I'll have to see you tonight."

The President glanced at his watch. "We're midway in the concert. I can shake loose in forty minutes."

"I'll be waiting in your office. It might be a good idea to have the Joint Chiefs stand by."

"Right, Marsh, we'll have them rounded up."

"Thank you, Mr. President."

André Devereaux received his own summons very late that night after a return from a formal dinner at the British Embassy. He arrived at Foggy Bottom in slacks, sport shirt, and loafers and was led directly to Nordstrom's main conference room. The carnage of the day's battle was in evidence: dishes of hastily eaten hamburgers and half emptied coffee cups and uncountable cigarette butts and stacks of notes and photographs still not assembled.

The three men remaining in the room were weary. Even the impeccably groomed Marshall McKittrick looked seedy.

"First, we want to thank you, André," Michael Nordstrom said. "No need in repeating how important this is."

Hooper sucked halfheartedly at an almost

97

empty pipe. "We believe that the Rico Parra papers are authentic."

"I felt they were authentic," André agreed. "I couldn't find a plant anywhere."

"It is our conviction," Hooper continued, "that the Soviet Union is up to something, very possibly the introduction of offensive missiles into Cuba."

"That's a very good bet," André said.

"I met with the President a few hours ago," McKittrick said. "He's ordered a sharp increase in U-2 flights."

"Of course, you are aware," Hooper interjected, "of our routine U-2 activity over Cuba for the better part of a year. This Finca San José has been spotted in general terms. The Rico Parra papers mesh perfectly. Take a look here."

Hooper's aged hands spread a number of aerial reconnaissance photographs before André, who lifted a magnifying glass and studied them.

"We're concerned with all the construction going on," Hooper said.

"I know the area. It would make a good missile site," André ventured.

"That's our guess."

"The President does not feel we can have a confrontation with the Soviet Union at this moment," McKittrick said. "On the basis of this evidence alone the Russians can claim it proves nothing."

André looked from one to the other. The Americans were grim. He was way ahead of them now.

"You are suggesting that you must have positive knowledge from inside Cuba," André said.

"Yes," Nordstrom answered.

"And your own intelligence resources are not sufficient on the island."

"You know that."

"I take it you are soliciting the help of France?"

"The help of Devereaux," Nordstrom answered.

"I'm not to tell Paris about Kuznetov and I am to apologize to Paris for a dozen requests for information that sit on your desk unanswered. I think I have had my fill of this one-way street."

"André . . ."

"No, damnit!" He came to his feet, bent over the table and eyed them angrily. "I warned you about the Russian surface-to-air missiles in Cuba. Not only the SAMs but the Russian jet bombers."

"We have only the power to gather information, André."

"I warned you from the first day Castro came out of the mountains. I warned you, McKittrick, and you, Mike, I warned you Che is a Communist and Rico Parra is a Communist. But you played with them! Well, after this mess you made at the Bay of Pigs it may be too late to keep the Russian missiles out."

"André," Mike said calmly, "you know how we value you."

"To do your dirty work."

Nordstrom spoke slowly. "I haven't supplied you with intelligence information, because we're all afraid of SDECE leaks. I'm not asking you to agree, but I know you can't disagree. As for the intelligence on Cuba, two Presidents have been briefed on everything you've said or suspected. Besides," Nordstrom added, "what about you and President La Croix? How much have you convinced him?"

André walked to the door and knocked for the outer guard to open. "I'm quite tired. I've worked forty-eight hours on end over the Parra papers. I'll let you know about going to Cuba."

"By the way," Nordstrom said, "I saw Kuznetov yesterday. He sends his regards. He's making an excellent recovery."

"I'm not certain whether he's lucky or not," André said.

The three Americans were unable to look at each other for some time after André departed.

"Jesus Christ!" Nordstrom finally sputtered. "I hope to God we can make it right for him someday."

(11)

UNLIKE HIS delicate performance at the Legion of Honor dinner, Ambassador René d'Arcy bit off the end of his cigar, spit it into an ashtray and lit it with quick, violent puffs. SDECE had contacted him regarding André's pending mission to Cuba, and the French President's office was pressuring him to influence Devereaux to change his tack.

"I must say, Monsieur Devereaux, I personally frown on your going to Cuba."

"Are you frowning officially or unofficially?"

"Well, the gist is that this is solely an affair between the Cubans and the Americans."

"Perhaps . . . perhaps not. I have a different interpretation, Monsieur l'Ambassadeur. There is an apparent threat to a NATO ally. France is still in NATO, you know. Unless you are ready to issue me orders on the matter, I intend to go forward with my plans."

D'Arcy rolled his cigar in pudgy fingers and

bolted out frustrated puffs of smoke across his desk to where André sat unmoved.

Despite Devereaux's unfortunate leanings, one would have to think more than twice about removing him from office. The skilled organization he had built in the hemisphere could collapse in lesser hands. Certainly Devereaux was one of the most competent intelligence officers in the SDECE. Furthermore, the Americans would turn completely cold to a new man. The pendulum had swung, sweeping away key personnel, and the pendulum had returned with La Croix people. André Devereaux had withstood the purges without politicking or kowtowing to the personal regime of a French President who was still under the influence of his personal sensitivities from twenty-five years earlier and his extraordinarily parochial advisers.

D'Arcy folded, unfolded his hands, tapped his fingers, balked. A large portrait of Pierre La Croix hovered behind him, glowering down on his back. "This whole undertaking is solely in the interest of the United States. I am going to be candid, Devereaux."

"That should be novel."

"There are unpleasant rumblings in both SDECE and the President's office about your overt pro-American attitude. The entire orientation of your office calls for a drastic change of thinking."

"Just what kind of change do you have in mind, Monsieur l'Ambassadeur?"

"To certain basic facts. France will not have her life and death dictated to by the Americans. France is the mistress of her own destiny."

"Or, better spoken, the master of her own destruction." André held up a hand to halt

D'Arcy's rebuttal. "No nation on this earth with a population of fifty million has the slightest chance of defending itself without an alliance with one of the two major powers. Without NATO and America we have nothing to deter a Soviet move on us."

"You call our *force de frappe* nothing?"

"France has an atomic popgun," he answered with disdain, flicking an imaginary fly from his wrist. "It cannot be taken seriously, despite the ill-spent billions."

"And you call the Western European Alliance nothing!"

"An archaic dream of two old men. A day-dream of forming a third power in Europe that calls for us to sleep with the Germans. Are you ready to sleep with Germany after what they have done to France in this century? Ah, Monsieur D'Arcy, but even if we are ready to deceive ourselves into believing that we could control a Franco-German union, the Germans are not so ready to abandon America."

As André spoke words detested under this roof, his mind suddenly reflected upon Boris Kuznetov. Kuznetov, a Russian who loved his country as he himself loved France. Kuznetov had paid the price for daring to be honest. How long could he, André, continue to hold these unpopular views?

"The return to glory," André said, "is an illusion. The attempt to break NATO and the medieval mentality of our foreign policy to play one great power against the other with little power pools is establishing exactly the same conditions that led to the destruction of France twice in our lifetime. Oh, yes, President La Croix and company play their cards like masters. I predict they will

102

go as far as to attempt to make France the broker between a union of Russia and Western Europe. And this will keynote tragedy for they don't understand . . . no one plays poker with the Russians. What keeps Soviet ambitions in check is not Pierre La Croix's international table-hopping but the power of the United States."

"That's quite enough, Devereaux," D'Arcy said, springing to his feet.

"Don't count on me as a party to the destruction of NATO. As a Frenchman, I say there is no way, no way at all, that Western Europe can survive without the presence of the United States." André arose and smiled. "You see, in fact, America is our leader."

D'Arcy's fist thumped on the desktop and his knuckles hurt. His round face turned apple crimson. "Such treasonous opinions have no place in French life today."

"You mean, Monsieur l'Ambassadeur, that no opinion other than La Croix's has a place. I beg to differ. That is not my France."

(12)

IT WAS GOOD to capture a moment of romance. Nicole looked radiant tonight in a lacy dressing gown on the other side of a candlelit table.

As the maid cleared the dishes, André leaned over and kissed his wife's cheek and thanked her, then luxuriated with a Jamaican cigar and a snifter of cognac.

"Darling, is this trip really necessary?" Nicole asked.

"I'm afraid so."

"Dr. Kaplan doesn't think it is."

"He doesn't run an intelligence establishment."

In his business few details were shared with his wife. Nicole usually knew better than to ask.

"You're going to Cuba, aren't you?"

André grunted a little laugh and pinched her cheek.

"Well?"

"You've a good nose for intelligence."

"Your health is not the only thing that disturbs me. The hostility against you at the Embassy is becoming quite apparent. I hear things and sense things that upset me. They say the Americans are just using you."

"Indeed they are. However, I've always been perfectly willing to be used in the interest of France."

"You and your twisting words. Lord, how I envy those people who live and breathe around us and who know a day of peace. Do you realize, André, since I've known you you've never really spent a day that you weren't in battle? For twenty years, day in and day out, this war you're in never stops. You bring it home with you, into the dining room, into the bedroom. As often as not I'm made to feel I'm looking at a detached stranger."

"Well, darling, better luck in your next life. Maybe you'll find a Tucker Brown IV."

"Why does it always have to be you who does it? What about the others? Why are you the one always in the middle?"

"President Truman had a little sign on his desk. I've always admired its philosophy. It read: THE BUCK STOPS HERE. I've envied certain people, too, the great majority of my colleagues whose sole mission in life is to attain the goal of mediocrity. They sail into a safe harbor, button up and con-

veniently and quietly sort their paper clips, avoiding responsibility and decisions. I can't explain,
Nicole, why I was singled out and am unable to
avoid conflict, but I can't run or plug my ears or
close my eyes or turn my back. I often envy those
who can."

She looked at him blankly, not drinking in his
words, but only feeling their thud as another of
his well-phrased rejections.

"I'm going up to see Michele," she said tersely.
"I'm thinking of going off with her on a trip."

"Where? When?"

"I don't know. France, to your father's. Switzerland, Outer Mongolia. Some place where I don't
have to be a daily witness to your demise."

Coming home these days, he thought, is not my
idea of heaven, but I never thought of a home
without Nicole. If I don't know how to quit and
if you love me, then, God, woman, accept it for
what it is and try to make things a little easier.

"For whatever it means," André said, "I still
love you dearly and I don't want to go through
life without you."

Nicole took her hand out of his, folded her
napkin, and stood. "Give Juanita de Córdoba my
regards," she said.

André watched her leave the room, stinging
from the slur. Damn it! Juanita de Córdoba had
no place in this conversation! It was the unpre-
dictable quiltwork of a woman's mind, the determined illogic of ending up with a stab.

Or was it so illogical? André ticked the ash
from his cigar and spun his cognac around slowly.
Wasn't this the real heart of the matter and
wasn't Nicole's intuition perfect?

Lord knows he had tried to keep the affair with

105

Juanita from his wife and Lord knows he was a fool to think he could. He had intended to live with Nicole forever and let things go on as they were. Yes, even to love Nicole in that certain way that two decades of marriage dictated.

But his real love, though denied and buried, belonged to Juanita de Córdoba. How many days and weeks and months had he gone on without daring to think about her, shutting this longing for her out of his life?

But the thrill and the hunger for Juanita never failed to renew itself.

In this moment of honest appraisal, Nicole understood perfectly.

André had tossed around his decision of whether or not to go to Cuba for the Americans. In the end the scale tipped in favor of the trip because Juanita would be there. And even though he denied it to himself and justified it otherwise, this was the truth.

His lips touched the cognac snifter. . . . "Juanita . . . yes . . . I am afraid I love you very much . . . I am sorry for that . . . for both of us. . . ."

He drew himself from the table and made his way slowly to the head of the steps. A ray of light from Nicole's room fell over the hallway and down the stairwell. He stood motionless, waiting until her door closed at last.

"Nicole," he whispered to himself, "please, please understand. Juanita is an unreachable dream . . . an illusion . . . but I must be allowed to dream. It means nothing between you and me. You are my wife and I love you . . . in a different way. . . ."

André found himself standing before Nicole's

door knowing it was not locked. Somehow he could not bring himself to open it and go to her with his thoughts flooded with Juanita de Córdoba and the coming nights with her.

Nicole lay in her bed tensely, listening for his every movement, praying the door would open. Praying to see his shadow move to her, stand over her, sit by the edge of the bed. She wanted the touch of his hand stroking her head, for him to draw back the sheets and come beside her.

Much of it tonight would be a lie, she thought, but God, I want him.

And she fell into despair as the sound came of his door shutting and wet tears formed on her pillow.

It turned midnight. André continued to toss in the dark, unable to sleep. The phone rang. He switched on the lamp and lifted the receiver. "Devereaux."

"Hello, Daddy."

"Michele. How are you, darling?"

"I'm fine. I understood you were going away. I just wanted to say good-bye."

Her voice sounded strange and shaky.

"I mean," she continued. "we've been missing each other and really haven't had a chance to sit and talk for months."

"Yes, come to think of it, it has been quite a time. Well, you know how my work goes."

"Of course, I realize. I'm not complaining."

"Come now. What's really bothering you? The quarrel with Tucker?"

"We're through and I couldn't care less. I just missed you tonight and wanted to talk to you . . . and to say . . . I love you very very much."

"Thanks, Michele. Maybe we'll be able to get

107

away later." But these were meaningless words, for he'd promise and disappoint her again as he had done before. How many disappointments did the rules allow him?

He fell back on his pillow with the light on, then went to Nicole's door and opened it softly and made to the edge of her bed and felt for her hand in the darkness. She was awake, but there was little warmth in her response.

That crazy recurring thought came to him that it would serve him right if some other man took her. He could envision the details of her love-making, her enjoying it madly. For that instant, he did not object to the sensation that swept through him. He wanted it to hurt and he wanted to be punished for Juanita de Córdoba and all the others.

He returned to his room.

André Devereaux and Brigitte Camus made for the National gate as the Miami flight was announced. He mumbled instructions she knew by heart.

She waited until he was in the plane and out of sight before she cried.

For twelve years André had come and gone, and Nicole had always taken him to the gate to see him off. André had looked for her in vain, and when the flight was announced Brigitte saw a desperation seize him. Oh, damn you, Nicole Devereaux! Don't you know he must do what he must do?

"Cocktail, sir?"
"Bourbon, please."
He watched land's end below. The layover in

108

Miami would be a short one until the KLM flight to Havana. It was painful to go there these days. Havana had turned old overnight, like a beautiful woman who had undergone major surgery at the hands of a butcher.

At least, Juanita de Córdoba would be waiting. Beautiful Juanita . . .

(13)

FROM THE EARLIEST memory she had been known as La Palomita, "The Little Dove."

Her name was Juanita Ávila de Córdoba. Her grandfather was Manuel Ávila, foremost among the lieutenants of the national liberator, Martí. During the ten-year war that freed Cuba from Spain, Manuel Ávila was to immortalize himself among his people as "The Poet of the Revolution."

Juanita Ávila de Córdoba's father, Jorge Ávila, had become Cuba's greatest composer and a guitarist of world renown. It was his composition, a lullaby to her, "Don't Weep, Little Dove," that was to give her the identity that would remain all of her days.

When Héctor de Córdoba, scion of a great family of landed gentry, took the Little Dove in marriage, it was an event long remembered in Cuba as one akin to a royal wedding. The couple were of the aristocracy, by both fortune and achievement.

Héctor de Córdoba preferred the electricity of life in Havana and the international sparring grounds of diplomacy and the world's sporting places to the bondage of the family holding near Santiago.

In the mold of a staunch independent thinker and somewhat of a black sheep, Héctor's interest in family affairs remained nominal, Actually, he was in constant battle with his family, deploring the exploitation of the peasants and the other social injustices upon which the family had been able to build and hold an empire.

The pull and tug of Cuban politics had always been a deadly game. Héctor de Córdoba, a liberal in days of reaction, achieved a stature so great that he rose above that small army of bickerers and became one of Cuba's foremost diplomats, mainly as a roving ambassador and negotiator. His value was great enough to pass him through seasons of disfavor with Batista, although, over a period, his relations with the dictator turned to ice.

He rejected a Batista attempt to bury him in a remote, obscure diplomatic post and chose to practice law and live in *de facto* political exile in Marianao, a suburb a few miles west of Havana in the hills overlooking the sea.

When Castro swept from the Sierra Maestra Mountains into Havana, it was Héctor de Córdoba who embraced him beneath the monument to Martí. It could now be known that Héctor had been one of Castro's manipulators and backers in the capital who hastened the collapse of Batista.

A month after the liberation of Havana, Héctor de Córdoba was killed in a tragic airplane crash en route to his first diplomatic mission under Castro.

Raul and Fidel and Che Guevara and Rico Parra all wept openly as the Little Dove was handed the flag of Cuba that adorned her hus-

110

band's coffin. In shaken voice, Fidel Castro named Héctor de Córdoba a martyr of the Revolution.

Juanita then retreated with her two sons into mourning in the pink marble villa in Marianao.

In the days that followed Castro's victory, great estates were broken up ruthlessly, with the former owners receiving a pittance of their true value.

Fidel Castro personally interceded in behalf of Juanita and arranged a large and admirable settlement on the de Córdoba holdings. The Little Dove of Cuba was that kind of aristocrat who could transfer from one regime to another and become an aristocrat of the Revolution.

When the time for weeping was done, Juanita emerged from her villa and continued the good works that had been part of her training and heritage from childhood. She walked among the impoverished and battled for the orphan.

She was swept into the swirl of state functions.

She was a woman who made a man feel good. To pour his liquor, to light his cigar. To dance with him till dawn.

She campaigned for greater sanitation in the villages.

The disenchantment with Fidel and his Revolution set in almost at once.

Lifelong friends were rounded up in a terror that soon filled the dungeons of Morro Castle and the moats of La Cabaña.

And many ended up in the Green House of G-2 on Avenida Quinta, to be doled the cruel mercy of Castro's chief inquisitor, Muñoz.

Juanita de Córdoba's reaction to the rape of Cuba and the murder of her friends filled her with unbounded hate of Castro. And she set out to do something about it.

111

Many years before his death, Héctor de Córdoba had attended a conference in Washington as an adviser on the sugar quota.

André Devereaux had also attended in behalf of France, both because he was knowledgeable in matters of the sugar quota, and because it was a good place to obtain intelligence information.

In the course of their daily contact, a friendship was struck up between Devereaux and Héctor de Córdoba, and also between their wives.

In his subsequent visits to Cuba, André continued his friendship with the de Córdobas and never failed to visit them at Marianao. Through his sources in Havana, André learned that Héctor was secretly working for the Castro band, which was then still in the Camagüey Mountains.

"I must warn you, Héctor," André told him over sunset drinks on the veranda, "that you will be disillusioned with this Castro. I know you detest the present regime, but those boys up in the mountains smell like Communists."

"André . . . ugh! . . . what will I do with you? You smell Communists behind every tree, under every leaf. It is a mania with you. I have known Raul and Fidel since we were children together in Santiago. Fidel is radical, yes. But a Communist, never. And, my friend, after this bastard Batista is thrown out, Cuba needs radical thinking."

"So the Castro brothers are pure Cuban. How about that South American devil, Che? And what about Rico Parra? Parra is straight out of the Soviet system."

"Yes, André, and how about the Americans? The damn Yankees do business with the Peróns, Trujillos, Batistas and Jiménezes, but let anything smack of desperately needed reform and you denounce it as Communist."

Juanita listened to it all quietly, attending to the level of their glasses and saying little.

"Mark it down, Héctor. Fidel Castro will become a menace. Even the Americans refuse to listen to me now, but they'll learn."

"Nonsense. The Cuban people will never choose Communism."

"They won't have to. The choice will be made for them."

Héctor died before the prophecy was fulfilled. Juanita had marked the Frenchman's words.

On André's first visit after Héctor's death, he went to the villa to pay his condolences. The Little Dove had already begun having her misgivings on the Revolution.

Old friends were gone. Of those who were left, one had to be suspicious. André was one of the few with whom she could share her feelings of sorrow and disgust over what was happening in Cuba.

Each visit thereafter, Juanita's feelings against Castro had grown darker and darker.

André sensed an opening upon which to build an important contact. She was a woman of prominence, above suspicion, and highly placed in the inner circles. He held back at first. Then, as the American intelligence organization in Cuba was broken, he proceeded to feel her out with caution, for as the Cuban government drifted toward the Soviet Union, new sources of information would be desperately needed.

André became a frequent visitor. At first he was looked upon from the outside as a good friend, and later rumor had it that there was a romance.

What André was romancing was the careful buildup of an espionage ring, and its heart was Juanita de Córdoba, the Little Dove.

He trained her expertly and sent her out on a mission. Since she was free to travel throughout Cuba at will, Juanita's appearances were considered good for the image of the Revolution. In trips around that country she recontacted some of those friends who had escaped the Castro terror and banded together a small, select group of patriots placed in every part of the Island.

André guided her in establishing communications through dead-letter drops in hidden places around the country.

When a message came back to Juanita de Córdoba, she would then pass it on to the French Ambassador, Alain Adam. Usually the messages were passed at cocktail parties or formal dinners and, at times, in broad daylight at public rallies right under the very beards of Fidel and Che and Raul and Rico.

André Devereaux had an excellent eye on Cuba, indeed.

(14)

MICHAEL NORDSTROM lined up the shot, drew the billiard stick back and tapped the cue ball. It slid off the six ball with a trace of side English. The six ball dangled, then dropped reluctantly into an end pocket.

"Eight ball in the side pocket." Mike chalked, made his shot, straightened up and beamed at his son, Jim. "Your old man didn't get a reputation as a good pool hustler for nothing. Earned all my spending money at Stanford doing this."

Jim was glad his dad finally won for his dad was down three games. Mike tousled his son's hair, replaced the stick in the rack, rolled down his sleeves, and walked up from the recreation room to the kitchen.

Liz had come in from her sunbath. She still looked great in a bikini. He watched her as she flitted about the kitchen setting a light under the pot of stew. As she passed, Mike grabbed her, reached under her robe and rubbed her warm flesh. Liz stopped long enough to lean back against him and purr.

"Hon, I'd like to take in the movie tonight with the Bowmans."

"What's playing?"

"*Lolita* with that deliciously decadent James Mason."

"Sure."

Liz put a tall iced tea before him as he thumbed through the Sunday papers, stopping at "Peanuts." He laughed and commented that Snoopy fractured him.

"The stationwagon is on the blink again," Liz said.

"Well, get it fixed."

"It spends half the time in the garage. Hon, do you think we'll be able to trade it in by the end of the year?"

"Huh?"

"I said I'd like to trade it in."

"Well, maybe. This Koufax is something. Struck out ten again last night."

Liz tasted the stew testily, adding a pinch of

115

onion salt and replacing the lid. Mike was in earnest in the sports page.

"Put the paper down, hon."

"Liz, don't talk about the car now."

"How are things with the Devereaux?"

"So-so."

"I dropped in to see Nicole this morning. I guess André had just left the house on his trip. She didn't take him to the airport."

"That's not a federal offense."

"It is with them. She was a little tight. Not drunk, just tight. A lot of tears and babbling. I've never seen her that way. I spent quite a bit of time with her . . . that's why lunch was late."

"You know how it is. He's under pressure, she folds."

"What about his women? I understand he has a lot of them."

"Not a lot, just enough. When he travels he gets down, tired, lonely. You know, like a human being. Hasn't got a damn thing to do with loving your wife."

"She's at an age where she's very uncertain about herself."

"For Christ's sake, Liz, what does Nicole want? André hasn't let any women give her a moment's worry or challenge her position. He's discreet and he hasn't dumped it on the doorstep. Nicole writes much more into this than she should."

"Yes, I suppose you're right."

"Right for Nicole's husband, not yours. Come on, Liz, we've played out the same damn scene. She's got him feeling guilty about things he hasn't done wrong."

"Are they going to make it?"

"I don't think so."

116

"Lord, I wish there was something I could do."

"People don't change, Liz. One by one the reasons to remain married fade. Most families hang together out of economic necessity. Then there's the children. Or the dread of loneliness. But there comes a saturation point where none of the fears equals the torture of a deteriorated marriage. I think she's pushed him over the edge."

"Nicole said something very strange. She said that she was getting the feeling more and more that he wants her to have a lover."

"We all go through that," he answered.

"Mike, it scares me to see this. Are we all right?"

"We're all right."

"It's not easy to learn, but I came to know that all the rest of it means nothing if you don't deliberately hurt me. I've really tried to make things more comfortable for you."

"You have, Liz."

The dreaded sound of the phone ringing stiffened Liz, then she answered and handed the receiver to him and saw his face grow tense and heard him say he'd be right down. Oh, *damnit!* Why can't they leave him alone just one Sunday?

"Something came up. I'm not sure when I'll get in."

"Of course, dear."

"You go on to the show. I'll heat up the stew."

"No, I'll wait for you, Mike." She put her arms about him and rested her head on his chest. "Try not to be too tired when you come home," she said.

(15)

SANDERSON HOOPER arrived at the Bethesda Naval Hospital simultaneously with Nordstrom and they proceeded together quickly down the corridor toward the guarded wing housing the Kuznetov family.

Boris Kuznetov was propped up with pillows. He smiled wanly as they entered. The Russian appeared much better. Some of the chalk had faded from his cheeks. "I regret to inform you I am making excellent progress," he said, "although American television is no help. It's quite bad."

Nordstrom pulled a chair close to the bed so Boris would not have to labor while speaking. Sanderson Hooper fingered his pipe in his pocket but remembered not to light it.

Kuznetov looked at both of them seriously. "I've come to a decision," he said. "That terrible pain hit my chest and darkness overcame me. Then I awoke under that oxygen tent. As the days passed with nothing to do but think, many things became very clear for the first time. I realized that if I could live, above everything else I had to live for my family. But I did not want to die. . . . I just didn't want to die. . . . I still love Russia."

He stopped and tears came down his cheek at the mention of his mother country.

"It's also unjust to take this country as my home and betray it from the beginning. Well, Nordstrom, you should be proud. I'm going to tell you everything."

He blinked a moment and waited to reinforce his meager strength. "You can start your Americanization program with Olga and Tamara."

118

"I keep posted about your condition every day," Michael said. "We'll have to take it very slowly. Soon as the doctor gives the green light, we'll start."

"Yes, take care. I'm a valuable piece of merchandise. . . . I insist that Devereaux be present."

"He's on a trip. Will you agree to the preliminary interrogation without him?"

"Yes, that should be all right."

"Try not to brood," Nordstrom said.

Nordstrom drove back to Washington, taking small consolation in the victory over the Russian.

"I suppose things do become clear inside an oxygen tent," Sanderson Hooper said. "Mike, you haven't spoken a word."

"Just thinking."

"About Boris Kuznetov?"

"About him . . . mostly about Devereaux. What's the connection? Why does Kuznetov demand André?"

"Points to the fact that Kuznetov has been on a mission against France."

"Or maybe he is deliberately using Devereaux."

"We all seem to use Devereaux," Hooper said.

"He's in a lot of hot water, wife and country. Hoop, I got a line on his health. Maybe we shouldn't have asked him to go to Cuba."

"Sorry about all his bad luck," Hooper answered coldly, "but we have to think of ourselves."

(16)

JUANITA DE CÓRDOBA pulled her car to a halt before the carved wooden door of the villa. In a quick, graceful movement she spun out of the

119

driver's seat, gathered up her packages, and shut the door with a push of the heel.

Emilio, the houseman, rushed out and took her packages. The instant she walked into the foyer the odor of potent cigar smoke was present.

"Rico Parra, señora," Emilio said, "he has been waiting for over an hour."

She hid her displeasure, lowering her eyes. "Very well."

At the end of the foyer she could see past the French doors to the veranda which hovered above the sea. Rico Parra, boots propped on the rail, sat munching a large mouthful of banana from a fruit bowl. He flipped the peeling over the rail, swallowed the load, and lit another cigar.

She studied him. The green dungarees were new and pressed, his boots polished to a high sheen, and even the unruly mop of hair and beard had been put into order for the occasion. As she approached she could smell a second odor. He reeked of cologne as though he had bathed in it in a clumsy attempt to make himself presentable.

Rico heard her dartlike footsteps, dropped his boots to the tile floor with a thud, and came to his feet. Juanita moved through the French doors without a word and his eyes followed her with obvious longing.

"I happened to be in the neighborhood," he blurted. "I . . . uh . . . there are a number of public events coming up next month and I thought I could be your escort."

There was no answer from her.

"Well, for Christ's sake, I could have more of a welcome. I've been gone a long time. Did you get my letters?"

"Yes."

"Paris, Moscow . . . head of the Cuban delegation in New York. Not bad for a peasant's son, eh?"

She continued to bear his unwelcomed presence with a quiet dignity that made the contrast between them even more apparent.

"Look, I brought some things from Paris," he said. "France," he continued as an afterthought. "Perfume, real French perfume and a case of champagne. And here, a needlepoint handbag. It is very expensive but it says to me . . . Little Dove . . . and I knew you should have it."

"I will not accept gifts from you," Juanita said and watched his face grow dark.

"Why do you always make me feel like dirt?"

"Rico, this business has been going on for a year. I have made my feelings clear. It embarrasses me to be put into this position. Please leave me alone."

He flung his cigar to the floor and squashed it under his boot and moved to her, breathing unevenly, then shoved both hands in front of her eyes. "See! My fingernails are clean! They are manicured just like yours!"

She turned her back on him and walked toward the living room and he followed, pleading . . . "Juanita . . . please . . . you are making a great mistake. I am now one of the biggest men in all of Cuba. Fidel depends on me from morning to night. You know how I crave you."

She stopped her retreat and stared into the black wounded eyes and the revolutionary quaked before her. "I have no feeling for you, Rico," she said firmly.

"Because I am a peasant!"

121

"No. There are many beautiful peasants in Cuba. They live and die with dignity. What you really want from me is respectability. There is no way you can buy it."

"Why?"

"Because you are scum."

His eyes watered and he giggled half madly. "But André Devereaux is a gentleman, isn't he! He kisses your hand and dribbles little whispers into your ears. Oh yes, the great French lover is coming to his Little Dove and you cream!" Rico thumped his fist against his chest. "But he will never be a man like me! Yes, and what about the others . . . the great Señor Iglesias with his Venezuelan oil and his yachts taken from the blood and the sweat of the people! And the Italian wop bastard aviator. Very brave when it comes to bombing defenseless Ethiopian villages. . . . Well . . . I thought as long as you were passing it out so freely you might give a few of your countrymen a break." He grabbed her arms and pressed his fingers until his knuckles turned white. "Behind all of that crap . . . that nobility . . . you're just a slut."

"Good day, Rico," she said softly, "Emilio will see you out."

(17)

KLM FLIGHT 431 terminated at Rancho Boyeros, with the stairs being rolled to the DC-6B. A trio of immaculately white-clad Cuban musicians stationed themselves to greet the debarking passengers with rumbas, cha-cha-chas, and sambas. This was Castro's proof that there was still a "beat" in Cuba.

However, the "beat" began and ended right there.

André stepped into the suffocating terminal, where the air-conditioning had long been out of function for fear that explosives would be set into the ducts.

The old health officer, a relic of Batista days, recognized him and called him to the desk ahead of the others, where he was waved through to the immigration booths.

These were now manned by a half-dozen Castro militia clad in ill-fitting faded green fatigues. A Negro militiaman, who attempted to identify himself with the Revolution by a growth of straggly beard, took André's passport and thumbed the fully stamped pages with confusion. André reached over, took the passport and handed it back, right side up.

"Diplomat," André said.

The guard stared angrily, then gave the passport to an assistant who could read. A blank space was sought out and stamped with vigor.

André stood by his own immune luggage as more militia poked through the baggage of the others, confiscating all English-language newspapers and magazines, both pro- and anti-Castro.

The customs chief, a short, fat, big-bottomed woman, appearing ridiculous in green slacks, waddled over to him and placed the necessary stamps on his bags.

Outside the checking rooms, the French Ambassador to Cuba, Alain Adam, greeted André warmly. The chauffeur gobbled up his bags and they made for the car.

Alain Adam was a member of that dwindling band, a ranking diplomat who had escaped President La Croix's axings and, like André, continued in office on borrowed time.

They had gone in dozens. Good men. Good Frenchmen cast out of the services with objective ruthlessness and once out were usually unable to place themselves in compatible jobs in France and unable to survive on their meager pensions.

This was André's first return to Cuba in several months. The drive into the city showed, without words, that things had gotten still worse.

The row of factories, beginning with the Goodrich and International Harvester plants, was all but defunct.

The stadium was once again turned into a concentration camp, crammed with real or imaginary enemies rounded up after the Bay of Pigs.

André left Alain Adam at the Chancellery, taking an Embassy car by himself to let his professional eye appraise Havana.

The "beat" was gone.

Havana! The city of romance, rhythm, rum, roulette!

The "beat" was gone.

Gone were the shrill voices of the bookies in their lottery stalls where any Cuban worth his salt would bet on the next pitch or at the cockfight or at the *jai-alai frontons*.

That nervous movement of the Habanero taking his spoon-sized cup of potent sweet coffee in a single quick sip twenty times a day at the little open stands.

The beat of barter at the cheap brothels set in near the docks waiting for the French, American, and Italian fleets to unload their cargoes of swaggering sailors. This, too, was gone.

Gone were the clicking Cuban heels and swaying bottoms and the lust-filled eyes of the Habaneros, who seemed to have no other occupation but watching women's backsides.

And the beat of the promenaders who aired themselves along the Malecón sea front all dressed in bleached white.

Gone were the shiploads of tourists seeking sin, making off for Sloppy Joe's, where a dozen bartenders played out magnificent drama in the fine art of mixing drinks.

And El Floridita, where those in the know waited to ogle at the bearded pundit of American literature. El Florida, which acquitted itself nobly in its sacred mission of saving the daiquiri formula during American prohibition. And, during prohibition, the luxury yachts came to avail themselves of the pleasures of the Sodom of the Western Hemisphere.

Gone now were the delights of the lady tourists in that place where they could be improper. The pornographic movie houses and human male stud shows.

Diminished were the world's greatest night club, the Tropicana, and the splendid restaurants, the Monseigneur and the Crystal Palace and the rest where justice was done to the delectable Morro crab with mayonnaise made before one's eyes at tableside.

All these things that had made Havana a center of sin and gave her her "beat" were gone.

And in their place the arcaded streets were patrolled by angry, bearded, bereted revolutionaries.

The whores had all been rounded up and interned in the once elegant Hotel Nacional to be reenlightened to live as productive citizens of the new society. They were turned loose as drivers, and soon the highways and roads were littered with the wreckage of trucks that had died of abuse.

Smart shops once bulging with alligator and tobacco and liquors and other national products that lined the Paseo de Martí on Prado Boulevard were either seedy, empty or shuttered.

The nation's Capitol building, an edifice built after the Capitol in Washington of marble and rare woods and gilded bronze, had degenerated into a grotesque house of barter.

Departing refugees were forced to turn in almost every personal possession. These were dumped, sorted, and sold in the foyers, halls, and galleries of Cuba's Capitol. Baby shoes, eyeglasses, trousers, brassieres, sandals, Panama hats, jewelry, all stacked in marble corridors like the warehouses of Auschwitz.

André drove through the harbor tunnel to the Morro Castle and La Cabaña Fort. Thousands of Cubans stood in tragic silence waiting for a glimpse of a relative imprisoned in the former national shrines. The dungeons of Morro Castle were once again crammed. And thousands were shoved into the dry moats of La Cabaña, the black hole of the universe. They were left to die in the blazing sun with almost no water or sanitation, and they fought like rats for scraps thrown down to them by the militia.

Old people were in these moats. Old people who had come to Cuba to finish out their lives in the sun. Now they were enemies of the Revolution. Many Americans had been among them.

Castro made no attempt to hide prisoners. They were stuffed everywhere. Thousands and thousands and tens of thousands. The once luxury hotels were walled in by barbed wire and had decayed to lice-riddled flophouses.

In a final symbol of hate, the monument to the battleship *Maine*, a testimony to American help in the liberation from Spain, had been dismantled.

And all of it made the brute dictator Batista a pale, benevolent tyrant alongside the massive rape of Fidel Castro.

André Devereaux returned to his room in the Embassy to unpack. Alain Adam personally came to deliver him a message. André smiled as he read it. It was from Juanita de Córdoba and she was waiting.

(18)

Muñoz, the personal butcher of Havana and hangman of the Revolution, held court in his office in the dreaded Green House of Avenida Quinta near the sea.

Muñoz had innocent brown eyes and baby cheeks and an almost sweetness about him that belied the brutality with which he served Castro. The G-2 headquarters had been converted into a chamber of horrors reserved for the more prominent enemies of the Revolution. Here confessions were extracted in rooms that threw off a horrible stench.

Muñoz was no longer aware of the odor for the smell of death was a part of him. The personal torture of his victims had demented him beyond human feelings.

His visitor was Oleg Gorgoni, Resident of the Soviet Embassy in Havana and second ranking KGB officer in the Western Hemisphere.

"André Devereaux must be taken care of," Gorgoni demanded. "You know his history and his sympathies. Furthermore, we suspect this woman he consorts with. This Juanita de Córdoba."

Muñoz looked up with such menace that Gorgoni was suddenly struck wordless. "You suspect everyone. But you are not running Cuban G-2, Comrade. Unless you are ready to supply proof against Juanita, I advise you to be quiet about her."

Muñoz had extended himself to the limit of his powers. He could bully and persecute underlings and small fish, but one did not murder a ranking French diplomat, nor did one toy with Juanita de Córdoba. Fidel would feed him to his own sharks if he made a mistake. True, the Comrade Resident had sound suspicions, but it was a decision beyond his hands.

"We are entering a critical time period," Gorgoni persisted, "and how can we be certain that he Inter-NATO Intelligence didn't deliberately send Devereaux to spy during the transfer of missiles? What if he discovers them before they become operational?"

Muñoz was not about to get himself caught in the middle of this business. He stared long and wistfully out of the window to the iron fence that surrounded the Green House.

He could go directly to Fidel for instructions but the matter was complicated by Rico Parra and his lust for Juanita. If I take Juanita into custody,

Muñoz thought, that bastard Parra might seek vengence on me, and he is a madman.

On the other hand, Muñoz reasoned, Parra would certainly like to do in the Frenchman. Of course, Juanita did not limit her affections to Devereaux, but with him out of the way her resistance to Parra could lessen.

At any rate, Muñoz concluded, it was all Rico Parra's business and he intended to dump the whole matter on him.

"Very well, Comrade," Muñoz said to the Russian, "I will follow through."

(19)

THE NURSE wheeled Boris Kuznetov into a large room which had been converted for conference purposes. She set his chair at the head of the table. The nurse spoke Russian and had been specially deputized into ININ. She placed herself nearby in the event Kuznetov needed attention.

Boris looked down the table, sizing up his adversaries. Michael Nordstrom, who he felt was considerate, was at the opposite end. Certainly Nordstrom could not be present at most of the conferences. He would be missed.

Between Nordstrom and Kuznetov were placed four men, two on either side of the table, armed with the full complement of foolscap pads, pens, ashtrays, drinking water carafes, and reference books and maps.

Nordstrom and his team had been warned strongly by the doctor not to grill Kuznetov too hard or to upset him, so the interrogation would have to be held on a far milder tactical level than normal.

129

"Mr. Jaffe, French desk at ININ," Nordstrom said. He wouldn't mind Jaffe, Nordstrom thought.

"Mr. W. Smith, Russian desk of ININ." W. Smith, Kuznetov had heard of and would be hearing a lot from.

"Dr. Billings, our Soviet economic and military expert." Billings had that soft-spoken appearance, but he would be deep and incisive in his questions.

The last man was introduced. "Mr. Kramer, counterintelligence." Always the foe.

Dr. Billings spoke first. Indeed, his manner was mild. "My colleagues and I are all fluent in Russian. Mr. Nordstrom is only adequate in the language but will not be with us often. The interview will be conducted in your language."

Kuznetov nodded.

"Everyone is well aware of your position," Nordstrom said. "We're not in a hurry, and if you become tired, just tell us."

"You have advised these gentlemen there is much information I will not speak about unless Devereaux is present," Boris said.

"We're all informed of that," W. Smith said, leaning on his elbows as if to get a better look into Kuznetov's eyes. "Does cigarette smoke annoy you?"

"The only tobacco I'm allowed to get near is that other people smoke in my presence. So kindly exhale in my direction."

"You see the tape machine here, of course," Nordstrom said. "All tapes will be transcribed and also translated into English. You can make any corrections after you have read the transcription. Is that agreed?"

Boris agreed quickly, grateful that the whole

business would be carried out without police-state tactics or menace.

"He's all yours, gentlemen," Nordstrom said.

"I'll begin," said Kramer of counterintelligence, scanning his note pad.

"Name?"

"Boris Alexandrovich Kuznetov."

"Aliases?"

"I have many, but that comes later."

"Birthplace?"

"Smolensk."

"Year?"

"Nineteen-sixteen. A baby of the Revolution."

"Family?"

"My mother died when I was three. There was left my father, a sister, and an older brother."

"Was your father active in the Revolution?"

"No, no interest. He was a carpenter, like Jesus' father."

As Kramer was forced into cracking a smile, Dr. Billings picked up the questioning, more slowly and softly.

"About your formal education. Where did you attend primary school?"

"Smolensk."

"What was the number of your school?" W. Smith fired out down the table.

"Sixty-two."

"Where was it located?" W. Smith snapped.

"Pushkin Boulevard near Brofka Avenue."

"There was a tobacco factory about a block away, was there not?"

"No. No tobacco factory."

"My records show a factory."

"Your records are in error. It was a residential neighborhood."

"Your school was a four-story building," Kramer said.

"No, two. It needed paint badly."

"Would you name the restaurants in your area?"

He did. Smolensk was thoroughly scrutinized, street by street.

They brought him through a round of questions to establish a normal, poor, hard-working family unit quite devoid of deep involvement with early Soviet politics.

"When did you become interested in Communism?" Dr. Billings asked.

"Well, in those days one had to make a choice. During the counterrevolution we sympathized with the Reds against the Whites. First my brother, then I, became members of the Pioneers in normal course as the Reds won control. However, the Pioneers, or youth movements, were not highly organized in the beginning. My first real interest was when I entered gymnasium, similar to your high school, in 1931. I joined Komsomol, the Young Communists, and was quite active in our unit."

"You went to gymnasium in Smolensk also?"

"Yes."

W. Smith, the Russian expert, dominated much of the questioning, feeding a great deal of false information. Boris remained calm, occasionally displaying barbed humor to slap their wrists.

"Now what position did you hold before your defection?" Kramer asked suddenly, skipping ahead.

"First, Mr. Kramer, I did not defect. One defects out of choice. I fled for my life without

132

choice. Second, I will not answer that question until Mr. Devereaux is present."

Both W. Smith and Kramer displayed detailed knowledge of Russia as they led him through his secondary education. At the end of the fourth hour he looked hopefully to Michael Nordstrom. His nurse quickly picked up the signal and indicated that that would be enough for the day.

(20)

SEVERAL MONTHS before the Bay of Pigs there came that moment in Juanita de Córdoba's villa that seemed a natural extension of the relationship between herself and André.

Juanita was having a sinking spell, depressed over the departure of her sons for schooling in Switzerland.

André was in a funk of his own. The first attack of narcolepsy had been followed by a severe round of arguments with Nicole. He was terribly down when he arrived in Havana.

Juanita de Córdoba was a striking woman, able to carry off severe hairdos, exotic colors, and large jewelry that gave her a look of total Latin femininity.

They sat quietly that night for a long while on the terrace watching the sun put on its closing display. It was an old place to them. They had sat there many times when Héctor was alive and later, when André cultured and tutored the espionage ring. Shadows came, and with them Juanita's sudden tears.

André put his arms about her to offer comfort, but beyond his motivation of compassion he was stirred by the touching, the silk, the scent, and the woman's softness.

He held her off at arm's length and stared at her, puzzled. "Juanita."

She nodded "yes," that she felt the same thing. It was simple and so very natural.

André, who was a sophisticated and traveled man of many nights, had known the enchanted routes of Europe and Latin America and North Africa. It would not seem likely that he would be so moved by just another affair. Yet he loved Juanita de Córdoba in a way that he was neither able nor desirous to discount. With Juanita he had broken his own rule that dictated he could not become emotionally involved with any woman. But even after the pain of the first parting he was unable to bring himself to cut it off.

Cubans are sensual children. When it was apparent that the Little Dove's mourning period had come to an end, it was looked upon by outsiders as permissible for her to take a lover discreetly.

Along with André Devereaux's worldliness, there was a strong vein of male vanity. She accepted the ground rules that she was to make no demands, keep her scenes reasonably quiet for a Cuban, and always anticipate an end to the affair and accept it gracefully.

Theirs was to become an affair of silent understanding without eternal pledges and devoid of an examination of its depth and meaning.

As convenient as the arrangement was for André, he somehow did not find it acceptable. Secretly, he admitted to himself he wanted to reach her deeply, have her think of him as he thought of her, wrest from her a kind of love that

134

would leave her lonely and wanting him when he was gone.

There was a rude awakening when she took up company with the Venezuelan tycoon, Fernando Iglesias, and on occasion served as hostess aboard his fabled yacht during its legendary cruise parties about the Caribbean.

There was another man often linked to Juanita. Manganaro, an Italian manufacturer who frequented Cuba. When his fabrication plant there was nationalized he opened a new one in Jamaica where she visited him.

André Devereaux's pride told him that he was the only man who really counted in her life. Yet he could not hide the hurt with his own common sense when he learned of the others.

He rationalized. Juanita was a needing feline creature. Perhaps she would be faithful if he could spell out his love. But with him out of Cuba most of the time, it was unrealistic for her to sit and wait for his ship to come in.

First, came the mission.

And so long as she was there for him alone when he was in Cuba and so long as she gave him the continued tenderness he could expect no more.

There was the terrible experience when he arrived unexpectedly from South America to learn she had gone off with Iglesias. André was wounded far more than a casual affair demanded. Moreover, he was making a basic error of an intelligence man. Never love . . . that was the rule.

But he did love her and he knew it then. And he had to remain quiet about it. He had no rights nor could he make any demands.

And in all eyes he simply remained a charming

135

French diplomat who breezed in and out of her life . . . among others.

After André had made his inspection trip of Havana and conferred with Alain Adam and the French staff, he knew there was going to be trouble for him this time.

The pressure of keeping the missiles a secret would dictate that the Cubans maintain a tight watch on him. If they got on to his game, they might try to do away with him. At the moment he left the Embassy to go to Juanita, his fears were for her. But, like his undeclared love, their danger was never talked about. She knew the risks from the beginning and they would not be discussed, ever.

And what about Rico Parra's unhealthy desire for her? It too could explode at any time.

As he drove into the hills west of the city he was consumed with a terrible sensation that his affair with Juanita de Córdoba was coming to an end just as their war together on Castro was also coming to an end.

She was there at the door when he arrived at the villa. The thrill was more intense than it had ever been. They embraced and swayed in the tightness of the way they held each other and they searched with their fingers . . . hers nervously clawing at his back and his fingers running through her black hair and over her cheek, and their lips sought each other out a hundred times. And at last the fervor mellowed to contented sighs and they were satisfied that it was all real that they were together again.

Juanita slipped him a note before he could talk. It read that he should be extremely careful as

136

she suspected the house was being watched and maybe tapped. He slipped the paper into his pocket, placed his arm about her waist and they walked lazily to the veranda and spoke of small things. Their fires had to be held in check for later.

In the evening they dined, as usual, in full view of everyone.

The only decent restaurant in a city once filled with fine dining places was La Torre, atop an apartment house. The Cuban government finally established it after numerous complaints by the diplomatic corps about the poor facilities.

With a majority of the diplomats visiting La Torre frequently, the room was profusely wired. This stratagem of Muñoz and the G-2 was crude indeed but André enjoyed using the opportunity to plant false information. Much of what he said was not bought by the Cubans and Russians but it could cause confusion.

Over their dinner, the small talk continued. Juanita spoke of the letters she had received from her sons in Switzerland. Their schooling was going very well and they looked forward to the ski season and her coming visit. Could André possibly be in Europe when she was there?

He no longer promised his time for he had had to break that promise too often.

They gossiped about the comings and goings of Washington and New York and the superficial social nonsense of Havana.

A stinging whistle brought all activity in the restaurant to a halt!

There at the entrance stood Rico Parra flanked by a half dozen Castroites of lesser rank.

Making certain his appearance did not go un-

137

noticed he yelled at a harassed maitre d', who nervously led the party toward their table. They made through the room with the fumes from their cigars fouling the air.

Parra stopped abruptly!

André came to his feet and extended his hand. It was not accepted. Parra glared from Juanita to the Frenchman. His clenched teeth caused a bulge of muscles about his jaw. A snarl changed to a strange giggle.

"I want to see you . . . now," Rico growled to Juanita.

André stepped slowly around the table so that he stood between Rico and the woman. "Not tonight, Señor Parra," he said quite softly.

The Cuban bullied with his eyes. André did not budge. Parra then let out a small cruel laugh, turned on his heels and walked from La Torre with his confused entourage trailing behind.

André returned to his seat, smiled reassuringly to Juanita, took her hand and kissed it.

"Hello there, mind if we join you for an after-dinner drink?"

It was the welcomed sight of the French Ambassador and his wife, Blanche Adam.

"I have a new travel film on the Cannes Festival," Adam said. "Why don't we all go back to the Embassy and I'll have it run."

"Not tonight, Alain darling," Juanita said.

"Don't be a killjoy. The cognac at my place is still French."

Juanita relented.

"By the way, Juanita," Blanche said, "the Chinese have a new First Secretary. Terribly clever chap. We're giving him a cocktail party next Friday. Perhaps you'd like to meet him. Now that France and China will probably be recognizing each other, we should get to know them."

"Yes, I'll be delighted to come," Juanita said.

"If you ask me, it's asinine of the Americans to withhold recognition of the Chinese. And they're not going to be able to keep them out of the United Nations forever."

There was further discussion of the conversation, made solely for the enlightenment of the G-2 wire taps. And then, the four of them swept from La Torre.

In the car on the way to the Embassy, Juanita allowed herself the luxury of becoming upset over the scene by Rico Parra.

"I would like very much," André said, "to have the pleasure of pulling his beard out, hair by hair, but I am afraid that my gallantry must be restricted in this country."

"He's the worst of the lot," Juanita cried. "He's a filthy beast and he's dangerous."

In the sanctity of the French Embassy, the charade of the day could be dropped. After Blanche poured their cognacs she excused herself from her husband's office.

"What is it, André?" Alain asked. "Something smelled rotten here for weeks."

"Yesterday," André said, "the port of Viriel was closed to all outside shipping. Clearing of the woods and other building activity at the Finca San José in Pinar del Río have been intense."

"What does it all mean?"

"The United States suspects that Russia is about to bring offensive missiles into Cuba, and I'm here to find out."

"Good God," Alain muttered.

"It could mean war," Juanita said.

"Yes, it could," André said. "The best chance there is to avoid a war is to detect the missiles and expose them before they become operational. Juanita, everything we've built in the past two years must pay off now."

"I see that we have our work cut out, my dear," she answered. "I believe in our people, André. We're not going to fail."

André nodded. "Alain, have Blanche figure out as many occasions as possible to have Juanita and me here together so I can give her instructions. It's impossible to do at her house anymore."

The Ambassador nodded.

"Information will be passed in the usual way. All other discussions will be held in this office. First priority is to cover that port," André said.

"I'll take a trip tomorrow and see our friends," Juanita said. "They're good boys, extremely reliable. Believe me that nothing will come into Viriel from the sea or out of Viriel into Cuba that will escape detection."

When the two men were alone and all the other business done, Alain Adam shoved all the papers on his desk aside and refilled the cognac snifters.

"She is a remarkable woman, André . . . a magnificent soul. . . . André, you and I have been comrades for a long long time. I sense something very different. Are you very much in love with her?"

André's face was drawn. "Yes," he whispered, "I am . . . and I've never told her and probably never will. What a shame. What a damned shame. Time has . . . just about run out on us."

The harrowing day was over. All the hungry

140

anticipation was done. Now, alone together as man and woman, there was neither wildness nor desperation. A beautiful calm descended over André and Juanita as they came together on the bed. They were at peace and grasped the rare instant of total contentment.

Not a word passed between them nor was any needed. . . .

Their hands, their mouths, their bodies spoke in a way more wonderful than it had ever been.

And when it reached its uncontrollable zenith, Juanita burst, at last, and trembled and cried for an hour and was unable to take her hands away from him until they loved again. He drifted into a euphoric dream with her fingers massaging away the tension in his back and neck.

He awoke with a cool chill passing over his body and saw the sea breeze blowing the curtain into the room. He had been in her arms, against her breast . . . all night . . . in the same position they had fallen asleep.

Juanita told him she loved him and she wept again and he asked why she was crying and she said it was from happiness.

André knew now that it was the same way with her as it had been with him. Wasn't it always that way? Hadn't she hidden her feelings to protect herself from heartbreak?

The sands of time had now run out. There was little left for them together. And, she need not keep her feelings from him any longer.

(21)

WHEN SHE HAD passed through Viriel a year

earlier, Juanita de Córdoba related to the Mendoza brothers the tragic news.

Carlos and Shuey Mendoza were to learn that their beloved father had been sent to Castro's concentration camp on the Isle of Pines after being branded, without trial, as an enemy of the Revolution. He was shot dead on the old ruse, "*la fuga*," the killing of a prisoner allegedly trying to escape. It was out-and-out murder and they all knew it, for one does not escape from the Isle of Pines.

After that, it was not difficult for Juanita to enlist Carlos and Shuey into the espionage group.

At one time the Mendoza family had had considerable interest in the shipping business of Viriel. Castro had confiscated their business.

But Carlos and Shuey had been born and spent their lives there, and they knew the old harbor like their mother's smile.

A day after André Devereaux arrived in Havana and gave instructions to Juanita, she traveled to Viriel and visited the Mendoza brothers and gave them cameras, field glasses, and orders to keep the harbor under scrutiny day and night.

On the third evening of their vigil four Russian ships . . . *Pinsk, Margrav, Georgia,* and *Vladivostok* . . . crept into the sagging harbor ahead of an onrushing storm. They were precisely the type of ship that the Mendozas had been told to look for. They had extremely wide beams, having originally been designed for the lumber trade.

All roads to and from the port area were sealed from the town by Cuban Army regulars. No Cubans were allowed into the port compound.

Russian troops debarked from the four ships in

battalion strength and took up guard of the port area as well as all stevedore duty.

At the Castro rallies one saw great portraits of the Russian and Cuban brothers clasping hands, embracing, side by side, fists upraised in play of white and Negro brotherhood. The marching brothers were grim in their determination. The embracing brothers smiled, comrades in this great new world of revolution.

But in Viriel the Cubans were puzzled, for the Soviets belied the posters by being standoffish and removed. So many strange things had happened since the Revolution. The local committees told the people the arrival of the Russian troops meant something for the better.

Yet the natives of Viriel remembered the brash Marines from Guantánamo and the American sailors when their little port was entered. They were different men. Wild and free, like the Cubans themselves. But one did not question these days.

The Russian entry had frightening overtones. Cubans were barred from their own places in their own land. They were kept from the hotels and bars in Viriel, where the Russians were billeted. Not even the prostitutes were allowed. During the day the four ships sulked at anchor. Only at night did they discharge their cargoes, while others slept.

But Carlos and Shuey Mendoza did not sleep. They crouched in the cliffs that surrounded Viriel. On the first night the storm hid the moon and bubbled the sea with increasing swells. During daylight they slept in shifts and used the long-range photographic equipment that Juanita de Córdoba had brought.

On the second night of the watch, the sea

calmed and it was moon-bright. Shuey Mendoza crept carefully from the hiding place and climbed down the jagged rocks to the sea. Alternating silent breast strokes and diving, he swam for a mile and ducked unseen under the pier pilings. He knew every cranny and hole. When the moon fell behind clouds, he slipped up onto the pier and hid in a lumber pile.

Carlos waited until two hours before daybreak, then made a shorter swim to the wreckage of an old ship which had piled up on the rocks just a hundred yards from the harbor entrance.

Each of them took a camera wrapped in plastic, and in short intervals shot film of the cargo which had been unloaded during the dark hours and now sat on the dock.

They stayed thus for twenty-four hours and on the third night retraced their steps, swimming back to the cliffs.

(22)

THE NEXT DAY, at the ancient graveyard of Matanzas on the road between Viriel and Havana, Rosa Mateos, wife of the local druggist, bought a bunch of flowers from the old vendor outside the cemetery walls.

She adjusted her shawl and entered. The wet ground and leaves sagged under her step. She looked about. The graveyard was empty.

Rosa Mateos walked to the third row of tombstones in the new section near the mango grove and counted to herself as she passed the tombs. Ten . . . eleven . . . twelve . . . thirteen . . . fourteen. She stopped and knelt, placing the flowers at the base of the stone.

144

Rosa patted the earth around the stone until her hand felt a crack in it near the ground. She pulled a loose fragment away and her fingers searched deftly, then found what she was looking for. She withdrew a plastic bag containing the film of the Mendoza brothers.

She slipped the packet inside her shawl quickly, replaced the piece of stone, prayed, made the sign of the cross and left the cemetery.

That evening her husband, Humberto Mateos, the druggist of Matanzas, left for his weekly trip to Havaná to requisition the drugs he needed to fill several prescriptions. It had been thus with the bureaucracy since Castro nationalized the druggists.

He personally delivered his requisitions to Amelia Valencia, a senior pharmacist at National Pharmacy No. 15 in Havana, along with the film.

During the afternoon break, Amelia Valencia visited the old market of Havana, as she often shopped during her time off. Her first stop was a futile attempt to buy some decent sandals at the sandal-maker, whose product had become atrocious since the Revolution.

The second stop was at the chicken stall of the butcher, Jesús Morelos. She passed the film to him.

Jesús Morelos put the packet into a chicken, sewed it up and set it aside.

Later in the afternoon, Maggie, Juanita de Córdoba's Negro cook of twenty years, also visited the stall of Jesús Morelos. The chicken and its messages then found its way to Juanita de Córdoba.

(23)

THESE WERE TO BE the longest, most harrowing days of André's life. For the intelligence chief there is no relief from the pressure. There are no fistfights, no gunplay, no swinging from balconies, no rescuing of maidens, no acrobatics, no karate chops, no miracle electronic gimmicks.

The pressure dictated silent courage and the brain-sapping work of outthinking and outmaneuvering a skilled and dangerous opponent.

As the moving force behind the mission, André had no choice but to wait in agonizing silence while his agents carried out his instructions. They were nonprofessionals for the most part . . . decent patriots ready to die at his command . . . and this responsibility weighted him down. André was able to hide the erosion of his innards, and publicly mask his tension.

Only his woman, Juanita de Córdoba, knew the truth when that ashen color came to his cheeks and his overworked brain betrayed itself behind a curtain of bloodshot eyes.

Fragments of information found their way back to Juanita and were passed to André. In the sanctity of the French Embassy he pieced the puzzle together, evaluated the scraps of hard-won intelligence, and formulated new plans.

The mission was moving along well enough, but a break was needed. Nothing of a conclusive or proof nature yet had been found.

It was a strange game. The cat and the mouse remained friendly to each other in public. As a

146

ranking French diplomat, André was greeted by warm handshakes of the Cubans and even the Russians. He attended long lunches and conferences on diplomatic and trade affairs and carried out the detail of routine government business with his adversaries.

Even though G-2 and the Soviet Resident, Gorgoni, suspected Deveraux was operating an espionage ring under their noses, they were simply unable to pin him down. But as the operation probed deeper, the chances for error and detection became greater and the pressure intensified.

André was able to establish that no phone taps or listening devices had been planted in Juanita's villa. He reckoned that G-2 was putting on a front to lull them into complacency. More likely, G-2 realized that André would soon discover the taps and use them to feed back confusing information. With the villa free of eavesdropping, it gave André and Juanita a welcome measure of freedom to speak to each other.

On the day of the French Embassy reception for the new Chinese First Secretary, three messages arrived sewn in a chicken from Morelos, the poultry merchant.

They were in a simple code and written on a special type of cigarette paper which Juanita had passed out months before. As he dressed for the reception, André placed tobacco on the papers and rolled them into cigarettes and put them into a half-empty Camel cigarette package.

Juanita studied him as they dressed. He was out of it again. His mind was on the frightful treadmill, thinking, thinking, thinking. She was disturbed by the obvious strain. The haggard expression . . . the sudden loss of strength that she alone saw in the bedroom.

— She helped him with his cuff links, her graceful fingers threading his shirt together, and he thought and spoke out loud. "We've got to move someone in close to the Finca San José. No damned way to get a camera there."

"Hold still, dear."

"Rico Parra has been invited to the reception tonight. It's our first face-to-face meeting since La Torre. He may want to talk. If he makes any overtures, give him rope. Try to be friendly. Sometimes he acts compulsively. Remember every word he says."

"Yes, dear."

André swept the excess tobacco off the dressing table into his hand and shook it off into the wastebasket. He put the message-bearing cigarette pack in his shirt pocket. Juanita smoothed his tie down, patted his cheek and told him he looked handsome.

As predicted and noted by the Cuban press, the new Chinese First Secretary was clever and filled with Oriental charm. The steady hum of Spanish, French, and English warmed the large living room of the Embassy. With Havana so drab these days it was an event when the French threw a party. Blanche Adam entertained with style. The Chinese were delighted.

Shortly after his entry with Juanita, André was cornered by Alain Adam and during their conversation Alain asked for a cigarette. André took the pack of Camels from his shirt pocket. Alain noted Camels were difficult to come by these days and André insisted he keep the pack. A few moments later, the Ambassador was called to the telephone. He excused himself, went to his office, locked the door behind him and quickly put the cigarette pack into the safe. The dials were twisted to secure the safe, followed by an enormous heaving sigh of relief.

Alain Adam had great affection for Devereaux but sometimes deplored his visits to Cuba. The intelligence game made him nervous. The Ambassador reentered the living room mopping his brow and nodding to André, who was deep in discussion with the head of the Soviet Cultural mission.

This night, Rico Parra seemed subdued by the elegant atmosphere. He admirably contained his desire to speak to Juanita de Córdoba, selecting a discreet moment when they could step out to the balcony out of earshot of the others.

Juanita noted his contemplative attitude. She was aware that Rico Parra was no fool. Much of his bluster was for public consumption and to instill fear into his flunkies. Behind that straggly façade was a man of enormous ability and native intuition.

"When a man such as I, Rico, comes into power," he said with uncommon softness, "he is apt to believe he can demand anything or get anyone. That is why you perplex me so, Juanita."

"You are being charmingly candid tonight," she fenced.

"You see, Little Dove. I have always observed aristocracy in a certain way. When I was a boy toiling in the canebrakes I vividly remember the haughty daughters of the Finca owner galloping by on their Arabian horses. Like a good, humble peasant I would take the hat off my head and bow

149

as they passed. But they inflicted a pain, here
. . . in my heart . . . which I will never get
over. When you are a monkey in a zoo behind
bars and are suddenly freed, you wish to hold in
your hands everything that was denied you."

He reached for a cigar, then thought better
of it.

"Do you know what I really want from Juanita
de Córdoba? Aside from your beauty as a woman
. . . aside from all the respectability?"

"Maybe."

"I want your power. De Córdoba and Parra.
That is power . . . yes . . . I know I disgust you.
I'm an animal. I disgust most women."

"You're not in keeping with yourself tonight,
Rico. What did you bring me out here to say?"

The Cuban managed a rare smile. "See the
Little Dove! She looks right through me. I cannot
win you as a man. But maybe I could convince
you by a more subtle means that a friendship
between us would not be so undesirable."

"Go on."

Rico Parra paced the balcony. All of the cunning and danger of the man was obvious to her.
The things which had made him a brilliant and
brutal guerrilla commander could not be under-
estimated. He selected his words with meticulous
care.

"Castro," he said, "has chosen me to keep an
eye on certain foreign diplomats who come in and
out of the country frequently." He stopped and
looked directly into her eyes. "Castro has also
given me a great deal of latitude and authority
to act in any manner in any given situation."

Juanita kept her composure. Rico Parra was
impressed by her show of skill. It was a skill he

150

wanted to have, to work for him. "I should say that Fidel has entrusted you with enormous responsibility."

"I knew you would understand," Rico Parra said.

André unzipped Juanita's dress and held her from behind at arms length and studied her back. She had a most beautiful back. Most women were either bony or angular or fleshy or marred. Juanita was perfect.

"Rico was in a rare behavior," she said.

"I'm queer for your back."

"We had our talk. He was subdued for a change."

"How did it go?"

"Nothing new, André darling. Parra's same old nonsense in a different presentation. I think he's a complete fool."

André dropped his hands from her and pondered. "Parra's no fool. Mistakes . . . yes. But no fool. I was getting a feeling that he had taken over some of the G-2 authority. I smelled his nose in our business."

"I couldn't sense anything like that," she said. Juanita went to him for the automatic response of his embrace. "Tonight," she said, "I want to make love to you."

"You always do, darling. You're unselfish . . . too unselfish."

"No . . . I mean . . . tonight I'm going to make love to you all night . . . and watch you while I'm doing it. I want to see your happiness. . . ."

THE VALLEY NEAR Pinar del Río brimmed with lush tropical foliage. This natural hothouse was a world wonder, a valley of rare fertility that gave the Cuban tobacco its unique and renowned quality.

A battered old Dodge, groaning from neglect, turned off the main road of the valley toward the Finca San José.

"WARNING!" a large sign read, "GOVERNMENT PROPERTY! GO NO FARTHER!"

The Dodge and its driver, Vicente Martínez, rattled and banged past the forbidding warning for almost two miles until the cane fields swallowed him up.

His eyes were glued to deep ruts and tire marks on the dirt road. He calculated their width and depth. This was what he had been told to look for. Monsters on wheels had passed on this ground.

Suddenly the main gate of the Finca San José loomed ahead. It had changed.

"Halt!"

Four angry Russian soldiers dashed from the guard shack, all yelling at him at the same time.

"What in the hell is this!" Vicente Martínez demanded, shoving the door open, getting out of the car and fanning himself with his wide-brimmed hat.

The Russians continued to jabber heatedly in a language he could not fathom. Vicente argued back just as heatedly in a language they could not fathom.

The old Dodge boiled over, too.

At last a Cuban officer was sent for. He arrived

on the scene growling. "Who are you! What the hell are you doing here!"

"Me! What am I doing here? What are you doing here? I am Gonzoles. I come here every month since I was a child to see my grandfather."

"Well, your grandfather is no longer here."

"He has been here all his life, señor officer. Why should he leave?"

"He has been relocated."

"What means by this, relocated?"

"He has moved. Did you not receive the letter?"

"Yes, I got a letter. But who can read?"

"You damn fool. Why didn't you get it read to you?"

"Well, I get the letter and I see all the government stamps and seals in it so I think it is an order for more crops. So I throw the letter away. I want to see my grandfather."

"You must go to the District Committee in San Cristóbal to find out where he has been relocated."

Vicente Martínez scratched his head.

A Russian officer pulled the Cuban officer aside. "He must be taken in for questioning," the Russian demanded.

"Oh, I don't think that is very wise Señor Captain."

"He may have seen too much."

"Señor Captain, you do not understand. This man is a Cuban peasant. The families are very close. If he does not show up at his home tonight, we will have ten more of his relatives down here looking for him. It is safer to send him off."

The Russian grunted reluctantly at the Cuban's logic. Perhaps he was right. It would be better not to risk having any more of them around or to arouse suspicion by questioning.

"Gonzoles" was ordered to leave the area and never return.

"I need some water for my old car," Vicente Martínez said.

They got him water. He poured some into the radiator and drank some. Then he turned and drove away, still mumbling protests.

Vicente Martínez was one of the finest lawyers in that part of Cuba. When Héctor de Córdoba practiced law in Havana, they had a number of joint clients and cases. Juanita de Córdoba was a good family friend of two decades' standing. He was one of the first recruited.

In addition to the telltale tire marks on the dirt road he was able to spot hundreds of Russian soldiers beyond the Finca gate.

He saw something else, too.

He saw the launching tower.

The information was written and placed in the little holder of a magnetic hide-a-key. The railing of the bridge outside San Cristóbal was made of hollow tube, like most of Cuba's bridges.

Vicente removed a loose knob at the end of the rail and placed the hide-a-key inside and returned the knob.

Later the dead-letter box was emptied and the message eventually found its way to the poultry butcher Jesús Morelos in Havana.

(25)

As THE TAPE came to an end, everyone stood and stretched. Kramer pushed the buzzer to call the outside guards and asked that the lunch dishes be cleared and a new pot of coffee brewed.

154

Dr. Billings spooled on another tape. "One, two, three, four," he counted into the microphone, adjusting the voice level.

In the second week of interrogation the atmosphere had relaxed. Boris Kuznetov had come to find the four ININ people agreeable and was less and less disturbed by W. Smith's rapid-fire, terse questioning. After all, if one had to speak, it was far better that it was under such circumstances. The continued absence of André Devereaux annoyed him, but Michael Nordstrom personally assured him that Devereaux would return within a few weeks.

One by one they came back to the conference table from the adjoining washroom, braced for another round of questioning.

Dr. Billings scanned his notes, then said, "In the purges of 1937 and 1938 you told us the Soviet intelligence system was badly disrupted."

"It was worse than that," Boris answered. "By 1939 NKVD, the forerunner of the present KGB, was a total shambles."

"What was your own status at the time?"

"I was the top student of my class in gymnasium. I went on to study for another four years at Smolensk University. And then I was invited for postgraduate work at Moscow University. I had strong recommendations."

"When did you go to Moscow?"

"In the first semester, fall of 1939. Here I also met Olga. Her name then was Cherniavsky. She was of the family of the Soviet General Cherniavsky, all ranking Communists."

"Her curriculum?"

"Art student."

"Your studies?"

155

"Required courses, mainly. No specialty or, as you say, no major."

"You were quite active with the Young Communists in Smolensk. Now did you continue this in Moscow?"

"Yes."

"Diligently or because it was required of all students?"

"Diligently. At the end of the first semester I was voted Komsomol unit leader. It is an extreme honor for a first-year student."

"Olga was in your unit?"

"Yes. A Soviet student has to fight for time to see his sweetheart. After Komsomol meetings was an excellent time . . . to discuss dialectics, of course."

They laughed.

"Isn't it hell on young people?" Kramer asked. "No apartment rooms, freezing weather outside, or during the summer the parks are filled with blaring speeches, no cars to park in."

"It's difficult but, as with boys and girls everywhere, we managed. You must remember revolutionaries are apt to be prim. We are quite Victorian in our morals."

"At the end of the first semester?"

"I was an honor student. My group leader . . ."

"Do you remember his name?"

"Tomsk."

"Go on."

"Tomsk instructed me to go for an interview at NKVD headquarters. I was asked to transfer from the university to the College of Intelligence. At first I did not like the idea, but the choice was limited and the rebuilding of NKVD was urgent . . . and my duty is my duty."

156

"When did you enter?"

"Immediately. Spring of 1940."

"Courses?"

"Politics . . . our politics and economics. Mainly we were indoctrinated in military intelligence and sabotage. Everyone in the school at that time held a reserve commission."

"What rank?"

"Few were over captain. You must bear in mind we were mostly Young Communists, all coming up together to take over the future intelligence system after the purges."

"How many years was the full course of study?"

"It was set up for four years, but the war interrupted and the need for military intelligence was desperate. After the first winter's siege of Moscow I was inducted into the Red Army as a captain. In the spring of 1941, April 15, to be precise, I was parachuted into Poland in the Lublin district, where the Germans had set up their government general."

"Mission?"

"Establish a small espionage network, set up radio communications, dead-letter drops, contacts. We had two people working inside German headquarters."

"How large was this group?"

"It varied. Never more than eight people. Our special job was to find out the time of the rail movements of German troops and equipment heading to the eastern front on the Brest-Gomel lines and its spurs."

"You remained in Lublin?"

"Until July. Then I moved back toward Russia on foot, stopping in cities along the rail line,

Brest, Pinsk, and so forth, to establish even smaller radio units. Eventually, advice on train movements would get into the hands of partisan units working in the Pripet Marshes. It was a good operation. We destroyed over ten trainloads."

"And you made it back to Moscow?"

"Not until midwinter. I lived in the Pripet Marshes." Boris Kuznetov related the brutal days of the Russian winter in which he lived with a partisan unit. They moved about in the bitter cold like hunted animals for whom there would be no mercy.

"As you know, I am missing three toes on my left foot due to frostbite. My eyes are also extremely sensitive to light due to partial snow blindness. By the time I reached Moscow I had lost twenty kilos' weight, over forty American pounds. But I am lucky. Most of that particular unit died of starvation or cold. The rest of that winter I spent in the hospital."

"No official duties?"

"No. Unless you call my marriage to Olga an official duty."

"And you remained in Moscow?"

"Only until the spring. Again in April of 1943 I was parachuted into Poland to establish another network east of the Praga River in the Vilna-Grodno-Kovno area. This time I was better at my work and I was able to get through German lines into Moscow by December. I was so good, in fact, I was sent out again after being home only two weeks to coordinate sabotage activities of the partisan units beyond the Second Baltic Front of Marshal Yeremenko. In February of 1944 I was captured with a unit of forty men in an ambush and we were sent to a stalag in Memel. By May of that year only four of us had survived the German brutality."

"I take it you were able to avoid being singled out."

"The men in the unit were of exceptional courage. No one told who I was and I was able to conceal my true identity."

"How long did you remain in prison?"

"I escaped in the summer of 1944 and reorganized a sabotage unit to coordinate with our summer offensive. When our forces passed my operation and moved into Poland and the Baltics, I returned again to Moscow. This time by train. For the rest of the war I worked at intelligence headquarters in Moscow, mainly in evaluation of information from German prisoners and information from our own sabotage units in Poland."

"You stayed till the war ended?"

"Yes."

"Decorations?"

"A few."

"Order of Lenin?"

"Yes, I think so."

"Then?"

"I was discharged as a reserve colonel and invited to study advanced intelligence at the Intelligence Academy in Moscow. I remained there for the next five years."

"Weren't the courses for three years?"

"I was a teacher for two years."

"How many were enrolled?"

"Three hundred, more or less."

"Women?"

"A few. It was an extremely difficult school."

"What percentage of people were dropped?"

159

"Not many. They were careful who they asked in."

Boris Kuznetov then recited a murderous scholastic ritual that converted a normal day's work into twelve to fourteen hours of study. At the academy he learned English, French, and German. There were intelligence courses in evaluation, analysis, coding, and ciphering. There were courses in geopolitics, psychology, advanced mathematics, art, and music. There were courses in military staff training. There was an intensive sports program and chess training.

"This, gentlemen, is the first time I came to learn about the West. I read Western literature and philosophy and religion. Along with general history we made an intensive study of each Western country, its political system and, most important, the lives and behavior of the Western leaders. We knew how they would react to each issue. And mainly, we learned their weak points."

The six-o'clock chimes played out "Rock of Ages" from Bethesda's chapel.

They all stood and gathered their notes. The four ININ men had come to respect Boris Kuznetov for he had sobered them on the depth, skill, and devotion of the enemy.

Boris smiled. "I look forward to seeing Olga and Tamara these evenings. Your Americanization program has given me two new beautiful women."

The tapes were locked into an attaché case. The room was thoroughly searched for loose scraps. Unneeded notes were placed into a basket shredder and chopped into a billion bits and mixed so they could never be read again.

They shook hands with Boris.

"Have a good Sunday," Boris said.

160

They left and Boris was wheeled out. The room was sealed.

(26)

MAGGIE, THE COOK of Juanita de Córdoba, made many trips to the stall of Jesús Morelos in the three weeks André Devereaux had been in Cuba. As often as not she brought home a chicken containing a message sewed up in its innards. Each new message gave another clue indicating that the Soviets were indeed bringing missiles into the country.

Yet the key link of an actual eyewitness remained missing.

The four Soviet ships left Viriel and were replaced by four others. André knew that the missiles would soon leave the Viriel docks on their trip to Finca San José. He became enormously anxious about what appeared to be a major Cuban and Soviet blunder.

In mapping out the routes to Finca San José there was but one choice. The missile carriers were compelled to travel from Viriel to Havana, through the edge of the city, then south on the airport highway.

Traffic into Havana was on a road that ran between Morro Castle and La Cabaña, then under the harbor through a tunnel. The tunnel emptied into Havana on the sea-front road, the Malecón.

By his own calculation of the size of the suspected missiles, they were too large to fit into the tunnel. This miscalculation would force the carriers to take a secondary road into Havana that led right into the old city. Here the missiles would have to travel through a labyrinth of small narrow streets.

If André's reckonings were true, it was just possible the error would force the Russians to parade their secret cargo under their very noses.

In addition to Jesús Morelos, a number of other friends of Juanita de Córdoba lived in the old town. She told them what to look for and to sleep with one eye open.

The word passed from Viriel that the cargo had left the port under heavy guard on large carriers and was heading for Havana.

A young medical student, Arnaldo Valdez, lived with his parents in the La Lisa section of Havana, but often spent his nights with his sweetheart, Anita, who had a small apartment near Avenida de Agua Dulce in the old city.

During the day curious activity had taken place on the streets near her flat. Anita and Arnaldo spoke about it when he arrived in the evening, and they both concluded that it could be the clearing of a route.

It was after midnight, as Anita slept and Arnaldo studied at the desk in her bedroom, that he heard a distant sound of motors.

As he buttoned on his shirt, Anita awoke, frightened.

"For God's sake, Arnaldo," she pleaded, "don't go out on the streets."

"I must. You know what our instructions are."

"But I'm afraid."

"Shhhh. It will be all right."

He left her stunned on the landing, looked up the stairs, blew a kiss and disappeared out onto the street.

In the old days something would be going on

162

all night. Raucous revelry, laughter, whores, fights. But since the Revolution the streets were empty and listless soon after dark.

In the shadows of the arcaded sidewalks, Arnaldo wove his way through a maze of streets and alleyways past sleeping dogs and howling cats, moving ever closer to the sound of the motors.

Even as the streets began to rumble under the weight of abnormal loads no one was curious these days. The lights of Havana, save for a few squalid joints, remained dark.

"HALT!" the sign before him warned. "THIS STREET IS CLOSED FROM MIDNIGHT TO DAWN!"

Arnaldo peered around the corner of the arcade and pondered his move. There were no headlights, but the convoy could not be more than a few blocks removed.

Across the darkened avenue he could make out the wooden booth of an old lottery stand. He darted out and crossed the street and dived under the counter. There he crouched into a ball and labored to quiet his gasping lungs.

Now he peeked around the tight confines. The stand was dilapidated. He poked with his penknife and pried a couple of boards apart, allowing him enough of a crack to see the street.

A platoon of motorcycles was almost on him, gunning up a roar, followed by the shuffling feet of soldiers at fixed bayonets probing around for loiterers or watchers.

Arnaldo curled into a ball of fear, mumbling prayers as the rumbling grew more pronounced. With a face of frightened sweat he lifted his eyes and knew he was going to dare a look.

An enormous tractor, the largest vehicle he had

ever seen, pulled a trailer of six axles. Each axle had eight wheels, In a blur of cold excitement, he tried to remember his instructions from Juanita. Look at the tires! Look at the tires!

Yes! See! They are squashed half flat under the agony of the load. The great tube lay on the trailer bed. It was two arcade lengths and covered with canvas, and as it inched along the street was indented by the tire marks.

The tail was uncovered. Arnaldo tried to draw a picture in his mind of its size and shape.

But he could no longer see. The caravan passed on, with a dozen armored cars and an open truck of Russian soldiers following the missile carrier.

He waited for total silence, but there would be none for his own breath and heartbeat were audible. At last the motors faded from earshot.

He was about to crawl from his cover but hedged. For certain, G-2 men would be sweeping the area. The thought of the Green House sickened him. That was where his brother had been beaten to death.

The lottery vendor's stall seemed to be the safest place. Tuck in and stay till daylight. Anita would be frantic, but it was all for the best.

In the old days before the Revolution it was a common sight to find drunks asleep in the streets. But this morning Arnaldo Valdez was discovered by a pair of militiamen and dragged to his feet and shaken rudely.

He played the part of a sick man with a hangover and grinned at his captors sheepishly. "I am a medical student, comrades. Please let me clean up and get to the university."

"Drunks are a disgrace to the Revolution. You

164

are going to the police station. They'll sober you up all right. Pancho, call for the wagon!"

"I beg you, señores. If you don't give me a break, I'll be thrown out of school." Then Arnaldo wept, and not all his tears were phony.

"Who wants doctors like you in Cuba?" the militiaman scorned.

"Let the stupid bastard go," the second said. "Who wants to fill out all those damned reports?"

"No! A medical student should not behave like a drunken pig."

"Oh, very well. I'll call for the wagon."

Anita appeared on the scene. She walked to Arnaldo and slammed him over the head with her purse and kicked his shins.

"Dog!" Anita screamed.

A delighted crowd gathered.

"You leave me for that other woman and get drunk! Liar! Dog!"

She grabbed his ear, literally jerking him free of the militiamen's grip.

"I worked to the bone to send you through medical school and this is the thanks I get! Bum!"

The crowd laughed and whistled as she banged him around the arcade. Arnaldo doubled up, shielding his face and stomach.

"I promise I'll study. Day and night I'll study!"

"He goes to the station." One militiaman asserted his authority.

"No," the crowd groaned. "No!"

"He's getting a beating enough."

"Dog! Bum!"

"Let him go," they chanted.

Anita kicked him down the street and around the corner as the crowd gathered around the militiamen and argued heatedly. By now the police were dumbfounded. As they shrugged and continued their rounds, they were applauded for gallantry.

In her room, Anita wept and kissed him for every blow she had rendered. "I almost lost my mind," she cried, "I almost lost my mind. Oh, my darling, darling, darling."

They kissed and rolled in the bed and fell to the floor. He laughed convulsively. "I saw them! I saw them!"

And she sat beside him on the floor and laughed with him until their sides ached and tears drenched their cheeks.

(27)

THE APARTMENT OF Teresa Marín was but a block away from the French Chancellery. Teresa was one of Fidel Castro's most trusted personal secretaries. In fact, he had her placed in the exclusive building in order that she might oversee an apartment on the floor below belonging to Fidel. It was a place where he entertained his mistress of the moment.

The first loyalty of Teresa Marín, however, was to the activities of Juanita de Córdoba.

Midway between the French Chancellery and Teresa's apartment house stood the Chinese Embassy on an acre of land surrounded by a high pink wall. Its flat roof held a field of radio antennae, which delivered high-frequency transmissions around the clock to China.

With the Chinese cluttering up the air, it was impossible to monitor the area. What better place than in the apartment of Teresa Marín for the

166

French espionage ring to place their own transmitter?

Near the end of the third week of André's visit to Cuba, Juanita paid what appeared to be a normal social call to her old friend, Teresa Marín. One floor below, Fidel Castro made love to a new woman.

At the moment Fidel was making his conquest, a high-speed, low-frequency transmitter came from its hiding place in Teresa's apartment and flashed a message to a receiver in Miami:

CONFIRMING THE INTRODUCTION OF SOVIET INTERMEDIATE RANGE MISSILES AT FINCA SAN JOSÉ AND PERHAPS REMEDIOS AREAS. MISSILES NOT YET OPERATIONAL. BASES APPEAR TO BE IN EXCLUSIVE HANDS OF SOVIET TROOPS.

The message was signed with André's ININ code name, Palomino.

(28)

MUÑOZ AND THE Soviet Resident, Oleg Gorgoni, stared into the eternally black, angry eyes of Rico Parra, who appeared intense even when drinking his morning *cafecito.*

The Russian hammered home his position. "Both Devereaux and the French Ambassador have a history of complete sympathy to the Americans. Devereaux has been in Havana almost three weeks. For what?"

Rico played with his beard. "Routine business."

"In the light of our present activities," Gorgoni continued, "we cannot consider his visit to Cuba at this time as coincidental."

167

"Well, Muñoz," Parra said, "you've had him under watch. What do you think?"

"We could find nothing specific. Only suspicions."

"Since when do we let suspicions stop us?" Gorgoni demanded.

"Since we started playing with high-ranking diplomats, Comrade Gorgoni." Rico threw up his hands. "I have no love lost for the Frenchman but I am reluctant to act without proof."

"There will be proof enough when you open his attaché case."

"And if there isn't? He's just hot for Juanita de Córdoba, and when he gets to Cuba he finds reason to stay."

"Is their affair such an innocent little game?" the Russian said.

Rico's eyes seemed even blacker. "You're treading on quicksand, comrade. She is a great and respected woman. But . . . suppose we do get rid of Devereaux. What about French-Cuban relations?"

"Did Castro give you authority to act or not?"

"Yes, but I'm giving the damned authority right back to him."

"Comrade Parra! The Frenchman cannot be allowed to leave Cuba with a suitcase filled with intelligence."

Parra shrugged and gestured. "So, what if the Yankees discover the rockets? Just what will they do? What did they do when the surface-to-air missiles were installed? Eh? Nothing, they did nothing."

"SAM's are defensive weapons," Gorgoni answered; "this is different."

"What about the Soviet jet bombers in Cuba?

168

Are they defensive? Again the Americans didn't do anything, and they won't do anything now," Parra bragged.

"Moscow is very concerned. Once we make the missiles operational it will be an accomplished fact. But they must be made operational first. You know as well as I of the increased American U-2 flights over Cuba. What are they looking for? Bananas?"

Rico Parra slammed his fist onto the desktop. "Do the Yankees have missiles in Turkey pointing at the Soviet Union? Yes or no?"

"One question does not answer the other. We must have time to make them operational. Devereaux leaves tomorrow. What will Castro say to you when the Americans threaten to invade Cuba? What will become of Rico Parra then? Think, comrade . . . think of the consequences to you if Devereaux carries out information of this."

Rico Parra thought. "Uribe!" he shouted.

His fragile secretary, Luis Uribe, hurried into the room.

"Did you reach Castro?"

"I called the apartment, also Che and Raul. He is on his way to Santiago for a speech but apparently stopped off en route to see one of his woman friends. He can't be located."

"What kind of crazy country are you running here when you can't find your own President!" the Russian said angrily.

"Comrade Gorgoni," Parra answered indignantly, "we are Cubans. Uribe, keep trying to locate Castro. Muñoz, you will go to the airport tomorrow. As soon as Castro gives me the green

169

light I will call you. Pick up Devereaux and take him to the Green House."

A slight smile crossed the baby face of Muñoz.

"And when you get him there," Parra continued, "save him for me. I have an account to settle."

(29)

ANDRÉ KNOTTED HIS ROBE, perched on the rail, and gazed toward the sea consumed by the terrible feeling that he would never see Juanita de Córdoba again. His fear for her life took his thoughts away from his own thorny problem of getting out of Cuba in the morning. He was not certain he would leave the country alive. Desperate men were obviously making plans for him. But he was more frightened about leaving her behind. This then was to be the final reward but one does not whimper about the cruelty of it all. You win . . . you lose. The game goes on. The angel of death circles overhead.

Juanita came to the veranda in a hostess gown looking particularly stunning. He was always amazed at this soft woman who never gave up being a woman in the company of cutthroats. She poured their cognacs with her particular grace and they hemmed in and contained the flooding desperation to cling to each other and weep.

"Well, here's to your next trip," Juanita said. "When do you suppose that will be?"

"It's difficult to say."

"Difficult to say when, or just difficult to say?"

"You're the one woman who doesn't play games. You know that I'll never get back into Cuba."

"Yes . . . I know. . . ."

She fitted into his free arm in a way that blended them. A way of saying, look how we belong, you and I. And she said, "We've had so many wonderful nights here. How nice it is when you make a woman believe that you and she are the only two people who can sleep together in a single bed with room to spare. I think of all the wonderful things you taught me and you brought out of me. Thank you."

"Juanita . . . I won't accept this finality."

"May I break our pact? About wives and sentiment? You are not going away without knowing that I've loved you completely. When we started this work I would have waited for you forever or taken scraps without complaint or condition. But . . . if I had loved you so obviously there would have been suspicion cast on us. And if I had declared myself to you I was a bit wary that you, as a man, would have been too proud to consent to what I could impose without your permission. I took up company," she said shakily, "with other men in order to protect what we were doing. I did it to keep suspicion away from us . . . so that I could go on seeing you. But there was never a moment I didn't long for you. . . ."

". . . Juanita . . ."

"It was no sacrifice. It's only a part of the way I love you. André . . . no man, not even my husband, has given me what you have."

Juanita's eyes were glassy from the ordeal of her words. She kissed the fingers that touched her cheeks and traced the lines of his neck.

"I love you that way too and I don't intend to give you up. Now listen . . . the minute I arrive in Miami I'm setting up plans to send a boat for you. Alain Adam will know the time and place."

171

She put her finger to his lips to stop him and she shook her head. "Don't you understand that I can never leave Cuba?"

"I saw the destruction of my own country but I left France in order to fight for her. You have to do the same thing now. You are more valuable to the cause outside Cuba."

"I will make that decision. . . ."

"What about your sons?"

"André . . . don't ask me anymore."

"Yes, I will, and you're going to promise me."

"I will promise you that I will believe in you and love you. If God wills it, then perhaps there is a life for us, together . . . but don't dream."

"I want to know your reasons."

She shook her head. "My dear . . . please don't sound like G-2 on our last night together."

"I'm sorry."

"I suppose that all I really wanted for us was to have just one week alone. There are islands in the Caribbean where two people can be away, except to each other. You know them all."

"I've only seen them," he said. "Other people know them. Oh Lord . . . I wish I could believe there was one for us. . . . I'd give anything . . . oh, Lord. . . ."

She saw her man waver for the first time. And she was stern.

"Come now, darling. We knew from the first day that we would have to come to this night and face it."

"That doesn't make me like it!" Then, shamed by her strength, he managed a smile. He took her hand and held it long and patted it, then put it to his lips. "You are a beautiful lady," André said.

The alarm rang at four-thirty in the morning. The KLM flight was not due to depart until noon, but it was obligatory under Cuban regulations that all passengers present themselves at the airport six full hours before departure.

They took breakfast in total silence, then finally got around to a last-minute bit of business. André always carried out a briefcase of letters to Cuban refugees to be delivered in Miami and elsewhere about the country. A valise of tears and hope. The authorities would examine the letters before delivery, then see that they got to the rightful recipients. Juanita gave him the locked valise.

"The mail," she said.

André hefted the valise, then looked at her curiously. "What the hell have you got in here this time? It weighs a ton."

Juanita shrugged. "Who knows? The mail just gets heavier as the revolution goes on. This time, please don't wait. Open it as soon as you can after you arrive in Miami. You'll understand."

What André understood without question was that he had received an instruction and would follow it. He nodded that he would comply.

At a quarter past five there was a knock on the door of the villa. Juanita was stunned to see Alain Adam waiting with the Embassy car. It was the very first time he had ever arisen at that early hour to take André to the airport. Obviously, she thought, something was wrong . . . and a sickening wave of fear passed through her . . . they are going to kill him!

His bags were loaded into the car in silence, the only sound being their feet shuffling on the gravel and the slam of the trunk lid.

André kissed her cheek. "When I send for you

173

. . . come." He got into the front seat next to the Ambassador, dared a last look at her, and closed the car door.

She grew smaller and smaller as the car pulled out of the circular driveway past the iron gates. He looked back desperately and caught the last wave of her hand.

"*Vaya con Dios,*" Juanita de Córdoba whispered as they passed from sight. . . . "Go with God."

In a moment a pair of G-2 men down the way in an unmarked car radioed the information that Devereaux had left the villa. Muñoz received the message at the Green House. He called Rico Parra at his office.

Parra had been up all night trying unsuccessfully to reach Castro. He was bedraggled and given to fits of temper.

"Devereaux is heading for the airport," Muñoz reported.

"You get down there," Parra snapped, "and you wait. Wait for my call. And God damn you, Muñoz, don't screw it up."

"Yes, compadre."

"Compadre, my ass. . . ." He hung up. Luis Uribe, his secretary, set a *cafecito* before him. Uribe's family had somehow skipped Cuba but he had no time for the man now. Rico bolted down the *cafecito* with a flick of the wrist and grunted. "Fidel!" he screamed, "where are you, you bastard!" He stared long at the unanswering telephone. "Uribe. Have you called all of his women?"

Uribe made a gesture of total helplessness.

Rico Parra cracked his knuckles nervously. Everything to take care of Devereaux was planned and in motion. He only needed Castro's signal to

174

go. When the phone rang, Rico heaved a sigh. Uribe lifted the receiver, answered, looked puzzled to his boss.

"It's . . . Señora de Córdoba. . . ."

"Juanita . . . at this hour . . . of course."

He snatched the phone and waved Uribe out of the room. "Hello, Rico Parra speaks."

"Hello, Rico. This is Juanita de Córdoba. I wish to see you."

Rico waited until the thumping of his heart slowed. "I'll see you later, at a more decent hour."

"No. I must see you now."

"Very well. Come to my office."

"No. I want to see you alone . . . to discuss something confidential. Could you come up to my villa?"

It smelled bad to Rico. A trap. He crouched in his chair and drummed his fingers on the desktop. "Juanita," he said. "Do you know the Bahía del Sol?"

"Yes."

"I have a villa there. You will come?"

"Yes."

"At the entrance take the right fork and follow the bay for exactly two kilometers. You can't miss the place. A big white stone wall and the name Casa de Revolución over the gate. In front there is a caretaker's house. He will give you the key. Women have waited for me before, so it will not seem unusual. If you leave Havana now you should be there within an hour."

"I will see you there."

Parra hung up, puzzled. "Uribe!"

"Yes, Señor Parra."

"I am going out for a while. If Muñoz calls,

175

nothing is to be done until I personally give the word."

"Yes, señor."

"You keep trying to reach Castro."

"Yes," Uribe said, retreating to the adjoining office.

Parra placed a telephone call to Casa de Revolución which was answered by the chief of the guard detail. "It is Rico," he said. "I am expecting a woman to arrive in an hour. Take her and search her for weapons, then hold her in the main building until I arrive. Stake out the guards around the grounds."

"What is up?"

"It may be a trick of the underground . . . maybe not." Rico Parra took his pistol belt from the hat rack and strapped it to his waist and left his office.

(30)

BORIS KUZNETOV developed a passion for Pepsi-Cola. As often as not he put away a six-pack during each interrogation session. He drained the bottom of his glass, asked the nurse for another, and looked into the familiar faces of Jaffe, Kramer, W. Smith, and Dr. Billings.

"In 1950," he continued, "I was assigned to East Berlin as the Resident of the Soviet Embassy under the cover of being a member of the purchasing commission. Under my office, the communications, dead-letters boxes, and control of operations were directed. I also kept surveillance over all the people working in the Soviet Embassy."

"You directed espionage operations?"

"Yes. Mostly in West Berlin."

176

"Outside of West Berlin?"

"Not much. I recruited illegals."

"Will you explain that?"

"We looked for young Germans of fifteen to twenty years of age whose parents had Communist backgrounds or ones who were otherwise suited for illegal work. These people were sent back to Moscow to a special German school for training that goes on sometimes for a decade. We have such schools for illegals from most Western countries. The master plan is to slip these people into Western Germany or Italy or France for a year to familiarize themselves completely with the area where they will work later on. Then after another eight years they will go back to the West with a complete set of false documents. They will be skilled enough to obtain highly placed positions in government, science, industry, or the military. With the planting of this seed of illegals there will be a great harvest of agents in the future of a caliber better than anything known."

"How many did you recruit?"

"Fourteen."

"Were others recruited from Germany?"

"I think the school in Moscow has forty Germans."

"The French school?"

"Probably the same number."

W. Smith and Kramer began an extensive round of questions to detail Kuznetov's Berlin operations.

They were suddenly interrupted by the appearance of Michael Nordstrom and his evaluator, Sanderson Hooper. The two had been coming more frequently, stopping the regular interrogation to ask questions about the NATO documents

Kuznetov had turned over at the time of his defection.

Boris realized that the Americans were coming upon something important.

"Do you mind if I question you in English?" Nordstrom always asked.

"It's all right."

"Would you identify this document?"

All the telltale numberings had been removed from the documents. Kuznetov adjusted his glasses and scanned the paper for a sparse ten seconds.

"This is in your twelve-hundred series, contingency plans in the event of Soviet troop movement in the direction of Norway."

"This one?"

"Class B document on defective ammunition."

"This one?"

"Purchase order for shoes. Special cold-weather materials involved."

"This one?"

"Alternate plans in the event airfields in the former British Zone become inoperative."

"This one?"

"It's a fake."

"Why do you say that?"

"It deals with Swedish air cooperation with NATO. Our sources inside Sweden tell us there is no deal between Sweden and NATO."

"Who are your sources?"

"I don't know. I believe it is a Swedish officer, probably of staff rank."

"What makes you think so?"

"A rendezvous in Moscow kept by one of our generals. A General Samov, Fyodor Samov. His real name is Pyotr Pavlovich Rogatkin. He had a

178

lot of dealing with the Swedes. My opinion is that he had highly placed contacts in Sweden."

"This document?"

"Placement of Polaris submarines in Soviet waters and the Baltic. Let me see . . . this, this, and this is correct. Paragraph F is a fake."

"How did NATO documents come into your hands?"

"From the Soviet Resident in Paris."

"Who is he?"

"Gorin."

"How were they transmitted?"

"Through normal channels. Almost any NATO document we requested was in our hands in Moscow within a week."

"Who was turning them over to Gorin?"

"I'll discuss that matter when Devereaux returns."

Nordstrom cut the session short. Boris detected a sense of urgency as he was returned to his quarters.

Jaffe of the French ININ desk was asked to remain with Nordstrom and Sanderson Hooper after the others had departed.

"We've made a significant breakthrough as of yesterday," Nordstrom said to Jaffe. "We've narrowed the NATO documents that Kuznetov turned over to us down to six common readers. Three of them belong to other countries, and we've got them under watch. The other three are Frenchmen."

"Who?"

"Colonel Galande in Air Planning."

Jaffe nodded in recognition.

"Two civilians. Guillon, Technical Adviser in the office of the Chief of Staff."

"Know him slightly. He'd be a surprise."

"Jarré, NATO economist."

Jaffe toyed with his massive mustache. "Colonel Galande, Guillon, and Jarré," he mused.

"We're nervous about going to French SDECE with this," Hooper said.

"You've got reason to be," Jaffe agreed.

"There's no way we can put a watch on Frenchmen ourselves," Michael said.

"Léon Roux, Chief of the Department of Internal Protection of the French Sûreté," Jaffe said. "The interior police are a different cup of tea. Roux has always played ball with us and, frankly, he's not too fond of much of the crowd at SDECE."

"Fly to Paris tonight. Talk to Roux and try to get him to put these three suspects under watch and do an investigation of their backgrounds . . . and keep the goddamn thing quiet."

"Roux will buy that."

Sanderson Hooper emitted a long, sorrowful breath. "I wonder what Kuznetov is finally going to come up with."

"We'll know pretty soon. Devereaux is due back in Miami."

"If he gets back," Mike said.

Jaffe got up from the table, thinking ahead of packing, catching the ININ plane at Andrews, working out his schedule to hit Paris and see Roux right away. "Hoop, Mike, put a big circle around Jarré's name."

"Why?"

"Just my thoughts at the moment."

THE LIMOUSINE OF the French Embassy stopped before the Rancho Boyeros Airport terminal. Ambassador Alain Adam walked in with Devereaux to the KLM counter, the sole scene of activity.

"What the devil do you have in this valise?" Alain asked of the bag that Juanita de Córdoba had given André.

"Just the mail. Hold onto it while I check in."

André feigned indifference as he spotted the man with an ill fitting KLM jacket working behind the ticket agent. He was Cuban G-2 and might as well have been wearing a sign.

André set his suitcases on the scale and observed the scene of the ticket agent fingering down the passenger list, then turning to the G-2 man behind him.

"Those two bags," the G-2 man said.

"I'll carry them aboard."

"They are too large."

"I'm a diplomat."

"Sorry."

"I don't intend for them to leave my possession."

"Put them on the scale."

"No."

"There have been bomb scares. All luggage will be weighed and inspected."

"Sorry."

The G-2 man stared. André yawned, bored. "Check him in," the G-2 man finally said.

The ticket agent's hand trembled as he went through the business of validation. "Down the corridor, sir. Departure Room Number 3."

André held his valises and began the long,

slow walk with Alain Adam. He was stopped abruptly by a guard at the head of the hall.

"You will say good-bye to your friend here. No visitors in the waiting rooms."

André glanced about, saw the scattering of G-2 men sloppily placed everywhere. Two of them moved up behind him to cut off an exit. All the other departing passengers were being put in Departure Rooms 1 and 2. He would be in Room 3 alone. Obviously, he carried something in Juanita's valise to implicate her, as well as a hundred other Cubans.

The gambit was opened! KLM flight lands in Miami. French diplomat missing. The Cubans would play dumb, show a passenger list without his name on it, apologize and promise an investigation, and the affair would die in mystery.

André played his first counter-card. He pulled Alain Adam aside quickly and spoke in cryptic French, "You see what's coming off?"

Adam nodded.

"Get back to Havana immediately. Pick up Juanita and have her claim political asylum in the Embassy. Then get to Castro, Parra, or Che Guevara and warn them we are on to what is taking place. Now go."

"André, I don't want to leave you here alone."

"Go. Get their officials confused at the highest level. Threaten to expose them. It's our best chance. Now go."

Adam tried to blurt out a proper word but grabbed André's hand tightly, nodded, and turned. André watched the Ambassador leave the terminal and saw the limousine pull from the curb and out of sight.

The circle of G-2 men closed in on him. "You go

182

to Departure Room Number 3," one commanded.

The one who spoke seemed to be in charge. André approached him slowly and shook his head, No. "Your boss, Muñoz, is no doubt waiting in one of the back offices. Now you just run in there and tell him that we are on to his game and the French Embassy here cabled to Paris last night about this situation. Until he wishes to discuss it with me I intend to wait in a departure room with the other passengers."

With that, André shoved past the man and entered Room 2, which was filled with activity. The confused Cuban ran to Muñoz in a back office and reported Devereaux's words. Muñoz betrayed his own sudden confusion with shaky hands and nervous breaths. He chewed his bottom lip, then snatched the phone.

"Put me through to Rico Parra!" he shouted.

(32)

RICO PARRA FLUNG OPEN the door to Casa de Revolución. The living room had deteriorated from the days of its former owner. Juanita de Córdoba was seated on a high-backed chair. The chief guard, Hernández, hulked behind her with a sub-machine gun at her head.

"She has no weapons," Hernández said.

Rico signaled the man to leave with a jerk of his head.

"I am flattered by your display of arms," she said, "but it was unnecessary. I am quite harmless."

"You are as harmless as a cobra," Rico answered.

"As you wish."

"Yes, as I wish. I did not survive as a guerrilla fighter in the Sierra Maestra Mountains out of stupidity. Well, what the hell do you want?"

Juanita unfolded her legs and stood, running her fingers over an antique desktop. Even in this tense atmosphere, the dark unkempt room, the devouring woods, even so he was aware of the female opposite him. Her body was closely hugged by a pair of silk slacks, the buttocks round yet firm. The long polished nails, the flair of her jewelry, the severe hairdo, her scent. Rico's eyes played on her bare midriff and to the halter top of thin enticing material, quite open and only tied in a bow loosely to hold her bosom.

"Of course you must know why I am here," she said.

"It's too early in the morning for games. You tell me."

"You told me you have control over certain foreign diplomats. I wish to bargain for one of them."

Rico slipped a cigar from his dungaree pocket, bit off the end, and spat it to the floor, then chewed on it without lighting it.

"André Devereaux is to leave Cuba safely."

"If he does?"

"You have yourself a Little Dove." She walked to the bedroom door and opened it.

Rico knew she would always hate him as intensely as she loved the Frenchman and all that he would really have of her was a shadow.

"Well," she said, "this is what you want, isn't it? Let's seal the bargain."

He giggled his strange giggle, then lifted his bearded face and laughed. "Do you really think I'm going to let him out of Cuba!" he bellowed.

"He's a spy for the Yankees. And what about you and this sacrificial act of yours? Maybe you're out to save your own damn skin. Well . . . Rico Parra is not going to be used like that. I don't protect traitors!"

"I don't know if André Devereaux has been here on an intelligence mission or not," she said.

"Liar!"

"I don't know," she repeated. "But if he has, then certainly he would not carry information out of the country on his person, would he? Wouldn't he have already sent it by radio or through diplomatic courier?"

"You're too damned logical for a woman."

"In any event, Devereaux can do you no more harm unless you are foolish enough to try to kill him. Then, indeed, there will be consequences. As for me, Rico Parra, I am not a traitor to Cuba."

"And if he goes . . . he tries to send a boat for you . . . yes!"

"I'm certain you will replace my servants with your own. I expect to be under constant watch as part of the bargain."

"You've really thought this out, haven't you?"

"I never took you for a fool." She walked into the bedroom. Rico trailed after her gnashing at his unlit cigar. He leaned against the doorframe and tucked his thumbs into his pistol belt and glared.

Juanita stood beside the bed and undid the bow of her halter. It opened. She let it fall to the floor and stood proud in her nakedness.

Rico flushed. Currents of lust and anger and confusion ran together within him. Juanita walked to him surely, took the cigar from his

185

mouth and tossed it away. She took his crude hand and lifted it to her breast.

"As long as we're going to do it," she said, "we might as well enjoy it."

His free hand raised suddenly and slapped over her mouth. "Pig! Aristocratic pig!" Her head snapped back from another blow and her hair was strewn awry. He slapped her again. Her head trembled but she neither retreated nor cried. Rico flung her on the bed hard. "You hate me! All right, woman! You want an animal!"

He leaped on her and tore her slacks off and flung her around the bed. Juanita broke into a half hysteria and reached up desperately and grabbed his beard. With a surge of strength she pulled him by the beard until he was forced to lower himself on top of her. Her teeth sank into his shoulder, cutting through his shirt. He screamed in pain.

"I'm an animal too!" Juanita cried and she bit into him again forcing him to stop his attack.

They lay side by side laboring for breath, then laughing and crying half madly . . . then tore at each other again and wrestled to the floor. She traded savagery for savagery, her nails found his face and clawed and she ripped his beard and she bit until he pinned her down. The blood spurted from his wound on to her face and neck. He held her solidly, both of them panting and groaning . . . and after a time . . . they quieted.

And suddenly Rico Parra began to weep. "I can't do anything. I am unable to now. I have this trouble all the time." He released his grip.

Her fingers went into the tangle of black hair, this time tenderly and she stroked him softly. "Rest and then I will help you."

"I can't."

"I'll show you how. I'll teach you everything."

They both became aware of someone else in the room. Hernández, the guard, stood open-mouthed over them. Rico staggered to his feet and Hernández backed out of the room quaking. "Com-padre," he begged, "I did not know. . . ."

"What the hell do you want!"

"Uribe telephoned from your office and asked if you were here. He said it was very urgent . . . from Muñoz at the airport."

"What did you tell him!"

"Nothing. . . . I did not tell him you were here. I swear it!"

"Get out!" Parra screamed, kicking Hernández in the backside.

He swayed for a moment and wiped the blood from his face with the back of his hand and looked down on the floor at Juanita, then staggered toward the telephone and lifted the receiver.

"Don't call," Juanita de Córdoba pleaded . . . "don't call."

(33)

AN HOUR PASSED.

A second hour passed. André sat on the wooden bench in Departure Room 2, holding the valises on his lap, with the cold glare of G-2 men never leaving him.

The room stifled and smelled from lack of air, while the officials and militia played out a sordid departure ceremony for the Cuban passengers.

An ugly, harsh woman from G-2 shrilled out their names. Immigration officials called the refugees up, and police went through a set of forms to list next-to-kin still in Cuba.

A representative of the National Bank cleaned their financial slates.

Terrified Cuban families were ordered into side rooms and stripped naked for inspection.

A pile of confiscated clothing, jewelry, watches, wedding rings, religious medallions, and literature grew higher on the counters. Much of what was there would be picked over by the militia and officials later. The rest would end up for sale in the foyer of the national Capitol.

"Your attention, please! KLM Flight 438 for Miami will be delayed for technical reasons."

A groan went up from the weary, and in a moment rumor spread of a bomb plant. Hunger and thirst took its place alongside of fear among the passengers. They lined up to be able to use the toilet one at a time in the presence of a guard.

Muñoz's face was wet with perspiration in the suffocating office. The KLM representative argued heatedly over the further delay of the flight.

Muñoz stared out of the window at the standing aircraft. "I said I would tell you when the plane can leave. Now get out!"

Large rings of sweat circled down beneath the armpits of his shirt. He tried to find a fingernail which had not been chewed to the quick. When the phone rang he grabbed it so quickly the receiver slipped out of his moist hand.

"Hello!"

It was Luis Uribe again, for the tenth time.

"Have you found Rico?"

"No, but something else has come up. Che

Guevara has just called," he said in reference to another of the strong men of the regime. "He said that the French Ambassador had just visited him and told him he knew there was a plot to kidnap Devereaux."

"Well, what were Che's instructions?"

"He told me to tell you that in the absence of Parra and Castro it becomes your decision as head of G-2."

Muñoz hung up slowly, walked to the door and opened it and called in his waiting lieutenant.

The reeking man on her emptied the last of his strength into her.

Juanita wept softly.

"I disgust you," Rico mumbled in exhausted self-pity.

"No . . . I am crying because I am happy," she sobbed, "because I am so happy."

"Attention! Attention! KLM Flight 438 for Miami will depart immediately. Passengers may proceed to the boarding gate."

(34)

ANDRÉ CLEARED MIAMI CUSTOMS and went directly to the lobby on the main floor and checked into the Airport Hotel under the name of De Fries.

Within a few moments Michael Nordstrom made an appearance at his door with a bucket of ice and a bottle of bourbon.

"Hi, Mike . . . how are you? Good to see you."

"Good to see you. Some of us were getting a little worried."

André shrugged, closed the door behind them. "Have you received everything?"

"Two rolls of microfilm and four radio messages."

"Splendid," André said. "I have a lot of loose ends in my briefcase, a few more photographs. It's going to take a few days to complete a report." He threw his jacket on the bed, loosened his tie, rolled up his sleeves and made to the bathroom and dunked his face in a sinkful of cold water.

Mike handed him a drink as he flopped into an easy chair. He sipped and sighed wearily.

"How'd it go?"

"Routine. Nothing much exciting. But I guess you'll have to look to other sources for information out of Cuba. I'm afraid I've worn out my welcome. We're all done, Mike."

"I hope none of your people were taken."

"Not as far as I know but they've become a body without a head. With any luck they can fall back into anonymity."

"It was a hell of a job, André. A hell of a job. I don't have to try to tell you how much you've done for us. As for your people, how damned fortunate they weren't shot down against some cemetery wall."

"It was Juanita's skill."

"She must be some woman," Mike said.

"Yes, there's no other like her. I'm going to need a boat for her. She's in more danger than she's letting me know."

"You can count on our help."

"Thanks."

It was clear to Mike that André had gone very far with this woman. It was stupid for him to get involved. He was sorry for André but even in this business men remained men.

André set his drink on the coffee table next to the valise Juanita had given him. "Oh, here's the mail. I was instructed not to wait, but to open it right away." He turned the key in the lock and opened it wide, then stared, stunned. "My God!"

Michael Nordstrom stood open-mouthed as André dipped his hand in and pulled out a fist filled with jewels. Diamond and ruby and emerald stones on chokers, bracelets, watches, rings. More were wrapped in old newspaper and oilcloth. Each piece of jewelry was tagged and bore a note:

PLEASE DELIVER THIS TO MANUEL SÁNCHEZ, MIAMI—FROM HIS SISTER, CECILIA.

DELIVER TO DR. P. DARGO, MIAMI—FROM HIS MOTHER.

I BEG YOU TO SEE THAT SAMUEL LOPEZ Y GARDOS RECEIVES THIS—IT IS FROM HIS BROTHER ARTURO. I BELIEVE HE IS IN DENVER IN COLORADO.

There were over fifty pieces, each containing delivery instructions. A potpourri of sparkling tragedy.

André started to refill the bag, then stopped as he eyed something near the bottom. It was a pearl necklace bearing a sapphire pendant set off in diamonds. He knew it! A ring beside it—he knew this also! A dozen pieces at the bottom of the bag were familiar and recognized. They belonged to Juanita de Córdoba.

191

There was a letter written to him. He opened the envelope.

ANDRÉ MY BELOVED,
Please use these for the education of my sons. Look in on them once in a while if it is possible. They are fine boys and have the courage of their father and I know they will become fine men.

My darling, my wonderful man, you must know now that whatever comes I love you, I love you alone until the day I die. Do not look back and do not weep for me. If it were to be all done over, I would not have done anything differently. Love . . . love . . . love.

JUANITA

Mike watched a desperation seize André. He had never seen him like this.

"Oh my God!" André cried. "She hid it from me, Mike. Oh God. She knew and she wouldn't tell me. Oh God! What am I going to do! Juanita . . . oh, my darling . . . Juanita. . . ."

"Steady, André . . . steady . . . steady. . . ."

192

PART III

Topaz

~~~~~~

(PROLOGUE)

THE PRESIDENT pushed off with his toes, setting his rocking chair in motion. Near him on the leather couch sat Lowenstein, his most trusted political aide, and Marshall McKittrick, his intelligence adviser. General St. James, the Chief of Staff, fine-tuned the television set and paced.

The man being watched on the screen was Congressman Brolin of Ohio, who had mushroomed into national prominence. After his introduction as speaker before the Convention of The Society of American Veterans, Brolin advanced to the rostrum and the bank of microphones . . . there was a flashing of light bulbs along with the thunder of the ovation.

Congressman Brolin had sounded the first alarm in midsummer in a series of public addresses warning the nation about the Soviet arms buildup in Cuba. At first, his speeches and articles were considered crank value, political in nature and posed to embarrass the Administration. This was no longer the case. Brolin's words were now being heard loudly and clearly with what proved to be obvious access to inside information.

The four men in the President's study watched intently as the white-haired solon pointed, seemingly right into the room. He charged increased Soviet shipping of arms into Cuba. He demanded that the President go to the American people or a Congressional investigation would result.

The President's study was dead quiet for a long time after the set was cut off silencing the cheering of the audience after Brolin's speech.

"He's speaking in the Congress Tuesday," Lowenstein said, "then Face the Press next Sunday."

No need to spell out Brolin's effect. The mail was becoming ponderous. New intelligence had just come in from the French on Cuba. That the Soviets had sent missiles now seemed to be a fact. The terrifying question of when they would be operational still hovered. Earlier that day, the President had met for two hours with a special Soviet emissary whose mission it was to promise peace and assure that the Soviet intentions were being misread.

"McKittrick," the President said. "I want Cuba photographed from one end to the other at once. I want the job done within days. Pull out all stops." Then, he got out of his rocking chair and looked to General St. James. "Bring in the contingency plans for the invasion of Cuba," he said.

(I)

SÛRETÉ, THE NATIONALIZED French police, was headquartered in the Interior Ministry over the way from the Élysée Palace.

Department of Internal Protection, a division of Sûreté, functioned with much the same duties as the American FBI. The division was headed by one Léon Roux, an old-time career officer. He ran a highly skilled, professional police operation relatively free of the heavy hand of President Pierre La Croix.

Roux refused to become one of the new, fashionable American-baiters and greeted Sid Jaffe, an old friend, as an old friend.

The Frenchman's movements were quick and jerky like a hummingbird's, but otherwise his face was a prune of wrinkles, expressively cynical from years of police work.

There were coffee and amenities before Sid Jaffe got down to the business that had brought him to Paris.

"NATO documents," Jaffe said, "dozens of them, have been stolen here and copies have been transmitted to Moscow."

Léon Roux grunted, palmed and massaged his wrinkled face in terrible concern.

"We have the Russian translations of many of them turned over by a defector," Jaffe continued. "We've broken it down to six common readers: three French, three non-French. The non-French are all back in their native countries. Nordstrom sent me here to seek your cooperation in putting the French suspects under surveillance."

Roux nodded.

"We want it kept as quiet as possible," Jaffe said, implying that both SDECE and President La Croix should be kept out of the immediate picture. Of course, Sid Jaffe knew of Roux's continued fights with SDECE, and it played in his favor.

Roux looked up at the ceiling and thought out loud. "Let's say Jaffe did not visit me with this information. Let's say I received it as a tip through my own sources. Therefore I would be within my prerogative to act on my own. No one else would have to know for the time being, would they?"

Jaffe smiled. "You didn't hear it from me."

"Well now, what good Frenchmen are suspect?"

"Colonel Galande, Air Planning."

Roux pouted his lips and waved his hand palm down with a *comme çi comme ça* . . . maybe yes, maybe no . . . gesture. "Possible. He was a Vichy French officer whom La Croix pardoned years ago. His wife was once a Communist; however, that is not a crime in France. Possible, possible."

"Guillon, Chief of Staff's office."

"Extremely doubtful, eh, Jaffe?"

"You never know."

198

"Who else?"

"Henri Jarré, NATO economist."

Léon Roux's silence was tip enough. He called for files on the three men and asked that Marcel Steinberger be called in.

"I'm giving this to Inspector Steinberger. You'll meet him now. Half Jew. After Auschwitz he ended up in Dachau. The Americans liberated him. He worked in your military government for four years. He is extremely pro-American, has a tight mouth and a quick mind."

The files of the suspects and Inspector Steinberger arrived together. The Inspector was introduced to Jaffe, who watched him closely as Roux explained the mission.

Steinberger was a smallish man who outwardly showed little of the years in two concentration camps except for a tinge of madness that sparkled from his eyes now and again. It was a hollow expression of sudden detachment, a reversion that Jaffe had come to know set concentration camp victims apart from other human beings.

When the briefing was done, the three of them scanned the files. Léon Roux tore two pieces of paper from a scratch pad and passed them over his desk to Jaffe and Steinberger.

"Write the name of the man we want and I'll do the same."

Jaffe made a crib of his hand over his paper and scratched two words, as did Inspector Steinberger. Roux cradled a pen between his forefinger and third finger and scrawled with a flourish. The papers were passed back to him, face down. He tore off his own sheet, then turned the other two over.

199

All three of them carried the same words:
HENRI JARRÉ.

(2)

ANDRÉ BACKED THROUGH the door and set his suitcases down. There was an instant feeling of
emptiness without the usual greeting of Picasso
and Robespierre. The living room was dark except
for a small lamp between the pair of Louis XV
chairs.

Brigitte Camus sat sullen in her trench coat
and tam.

"Hello, Monsieur Devereaux," she said.

He knew but feared to ask.

"Madame Devereaux is gone," Brigitte said.

"When?"

"Right after you left for Cuba. There's a note
on the desk from her, and several letters from
Michele at the office."

He went to the desk, clicked on the lamp, and
opened the envelope.

MY DEAREST ANDRÉ,
  What was once love between us has turned to
something else. We are saturated. It seems the
days go by with a never-ending digging of barbs.
There is always an air of hostility very close to the
surface, waiting for the word to erupt.
  I detest the slavery of your position. I've wanted
to understand and hold up my end of things, but
I cannot watch you die before my eyes.
  Oh, how I long for time we cannot buy back. How
I wish we were not so far down the path and committed to our unalterable ways. If we had known
then what we know now, we might have been able
to bring out the best in each other instead of the
worst. I cannot condone what you have done with
other women. I've lived with it, but I've never
liked it. There is my part in this, too, I suppose,
in not bringing you fulfillment.

I know I must have time to think and space away from you to think, for when I see you or hear you, I tremble with weakness.

Michele and I have been living in the apartment in Paris, and I have been visiting your father on weekends in Montrichard. He has been quite decent, considering his general opinion of all women and, thus far, has spared me being told that I am but further proof.

Michele is totally finished with Tucker. She has enrolled in the Sorbonne here in Paris and has met a young man, a François Picard, who is a journalist and also works for national television. He is quite intense and dedicated, and in many ways reminds me of you when we met. He and Michele see each other constantly.

André, my darling, if I have hurt you by this separation, I believe I would have hurt you more by remaining in Washington in our failing state.

Love,
Nicole

The letter lingered in his hand.

"Are you hungry, Monsieur?" Brigitte asked.

"No."

"A drink?"

"No, no thank you, Madame Camus."

She took the letter from his hand and read it. "She is not fair."

"I am afraid Nicole is quite correct," André answered.

"No, she's not right. Her life should be you. Your life is the whole world. She has to be here, to stand alongside you no matter what discomfort it causes her. But Nicole is in love with her own misery. She rejects her duty as a wife by failing to smile to you when you are weary, to give you her strength and share your fears, to give silent compassion when you are done in with tension. What she deserves is a Tucker Brown."

"That's enough. . . ."

201

"I'm sorry, but I've seen you come out of the battlefield in your office into the battlefield in your home for too many years."

"Yes, how inconsiderate of Nicole to leave me at the very time I am trying desperately to get my mistress out of Cuba. Pity of Nicole not to be broad-minded enough to understand."

"If the situation were reversed, would Juanita de Córdoba understand?"

"Yes . . . how well she would understand."

"Then, that is the kind of woman you deserve."

He slumped at the desk and rubbed his eyes with the heels of his hand and spoke in a mumble almost incoherent. "I made up this cable on the way here. It's to Ambassador Adam in Havana and concerns a boat from Miami to Cuba. I'm going on it to bring Juanita out. I . . . just don't care to look over the mail tonight . . . we have a long report to work up so we'll be at the office late for the rest of the week . . . just make sure the cable goes out in the morning. . . ."

"You've had enough," Brigitte said. "Now, shut it off for a while." She unbuttoned her coat, deliberately. "I'll make you something to eat."

"No, you go home."

"Please. . . ."

"No, you worry too much about me as it is."

"I'll take your daughter's room," she insisted. "I want to be nearby if you wish to talk or need something. There are times when a man should not be left alone."

(3)

THE DOOR BUZZER SOUNDED in the Devereaux

apartment on Rue de Rennes. Nicole let in François Picard, led him to the living room, and poured him a Pernod and herself a bourbon, a carry-over of her Americanization.

"Michele will be ready shortly."

François was piqued. "Why the devil isn't she ever ready on time? I've never seen a woman who is always, always so late."

"You've been spoiled, François. But for a girl like Michele, one has to pay small prices."

He grunted, she laughed. Nicole liked this testy young man. He was in his late twenties, dressed nicely but in an unconcerned way, and sometimes in mid-conversation his mind drifted to something far away. He was as a dreamer should be.

"I read your article in this week's *Moniteur*. You have a very barbed pen. I'm sure you made President La Croix quite unhappy."

"Unfortunately, he does not read me."

"I rather think your opinion will get back to him."

François let out a deep sigh that reeked of frustration. "It's not only La Croix and the people around him. The worst of it is the French people are deaf to what he is doing. A nation of fools. Eternal parade-ground soldiers. But we must go on trying, mustn't we, Madame Devereaux?"

Nicole lowered her eyes and tucked her legs beneath her on the couch. "Yes, I know someone like that."

François carried out the smoking of a cigarette with the same intensity that he did everything else. François Picard was a rebel in a futile cause . . . quite like someone she knew. But there was a light side to him and Michele was able to bring it out.

"Are you and Michele serious?" Nicole asked abruptly.

"Would you mind if we were?"

"I never object to anything Michele does, but I will give my opinion."

"Please."

"She's lived her life a certain way. Michele is very sheltered and conscious of . . . well, the emphasis has been on the social side of life."

"I understand what you're saying."

"Don't be offended, François, but this sudden new change of climate may not work out as easily as you think."

"I'm not offended, Madame. I'm without station in life or what you call station. Moreover, I suspect that my anti-La Croix attitudes will eventually get me fired from Télévision Nationale. Then I'll really be a struggling journalist. One does not live well on a column a week in *Moniteur*."

"Enter Bohemia?"

"As long as Michele sticks, I'll try."

"But you've only known each other such a short while."

"She does something that no one else can make me do. She makes me laugh. When I come into the room, she looks at me in a certain way and always smiles and gives me the feeling she is happy because I am alive. I've had my share of girls. Michele is very young, but she is more of a woman than I've ever known. She dresses like a woman, looks like a woman, smells like a woman. She is a total woman, like her mother."

Michele made her entrance with a weekend bag. They would drive to the coast to a place he knew near Dieppe. More than likely the Channel weather would be too foul for bathing or sunning,

204

but there would be long soulful walks on the beach and a pleasant cottage and fireplace. They would listen to music and talk. They seemed to be able to talk endlessly.

François and Michele exchanged smiles.

"Sorry I'm late."

"We'd better be off to beat the traffic out of Paris."

"Have a nice weekend. I'll look for you Sunday night."

François assured Nicole he would not speed his sports car recklessly through the countryside, and left.

"I hate to leave you alone, Mamma."

"Nonsense."

"Why don't you go down to Montrichard?"

"I'm not up to Grandfather Devereaux this week. Go on, don't keep your young man waiting."

They touched cheeks. Nicole turned at the door. "Is he wonderful, or am I mad?"

"Yes, he's wonderful, and he'll give you a life of . . ." She stopped before saying "loneliness and pain."

"Don't, Mamma. I'm so happy."

Nicole looked out of the window down to the pavement and watched them drive off into a world they were now able to create just for themselves. They would be oblivious for a while of that other world that would gobble them up and shatter the bliss.

She began a nervous pacing accompanied by a cigarette and a bourbon. She stopped before the record player and read the album covers. Somehow, every damned bit of music these days reminded her of André.

She looked toward the phone. Call a girl friend

and have lunch and gossip? Nicole had become bored with this waste in just a few weeks.

Dinner and theater? There were standing offers from the many friends they had in Paris. *They.* She was a third wheel now, and the invitations were predicated on friends feeling sorry for her. She would stand no more of that.

The walls of loneliness closed in on her.

A good book. Hell, there aren't any good books anymore.

Loneliness was the plague. You drift to second-rate company and seat yourself with a known bore in order to evade being alone.

But you cannot escape that fear that comes when the lights must finally be turned off, or that emptiness when you awaken fitfully and the bed is empty.

The void is there all the time, even in a crowd.

She lit another cigarette and tried to thumb through a magazine. It went into the wastebasket.

The decision that Nicole had hoped to reach by the separation had not been reached. Things were more confused than ever. Once, when she and André were young, she had felt he could not live without her. Now, with each passing day, she knew that just the opposite was true. He would continue his work . . . perhaps a bit sadder and wearier, but he would go on as a living, vital human being.

Nicole had reduced herself to a static, cigarette-smoking stone, totally consumed by her own problems and misery.

The sound of the phone had a blessed ring.

"Hello."

"Nicole darling, this is Jacques."

It was Granville, the oldest and closest friend of hers and André's.

"I'm a bastard," he said.

"Of course you are, darling. That's nothing new."

"No, no. You see, I knew it was a weekend and if you weren't going to Montrichard you'd be booked up. I really hesitated to call."

"As a matter of fact, I planned a quiet couple of days of records and catching up on some back reading."

"You must do me an enormous favor. Do you remember Guy de Crécy?"

"Yes, we've met here and there. Ambassador to Egypt, isn't he?"

"Right ... or he was until last week. We've recalled him to Paris. Poor devil only arrived yesterday and I'm shooting him out to the Far East on some special business in a few days. I'm throwing a little dinner party for him at my apartment. Intimate, you know, just five or six couples."

"Isn't he still married?"

"Widower. Lost his wife about a year ago."

"Oh, I didn't know that."

"Be a dear, Nicole. Please come."

"Just for you, Jacques."

"I love you, I love you. De Crécy will call for you around eight."

Nicole hung up with a great sense of relief that the loneliness would be reprieved for an evening. Then strangely she felt herself pleasantly anxious at the idea of meeting Guy de Crécy again.

207

NICOLE WAS READY well in advance of Guy de Crécy's arrival and kept him waiting for only a few judicious moments. She had made herself utterly radiant and was pleased that he was pleased at the sight of her.

He was a man of fifty, not in the least handsome, but with that kind of strong face often more desirable in a male. De Crécy carried himself with the suave assurance of a man at ease, seasoned by years of fencing on the diplomatic fields of honor.

Conversation on the way to Granville's apartment was easy between them. He had a grown son and daughter. Life was quite lonely after his wife's death. He was happy to get out of Egypt and damned mad to be hustled off to the Far East after only a few days. Oh, well, there would be a few months in Paris, later.

She did not talk of the separation with André. She had returned to Paris to get her daughter started at the Sorbonne, and catch up with things in France. Love Washington, she lied.

When André was in one of his pointed moods, he had told her more than once that a Guy de Crécy was the kind of man she should have married in the first place. He would never die from overwork, would always be on the correct side of the political fence, never allow himself to get cornered into making a crucial or unpopular decision, and he thrived on the round of parties and pomp of officialdom and adored all the outward signs of success.

Jacques Granville's apartment was in the Meurice Hotel. As Deputy Aide to the Presidential

Executive, who ran the offices of the President, Jacques Granville had risen from a lowly office during the war to one of the most influential positions in France.

The elegance of his Paris place in the Meurice testified to both his position and personal wealth. Paulette Granville, his fourth and youngest wife, greeted them in the foyer. And Jacques, a charming silver-haired fox, warmed the welcome with a Gallic outburst.

The sitting room was soon filled with gossip, larded with the special wit of diplomats and exquisite champagne. All of those present were men high in the La Croix entourage except Henri Jarré, one of NATO's top economists.

The conversation quite naturally drifted into an anti-American dissertation.

Henri Jarré, with a great shock of black hair, thick eyebrows, thin bony pale face, pursed his lips like the cynical intellectual he was and was most vocal and venomous. "I say damn the Americans. It's not the diplomatic blunders or even their total lack of diplomacy. It's the Americans holding the trigger of the atomic gun. I'll be damned if I want these upstarts to call a move that can destroy France without France's consent. Well, we can all be thankful President La Croix is in the Élysée Palace. By God, he gave them a jolt with his demand on the gold payment."

Guy de Crécy was what one might call a total diplomat, without strong feelings on any subject. Other than Nicole Devereaux, who remained properly silent, the room was without a champion for the maligned Americans.

She drank her champagne, a few glasses too many, and quelled the temptation to throw out one of André's assorted barbs just to see the stupid expressions that would envelop their faces. Jarré, in particular, needed some cutting up.

How strange it was that in this room she fully shared André's views. It annoyed her. It annoyed her, too, that she had loathed Washington but could not find happiness in Paris or Montrichard.

Nicole was pleased by Guy de Crécy's attention. While others around him raged, his gestures and mannerisms were refined and his voice smooth, his words carefully chosen and properly spoken.

Paulette Granville mercifully seated them together during the dinner, and the sympathy between them heightened. He showed he was aware of her with the slightest hint of a smile, a brushing touch, a lingering look.

Nicole wondered as she flushed, Is he playing the subtle art of seduction or am I reading him wrong? Is he merely being polite? What if I am mistaken and rejected? The word "rejected" stayed with her. Am I desirable enough for him? I'm not . . . I'm too old. . . .

"More wine?"

"Yes, please."

No, damn it, she thought. Don't be like an American woman and drink yourself into a justification! She covered her wine glass, changing her mind.

In the car on the way home, Guy de Crécy took her hand in both of his in a most innocent manner and spoke of how nice the evening had been and how grateful he was to Granville for making his short stay pleasant.

In this game they were playing and in the way they played it, there was no such thing as a man taking the woman. Mauling before the door and empty words were for children. In the end it would have to be her choice. And the man who played the game well, as Guy de Crécy did, would have presented himself and his case, as he had, with great charm and now would have to await a sign from her.

Nicole, too, had played the game, to a point. She played it as long as no one became offended. Others had waited for the sign as Guy de Crécy waited now. She had never given it because Nicole never wanted or needed more than her husband.

The car pulled to a stop at 176 Rue de Rennes. The chauffeur came around to open the rear door.

"Thank you for a lovely evening," she blurted as though she had no control of the words leaving her mouth.

He showed no trace of displeasure as he walked her to the lobby door. Nicole handed him the key, avoiding his eyes. He unlocked the door, shoved it open. She gave him her hand.

"Please forgive me," she said.

"I quite understand, Madame Devereaux," Guy de Crécy said. He kissed her hand and left.

Nicole closed her apartment door behind her and leaned against it breathing erratically. She took off her wrap slowly and let it fall over the back of a chair. The room was so horribly quiet. As she heard the motor drive off she damned herself.

Down the hall, into the bedroom . . . the empty bed. She sat before the dressing mirror for a timeless period looking at herself as though through a veil, seeing a diffused stranger in the half-light. And tears fell down her cheeks until none were left.

211

JACQUES GRANVILLE ENTERED Nicole's apartment drenched from the driving rain. He had found no parking space closer than two blocks away.

"Poor dear," Nicole said taking his coat. She hung it over the heater in the entry to dry.

Jacques rubbed his icy hands together, shook his head like a dripping dog, and made straight for the liquor cabinet in the living room.

"I'm glad Michele phoned so I could talk her out of driving back from Dieppe tonight."

"Ahhhh," Jacques said as the cognac hit the spot. "Well, I'm a bachelor. Paulette left for Normandy early this morning . . . in a huff I'm afraid. Now that I've got you all to myself why don't you let me take you out to dinner?"

"I have a better idea. Let's not go out in the mess. I'll cook something here."

"Beautiful." Jacques phoned his office to give his whereabouts, then unlaced his shoes. His socks were soaked.

"You're half drowned," Nicole said. "Trot on back to André's room. Raid his closet and make yourself comfortable."

When Jacques entered the kitchen, Nicole was aproned and flitting about in preparation to assault the oven. She approved of the baggy velour shirt, old trousers, and André's slippers.

"Nothing serious with you and Paulette?"

"Frankly, we're heading for the rocks."

"Not again, Jacques."

"It's a talent with me," he berated himself. He sat up to the kitchen table, poured a glass of wine. Nicole opened the refrigerator and studied.

"You can have a choice of . . . ummm . . .

212

let's see . . . lamb, but that will take a while, or sweetbreads or, yes, I have some scallops."

"Surprise me." He picked up a magazine on the table whose cover was adorned by the lord and master, Pierre La Croix. After a quick thumb-through he set it aside. "How'd you get on with Guy de Crécy?"

"Oh, fine. Charming man. Shame about his wife. Pour me a little wine."

He set her glass next to her at the sink where she peeled potatoes. She finished her chore, wiped her hands on her apron, brushed back some fallen strands of hair and saluted with her wineglass.

Jacques became rather grim. "I wanted to see you because I'm worried about André."

"So am I," Nicole said.

"Nicole. I'm going to confide in you and tell you some things I shouldn't be speaking about, but I trust you implicitly."

"Don't worry, my dear. I've been married to an intelligence man for a long, long time."

"You know, of course, André has been in Cuba."

"Sometimes he tells me where he is going. Other times he doesn't. In this case it wasn't hard to figure out."

"Against a lot of opposition he took it upon himself to do a job primarily for the Americans," Jacques said. "His report has arrived at SDECE. We conclude he found evidence of Soviet offensive missiles."

"That's frightening."

"An understatement. If it's true, the Americans are going to have to act and act soon. God knows what it can lead to. But André's part. He is a French official. By his action he may have put

213

France into a precarious position, involving us against our will."

"That's our André," she said with a crisp tone of irony. "I'm certain he was wise enough to figure out the consequences in advance."

"Even if his case is strong enough to justify it, he's in the same tub of hot water he's been in for five years in this continuous waltz with the Americans. NATO is unpopular and his views are unpopular. You know Admiral Brune. Brune is the prime mover of the Secret Service and he's out and out to get André. I know my title as Aide to the Presidential Executive sounds impressive as hell but I'm just La Croix's errandboy. I've managed to stop a lot of reports downgrading André from reaching La Croix."

"As his oldest and dearest friend," Nicole said, "then you know his damn martyred dedication."

"Nicole. There's also a report on his health I've been able to break and this little finger of mine can't hold back the flood."

"How can you get him out of Washington . . . feet first?" she said bitterly.

"André has friends throughout the whole spectrum of the government. His reputation is almost like that of a holy man. I've talked around. We can get him out of this, honorably."

"I'd give anything," Nicole whispered.

"There's an Ambassadorship opening soon. It's his if he'll take it."

"Where?" she asked shakily.

"A bit far away but it's quite decent. And mainly, it's peaceful. New Zealand."

Nicole turned her back and held her face in her hands, then quickly controlled herself before she came to tears.

214

"You must help me convince him," Jacques said.

"I don't even know if I have a husband. We're in serious trouble."

"André will come back to you," Jacques said firmly.

"He may be involved with another woman."

"I know my man," Jacques said, "he's no Granville. He'll come back."

Nicole calmed herself and returned to preparing the meal. Jacques refilled his wineglass and stared long and hard at her.

"I'm glad it's raining," he said. "And I'm glad Michele won't be back tonight and I'm glad Paulette is in Normandy. I've never been anything but a bastard all my life and I won't change this minute. Nicole, I want to take you to bed."

She accepted it calmly, then smiled and tweaked his nose. "After three young beautiful wives, what do you want with an old girl like me? I know you're just doing it to comfort my sorrow and I'm flattered you asked."

"Now, damnit, Nicole. I've had a thing for you for a long time. I've behaved for twenty years, but under the present mutual circumstances I don't think we have to moralize the situation."

"Jacques . . . I believe you're serious."

"I want to make love to you, Nicole. You can turn me down, but don't take me lightly."

The man before her was far too handsome, far too smooth. He was a beautiful rake and she was sure that her name would be forgotten among his lost legion of mistresses. She put her arm about his neck and kissed him.

Sooner or later the piper would be paid. But for

now she handled it all with discretion . . . in the French way.

(6)

SEVERAL DAYS AFTER his return from Cuba, André had fully indoctrinated himself on the Kuznetov interrogation and was ready to sit in attendance in what was obviously to be the crucial moment of revelation.

Boris Kuznetov asked to see him alone before the session began and was wheeled into a private office. He shooed the nurse out.

"Well," André greeted him, "you look much better than the last time I saw you."

"I wish I could return the compliment," the Russian answered. "It appears that you've had a difficult journey."

"You might say that."

"The concept of a next life beyond this one is a delightful hoax, but if there is one, I'm certain we'll both choose a different line of work."

"Mind if I smoke?"

"Please."

"You've read the interrogation to date?"

"Yes."

The lighthearted manner that Kuznetov had developed during the weeks of questioning suddenly faded, and he was again the same fear-filled man as in the days following the defection.

"I wanted to talk to you alone," he said, with a sudden lurch of desperation. "I'll come right out and ask you. Will the Americans keep their bargain with me?"

"Do you have any reason to suspect they won't?"

216

"No, nothing concrete. But, on the other hand, I haven't told them much of value yet."

"I personally have never known Michael Nordstrom to go back on his word."

"I'm convinced of Nordstrom's good intentions," Kuznetov answered, "but he doesn't have the final word. Suppose there is a policy change, or suppose a superior backs off. Whom do I turn to if Nordstrom suddenly can't deliver? What if they decide to get rid of me?"

"You know damn well they don't play that way. Look, Kuznetov . . . Boris . . . your apprehension is natural, but you made a deal and you'll just have to go through with it and trust them."

"All right, suppose I do? Now let me ask you about yourself. With the information you are about to learn, you may be put in a very difficult position with your own government."

"That won't be anything new."

"But you also may need American help. Are you so certain they won't turn their backs on you after you've been used for all they can get out of you?"

André gave it a long thought. Kuznetov was warning him they were in the same boat, and now he showed the same kind of hesitation the Russian showed.

"Whatever," André whispered, "we're both committed."

"If I were of religious conviction," Kuznetov said, "I'd suggest we pray for each other."

The interrogation room was as familiar to Boris as a second home. He knew every grain in the big table, the way the curtains hung, the sway of the leaves of the maple tree just outside the window. He knew every nuance and gesture

217

of the men he nodded good morning to. In addition to Kramer, Jaffe, W. Smith, and Billings, Michael Nordstrom and Sanderson Hooper were in attendance. Never before had there been such tension.

He was wheeled to the head of the table. The nurse took her station as the four interrogators scanned their pads and the thick book of his testimony to date. Dr. Billings turned on the tape. There was a moment of confusion until they decided to continue in English because of the newcomers.

"In 1952," W. Smith began, "you were the Soviet Resident in Berlin and you were recalled to Moscow. For what purpose?"

Kuznetov hedged, looked rather pathetically toward André. He poured his Pepsi-Cola slowly. They waited expectantly. "I would like a large blackboard," he said.

It was sent for and placed next to Boris so that everyone in the room could view it. Boris pushed himself out of his wheelchair over several objections. He assured them he had the doctor's permission to stand and walk for short intervals. Chalk in hand, he drew a number of squares which were obviously to show the chain of command in some kind of organization.

"Do you know what this is, Devereaux?"
"Perhaps."

Across the top of the board he chalked in the letters "SDECE," the initials of the French Secret Service. Slowly and meticulously, Kuznetov began filling in the squares, starting at the top with the Director's office. Then he turned to the squares on the left side of the board.

"R—1 is your intelligence service." Under this he filled in the following boxes:

R—2 EASTERN EUROPE
R—3 WESTERN EUROPE
R—4 AFRICA
R—5 MIDDLE EAST
R—6 FAR EAST
R—7 AMERICA—WESTERN HEMISPHERE

Under each of these he proceeded to enter the names of the directors, the deputy directors, and their code names. Then he moved to the center of the blackboard and again filled in a new set of squares.

"French Counterintelligence is known as Service 2," Boris said. He listed the various divisions of the worldwide organization, including the highly secret "3/5—Communist Section," and named its chief and principal deputies.

On the lower right side of the board he filled in a single large square: "Service 7—Administration."

On the far right he wrote, "Service 5—Action."

Subdivisions under the Action Section were "A/1—Paramilitary" and lastly "FFF—Secret Operations."

Kuznetov set the chalk down, brushed his hands clean, and was assisted back into the wheelchair. Then he addressed André.

"FFF, your Secret Operations Section, is directed by one of your closest friends, Robert Proust. His code name is Panorama."

The silence in the room remained intense, and André bore a stone face.

"FFF has particular interest to us all, as you

219

will soon learn. FFF has sprouted a baby, a new subsection. Your friend Robert Proust has as his chief henchman one Ferdinand Fauchet. Do you know Ferdinand Fauchet?"

André nodded faintly.

"Well, let me enlighten our American friends. Ferdinand Fauchet keeps his office at Orly Field under the guise of a customs control. Actually, his office is rigged out with some remarkable listening apparatus, camera equipment, and ingenious devices for picking locks and breaking seals. He is an expert at opening and photographing the contents of diplomatic pouches which are not properly sealed. So be careful when your diplomatic mail passes through Paris."

André felt shaky but controlled it.

"Let me tell you some more about Robert Proust and his henchman, Fauchet. Fauchet is the SDECE liaison with certain French gangsters and underworld people who carry out most of the actual kidnapings, beatings, and killings for Secret Operations. Two years ago, Fauchet purchased a small but exquisite hotel, the Miami, located on Rue Montparnasse. But, you see, it does not belong to him. It belongs to the French Secret Service."

Sid Jaffe licked his lips, remembering that he had visited the bar and restaurant of the Miami on a number of occasions, once with Michael Nordstrom, who now exchanged a glance with him.

"The underworld has supplied a number of very high-class prostitutes who are extremely well trained. They work diplomatic receptions for the SDECE, usually under the guise of being models or even housewives. An amorous or drunk diplomat is apt to leave the reception in the company of one of these young ladies and be taken to the Miami. Or a married diplomat may want to rendezvous with a so-called married girl in this group and she'll also take him to the Miami. Every room is wired and can be photographed by hidden cameras."

Kuznetov scratched the end of his nose, trying to recall a figure. "If memory serves me correctly, there are twenty-two thousand phone taps in France and four thousand in Paris off a central switchboard. But back to Ferdinand Fauchet. Sometimes he doesn't use gangsters, but instead asks a fanatical right-wing organization to carry out assassinations. For example, the three German industrialists who were murdered last year in Switzerland in what appeared to be an automobile accident. Because of their sudden demise, a French firm was able to get a NATO contract for short-range rockets and carriers that had been about to be awarded to the Germans."

Kuznetov continued to detail other murders and operations that could be known to someone with remarkable contacts. André managed to maintain his outward appearance of calm, but inside him a storm was raging.

"All you have told us." André said, "is that you have some extremely good sources of information about the workings of the SDECE."

"Then there isn't anything you wish to correct?"

"There is nothing I wish to comment on."

"Would you say that this organizational chart of the SDECE is accurate?"

"Perhaps."

"Do you find anything missing?"

André studied the diagram for several moments but did not answer the question.

"There is something missing," Kuznetov went on. "It is part of Robert Proust's Secret Operations which will be put under the direction of Ferdinand Fauchet. It will be known as Section P and be composed largely of a group of French scientists now in training who will be placed in American research and industry."

"America is our ally. We have a regular exchange program of scientists."

"But Section P has a totally different purpose."

"What purpose?"

"Not just surveillance, carried out by every country even on its friends, but actual spying. Section P will conduct industrial and scientific espionage on the United States."

André felt the eyes of the others hard on him. "It is a lie," he said softly.

"Section P will spy on the United States as though the United States were the enemy of France," Kuznetov repeated.

"You are telling me that as national policy in 1962 the government of France is deliberately organizing a unit to commit espionage on America?"

"Yes."

"It is a lie," André repeated. "It is unthinkable."

"It is also good intelligence to think of the unthinkable."

André's humiliation before friends and colleagues was becoming total. He knew he had to keep his composure at all costs. Then he was stricken with the sickening thought that Boris Kuznetov's information had thus far shown itself to be foolproof.

"I may continue?" Kuznetov said.

"Of course."

"On your next trip to Paris either Robert Proust or a superior in SDECE will advise you of Section P and order you to implement this operation through your office in Washington."

"If what you say is true, everyone knows my attitude."

"Precisely. Nordstrom, McKittrick, the head of CIA. You are completely trusted. That is why Section P can become a masterpiece of deception. In Moscow KGB likes the operation so well they plan to use it as the key to their own industrial espionage in America."

For the first time in two decades, André Devereaux became unraveled before an adversary. He stood livid and cracked his fist on the desk. "You are trying to mortify France! You dare accuse my country of collaborating with the Soviet Union! You lie!"

André hushed abruptly, shocked by the sound of his own voice. He had committed a grievous error before men of his own breed. "It's fantasy," he said harshly.

"We deal in fantasy, do we not?" Kuznetov answered, taking off his glasses and setting them on the table wearily and rubbing his eyes. He felt sorry for what he was doing to André Devereaux. He put his glasses back on and searched the faces of the Americans he had come to know. They were hushed with disbelief.

"I am Boris Kuznetov," he said in almost a whisper. "At the time of my defection I was chief of an ultrasecret division of KGB, the Anti-NATO Section."

No one present had known of its existence and they were dumbstruck.

"The information gathered by Section P will get back to Moscow in the same way we received the NATO documents. Topaz," he said slowly, "is the code name for Frenchmen working inside the French government as agents of the Soviet Union. They are everywhere, in every department in the military, in every ministry. The SDECE is riddled with them. Members of Topaz go clear up to the top level of government. Topaz No. 1 is a man who carries the code name of Columbine. If you find out who Columbine is, then you will have uncovered a person who is extremely high in the personal entourage and has the ear of President Pierre La Croix."

"Are you charging that the President of France is being advised and briefed by a Soviet agent?"

"Precisely," Boris Kuznetov said, "precisely."

(7)

SNATCHING PROMINENT CUBANS from the "fatherland" was routine these days. The refugee trade was brisk. After André turned the valise of gems over to the FBI for delivery to their new owners he set out, with Mike Nordstrom's help, to arrange a boat for Juanita de Córdoba. A simple plan was evolved, built around an extremely fast boat manned by a crew and skipper who were old hands on the Cuban run. They knew the place to land, the time, the Cuban patrol schedules. They could be in and out of Cuban territorial waters in short order under cover of night, and, if trouble came, could outrun any pursuers.

In one of the paradoxes of Cuban-American relations, it was still possible to speak by telephone between the two countries. With the escape plan locked up, André spoke with Adam by prearranged code then returned to Washington and dispatched the plan by diplomatic courier and waited for the green light by return diplomatic mail.

Brigitte Camus entered André's office, stopped before his desk. He glanced up to his secretary, a woman obviously filled with displeasure.

"Has the courier arrived from Havana?"

"Yes," she answered, "he is on the way in from the airport. He'll be at the Chancellery at any time." She continued her display of annoyance by slapping an airline ticket on his desk loudly.

André pretended to be unaware and examined his round-trip ticket from Washington to Miami. "If all goes well," he said, "I'll be back at my desk in seventy-two hours."

"If all goes well," she snapped.

Brigitte Camus had been a most dedicated, closemouthed and loyal associate. In the decade of their relationship she was party to most plans, undertook important responsibility, and on occasion André even sought out her advice.

On rarer occasions, Brigitte Camus volunteered advice whether it was solicited or not.

"You will kindly not hover over my desk," André said.

"Before you fire me," she always opened such conversations, "I have something to say and I intend to say it."

André flipped his pen down, took off his glasses, and leaned back in his leather chair resignedly. "In that case, you might as well sit down and be comfortable."

Brigitte remained standing. "It is dangerous for you to go back into Cuba."

"What makes you think I'm going into Cuba?"

"Why haven't we contacted any one of a dozen agents in the Florida area who could go in and bring Juanita de Córdoba out? How about Pepe Vimont?"

"Perhaps I plan to speak to Pepe in Miami. Did that occur to you? Did it occur to you I might just want to be present when the boat returns?"

"You may be the best intelligence man in the world but to me you are a very bad liar. And you know full well that a man in your position does not take part in these operations. It violates every rule in the business."

He was properly exposed. No use to try to fool this woman. "For years," André said softly, "I have planned operations and rotted inside . . . waiting. There have been times, you know them, when I have sent men and women to their death. What if I had been there in place of them? I could have come through it every time. Brigitte," he continued with uncommon familiarity, "Brigitte, this once I must do it myself. If anything should go wrong. If she is lost and I'm not there . . . then maybe I wouldn't want to go on, myself."

Brigitte's anger softened to pity. "I'll have to understand, Monsieur Devereaux."

"The Ambassador is not to know."

"Yes." She began to leave, then stopped. "There is another letter on my desk from Madame Devereaux. This time she addressed the outer envelope to me and pleaded that you do not return it unopened as you have the others. Before you go to Miami, please read it."

226

"No."

"If anything should happen, please don't leave her with an unopened letter."

"She left me with cause. It still exists. I will not be a hypocrite so long as the most important thing in my life is to get Juanita de Córdoba out of Cuba. I know we're star-crossed but I can't stop this illusion of mine of a life with her. . . ."

"And if the illusion dies?"

"Why should Nicole be the butt of my folly? She's still young and handsome enough to make for herself the kind of life she can deal with."

"Don't you know that Nicole will take you back on any terms and she'll be damned lucky."

"Return the letter."

Brigitte shook her head. "How can such a wise man be such a fool?"

"I have dealt in logic all my life. This time I intend to be a complete fool."

The secretary from the message center knocked and entered. Brigitte signed for a bundle of letters. She fingered through them quickly, found the courier message from Alain Adam in Havana and zipped it open.

André adjusted his glasses.

My Dear André,

I am sorry our telephone conversation was so frustrating but I can say that I was happy beyond words to hear your voice and know you had arrived safely in Miami.

I have your letter of instructions about getting Juanita to Point Lucia on the Cape Saturday night and although the fishermen you mentioned are prepared at this end, there are other events that have to be explained.

When I left you at the airport I went immediately to Juanita's villa to take her to the sanctuary of the Embassy. She was not there and I could get no information on her whereabouts.

227

I had to turn my efforts to the balance of our plan. After several futile hours I literally bullied my way into Che Guevara's office and warned him we were on to a plot to kidnap you.

The rest of your departure from Cuba is history. Thank God you made it.

I tried hourly for the rest of the day to reach Juanita without success. Next morning I phoned and was answered by someone new in the villa who informed me rather tersely that she was not available.

I sent Blanche to the villa in an Embassy car on the pretext of a social call and there she relates a bizarre turn of events. Juanita was apparently not herself and barely hospitable to Blanche. She begged off outside social engagements on the pretext that she was feeling ill. Blanche was hopeful that some sort of note or sign could be passed but it was obvious the encounter was being closely watched.

Next day I went to the villa myself. A pair of militia were at the gates. I was unable to establish much except that her houseman, cook, and gardener had all been replaced. She seemed a virtual prisoner.

The day before yesterday she made her first public appearance since your departure. The occasion was the dedication of a new hospital. I made it a point to attend the ceremony in the last hope of being able to establish contact and inform her about the boat.

André, my dear comrade. I choke with pain as I write these words. Juanita showed up on the arm of Rico Parra. She was closely guarded at all times, making it impossible for me to speak to her more than a perfunctory greeting. I loathe having to tell you this but the rumor is around that she has become Parra's mistress.

It appears, my dear André, that Juanita bargained for your life and is now paying off her end of the bargain.

Blanche and I share your grief.

Your affectionate friend,
ALAIN ADAM

André sat like a wax statue. "Cancel the flight to Miami," he mumbled harshly. "I swear . . . as long as she is alive I will find a way to get her out of Cuba. . . . I swear it . . ."

8

INSPECTOR MARCEL STEINBERGER parked his car on Boulevard Murat and proceeded on foot to his flat some two blocks away. With so many new cars, parking had become a large headache in Paris these days.

He walked, hands clasped behind him, head bowed, consumed in thought and oblivious to the game of kickball being played around him by surging, screaming youngsters.

The odors of the variety of foods being cooked seeped into the stairwell and hallway as he climbed the winding stairs to his flat.

Sophie greeted him at the door, took his hat, coat, scarf, umbrella. He bumbled off absent-mindedly to the kitchen, took the lid off the pot of steaming pungent cabbage borscht, their usual Thursday night meal, and passed his blessings on it as he always did.

His wife was of Polish origin. They had met as inmates of the Dachau concentration camp. Some fifty of her immediate family had perished in the extermination ovens, leaving her as sole survivor. After the liberation they were separated in that confusion of human movement. By some miracle they found each other again when Marcel read one of the hundreds of thousands of messages desperately and pathetically pinned on the walls of the refugee centers:

MARCEL STEINBERGER—I AM ALIVE, IN VIENNA AND AWAITING TRANSPORT TO PALESTINE—CONTACT ME THROUGH HIAS (HEBREW IMMIGRANT AID SOCIETY), VIENNA—SOPHIE PERLMUTTER.

Like most concentration-camp couples they felt that their son Émile had to live in the name of a hundred murdered relatives. He was considered by them a very special gift of God to enable the continuation of a family name that was once believed destroyed, and like most concentration-camp couples they tended to be overindulgent. But young Émile grasped the meaning of his own existence and took little advantage of it. Tonight the father and son worked together on math problems the boy had been saving, until they were called to the table.

Émile and Sophie were talkative, but Marcel had detached himself and toyed listlessly with his food. He was immersed in the puzzle of his mission.

Marcel had spent six years directly after the war hounding down wanted war criminals. He was relentless and dedicated, and he now assailed his present assignment with the same sense of vengeance.

So far, Colonel Galande and Guillon showed no reason to be suspect. Further reports from ININ had come to the Sûreté to the effect that nothing could be found out of order on the three non-French.

Everything pointed again to Henri Jarré, the embittered, vitriolic American-baiter, as the man passing the NATO documents.

"Marcel, eat your borscht, it's getting cold."

He complied noisily.

But how? Inspector Steinberger was reputed to be the best second-story man in the Sûreté. He had waited for a weekend when Jarré and his wife would be out of Paris and personally entered and tooth-combed the Jarré flat.

No library book, pipe fitting, closet, coat lining, light fixture, cabinet, bed, desk, or radiator went unsearched. He placed ingenious bugs in every room and attached phone taps.

But nothing turned up. Henri Jarré was tailed day and night and led them nowhere.

Yet Marcel was convinced that Jarré must be the traitor.

Marcel was dunking his bread in the bowl and stopped abruptly. That strange look came to his eyes. "Of course," he whispered to himself. "I've been a fool!"

He shoved the chair back from the table and without adieu kissed his wife and son and mumbled that he would return later. It was a situation they had come to live with.

Steinberger made a hasty call to a person with whom he had worked on many occasions, Colonel Jasmin, the Head of Security of NATO headquarters in Rambouillet, and in a few minutes was speeding out of Paris to that town, fifteen miles south of the capital.

Jasmin was in lounging attire on the patio of his cottage on the edge of the NATO complex and greeted Steinberger gruffly, speaking from behind a fat cigar. "Well, who is Sûreté after?"

"Jarré," he answered tersely.

"What for? Giving bad speeches?"

"We suspect him of passing NATO documents to the Soviets."

Jasmin grunted a laugh. "Well, anything you suspect of Jarré is reasonable. I've never understood how such a violent anti-American could remain as one of the Chief Economists for NATO."

"Another of President La Croix's forceful appointments."

"Yes, La Croix is good at that. Well, what's this all about, Steinberger?"

"Jarré comes into contact with innumerable documents in many classifications of secrecy."

"Yes."

"He is a known, highly placed official, so his movements in and out of the grounds are accepted without suspicion or inspection."

Jasmin nodded.

"In theory, then," Steinberger said, "Jarré could drive his car through the gates with an attaché case filled with secret papers."

"Only in theory," Jasmin corrected. "Any classified document has to be signed for by him and returned to the security vaults before the end of the day. Or he must return documents to the vault if he leaves the grounds that day."

"But, my good Colonel. Suppose Henri Jarré reproduced copies of these documents in his own office, returned the originals to the security vaults, and carried the copies out."

Colonel Jasmin's face turned to stone. He lifted the phone and ordered the keys to Jarré's office building to be sent to him immediately.

In a few moments the two men arrived at the temporary barrackslike structure that housed Jarré's offices. They unlocked and entered, and closed the door behind them, switching on the hall lights. Jarré's office was a large one at the far end of the corridor.

Jasmin found the key. The desk was cluttered and the room filled with books and haphazard furnishings in aging leather.

232

Steinberger's trained eye moved from floor to walls, looking for something in particular.

"Let's start with his desk," Jasmin said.

"No. He won't oblige us by conveniently leaving a camera here."

"Do you think he could have been carrying in a Minox or Tessina?"

"That's not the way he does it. Film can be tricky and dangerous. I've looked into his personal photography. It's of very poor quality. His camera store shows no unusual purchases of film for the past several years." Steinberger pointed questioningly to a door.

"Secretary's office."

Steinberger tried the knob. The door was unlocked and revealed a small office, neat in contrast to Jarré's. Steinberger pointed again, this time to a curtained-off alcove.

"More than likely a supply room of some sort. It's standard in these barracks buildings."

"It's in there," Steinberger said, smiling.

"What's in there?"

The Inspector pulled the curtain back and pointed to a duplicating machine. It was a simple wet-process copier, of a type used by millions of offices in the world to make a duplicate from an original.

"Ingenious," Jasmin muttered, "ingenious. We must have a hundred of these machines on this compound."

"Now we will have to discover if his secretary is in league with him. If she's clean, she'll help. Otherwise, she'll help in order to save her own neck."

9

THE PRESIDENT WAS an extremely vigorous campaigner who received great exhilaration from the thunder of ovation, the stretching hands and the jostle of the crowd, and his ability to inspire his countrymen. He constantly broke standard security in his appearances, to the everlasting worry of his Secret Service guards.

On this day in October the President had made three speeches in three state capitals on behalf of candidates of his party, then returned to the White House by helicopter. But along with the cheers he could sense an undertone, a growing ground swell demanding action on the Cuban arms buildup. One poster which read MORE COURAGE—LESS PROFILE caught his eye and stung him.

Now, past midnight, the thrill and trial of the day faded, he sat in pajamas and dressing gown cross-legged on his bed glancing through the late newspapers strewn around him.

His two closest confidants, Lowenstein and McKittrick, sat bleary-eyed before the coffee table holding the latest batch of U-2 photographs.

The President got off the bed, put his feet into his slippers, and his mood turned grim.

"Do you believe Devereaux's report is hard enough to make a confrontation with Khrushchev?"

"I do," McKittrick answered. "And today's photographs show a tent city springing up in the Finca San José. These slashes in the earth represent further clearing. In the past they've been a positive identification for Soviet missile sites."

"The information is hard enough for me too," Lowenstein agreed.

"Policy will be framed in the next several days," the President said. "Tonight, I want your opinion straight from the shoulder."

McKittrick came to his feet and jammed his hands into his pockets and hesitated.

"Lay it on the line," the President insisted, "and don't spare me."

"All right. I pleaded with the last administration to do something about Budapest. I know there was no way to get into Hungary. The Soviets held the cards. On the other hand, there were places in the world they were vulnerable and we should have retaliated."

"Go on."

"I asked you to retaliate when they built the Berlin Wall. As long as we let them bully without fear of retaliation we're always going to be faced with things like this missile business."

The President brushed back his rumple of hair. He recalled his meeting with the Soviet Premier in Finland. Khrushchev bullied, berated, and threatened him over the Bay of Pigs fiasco.

"Khrushchev knows," Lowenstein said, "that we have them outgunned. But he also believes we won't dirty our hands."

A classical and historical error about the determination and temper of the American people was about to be compounded once again, this time by the Soviet Union.

Now that the hour of decision was coming, the young President was calm and determined. "Lowenstein," he said in a tone that spelled decision, "keep all my appointments running. I want everything to appear as normal as possible. Mac, you keep me on a minute-to-minute briefing about any new intelligence. I go with you. The Devereaux report makes it hard. Now, we'll see what kind of poker player Khrushchev is."

Marshall McKittrick's face broadened in a smile.

"This week," the President said, "I'm going to earn my salary."

(10)

MICHAEL NORDSTROM RANG the bell of the Devereaux home in Georgetown. He was baggy-eyed and yawned.

André opened the door, punctual and ready to go, a habit reluctantly learned from the Americans. They shook hands, exchanged good mornings. André grabbed his briefcase and they continued down the steps to Mike's car.

Mike pulled out into the traffic stream, yawned and apologized for it. "Had a beef with Liz," he said. "She's after me for a new car. Anyhow, I got P.O.-ed and slept on the couch. My back's broken. I guess none of us got much sleep last night."

"To say the least," André agreed.

They were both silent a long while, still in a state of shock over Boris Kuznetov's revelations.

"André," Mike said at last, "I had a long session with my people yesterday. We all believe you were not aware of this Section P, or of the existence of Topaz. That goes for McKittrick, too."

André grunted an indefinite answer.

"What I'm saying is that no matter what else is revealed by Kuznetov, we want you to stick to your office. Stay with it, no matter."

"Are those my orders?" André said acidly.

"I said, we trust you."

"I'm a Frenchman, that's my first duty. Don't forget that, Mike."

The usual air of friendly exchanges was gone from the interrogation room. The atmosphere was cold, formal and stripped for business. When Boris was wheeled in, he glanced quickly at André and nodded, feeling the guilt a fighter sometimes experiences when he has beaten up an opponent badly. On this note of mutual discomfort the session began with the turning on of the tape.

"When I was recalled from my post in Berlin as Resident," Boris began slowly, "and was told to form the anti-NATO division of KGB, the first thing I did was to order an intensive study of the NATO countries, their political habits, their leaders, their military, their intelligence. My section is small, but elite."

"How many?"

"In Moscow, seventy to a hundred men."

"In the NATO countries?"

Boris shook his head. "We used only the Soviet Residents in each NATO capital and their existing espionage systems."

"You are saying, then, you don't know who any of the anti-NATO agents outside Moscow were."

"That is correct."

"You know no one in Topaz?"

"No one."

"You have no idea who this No. 1 Columbine, is?"

"No. It is standard intelligence for a division leader not to know his agents, is it not? In KGB we are even closer about it than the Western systems."

"Go on."

"By the early nineteen-fifties, the Soviet Union

237

had lost two of its prime postwar objectives. First, we failed to prevent the reunification of western Germany. Second, we failed to remove the West from Berlin."

He paused for his Pepsi and realized he would appreciate the day when he would be permitted a vodka.

"NATO is probably the most effective and ultimate military alliance ever devised. The breaking of the NATO shield has top priority in Soviet thinking, for as long as NATO stays intact the Soviet Union cannot encroach further on western Europe. In my study, I must find the weak link in NATO. It is France."

Boris chanced a look into Devereaux's burning eyes. "I regret it for your sake, Devereaux, but NATO will be broken by France, and here is where we have concentrated our efforts through Topaz."

André continued to avoid looking at the Americans. He became sullen for he knew what was coming from the Russian, and he knew the man would be telling the truth.

"My study shows me that France is traditionally unstable politically, and that Frenchmen are loyal only to themselves. Their arrogance is bottomless.

"The French dream of superiority and a return to grandeur is to them like an hallucinatory drug.

"Enter Pierre La Croix. La Croix is a man eternally embittered by the humiliation of France's defeat in the war. France's mortification at the hands of the United States has made him vulnerable to those who would use his bitterness. La Croix's weakness is a tool playing into Russian hands. Of course he is not a Communist, but he does Moscow's job."

The humiliation of France was a fact André

Devereaux knew only too well, for he had been part of the early days of the Free French. In those days he had looked upon La Croix as a savior indeed. Yes, Boris Kuznetov had conducted his study well.

"France is defeated in Vietnam, Morocco, Tunisia, and, most devastating of all, Algeria. La Croix has inherited a paper tiger and a people weary of bloodshed and a hundred years of defeats on the battlefield.

"But La Croix knows his Frenchmen. Use the word 'honor' to a Frenchman and you have struck the core of his being. How beautiful the word."

Kuznetov lifted himself from his wheelchair, stretched and paced along the table slowly.

"But his strength is questionable. Billions are poured into the French atomic force. As you know, gentlemen, no one takes the *force de frappe* seriously. La Croix must win his points by diplomatic blackmail. It is a game in which he is matchless. The core of French policy is to resist American domination. *What more could Moscow ask for?*"

The Russian returned to his chair and took up a volume from the table. The dust jacket read: *The War Memoirs of Pierre La Croix*. He opened the book to the first of many marked sections.

"I read you his words." Boris adjusted his glasses, fingered down the page, looked quickly to the ININ people and back to the page. " 'In Russian eyes there could be no third power playing Vichy France against Fighting France. America believed herself in the position to direct the French nation after centuries of French experience. Russia understood the position of Fighting France perfectly and honored it by recognizing the Free French Committee.' "

Further in the volume, Kuznetov explained, were La Croix's hurt, angry complaints against the Anglo-Americans for failure to recognize his Fighting French, for failure to consult them in planning strategy, for failure to arm them, and for having concluded international agreements concerning France without the consent and presence of the Free French.

" 'There certainly exists a kindred spirit between the French and Russians,' " Kuznetov read again, " 'the Russians being, in many ways, more in tune with a European hegemony and a union of Europeans than the Anglo-Americans.' "

Kuznetov closed the book. "Pierre La Croix has a long association with Russia, and in many ways feels the French, as fellow Europeans, are closer to the Russians than the Anglo-Americans."

Boris set his glasses down, played with his knobby fingers. "Once you accept the fact that France is under the thumb of La Croix and once you understand his basic hatred of the Anglo-Americans, it is not too difficult to see what is going to happen. He has experimented with the *force de frappe*, the nonsense of creating a third force in the world, made by an alliance among Europeans, which France intends to dominate. He has bullied his partners around in the Common Market, which France has succeeded in dominating.

"He will attempt to make France the broker of a Pan-European union to include both the Eastern and Western blocs. But no one plays poker with the Soviet Union. We intend to use these weaknesses to our benefit. As Germany used Pétain, we intend to use La Croix. I predict that within five years he will personally take France out of NATO, for what grates his innards is the American, who he believes robs France of her true destiny . . . or a sad old man's illusion of it.

"Topaz is rotting the understructure of France. It is child's play for the Soviet Resident in Paris to obtain intelligence. In France he inherits three million French Communists whose loyalty is to Moscow. La Croix has dealt with the French Communists in order to remain in power in the mistaken belief he can avoid the ultimate settlement with them.

"But anarchy, monumental anarchy, is on the planning boards in Moscow. With France out of NATO and the French Communists imbedded, when Pierre La Croix dies, a rage of confusion will sweep over France. It will be followed, gentlemen, by a Communist takeover."

(11)

DEAREST PAPA,

A great sadness has overcome Mamma. A kind of lethargy owns her. She's left Paris and stays in Montrichard all the time. I think something has happened to make her frightened to really search into herself because the truth may be too painful.

I've worried over Mamma so much. Mamma is a beautiful bird, but one meant to stay down in her own little part of the sky. If she tries to fly too high, her wings will break. She wants to soar to the heavens and fly through the high winds, but she cannot. She sees you reach up despite the risk and pain, but she cannot follow and she hates you for it and herself for her own inability. Is it wrong for me to think this?

I'm happy studying at the Sorbonne. When Tucker followed me to France to make his inept plea, I could see how shallow a life he was about to lead me into. Lord spare me from being the well-groomed, mechanical, basic functionary.

With François I want to dare to climb, to fly, to find the courage as you have. Papa, I want to be counted in this world and I want to count.

241

What a dismal day it is here in Normandy. François and I got back to the cottage ahead of a driving rain. There is a fire now and a background of Brahms. François is across the room framed in the window, terribly handsome, terribly intense. He leans over the typewriter, makes a correction, and grumbles as he writes his column for *Moniteur*. Papa, I am hopelessly in love.

Your
MICHELE

She folded the letter, sealed and addressed it. Then, after mending the fading fire, she walked up behind François's chair, folded her arms about him, laid her cheek on the top of his head, and felt beneath his shirt.

François stopped his pondering, took her hand and kissed it. She read the words in the typewriter.

FRANÇOIS PICARD'S COLUMN

What now, President La Croix! The new French demand for American gold on the balance of payments strikes another low blow to our jaded diplomacy.

But once again our President has struck out with a reckless tactic. One does not use a battalion of horse cavalry against a division of tanks in a frontal assault. This ill-advised attack on the American dollar, a move born of pure vengeance, is bound to backfire, for the stability of the world depends on the dollar.

If the American dollar is weakened, France can fall into a state of chaos overnight. And who will cry louder than a greed-riddled French public made fat by the good will of the ally we are trying to destroy?

How long will Frenchmen tolerate Pierre La Croix doing the Kremlin's work as though on orders . . .

Michele detached herself from him, looked at the wind-driven rain pelting the window, and sighed.

"What is it, Michele? You do not like it?"

"It's very good."

"What then?"

"It's also very dangerous. I become frightened for you."

"I cannot quit, Michele. I cannot quit."

"I wouldn't ask you to do that. I'll never ask it. Only don't ask me not to be frightened."

He shoved away from the typewriter and paced before the fire.

"François, never give a thought about how I stand. I'm with you in whatever you are trying to do. Darling . . ."

"Yes?"

"What have you been trying to tell me all weekend?"

"Am I that transparent?"

"Dreadfully. I don't think you could ever lie to me. You are like a little boy."

François pouted a moment, adoring this young girl who seemed to speak with a wisdom far beyond the innocent face, the nymph smile, the wide-eyed admiration.

"Michele, this is our last weekend for a time."

"Oh?"

"The first smells of pressure from our government-controlled television. The news department is sending me out under the guise of doing special coverage for a lot of minor nonsense in the south and then to Munich for the *Oktoberfest*. I have a feeling they'll keep me away until I quit or indicate I'm ready to fall in line."

She came into his arms and was held by him. "May I cry a little?" she said.

"Michele," he whispered, "Michele . . . Michele . . . Michele . . ."

243

Justine de Vore was offered a seat opposite
Colonel Jasmin. Inspector Marcel Steinberger
studied her from the sunken leather couch across
the room. She had slim ankles and shapely legs,
one of them adorned with a tiny gold chain. In
her early thirties, Justine de Vore cut the picture
of a chic Frenchwoman. She crossed her legs en-
ticingly to see if she had the attention of Colonel
Jasmin and Inspector Steinberger. She had.

"Mademoiselle de Vore, please meet Inspector
Steinberger, Department of Internal Protection,
Sûreté."

The two nodded to one another.

"We have some questions concerning security
matters in your department and solicit your open
cooperation," Jasmin said. "I mean, of course, if
you have no objections to answering our questions . . ."

"Certainly not," she answered in the sure voice
of a professional woman showing no shred of
hesitation.

Marcel Steinberger bounced from his seat,
scratched his head and paced. "Mademoiselle de
Vore," he said, "you have worked as the personal
secretary of Henri Jarré for how long?"

"Over three years," she answered.

He took the file on her from Jasmin's desk,
scanned it, and, prompted by the record, began
questioning her. Justine de Vore was established
as a woman with special qualifications to serve
under a top executive. She was from an excellent
family of upper-middle-class civil servants in
Paris, and had had good schooling, including the
Sorbonne. She was independent, well salaried,

and her record revealed nothing of an unusual nature.

Inspector Steinberger stopped his pacing suddenly. "Do you like Henri Jarré?" he asked abruptly.

Her unbroken string of answers halted. "What kind of a question is that?"

"Do you like him," Steinberger repeated, "as a person, as a human being, as someone to work for? Do you find him pleasant, friendly or difficult? Do you like his personal habits?"

She hedged, resorting to professional loyalty. "Monsieur Jarré is my superior. My position is such that I would perfer not to answer such a question."

"Hmmm," Steinberger grunted, "hmmm."

Colonel Jasmin lit his usual fat cigar ever so slowly, sending a billow of smoke over the desk that drifted to the tall ceiling of the château room. "Mademoiselle de Vore," he said deliberately, "at the beginning I stated it would be desirable if you volunteered the information we seek. If at any point in this questioning you are inclined not to answer, or if for any reason you toy with the idea of giving us an incorrect answer, then I had better advise you of your legal rights and we'll do all of this another way. Am I clear?"

"You are quite clear," she whispered.

"Well, what do you intend to do, mademoiselle?"

"I will cooperate, of course," she said. "I only hoped that it would not be unpleasant or put me in an uncomfortable position, but I'll cooperate."

"Do you like Henri Jarré?" Steinberger repeated.

"I despise him," she said.

"Would you explain?"

"He is a man filled with hatred and bitterness. He knows no pleasantries. His wife . . ."

"Yes?"

"He has a very unhappy marriage, he is a very sour individual."

Marcel Steinberger brought a chair up opposite her, sat on it backward, leaning his chin on the back. "You went away with Jarré on a number of occasions."

"On NATO business."

"Always?"

She looked for sympathy to Colonel Jasmin, who offered her none. "No," she confessed, "not always."

"On how many occasions did you go off with him when it was not NATO business?"

"A half-dozen, more or less. I'm not certain."

"To Cannes?"

"Yes."

"Normandy?"

"Yes."

"London?"

"That was for a NATO meeting."

"And all this time you despised him."

"Yes, I despise him."

"Why did you go away with him?"

"I live my life as I see it. Monsieur Jarré made it quite clear from the beginning that this might be a part of my qualifications. I am thirty-two. I was married once and do not wish to remarry. I care for my independence too strongly. I have even resumed my maiden name. As Colonel Jasmin will certify, I have an excellent position. So, if Monsieur Jarré makes this a condition . . . so what?"

246

"We appreciate your candor," Inspector Stein-berger said. "Now, we would like to be equally candid. We would like you to cooperate with the Sûreté."

"In what way?"

"To keep Henri Jarré under surveillance. You see, Mademoiselle de Vore, he is suspected of passing NATO documents to the Soviet Union."

For a moment she was stunned, trying to comprehend. Then a throaty little giggle emerged. "I'll be damned," she said and the giggle swelled into hard laughter.

"Well? Will you help us?"

"It will be a pleasure, Inspector Steinberger."

"Good," Jasmin said, "excellent."

"Now, Mademoiselle de Vore, we need to establish certain patterns, habits of work, routines, et cetera, et cetera. I'd like to ask you a few questions about the duplicating machine in your supply room, the one adjoining your office. It's a Repco, is it not?"

"Yes."

"You use it to complete office files, make needed extra copies to advise other persons, or send copies with regular correspondence when required. In other words, the machine is used in normal daily office work?"

"Yes, that would be correct."

"Who operates the particular machine in your office?"

"I do. For the entire building. As you can see from the way the supply room adjoins my office, I was annoyed in the beginning by people running in and out, so I set up an incoming basket for requests for duplicates. Generally speaking, at around three in the afternoon I run off copies and place them in an outgoing basket so they can be picked up in time for the late mail."

"Now, Mademoiselle de Vore. Does Monsieur Jarré use this machine? Does he know how? Have you ever seen him use it?"

"Yes, I remember quite clearly. We had an old Thermo-Fax up to eighteen months ago. It was exchanged for the Repco. A few days after the new machine arrived I returned from lunch to find Monsieur Jarré in the supply room cursing and trying to operate the machine. He had made a mess of the fluid bag and was quite confused over the positive and negative papers. He asked me to show him how to operate the machine."

"Did you think it odd?"

"Well, no. Some days I could be ill or for some reason not available when he needed copies of something. I didn't think it strange."

"Mademoiselle de Vore. Do you ever leave your office for long periods during the day?"

"Exactly what do you mean?"

"A half-hour, forty minutes, an hour?"

"Other than lunch?"

"Yes."

"Yes, I am out of the office frequently."

"Does Jarré send you out of the office?"

"Sometimes."

"Would you explain that?"

"The Press Building is a ten-minute walk. I often carry dispatches there for personal delivery. Or I may be called to another office to record the proceedings of a meeting. Then, for one reason or another, I may be sent to nearly any building on the compound. I even come here, Colonel Jasmin. I deliver security files at least once a month, anyhow."

248

"It would be safe to say, then, that you are out of your office at least once a week for a half-hour or longer?"

"Yes."

"Long enough for Jarré to come to the supply room adjoining your office and make, say, ten or fifteen copies, clean up the used positive and negative papers, and return to his own office?"

"That would be sufficient time."

"Do you recall ever seeing him in the supply room?"

"Once. I started out of the building, then returned to my office for my cigarettes. He was quite startled, but he covered it quickly. You know, I've always wondered why my Repco supplies ran out so fast."

Inspector Steinberger and Colonel Jasmin alternated questioning to further establish Jarré's working habits.

"He's at his desk promptly at nine-thirty," Justine de Vore said, "except Thursdays."

"Why not Thursdays?"

"He takes the commuter train from Paris on Thursdays."

"Every Thursday?"

"Yes. Sometimes he is late."

"Does he always take the train home on those days?"

"Yes."

"Did he ever tell you why?"

"He said he gives the car to Madame Jarré on Thursdays for her special shopping."

"Did you know he was an official of high enough rank to warrant a staff car and chauffeur?" Jasmin asked.

"Yes, I've sent for staff cars on a number of

occasions. He just told me he liked the commuter train once in a while, and I believed him."

Justine de Vore was given the secret mission of observing Jarré. The suspect supply room was wired so that use of the Repco machine would automatically light a signal in the office of Colonel Jasmin.

An adjoining closet was fixed with a two-way mirror. Its peephole was impossible to detect from the supply room. At any time Justine de Vore left the building, she first advised Jasmin and the observation closet was immediately manned by security personnel.

The surveillance was carried on with extreme vigor on Thursdays, commuter-train day.

The second Thursday after surveillance began, Henri Jarré copied four secret documents during the absence of his secretary. Marcel Steinberger personally rode the commuter train to Paris in the next seat behind Jarré. He observed a quick switching of attaché cases with a contact. But, under stern orders from his chief, Léon Roux, Steinberger made no arrest.

"Good work, Inspector," Léon Roux said to Steinberger.

"When will you let me pick the bastard up?" Steinberger demanded.

"Aha!" Roux answered with a twinkle coming to his eye.

"What game are you playing?"

Roux's prune face contorted into what might have been a smile. "Colonel Jasmin and I are seeing to it that Henri Jarré doesn't look at anything but fake documents for the next several weeks. So he will be feeding his comrades in

Moscow enough false information to confuse their military planning and counterintelligence for a year. At least, let Jarré undo some of the harm. When we feel the Russians have had their bellies full of confusion and are getting onto us, we'll plant the real articles on Jarré and close the trap . . . eh?"

Marcel Steinberger erupted in rare laughter.

"Eh, Steinberger, eh? We'll show those idiots at SDECE who is better, they or the Sûreté."

"Incidentally," Steinberger said, "we will have to pick the woman up. I am afraid Mademoiselle de Vore's bank accounts and spending and her salary do not jibe. Obviously, she has been in on it with Jarré from the beginning. Shame."

"Well, she's given us a hand," Roux said, "and she's betrayed Jarré nobly in order to save her own neck. So we'll see that she gets a light sentence."

(13)

COMMANDER FARROW, the Navy cardiologist in charge of Boris Kuznetov, left the Russian's hospital room in concern. He was followed out by Sid Jaffe. They crossed to the doctor's office, where Dr. Billings, Devereaux, Kramer, and W. Smith waited in a knot. The doctor closed the door behind him.

"He's bushed, strained. He's gone through sixty-odd interrogations and needs a complete rest."

"Is it serious?"

"It will be. If we push him any further, we're playing, if you'll pardon the expression, Russian roulette."

251

"But, Dr. Farrow," Jaffe said, "Kuznetov insists he be allowed to speak to us once more."

The Commander fiddled with his stethoscope. "Once more, in his bedroom, and keep it short. I mean that."

"Thank you, Doctor. Could we have your office for a moment?" When the doctor stepped out, Jaffe turned to the others. "Kuznetov demanded that Nordstrom, Sanderson Hooper, and the President's Intelligence Adviser be present today."

They nodded in agreement quickly. Jaffe put in a call to ININ at Foggy Bottom. "Mike . . . Sid Jaffe. Our friend is feeling under the weather. The doctor has given us an okay to visit with him, but he insists you be here with Sandy and Marsh."

"Right," Nordstrom answered.

The room was packed with the presence of the seven Americans, Devereaux, and two nurses. One nurse plumped the pillows up behind Boris Kuznetov to enable him to sit and the other repeated the doctor's restriction and issued a "no smoking" order.

Kuznetov was weary from his ordeal. He had been skidding for a week.

"I wanted to speak to you now for I must reveal to you a secret department in KGB responsible for the most ingenious and successful intelligence operation ever performed by the Soviet Union. I refer to the Department of Disinformation."

They were studied but taut as he searched their faces for a response. Disinformation was unknown to them, just as his own anti-NATO Division had been.

"The Department of Disinformation is under the direction of a KGB officer named Sergei Mike-

252

loff. The purpose of Disinformation is to invent and distort data and feed it into an enemy government through his own intelligence system. I repeat, through his own intelligence system. Topaz does our work inside SDECE. Let me impress upon you gentlemen, this is far more sophisticated and sinister than routine camouflage counter-espionage operations.

"False data are invented in Moscow, passed to the Resident in Paris, and given to Topaz agents in the SDECE. From there the information is filtered into the ministries, the Cabinet, or wherever we want it. These lies, stamped with the seal of authenticity by SDECE, are briefed to President La Croix by the man known as Columbine."

"How many times have you worked this?"

"Dozens. Tens of dozens. Nowhere as successfully as in France, the weak link. During the Algerian crisis we were able to implant reports inside the French Cabinet to the effect that the CIA owned the Pepsi-Cola franchise in Algeria as well as several newspapers and used these as fronts to feed money to the Algerian rebels. As you know, gentlemen, many Frenchmen believe America is responsible for Algeria. This is largely the work of Disinformation.

"Last year," Kuznetov continued, "during the Generals' Revolt in Algeria, Soviet Disinformation was able to establish enormous confusion about the threat of the Algerian French generals to land in Paris with paratroops and take over metropolitan France. The reaction of the American President was to offer aid. Thanks to Soviet Disinformation, this offer was interpreted by La Croix as an American attempt to meddle in a French internal affair, even as a springboard to introduce large numbers of American forces into metropolitan France.

"And so it goes. When President La Croix travels from France, often Soviet Disinformation is fed to him to the effect that the Americans are undermining his visits and plotting anti-French demonstrations. He is positive it is the work of the CIA.

"As you know, La Croix has very bad eyes and cannot read long documents. Therefore he depends greatly on verbal briefings. This makes him particularly vulnerable. We see to it he gets our share through Columbine."

"Who is he?" André demanded.

"Who knows?" Kuznetov said. "He may be in SDECE, the Cabinet, the military. I only know if we want Disinformation to reach La Croix, he gets it."

"My God," Michael Nordstrom blurted inadvertently.

"Kuznetov," Marshall McKittrick said tersely, "did you use Disinformation against us at Suez?"

Boris Kuznetov smiled. "You are getting the picture. It was one of our greatest triumphs."

"Of course!" André cried. "Of course! It was the only way, Marsh. We were tricked."

In the hallway, Marshall McKittrick pulled Nordstrom aside. "Get this transcript to me at the White House immediately," he said with obvious alarm.

254

THE PRESIDENT OF THE UNITED STATES reread his letter to the President of France.

The White House

October 20, 1962

DEAR PRESIDENT LA CROIX,

Sources we consider completely reliable have made us aware of a situation of such gravity I am taking the unusual step of writing this single-copy letter, which will be delivered by my Special Assistant Marshall McKittrick.

We have been informed of the existence of a vast espionage network of French citizens employed as agents of the Soviet Union. This network operates under the code name of Topaz. It appears they have been successful in deeply infiltrating all branches of government, particularly your Secret Service.

Employing a unique method termed "Disinformation," under the direction of Sergei Mikeloff of Soviet KGB and Soviet Paris Resident Gorin, they have been able to direct false information and confusing intelligence into your highest councils.

It is further revealed to us by our same source that a member, or members, of Topaz are among your personal entourage.

I urge you to send a team of experts to the United States to study all the information we have gathered and to interrogate our prime source of discovery.

We understand that the Topaz network is capable of supplying Soviet KGB with secret NATO documents and trust you will employ all deliberate action in joining with us to ferret out and destroy this operation.

With kindest personal regards,

The President affixed his signature to the letter and handed it to Marshall McKittrick, who folded it and placed it in his breast pocket.

"I'll seal it after Devereaux has read it," McKittrick said.

The President nodded. "I'll be calling the

French Ambassador in later today," he said. "You'll be on the way to Paris tomorrow."

"Right," McKittrick answered.

"Lord," the President said, "I hope La Croix doesn't take this for another trick."

(15)

As THE NIP OF autumn fell on Washington, an outward calm and normalcy blanketed the explosive inner struggle.

Doves and Hawks swept in and out of the West Wing of the White House in the uninterrupted flow of the hourless days. With the evidence of Soviet missiles in Cuba proved beyond doubt, the crisis heightened.

The Hawks and Doves debated their points of view; the consultants and appraisers and evaluators and advisers and gatherers of information consulted, appraised, evaluated, advised, and briefed.

And then the moment of awesome decision fell upon a single man, the President.

On a wet day late in October, Ambassador of France René d'Arcy received a request to come to the White House. He was passed through the bulwark of security men and receptionists and was led directly to the President's office.

The President greeted d'Arcy with warmth, coming from behind his desk and taking him to the comfortable arrangement of chairs and sofas near the fireplace. During the moment of small talk, Marshall McKittrick joined them.

"For the last several months," the President said to the Ambassador, "we have suspected and now have gathered irrefutable evidence of the in-

256

troduction of Soviet intermediate-range missiles into Cuba. You are no doubt aware of this situation through the work of André Devereaux and French Intelligence."

"Yes, I am aware," d'Arcy said, hoping the President would not detect his cigar as Havana.

McKittrick gave a detailed briefing of the sites, range, and estimations of Soviet strength now footed in the hemisphere. When he finished his dissertation, the President continued. "We have examined the situation from every possible angle. A decision has been reached. I have notified the British Ambassador, and within thirty-six hours we will have advised all our NATO Allies and then I will inform the American public."

D'Arcy felt fright, for the man before him could well be announcing a war.

"The most favorable course of action in my opinion will be a naval quarantine of Cuba for the present."

"Do you mean a blockade, Mr. President?"

"A quarantine . . . not a blockade of peaceful cargo, but to stop, search, and prevent further introduction of offensive weapons."

Perhaps it was the most temperate method, but nonetheless the fuse would be lit, and unless men became reasonable quickly, a hostile confrontation at sea or an air strike at a Cuban missile site could lead to the shaking of fists, an invasion of Cuba, and a prelude to a world holocaust.

D'Arcy knew that General La Croix would fume in anger at the unilateral action of the Americans, for they were dictating life-and-death policy without consulting their allies.

"What do you expect of France?" he asked.

"To look on our situation with sympathy, respect the quarantine, and share our point of view that we are in danger."

And drag France into a war against her will, d'Arcy thought without putting it into words.

"I am sending Mr. McKittrick as my personal representative to inform President La Croix, and the British Prime Minister. We ask you keep the matter secret until he reaches Paris."

D'Arcy said he would comply.

"One more thing," McKittrick said. "Because of André Devereaux's intimate involvement in the missile business, I would like to have him present in Paris. There is also an additional matter regarding Intelligence affairs that requires his presence."

"Yes, you may have Devereaux."

"Thank you, Mr. Ambassador. I'll be leaving by Air Force jet from Andrews in about two hours," McKittrick said.

As Marshall McKittrick and André Devereaux boarded the plane, great armed forces lumbered into position, poising along the eastern coast of the United States, and the fleet swung out into the Atlantic to cut off the sea lanes to Cuba. In the air, the bombers of the Strategic Air Command circled in readiness to unleash their atomic warheads, and in their earthen silos the awesome arsenal of missiles was alerted, with preselected targets in the Soviet Union, all prepared to unleash the most terrible catastrophe ever known to man.

(16)

THE AIR FORCE courier jet streaked past land's

end. Marshall McKittrick showed André the letter he was to deliver to Pierre La Croix. André read it and passed it back without comment.

Drinks and snacks were served, then a card table was set up. With a crewman as his partner, André gave McKittrick and the steward a sound thrashing in a rubber of bridge.

"Where the hell did you learn to play like that?" McKittrick asked.

"Once I used to play for a living, or at least to survive. On a good night we usually took in enough to buy bread and wine for a dozen comrades. Sometimes we could afford an extra pair of shoes," André answered.

"Where was that?"

"When I was interned in Spain. As a matter of fact, I met Nicole then," he said with a catch, for he realized he was heading toward her. "It's a long, long story, Marsh."

They were pensive for a time, neither of them broaching the gnawing thoughts, the implications of the trickery unearthed by Kuznetov's story.

"I've never carried on my work in vengeance," André said at last, "but for this, someone is going to pay. I'll find him and expose him if it's my last act on this earth."

"Watch out for yourself," McKittrick answered and went across the aisle to his own seat. He opened his attaché case, sealed the letter to Pierre La Croix, and placed it among his papers.

André warmed himself on cognac and became caught up watching the jet plunge into night. It was that time of transformation in an airplane when the liquor and the altitude and the sense of detachment have dulled and mellowed one enough to plunge him into a sense of timelessness.

Since learning of the Topaz conspiracy, André Devereaux's nights had been spent in restless fits of semisleep and angry pacing, in torment over the treachery of his countrymen. His own years of devotion and pain, born of love for France, had been vomited upon by men who would destroy her out of ignorance or sinister choice.

What nest of serpents would he have to do battle with now in Paris? Soon the trap would close on Henri Jarré, but there was another, above him . . . Columbine. Come heaven or hell, he was determined to flush out the supreme traitor.

The name of one man turned over and over in his mind, that of Colonel Gabriel Brune, a Vice Administrator of SDECE. With the revelation of Disinformation and how it had been used at Suez, the behavior of Colonel Brune had to make him the leading suspect.

André glanced over to Marsh McKittrick, who was dozing. How strange, he thought. It was seven years ago, almost to the day, that he and McKittrick had played out an almost identical drama during the Suez crisis.

The Israelis had poured into the Sinai Peninsula toward the Canal. André was in Paris at the time on other affairs. Because of his intimate relations with the Americans he was brought into the picture. After his briefing, they sought his counsel. André knew that Marshall McKittrick was in Rome on Presidential business and asked him to come to Paris.

October, 1956
André Devereaux and United States Ambassador Rawlins met Marshall McKittrick at Orly Field.

The matter was so urgent that the two Americans were briefed in the limousine en route to Paris.

"In four hours," André said, "we are issuing a joint ultimatum with the British for Egypt and Israel to cease fire and recognize a demarcation line ten kilometers from the Canal."

"A unilateral action?"

"Yes."

"Are you in league with the Israelis?"

"I don't know," André answered. "I am advising you that if the cease-fire is not accepted, a joint French-British Expeditionary Force, now gathering in Cyprus, will move in and seize the Canal."

The reaction of the Americans was to accept the news with studied calm and to digest it in terms of their own situation. France and Britain could well be dragging America into a war without consultation.

"You people might have given us a day's notice," McKittrick said at last.

"I would suspect we didn't want to be talked out of the action," André answered.

"Well, we've got a busy afternoon," the Ambassador said.

"What is expected of the United States?" McKittrick asked.

"As an ally, to recognize our position and understand that we do this in the international interest."

As Ambassador Rawlins and Marshall McKittrick plunged into the business of advising Washington and awaiting instructions, André reported to a Vice Administrator of SDECE, Colonel Gabriel Brune, that the United States had been informed of the pending action.

As one of the last shows of naked, old-fashioned imperialism shaped up, the information reached the President of the United States, who hastily summoned his advisers.

The position seemed clear. France and Britain were traditional allies, who needed international controls returned to the Suez Canal or continue to be at the mercy of the Egyptian dictator, Gamal Abdel Nasser. France had further brief to overthrow Nasser for his overt sympathy and help to the Algerian rebels.

The West, in general, was deeply concerned over Nasser's flirtation with the Soviet Union, the massive importation of Soviet arms to Egypt, and the frightening specter that the Soviet Union would break through to the Mediterranean.

As for Israel, the invasion of Sinai became a necessity for national survival, to stop the harassments from Egypt and to check the buildup of Soviet-supplied weapons. And finally, Israel needed to break open the blockade of the Red Sea for use as a sea lane to Asia.

The entire operation smelled of collusion between French-British interests and Israel. But this, obviously, was to remain a secret and a mystery for another decade.

Three and a half hours after his arrival in Paris and a half-hour before the cease-fire ultimatum, André Devereaux entered the Ambassador's office in the American Embassy.

"The position of the United States," the Ambassador said, "is to act as though we have not been informed of your intention to seize the Canal. After the cease-fire ultimatum and your invasion we will officially pronounce surprise and indignation. In any event, we must not appear partners to this venture. This will allow us the freedom to stand off the Soviet Union as fellow neutrals."

"Now for Christ's sake," McKittrick added, "take that god-damned Canal in the next seventy-two hours. It must be an accomplished fact, because after that we'll have to back any United Nations aggression charges against you. Get that Canal first and then we can talk it to death."

The American position was reported to Colonel Brune at almost the same moment the cease-fire ultimatum was being delivered to Nasser and Ben-Gurion.

Nasser rejected the ultimatum, and a war fever swept London and Paris as British and French planes bombed the Egyptian airfields in prelude to invasion while their joint expeditionary force set sail from Cyprus.

André's personal knowledge of these events ended with his delivery of the message from the Americans.

These were the days before La Croix's formal ascent to power. Although the official heart of the executive lay in the Premier's office, La Croix maneuvered behind the throne. In his nondescript post he was surrounded by a personal army of military leaders and Secret Service and ambitious flunkies who read the future and jumped aboard the bandwagon in preparation for a La Croix takeover.

His advisers were faithful to him ahead of the government, and as often as not La Croix was consulted even before the Premier.

As the Anglo-Franco forces neared the Canal, Colonel Brune asked for an urgent appointment with La Croix. Brune, a member of the General's clique, was La Croix's main source of power and information within the SDECE.

Jacques Granville, Pierre La Croix's personal aide, ushered Brune into the General's office at the moment of invasion.

"We have been following a desperate situation for several hours," Brune said. "I've been waiting for confirmations. We have them. Messages started coming into SDECE from our military and naval Intelligence shortly after midnight to the effect that American warships of the Seventh Fleet picked up our expeditionary force. Throughout the night destroyers followed us and their airplanes put us under surveillance. This morning as we entered Egyptian territorial waters warning shots were fired by the Americans over the bow of our troopships."

Without visible reaction Pierre La Croix took the dispatches, all stamped with the authenticity of the SDECE, and thumbed through them.

"Has the Premier been advised?" he asked.

"No," Brune replied.

La Croix nodded. "The Premier is so pro-Israeli we will have to act on this information without his knowledge."

"Yes, sir. But I can't believe it. The Americans gave their word."

"It's obviously a double cross," Colonel Brune said.

"I just can't believe it," Granville repeated.

Ambassador Rawlins was summoned to the Prime Minister's after he was finally informed. The messages of American treachery were shoved unceremoniously into the Ambassador's face, followed by an undiplomatic Gallic outburst by the Prime Minister.

Rawlins was thoroughly confused. With normal communications on Suez deliberately cut off, Marshall McKittrick was dispatched to Washington for clarification. It took several days to ascertain that there had been no American action against the expeditionary force and that the reports received by French SDECE had been false.

It had been the work of the Topaz ring, and the information General Pierre La Croix had been fed and in turn had fed to the Premier and Cabinet was Soviet Disinformation.

Moscow capitalized quickly on a hysterical situation by a saber-rattling threat to turn loose its missiles on Paris unless the French quit.

The seizure of the Suez Canal never came to pass, with only the Israelis achieving their objectives.

Following up the Disinformation coup, the Soviets convinced Nasser that the United States was really behind the plot to grab the Canal. And a final propaganda barrage put the blame on the Americans, in the minds of Frenchmen, forever.

It grew dark. Marshall McKittrick had fallen asleep.

But there was no sleep for André. Who had carried the Soviet Disinformation to La Croix and the French Premier during Suez?

The false dispatches had come from the SDECE. Who in SDECE was in constant communication with La Croix and Matignon? Who was doing the briefing on behalf of the Secret Service?

Who but Colonel Gabriel Brune?

The chiefs of SDECE were generally political appointees. Many were pro-American. They were largely functionaries totally dependent on their staffs. The real seat of power was with the Vice Administrators, the career professionals—as Colonel Gabriel Brune.

It was all in tune with a known Communist tactic of sneaking the actual power into the hands of a deputy working under a harmless figurehead.

And what of Brune's nature and his past? He had kept himself nondescript and out of the limelight. He had held a key post with the NATO intelligence network, ININ, and he was a friend of Henri Jarré. A further look showed him to be a hostile anti-American who deliberately slanted reports and opinions against them.

When the Americans balked strongly at sharing intelligence with the French because of leaks inside NATO, Colonel Brune was quietly moved from ININ to the French government as Vice Administrator of SDECE, where he cloaked himself in anonymity.

With access to top secrets and in a position to advise members of the government, Brune could cause unbelievable damage if he was indeed a Soviet agent.

When Pierre La Croix ascended to power, Colonel Brune's role and power increased. He was constantly at La Croix's side and had his ear.

The plane arched down toward Paris. André knew that if he made this fight, the chances were it would cost him his life. His foes were vicious and resourceful, and the head of his government was an obsessed, arrogant, aging dictator.

But he knew he would make that fight, regardless.

As land came into view below, André felt a moment of fright. Was this all too late and too useless?

GORIN FOUND A PARKING space for his Peugeot in the Place d'Armes facing the Versailles Palace and set out on foot to the broad avenues of gardens and fountains and forests toward the grand canal in this unsurpassed monument to extravagance. As Soviet Resident and head of Russian intelligence in France he was the prime mover of Topaz. His true position was veiled under the cover of the title of Assistant Cultural Attaché.

At the base of the mile-long, man-made, cross-shaped waterway he stopped and looked about to assure himself he was merely another inconspicuous stroller. Satisfied, he headed to the rendezvous.

Behind the Petit Trianon were clipped hedges and English-style gardens, then a maze of wooded paths that insured privacy. Gorin's pudgy fingers slipped back his shirt cuff. Five minutes to go. The air was chilly, the trees nearly bare. A stiff breeze blew a swirl of leaves around his feet. In the distance he could hear a sound of children running and screaming in their play. Gorin had a massive face and twinkling eyes. He was a gregarious fellow, outgoing. Rather an oddity among his somber colleagues. He slapped his cold hands together, then shoved them in his pockets and looked up the path.

A shadowy figure emerged moving toward him down the tree-lined walkway. It was the familiar figure of Columbine. He was taller than most Frenchmen, the collar of his overcoat turned up and buttoned around his throat to keep out the autumn nip. A dark hat was worn low on his forehead and his gloved hand held an ever-present cigarette. Columbine stopped before Gorin and nodded. The two men continued along the path side by side speaking in practiced softness.

"Something was wrong with the last four NATO documents," the Russian said. "They've caused a great deal of confusion in Moscow."

"What was the matter with them?"

"KGB thinks they may be fakes. NATO intelligence may be on to Jarré. If so, his usefulness to us could be coming to an end."

"Jarré is a despicable bastard," Columbine said. "I've never cared for him."

Gorin took the first of two envelopes from his pocket and gave it to Columbine. "This lists three documents in the NATO fifteen hundred series. Contact Jarré and instruct him to get copies. KGB has seen authentic copies which have come through other sources. If Jarré passes us anything different, we'll have to do something about him."

They stopped at a fork in the path and remained silent as an old couple hobbled by, then continued their walk in another direction.

"American U-2 flights over Cuba have been concentrating on the areas where our missile bases are being established," Gorin said, "they may know."

"What do you expect them to do?"

"Probably nothing." Gorin handed Columbine the second envelope. "In the unlikely event the Americans make trouble and stir a crisis, your instructions are in this envelope. Certain disinformation must be fed to La Croix to confuse the issues and create mistrust of American motives. The result is to be to neutralize France. France must not side with the Americans."

Columbine, a past master in this operation, took his instructions and nodded.

"A final matter," Gorin said. "The KGB defector may have revealed the existence of Topaz to the Americans."

"I was wondering about that," Columbine said. "I learned just before I came today that Devereaux is on the way to Paris . . . aboard an American Air Force jet."

"That could mean Topaz, the missile business . . . or both. What about Devereaux's movements?" Gorin asked.

"I was able to find out," Columbine said, "that several months ago he went on a series of weekend or overnight trips out of Washington. Apparently he did not travel far. He left and returned by automobile, often in the company of Nordstrom. One conversation brought out the words 'Maryland countryside.' In recent months his trips have taken him closer, a shorter drive, again often in Nordstrom's company. The only clue would be 'Bethesda Naval Hospital.' "

Gorin stopped, mulled. . . . "Bethesda Naval Hospital," he grumbled.

"It's close to Washington and is used by a number of Congressmen and high-ranking military. At times, American Presidents have been interned there. Therefore, elaborate security measures are commonplace."

"That fits with what we know," Gorin said. "The defector had a history of heart trouble. He could well be at that hospital. Your main objective, and this is imperative . . . is to totally discredit Devereaux."

"You know that's not so easy," Columbine said. "He has a spotless reputation and friends and he thinks fast. We've tried to smear him and set him up time and again. La Croix isn't being taken in so fast. Even though he and Devereaux have different politics, La Croix respects him too much."

"Well," Gorin said, "we'll make a deal with him. Devereaux will have to join us."

"He'll never make a deal. He's too damned honest."

"Big men have big blind spots," Gorin answered. "Devereaux has his and we know what it is. He'll deal."

Columbine stopped, stepped on his cigarette butt, took another one from the pack, flicked on his lighter and cupped his hands to keep the flame. He looked up, his gray eyes staring curiously at the Russian.

"Devereaux has a mistress in Cuba," Gorin said. "Juanita de Córdoba. She was probably a member of his operation."

"You're a fool, Gorin. He's too smart to get himself involved beyond a casual affair."

"Big men have big blind spots," the Russian repeated. "He's insanely in love with her. Why else would the head of an intelligence section personally attempt to take a boat into Cuba to get his woman?"

Columbine sucked at the cigarette without comment.

"When the time comes, he'll make a deal with us to save her life. I'll see you here next Friday."

Columbine watched the Russian disappear down the path in the fast-fading light. He wondered if at last he had found the elusive key to destroy his archenemy, André Devereaux.

PART IV

Le Grand Pierre

(1)

THE YEAR OF 1940

FRANCE HAD FALLEN!

The beginning for André Devereaux was his town of Montrichard in the Loire Valley, named for the river that flowed through this, the garden of France.

The Loire Valley, magnificent with its hundred great châteaux, their lakes, their formal gardens, their woodlands. The playground of royalty and a mistress of history for over a thousand years.

It was Orléans of Joan of Arc.

It was Charlemagne and his Abbey of Pont-Levoy, the oldest school in all of Europe.

It was the resting place of Leonardo da Vinci and the Castle of Chambord, enriched by the hand of his genius.

Oh, the castles of the Loir-et-Cher! Chaumont and Montrésor and Amboise, where da Vinci died, and the Castle of Chenonceaux with its five arches built over the Cher River itself!

It was the staggering rock at Le Puy crowned by the statue of the Black Virgin.

It was the hunt. The ride for the boar and

the fox behind the magnificent hounds of Cheverny.

It was the grape of Tours and the sparkling bubbles of Vouvray and the scrubby farms and goat cheese of Sancerre.

Montrichard, the home of André Devereaux, lay in the heart of this France. Cobblestone streets and dramatic cliffs fell to the white sand beaches of the Cher. The winery of Montmousseau on the edge of town had its vats dug deeply into cliffs built during the Roman occupation. Around it stretched fields of raspberries and strawberries to augment the grape.

Primitive ancient troglodyte houses built in the cliffsides were still used by the peasants during the grape-picking season.

Montrichard! The Hill of Richard the Lionheart, named after the King of England who stopped there on his return from the Crusades.

These days it sat in sadness, for France had fallen.

The nation was divided in half. A few kilometers to the south of Montrichard, where the Cher flowed in its gentle course to Chenonceaux, there was now a border. Montrichard was in Occupied France. Beyond the border, a sham government of collaborators with the Germans had established its capital at Vichy and was led by the once honorable Marshal Pétain.

When France fell, André Devereaux was twenty years old and an apprentice lawyer in his father's office. The elder Devereaux, a landholder of considerable means, was now the head of a long-honored family in the district.

The Château Devereaux stood on the west edge of town, on the road to the Castle of Chenonceaux, and consisted of twenty-eight rooms, modest as châteaux went in that area.

Life was orderly. As the only son, André lived in preparation to assuming the family responsibilities in an area no longer given to upheaval.

The only thing that marred this pastoral existence was the sudden, tragic death of André's mother which orphaned him as an infant. It was an automobile accident for which his father took the blame and an overwhelming burden of guilt.

As a sensitive boy, the longing for his mother, complicated by his father's self punishment, set off a conflict of emotions.

Some two months after the fall of France, André looked up from his desk late one morning to see his best friend, Robert Proust.

Robert's behavior seemed strange and nervous.

"What goes?" André asked.

"Could you come to lunch at La Tête Noire?"

"Certainly."

"There is someone I want you to meet."

"What's so mysterious?"

"You'll see."

Later, at La Tête Noire Restaurant, Robert led André to a secluded table. There sat a lean, handsome young man in his early twenties. He was introduced as Jacques Granville from the nearby town of Blois. Jacques had been an officer during the fighting, but had escaped capture and returned to his home.

"Robert said you are an old friend," Jacques said, uncorking the wine.

"Yes," André answered. "We went to the school at Pont-Levoy Abbey together."

Jacques poured the wine. "We are all school-mates then. It is my school, too."

Robert Proust, a small, plain, shy fellow, sipped the wine nervously. "Jacques, Monsieur Granville, has many connections in Blois to . . . help people."

"I don't understand you."

"Robert here said I could speak freely with you."

"But of course."

"We are helping Jews," Robert said.

"What do you mean, helping them?"

"I am half-Jewish, as you know," Robert said.

"I never really thought about it," André answered.

"Things are getting difficult, very difficult, for the Jews in Occupied France. The Germans are no-good bastards. First, public humiliation. Now their property, beatings. God knows what next. Many of the Jews in Occupied France are trying to cross the border into Vichy France. We are establishing an underground railroad."

"Why?"

"They are Frenchmen," Jacques Granville said eagerly, "and they are in trouble. Other Frenchmen are turning on them as things grow more difficult."

"That's disgraceful," André said.

"Robert suggested I see you because I understand your father owns several farms along the Cher River."

"Yes."

"Would you be willing to help Jews?"

"Of course," André answered without hesitation.

Proust and Granville drew deep breaths, exchanged looks. Jacques leaned forward on his elbows. "It could be dangerous business."

"The Germans can go to hell. I hate them," André said. "What do you need of me?"

"Can the tenant farmers on your father's farms be trusted?"

André mulled. "We have four small farms on the Cher. Two of the men I would vouch for."

"Good," Granville said. "Now, as you know, the Berry Canal runs parallel to the Cher River. The area in between is where the Germans have their border patrols. If we can observe the German patrols from one of the farmhouses and establish some kind of pattern, then we can slip the Jews over the river into Vichy France."

The idea was both fascinating and frightening to young André. He felt deep guilt because, unlike Robert who was a year older, he had not fought against the Germans.

"I will help," he said, "if you will agree not to tell my father."

Flamboyant Jacques Granville flashed a broad smile. Bland Robert Proust merely nodded.

"Welcome, comrade," Jacques said, and the three of them shook hands.

(2)

THE CHER WAS a lazy river with a slow, untroubled movement. In many sectors, centuries of sand had built up a network of shallow bars and submerged islets.

André and his friend Robert Proust had swum the river and fished and boated on it from earliest memory. It was a simple matter for them to know at what places one could wade all the way across.

Telling his father that he had found a girl friend in Blois, André set up an excuse to spend several nights a week studying the movement of the German patrols between the Berry Canal and the river. The Germans were unbelievably methodical. One could set a clock by their appearance.

In Blois, Jacques Granville acquired a half-dozen bicycles, which he hid in a barn. With the pattern of the German patrols established, André alternated with Jacques and Robert in coming to the barn, where five Jews from Blois awaited nightly. They cycled fourteen kilometers to the crossing place and were led over to Vichy France. A horse-drawn wagon picked up the bicycles and returned them to the barn.

Some nights all three of them worked along with other members of the ring from Blois, and two or three trips were made across the river. The operation became so successful that another ten bicycles were acquired.

In the six months that followed, nearly three thousand Jews and other illegals wanted by the Nazis were spirited over the Cher from Occupied France to Vichy France.

"André," his father fumed. "What is this monkey business? You are with that girl in Blois all night and you sleep all day. Either marry her or find a woman closer to home."

André yawned his apology.

When he became too worn out to do his job properly, he broke down and confided in his father, who approved of the activity with a great deal of pride. From then on, André worked with the people in Blois on a full-time basis. It was the true beginning of his intelligence career.

One night he showed up at the barn and there were no Jews. Robert Proust and Jacques Granville came in shortly after, frightened and excited.

"I received a warning," Jacques blurted, "that the Germans have been watching us for the last couple of days."

"Oh, God!"

"I'm sure they're waiting to learn our system and find all the underground stations before they close in. It will give us a chance to get away."

"Run?"

"Yes," Robert said shakily. "We must flee now. Everyone in Blois has scattered. I've packed some things for you."

"Papa! I have to tell him good-bye."

Jacques gripped him and shook his head, No.

"I must."

"It could implicate your father if you see him now. We'll get a message to him when we can."

"Who informed on us?"

"Frenchmen," Jacques Granville spat. "Frenchmen trying to kiss the asses of the Germans. And it's the French police looking for us along with the Germans."

"The sons of bitches . . ."

"Come on, André, let's get going."

That night they fled to Tours and were hidden in an attic which had been a station in the underground. By morning they learned that they, and the rest of the Blois ring, were the objects of a massive manhunt.

Each night they shifted to a new hiding place in Tours, awaiting help from the underground. After a week, a grizzled old man who was called Duval visited them.

"We've got you cleared as far as Bordeaux. The organization there will give you papers and certificates stating that you have tuberculosis. With TB papers you will be able to travel to rehabilitation centers in the foothills of the Pyrenees."

He spread a map on the rough-hewn table and squinted, leading his finger to the French-Spanish border.

"Here it is, Cambo. You will be able to make contact with a guide to take you over to Spain."

"From there?"

Duval shrugged. "I can only give you one name, that of a Miss Florence Smith in the British Embassy in Madrid. We believe she is MI-5, British Intelligence. She's helped a number of our people get to French North Africa."

Duval gave them money. "I'm sorry we have no papers. You'll have to get those in Bordeaux. It's going to be a hard journey. You'll have to walk by night and live off the land. And remember, the bastards in Vichy are just as bad as in Occupied France."

"We'll make it," Jacques said, with much doubt in his voice.

"Tonight I will come back and show you the way. And, boys, I want to thank you for what you have done. I am a Jew. You've taken my whole family over the Cher. God knows what would have happened if they had had to stay."

Two months later, André Devereaux, Robert Proust, and Jacques Granville arrived in the town of Cambo near the French-Spanish frontier. They were shabby, half-starved, and nearly penniless.

Before them loomed the monstrous barrier of the mountains known as the Pyrenees.

ANDRÉ DEVEREAUX SPENT his twenty-first birthday in Cambo. He had grown a beard, a rather
handsome one, that belied his age.

On the journey Robert Proust had proved the
weakest of the three, tiring, becoming dejected,
complaining of hunger constantly.

Jacques Granville, the eldest, kept up their
spirits. He was a born *bon vivant*, even in their
miserable circumstances always seeking out a
bed partner where they hid, in the haylofts, the
open fields, or the cellars of peasants' homes. It
seemed that if there was a woman to be found,
Jacques would find her.

Beyond the Pyrenees was Spain and perhaps a
path to the French Vichy forces of Admiral de St.
Amertin based in Casablanca. They were certain
that someday these French forces would quit
Vichy and turn and fight the Germans.

There was another group now based in London.
General Pierre La Croix, whom they had heard
on the clandestine radio, had denounced Vichy
and the Pétain regime and had actually rallied a
number of the French possessions to his Committee for the Defense of the French Empire.
They called themselves the Free French or Fighting France.

Certainly Pierre La Croix had more appeal to
the three comrades, but it seemed impossible to
reach him, so their goal became Casablanca and
Admiral de St. Amertin.

Cambo was filled with tuberculars from all over
Europe. Although the three of them carried false
medical certificates stating that they had TB,
too many escapees had passed the same route

with the same story. It was certain they would be found out.

For a week they were unable to make a contact. Their money was depleted and it was impossible to cross the mountains without a guide.

In desperation André went to the church and in the secrecy of the confessional booth spoke to the priest.

"Father," he said, "I am in Cambo with two comrades trying to escape to Spain."

"For what purpose?"

"To fight for France."

"Why are you fleeing? The truth."

"We are wanted by the Germans for helping Jews escape to Vichy France."

"Yes. News of you is known. It will only be a matter of a day or two and the police will come for you. You must get out of Cambo."

"Please help us. We are out of funds."

"That is your problem."

"But, Father . . ." André said harshly in disbelief.

"I'm fed up with the flood of escaped criminals descending on Cambo."

"Father! We are not criminals."

"If the law wants you, you are criminals. Either be out of Cambo by morning or I will turn you in to the police."

"Father! We are Frenchmen!"

"Get out."

André reeled from the church, running back to their pension. He tore up the stairs panting, flung the door open.

"The priest threatens to give us up to the police!"

Robert Proust trembled, then sat and wept.

282

"Shut up, Robert!" Jacques ordered. "God, let me think . . . that bastard . . . that bastard!"

There was a sharp knock on the door. They all looked to it in terror.

(4)

ANDRÉ OPENED THE DOOR. They saw a small, stout man who gave off an air of professional eminence.

"I am Dr. Aumont," he said, "the director of one of the sanitariums. May I come in?"

The curious visitor looked from one to the other. "You boys are escapees, are you not?"

There was no answer.

"Come, come now," Dr. Aumont said, "I'm not going to turn you over to the police."

André ignored Jacques' shake of the head. "What does it matter, Jacques? Yes, we are escapees."

"For what reason?"

"We are from along the Cher River. Our underground took Jews over to Vichy."

"All right, boys, you can be easy. I am the head of a group here in Cambo who keep an eye open for escapees. We have set up a fund to help our boys get to the fighting forces."

André leaned his face against the windowframe and the cheap lace curtain brushed against his beard and tears came to his eyes. "Thank God there are some decent Frenchmen left."

"All right, boys, you must leave immediately . . . now. You will make it to the village of Espelette. It will take several hours. Find the Berhard Inn. A waitress there named Geneviève will find you a hiding place and will obtain a Basque guide to take you over the mountains."

"Dr. Aumont, I can't tell you . . ."

"No time to tell anyone anything. Who is the leader?"

The other two nodded toward Jacques Granville. He handed Jacques a packet of bills, a hundred and fifty dollars in American money, and explained their worth in francs.

"Now you must bargain hard with the Basque guide," Dr. Aumont instructed. "He will take you over for thirty dollars a head, but halfway through the passes he will try to extort more money out of you on the threat of leaving you alone in the mountains. Give him a few more dollars and promise him a few more when you reach Spain, but hide part of the money. I suggest you tie it around your waist. Well, good luck."

They found Geneviève in the Berhard Inn, and she fed them and hid them in a corncrib. All save Jacques, to whom she took an immediate liking. He had another bed for the night.

At the first light of dawn, a gruff, blocklike, leather-faced man dressed in heavy sheepskin and fur leggings appeared at the corncrib.

"I am Ezkanazi, Basque guide. I take you to Spain. Three thousand francs each before we start."

As good Frenchmen they bartered and bickered before they struck a deal. Geneviève fixed them each a small sack of cheese, bread, and a bottle of wine. The party then headed toward the bleak, foreboding mountains.

The smuggler trails known to centuries of Basques were made for goats rather than men. They climbed into the jagged wilderness with a

284

howling wind beating the warmth from their bodies. Breathing became a struggle as they ascended higher and higher to the fringes of eternal snowfields.

The Basque cursed at their slowness but to no avail. By late afternoon, Robert Proust slumped to the ground, a beaten man. Heart pounding, throat caked from dryness, he mumbled that he could not go on.

Jacques and André dragged him to his feet. Then Jacques punctured him in the seat of the pants with a hypodermic needle that Dr. Aumont had given him filled with caffeine to sustain energy.

Darkness crept over the mountaintops. Ezkanazi stopped.

"More money," he said.

They argued frantically.

"More dollars or I leave you here to find your own way."

Jacques handled the situation masterfully, and paid some and promised some. The Basque snatched the money angrily and grumbled, then led them off the path into a high pasture where they came to an abandoned shepherd's hut.

A fire was built and they nibbled listlessly at their food. Robert was shivering and moaned himself into a fitful sleep filled with high-altitude hallucinations.

André and Jacques took turns sleeping and sitting with their backs propped against the door, so the Basque would not try to escape.

The next day when they reached a small farm and were shown to the corncrib, Robert was in bad condition, feverish, hacking and spitting. André and Jacques took shifts in soaking his forehead with wet rags and pleading with him to hang on for one more day. The night seemed utterly without end. The corncrib offered small protection against the elements. They greeted the morning in a stupor.

Ezkanazi appeared and ordered them to come into the farmer's house. A pine-box coffin sat in the center of the floor filled with smuggler's booty. It was nailed shut and sat on a pair of poles.

"We are in Spain," the Basque said tersely. "The four of us will carry the coffin to the cemetery in the town of Elizondo. The border guards and police will pass you as family."

Jacques collected the identification papers of his two friends and burned them along with his own in the stove on orders received in what seemed ages ago in Bordeaux.

They descended to Elizondo holding the coffin on their shoulders in a mock funeral. Robert staggered along with them. A few moments after they entered the cemetery, they were ordered to take off through a rear gate.

They made for the road. A half-mile outside Elizondo, four cars filled with Spanish border police descended on them bearing sub-machine guns. They were arrested and driven away.

(5)

THEY WERE FLUNG into the dungeon of a medieval prison and fed gruel and water once a day. The Spaniards refused to respond to a plea for a doctor for Robert.

At the end of a week they were removed in wretched condition to the penitentiary at Pamplona, where, at last, Robert was taken to the sick ward. Each of them had lost some fifty pounds in weight and was a sorry, weak specimen of the human race.

Their interrogation was perfunctory, for many others had come their route. They made the standard claim of being French-Canadians and were placed in the cell block that held a hundred other French escapees also claiming to be Canadians.

The penitentiary was a large affair crammed with Loyalist prisoners of the Civil War. Spanish sentiments were openly pro-German, with a Spanish Blue Division fighting on the Eastern Front against the Russians. The prison authorities dealt particularly harshly with the French, affording them a life of bare existence.

As weeks passed, Robert slowly regained some strength, but they all wallowed in futility. The only ray of hope came when Jacques was permitted to write a letter to the mysterious Miss Florence Smith at the British Embassy in Madrid.

When all hope seemed gone, a sudden wildfire of rumor swept the escapees' cell. It was true! A British-American delegation appeared in Pamplona to fulfill a deal made with the Spanish government to release the prisoners in exchange for a shipment of wheat and flour.

They were to leave in groups. Jacques and André went to the Americans and asked that Robert be allowed to go first because he needed medical attention. And so the comrades were separated. Two weeks after Robert had departed they received a short letter from him.

DEAR JACQUES AND ANDRÉ,

I am at an enormous camp at Miranda de Ebro. It not only holds military escapees but thousands of

Jews who have fled from Holland, Poland, Belgium, and, oh yes, France. By wonderful coincidence I've run into a few we took over the Cher River.

There is a permanent British-American committee bartering for our release, and we all feel there is a chance to get to North Africa.

I look for your arrival every day. Please get word to me through the Red Cross office.

I am sorry to cut this short, but they are only allowing a single-page letter. Life is marginal, but I am feeling much better.

Your devoted comrade,
ROBERT

André and Jacques were not to follow to Miranda de Ebro. Their train terminated at the spa of Arnedillo, where a number of smaller hotels and pensions had been leased by the British and Americans, who continued to pay ransom to the Spanish government.

In Arnedillo they were instructed not to try to escape, for if they did it would jeopardize the entire program. Under this honorary parole they were allowed to mingle with tourists from all over Spain who had come to the famous mud baths for therapeutic treatment.

One day André was walking past the ultraposh Balneario Hotel.

"You there," a voice called.

He looked up to a balcony, where a heavy-set, middle-aged man stood wearing a magnificent velour smoking jacket.

"Me?"

"Yes, you. Are you one of the internees?" he asked, speaking perfect French.

"Yes."

"By any chance do you or any of your comrades play bridge?"

"Yes, I play."

"We're short a hand. Would you mind sitting in?"

"Why not?"

André felt awkward and shabby in the splendor of the Balneario as he found his way to the man's suite. The stranger introduced himself as Victor Thibaud, a Frenchman whose business interests had been centered in Spain for a decade. André reckoned from the size of the suite and the stones in Monsieur Thibaud's rings that his business was considerable.

Madame Thibaud, he explained, was at the mud baths a good deal of the time and he was constantly looking for a bridge partner.

A snobbish-appearing but quite lovely girl, perhaps twenty, came into the parlor wearing riding habit.

"My daughter, Nicole."

She nodded curtly. "I'll be at the Valdez Ranch, Papa. They are running new bulls. I hear some are magnificent."

As André's eyes followed her, Monsieur Thibaud curtly announced his daughter was engaged to a member of an important Spanish banking family.

"Well now, young man. What kind of a game do you play?"

"Fair," André said, "just fair."

"We'll be a team. Try not to lose me too much money."

That night at El Torito Café, hangout of the French prisoners, André spoke excitedly to Jacques.

"It's a cinch," he said, "an absolute cinch. My father taught me to play bridge before I could walk. We were district champions five years running. These Spanish idiots here, Thibaud included, don't know a damn thing about the game."

"I don't know," Jacques said. "My game is really not very good."

"I'll teach you everything you need to know, plus a few signals during the bidding."

"My God, André, these people are filthy rich. They play for a peseta a point. We can't afford that."

"Hell, we'll be playing with their money after the first rubber. We need the money, they don't. God, I'd like a decent meal. Just to eat meat once more before I die. Come on, let's take up a collection from the boys so we can have a stake."

"It's madness, but you're the boss."

The two charming Frenchmen then proceeded to fleece the wealthy guests of the Balneario out of enough money for food, half-decent wine, and some clothing for twenty-five comrades at their pension.

Jacques Granville had the additional pleasure of servicing a number of ladies, from chambermaids to some of the wives of the guests.

But, despite Jacques' urging, André didn't seem interested in this diversion. He played with one eye on the door, waiting for the haughty Nicole to make an appearance. At first they exchanged a few clipped words, then a softening started in her.

Did she like him or was she merely bored with her parents' holiday? After all, the hotel was filled with older people. It was not much of a place for a young girl, and there was a romantic air about the ragged Frenchman from the other side of town.

Whatever her reasons, if André showed up early for the bridge game, she would be there.

290

Perhaps they would walk through the garden for a bit. Nicole was a master of flirtation and teasing, and played it to the hilt.

Jacques whistled as he divided the day's winnings on the table. André sat glumly on the edge of his cot.

"What a piece of ass I had tonight! That bastard of a husband came back an hour earlier than he was expected. I almost got caught. Look, I ripped my damn pants on the rosebushes outside her window."

"You're lucky her room wasn't on the third floor. One of these days you'll get killed. You know how jealous Spanish husbands are."

"Bah! Can I draw a few pesetas out of this without going to the committee? I need a new pair of pants. There's no place left to patch these."

"Sure, for pants. But you've got to stop buying so damn many presents for the women."

"But I love them all! Hey, André, what the hell are you so miserable about?"

"I think I'm in love."

"So why be miserable? People should be happy when they're in love. God, you make it so dreary. What a bore! Who are you in love with?"

"Nicole Thibaud."

"God in heaven! Women are falling out of the trees and you've got to go for that brat."

"She's not really that way at all. Maybe a little spoiled, but . . ."

Jacques dunked his face in the water basin, scrubbed and toweled vigorously, then admired himself in the steel mirror nailed on the wall.

"She's bad news, André. I know this kind of girl. All women are possessive, but this one is the devouring kind."

291

"You sound like my father. What's the difference? She's engaged to be married."

"You're lucky. Love comes in many packages, my friend. Some things which are called love are not love at all. What a girl like Nicole Thibaud thinks is love is total ownership. It's destructive."

André was beyond listening to his older, wiser friend. He unlaced his boots and let them fall to the floor with a thud. "We'd better let them win tomorrow. I think we're getting greedy."

That particular tomorrow never came for Jacques Granville. His freedom was purchased, and with a rousing farewell from his comrades he made off to join the Free French forces of General Pierre La Croix.

André alone was left of the three comrades, and he fell into a deep depression.

André answered a knock on the door. Nicole Thibaud stood before him.

"Hello, André."

"What the devil are you doing here?"

"Looking for you. Won't you ask me in?"

"It's not the Balneario. . . . Well, come in."

She scanned the cell-like room with its few pieces of cheap furniture. The walls had long needed paint, the windows were uncurtained, and a kerosene lamp on the table provided the only light.

"You haven't been around," she said.

"I've been quite upset since Jacques went away."

"Oh, I didn't know he'd left. Papa wanted you for bridge tonight. There is no telephone here so . . ."

"I was thinking of coming back. We're running out of money."

"Do you dislike me, André?"

"On the contrary."

"But you dislike things about me."

"I'm not in a position to like or dislike. I'm penniless and homeless. Besides, you're engaged to be married."

"Oh, that. I was going to call it off anyhow."

"Your fiancé might not like that."

"Too bad. Spanish men are too domineering anyhow. It was all arranged as a convenience for Papa's business. I planned to rebel shortly."

She pushed close to him so that he could feel and smell her for an instant, then she spun away. "Do come back to the hotel. I've missed you," she said, opening the door a crack.

"Miss me, or are you bored?"

"Mmmm, a little of both."

André reached over her shoulder and slammed the door shut. "You're a bitch and a tease," he said, grabbing her hands and pinning them behind her back. She struggled and tried to kick and bite. He avoided her movements deftly.

"I'll scream!"

With his free hand he slapped her face, then released her. "Someone should have done that to you a long time ago."

Nicole fell back against the wall, panting in a rage. She looked about, found some tin cups and plates to throw and missed him by half the room. Tears of anger brimmed in her eyes.

"Get out," André ordered softly.

Then suddenly her anger stopped and she stumbled to a chair and sat and hung her head and shook it and began to cry softly. "I don't want to go, André. Lock the door. . . ."

She was in his arms and they loved fiercely.

293

"I've never had a man. Please be careful . . .
please . . . please."

"I love you, Nicole."

"I love you. . . ."

"Well, good to have you back, Devereaux. I
haven't won a rubber since you deserted me. We'll
give the Valencias a lesson later, eh? Here, have
a drink."

"Thank you, Monsieur Thibaud."

"Montrichard, eh? Magnificent country. What
exactly did you do before the war?"

"I was an apprentice lawyer in my father's
office."

"Old family? Active?"

"My father, my grandfather, and my great
grandfather were all mayors of Montrichard. A
family responsibility I suppose I'll inherit."

"Really, how interesting. Then your family has
substantial interests in Montrichard?"

"We do."

"Land. Assets."

"Yes."

"And your schooling?"

"I am drawing a conclusion about this questioning, Monsieur Thibaud. Perhaps you will tell me
if I am correct."

"Man to man?"

"Yes."

"Devereaux, my daughter has taken quite a
liking to you. She has a disturbing temper . . .
disturbing! Very willful. Young man, are you interested in Nicole?"

"Yes, sir, I am."

"Then I'll be candid. Nicole returns your feeling, fully. I am in a position to get you out of here and fix you up with a set of papers. My business in Madrid could use a young chap like you with legal background and your knowledge of several languages. You see, we engage in international trade and . . ."

"Why, Monsieur Thibaud. I do believe you are proposing to me."

"Well, you want to get out of this mess, don't you? Do you intend to rot in this place?"

"I intend to fight for France. Good day, sir."

"Devereaux!"

"Yes?"

"You are not to call on Nicole again."

"That is her choice, sir. She knows where I live."

Nicole stood on the fringe of the outdoor patio of El Torito Café, where the men drank cheap wine and discussed news and rumors with a zest that could only sparkle from Frenchmen.

"By the end of the year all of North Africa will be in La Croix's hands!"

"Mark my words. La Croix will move his headquarters to Algeria, and then we'll see about Admiral de St. Amertin."

"I don't know."

"Well, you do know the bastard scuttled part of the fleet rather than deliver it to the Allies."

Nicole spotted André, twenty-one, filled with exuberance and handsome in his way. She caught his eye. He excused himself and they walked silently to the end of the street, which led to a country road and a meadow.

"I came to say good-bye," she said. "Papa is taking us back to Madrid tomorrow."

"I'm sorry."

She broke into tears. "I thought you said you loved me!"

"I do, Nicole."

"And after what we did together, you refused my papa's offer!"

"Making love is a natural expression of a man and a woman who desire each other. As for your father's offer, I'm not to be selected like a bottle of wine."

"After I have given myself to you, you'd leave me?"

"Only till I get my job done."

"What job? You have no job."

"Nicole. In Africa there are Frenchmen wearing the French uniform, fighting for France. Jacques and Robert are among them. This war is passing me by. Did you see the men in El Torito? We all exist for but one thing . . . to redeem the honor of France."

"I don't understand this rubbish of honor and this fanaticism for blood."

"You've lived in Spain most of your life. You don't even speak French to your parents most of the time."

"But I love you, André."

"The way to love is by giving, not taking. If you really love me, then get me my freedom and let me do my duty."

"Oh, God! I don't want you to go."

"That's what I'm going to do, Nicole."

"There's no choice then, is there?"

"None for me."

"Will you ever come back for me?"

"Yes, I want to."

"I'll . . . I'll see that Papa buys your freedom."

"Nicole, try to understand."

"No, I don't. But take me to your room . . . now!"

André arrived in Málaga, where a number of liberated prisoners from Miranda de Ebro slept in the bullring awaiting transport.

He boarded the ship with a mixture of elation and sadness, for his heart was filled with love for Nicole.

Operation Torch, the British-American landings in North Africa, had swept the coast and the tug of war was on between the two divided French forces.

The arrival at Casablanca set off a grand welcome. Bands and troops were there in the uniform of the Spahi Cavalry and the Foreign Legion.

Tears of joy streamed down the cheeks of men as they once again saw their beloved tricolor and once again heard the national anthem.

André Devereaux had arrived in the stronghold of Admiral de St. Amertin.

(6)

CASABLANCA, A CREATION OF French imperialism since the turn of the century, was suddenly thrust into world attention as a focal point of invasion by Operation Torch in November of 1942 and later as a meeting ground at the summit for the Allied leaders.

The upper-class European merchants lived in luxury along wide and endless boulevards that surrounded the now all-important port. Impoverished Muslims and Jews continued life in their miserable *medinas* and *mellahs*.

Casablanca teemed with fresh, untested American troops forming an admixture with the French Marines, the colonial infantry, and the Spahi Cavalry.

Within the walled city of Bous Bir, five thousand skilled prostitutes and superb belly dancers vied for the flood of soldiers' money in the most ancient way.

But all through the French North African colonies and in the Near East an inner conflict raged. The garrisons of a hundred thousand-odd French and colonials belonged mostly to the Vichy Government, the collaborationists of Nazi Germany.

Pierre La Croix and his Free French had fought a series of popgun invasions and expeditions under General Leclerc to reclaim French possessions from Vichy.

Starting with a landing in Cameroons in 1940, La Croix had rallied territory after territory to the cause of Fighting France: Gabon, French Equatorial Africa, Chad, Ubangi. Then in the Pacific and Far East, Tahiti and New Caledonia declared for La Croix, followed by Pondicherry and the French possessions in India.

Fearing an invasion of the Japanese, the British landed in Madagascar, and it, too, joined the swelling ranks of Free France.

Now Senegal, French Guinea, Ivory Coast, Dahomey, Niger, French Occidental Africa, and, in the West Indies, Guadeloupe and Martinique all declared for Fighting France.

Free France entered the field with the British in the Ethiopian campaign and tasted bitter blood at Bir Hacheim in Libya, writing a chapter of glory against Rommel's assaults.

In one of the great paradoxes of the war, Vichy France continued to be recognized by the United States despite its collaboration with Germany, and the Vichy garrisons sat tight in Morocco, Tunisia, and Algeria.

When Operation Torch opened the invasion of North Africa, the Germans were forced to retaliate by occupying all of metropolitan France and reducing the Vichy Government to the rankest of puppets. Vichy was virtually powerless.

Now it was a question of the Vichy garrisons. The American paradox became even more baffling when Vichy Admiral de St. Amertin was installed by the Americans as their handpicked commander of the former Vichy garrisons.

Pierre La Croix and Fighting France countered this by establishing headquarters and a quasi government in Algeria in late spring of 1943. From here, he continued to press his demands for recognition, the right of France to fight, the joining of his forces with the garrison forces and the formation of a joint national committee.

Free France was extremely unpopular, for the majority of Arab sympathy was for Germany and the Axis. The French colonists and settlers wanted to keep a status quo and continue the spirit of Vichy and not be dragged into the war by alignment with Free France. The major exception was the French Jewish population, who backed Free France in their personal desire to fight against the Germans.

Camp Boulhot stood midway between Casablanca and Rabat, thirty miles inland from the sea, and was filled with a collection of French and Moroccan soldiers of traditional colonial units.

André Devereaux, who had been a horseman since childhood, requested duty in a Spahi Cavalry regiment. The Spahis were a colorful lot, with their flaming red capes and high polished boots and light blue kepi hats bearing the crescent and star of Morocco.

But they were the forces of Admiral de St. Amertin, formerly of Vichy, and were to be kept by the Americans as parade-ground soldiers far from the cannons' roar.

In the weeks that followed, André received letters from Jacques Granville and Robert Proust, who were with La Croix in Algiers. With the picture terribly clear, André sought out La Croix men who had infiltrated de St. Amertin's ranks to recruit for Fighting France.

"L'Auberge de la Forêt" stood beyond the camp gates in a setting of jasmine trees and the raging color of the French colonial uniforms.

Captain Dupont found a quiet table with André and ordered thick, sweet coffee. The La Croix recruiter asked a number of questions of André.

"This place stinks of Vichy, Captain," André said. "All during the time we were struggling to reach here, I never thought it would be like this. They're Frenchmen. They've got to fight for France."

The Captain shook his head slowly. "It doesn't work that way."

"I don't understand," André continued, "why the Americans installed a Vichy officer over the garrisons or why they are so determined to keep us off the front or why they withhold recognition from Free France."

"They do not want us fighting," Dupont said,

300

"or the colonies reunified so that we will have no word at the peace tables."

"Why in the name of God do the Americans hate us?"

"Roosevelt has never forgiven France for bungling the phony war, sitting it out when Poland was attacked and then letting Germany crush us. He feels that France is incapable of leadership in Europe and intends to reduce us to a second-rate power. Only Pierre La Croix and a handful of Free French stand between the United States and its ambitions."

"I must join Free France," André cried. "I must get to Algeria. Will you help me?"

"Wait until you get a leave, then bolt. I'll get the information on you back to Algiers."

The tough, hard-nosed old colonials detested the proud young men in their ranks who longed to fight for Free France. André Devereaux was singled out for special punishment and humiliation. His nose was rubbed in every dirty detail and no means was spared to break his spirit. He was in a state of constant fatigue imposed by brutality. Somehow he continued to endure.

Finally, on a flimsy pretext, his commanding officer inflicted on him the most inhuman of punishments—the *tombeau*. André was compelled to dig a shallow trench under the flame of the desert sun, then lie in it. The trench was covered by a canvas. No food or water would be given him, nor would he leave until he pleaded for mercy.

André baked in the *tombeau* for thirteen daylight hours, and through the night he half-froze to death. The test of fortitude continued a second searing day. Through his agony his lips remained sealed. No plea came from him until a merciful unconsciousness consumed him on the third day.

When the canvas was lifted, he was carried off to the hosptial. All the years back, of flight, prison, and semistarvation, had taken their toll. He was a sick young man, needing long hospitalization.

At the end of his stay he was granted a short leave. With furlough documents in his hand, André Devereaux boarded a train and fled to Algeria.

At last he arrived in the headquarters of Fighting France!

(7)

ALGIERS ROSE FROM the sea, hugging the line of the bay for miles, while it climbed the steep hills in dazzling white terraces. From the Casbah with its fabled evil and twisted alleyways down to the broad boulevards that hovered over the quay lined with government buildings, public squares, and hotels, it swept up again to the university, which was now the seat of Fighting France in exile.

André turned himself in at once at the Arabian Bruce Palace that housed the Central Intelligence Bureau.

"We have been expecting you," he was greeted.

The bureau, run by a smattering of former military intelligence personnel, interrogated him thoroughly before issuing him temporary papers to the effect he was now a member of the Free French.

André left the Bruce Palace still in a state of disbelief.

"André! André!"

"Robert!"

The comrades embraced and slapped each other's backs sore.

"I phoned Jacques. He'll be waiting for us at the Aletti Hotel."

André patted the jeep bearing the Free French colors and Cross of Lorraine, and Robert pointed it downhill, babbling the while, trying to catch up in a single moment.

He had been appointed Chief of Western Hemisphere Intelligence in an organization being built from the ground up. As for Jacques Granville, he had fared even better. Jacques had been named one of Pierre La Croix's chief liaison officers.

As they raced down toward the harbor, André drew a series of deep, deep breaths. "Oh, God, this is so great!"

"Don't dream too much. It's full of Vichy here, and we don't get along with the Americans. The only real support we have is from the Jews."

Jacques Granville cut a magnificent figure in his uniform. They greeted each other affectionately, and all three headed to the Oasis Restaurant, a large open-terraced establishment on the second floor of the Aletti Hotel. For a while all three of them jabbered at once, then Jacques prevailed. "Now, ready for some news?" he said. "Hold your breath, André. You have an interview tomorrow with the General."

"La Croix?"

"Yes!"

"But . . . but . . ."

"But nothing. I told him you were the brightest fellow in all of the Loire, that you were the heart

303

of the underground ring. It's a great opportunity for you. We are very short of people and the sky is the limit."

"Tell me I'm not dreaming!"

"It calls for champagne," Robert said.

"There's another surprise."

"I can't stand another one."

"This one you'll stand."

The champagne came as André was recounting his life as a member of the Spahis. They lifted their glasses. He looked over the terrace and came to his feet. "Nicole," he whispered. "Nicole!"

"André!"

(8)

ANDRÉ WAS SO FILLED with the weary glow of love-making he was oblivious to the chatter of Jacques and Robert as they ascended the hill to the Villa Capucines, residence and office of General Pierre La Croix. The nearby Fromentin Heights held the girls' college, now the seat of the Free French Government.

When they entered the modest villa, one could sense the almost consecrated air of people moving about with silent urgency.

Jacques and Robert paced the outer office, alternately coming back to André to whisper suggestions as the nervous parade continued in and out of the General's sanctum. Then booming through the thin walls came the voice of Pierre La Croix!

"The dirty sons of bitches! Inform those bastards they'll do what is expected of them or I'll have their balls."

And thus, without formal introduction, André was to meet Pierre La Croix.

304

The voice within continued in the same lusty barracksroom vernacular, so bawdy that even Jacques Granville blushed.

"He expresses himself rather colorfully," Robert understated.

The recipients of La Croix's outburst fled the Office. One was pale, the other crimson.

André's palms felt damp and his mouth dried as they were summoned in.

Pierre La Croix, the maverick of the French military, sat ramrod-straight in an ornate mahogany chair before a paper-littered baroque desk. The Cross of Lorraine on a tricolor hung on the wall behind him. He neither stood nor smiled nor gave greeting as the three advanced to his desk and came to attention.

La Croix squinted at André through nearsighted eyes.

"Sit down, gentlemen," he said in the manner of a king granting audience. A secretary quickly set André's dossier before him. He scanned it for a brief moment and looked up.

"What do you have to say, Devereaux?"

"I am devoted to the cause of Fighting France. I have come a long way and I intend to prove myself."

"France expects nothing less than this devotion," he said. "I am assigning you to my intelligence staff. Proust here will acquaint you with your work."

"Thank you, sir."

"France welcomes you. That is all, gentlemen."

Outside the villa they caught their bearings as Robert pumped André's hand long and hard.

"Well? What do you think of him?" Jacques asked.

"I've never seen a man like that."

"He is France," Jacques answered simply.

André shared an office with Robert Proust in a villa on Rue Edouard Cat, plunging into his mission and living up to the demands of the General. He proved himself so at home in intelligence matters that he was advanced rapidly to the special title of "Chargé of Mission" and became one of the General's personal advisers.

Still in his early twenties, André Devereaux was immersed in the struggle of Free France, never ceasing to marvel at Pierre La Croix, who was capable of irritating his major allies as though he had fifty divisions of troops at his command instead of a handful of regiments.

But André's admiration was not total, as was Robert's and Jacques'. It was tempered with the fear that if one day La Croix came to rule, his strong-man traits could become undemocratic. Furthermore, his drive for power was a mania that could be channeled effectively by the less scrupulous of his staff.

With access to top-secret documents, André was able to trace La Croix's struggle and the wizardry he had performed in the name of France.

Free France had been shut out of all the top-level decisions in military and political planning by the Anglo-Americans. Innumerable documents seemed to bear out La Croix's fear that the British aspired to replace France as the dominant power in several areas of the Middle East that had traditionally been in the French sphere.

In the early stages of the war, Churchill continued to bow to Roosevelt's pressure by not arming or allowing the Free French to fight in Allied campaigns. Finally, La Croix made the blunt threat to send a division of Frenchmen to fight alongside the Russians against Germany on the Eastern Front. Only then was La Croix able to increase his military role.

His most painful affront came when the proud Frenchman was invited to Casablanca by the American President. La Croix and his staff were greeted coolly in Casablanca, without military honors. In this, a French possession, they were billeted inside barbed-wire compounds under the guard of armed American soldiers. The American President bluntly warned La Croix to place his forces under the supreme command of Admiral de St. Amertin.

But even with American backing, Admiral de St. Amertin was no match for the brazen Pierre La Croix, who outmaneuvered him at every turn. La Croix was splitting his forces from him, rallying the territories to his cause. And when negotiations opened for a merger and a national council, it was predestined that La Croix would emerge as the supreme head. No small part of La Croix's advantage was due to the fantastic intelligence network he built, and young Devereaux was one of its driving forces. La Croix's people seemed to have the tactical advantage and answer to every Anglo-American move against him.

Despite the ground swell of Free France, America continued to withhold recognition. Pierre La Croix had no embassy in Washington, only a mission.

Then André Devereaux obtained evidence of American intentions to "occupy" France. With the evidence at hand, he asked for an immediate and urgent appointment with the General and raced to the Villa Capucines.

"General," André said, "we have the proof here,

in their own orders, that the United States intends to install an American military government in France in much the same way they will occupy conquered Germany."

(9)

"FEEL THE BABY," Nicole said, pressing André's hand to her stomach. "It's kicking up a real storm today."

André kissed her cheek and petted her as they went out to the little balcony together to watch the sunset. Nicole was starting to waddle a bit as she grew larger. He adored the wonderment of the whole thing and hoped they would have child after child.

In a moment he became pensive.

"I found some beautiful lamb. A whole rack of it, and I'm making it just your way."

André didn't hear her.

"It's almost like a party when you get home for dinner."

"The General was in a rage today. I've never seen him in such a vile mood."

Nicole did not answer immediately, but her discomfort was apparent. "Darling, this is the first evening we've had to watch the sunset in so long. Let's not talk about him or Free France or the war or anything but us tonight. I saw the doctor yesterday. He says it's still safe to make love."

"You can't imagine how serious it's become. If the Americans go through with their plans to treat us like a defeated enemy . . ."

"La Croix," she snapped, "La Croix! Morning, noon, and night, La Croix!"

"Nicole, without the General, France will be

reduced to a puppet state after the war. The invasion of the Continent is coming very soon. It will happen in the spring or summer of this year. We have only a few months . . ."

"For God's sake, André! Darling, I have been patient, I've tried to understand. But we've been married seven months. Do you realize how few nights you've come home for more than a half-dozen hours' sleep? You're so tired most of the time I have to undress you."

"Nicole, we promised we wouldn't get in any fights about this."

She turned and waddled into the small room that held their bed and was, in addition, kitchenette and parlor. She stood with her back to him, staring blankly at a needlepoint on the wall she had bought in an Arab bazaar. "I sometimes feel like a stranger. And I think, all during those hours I'm alone, which is most of the time, that you're not happy I ran away from Spain to come to you."

"Nicole, you know how I love you. How can you say that?"

"There never seems to be any time for me."

"We're in a war."

"War! Don't say that word again."

"Nicole . . . Nicole . . . I didn't invite the Germans to invade France." He came up behind her, dreading to have to say his next words. "I came home early tonight in order to pack. I'm leaving with the General tomorrow for London."

Nicole turned and faced him slowly, glassy-eyed. "You'd leave me now?"

"I don't give the orders to General La Croix. He gives them to me."

"You'd leave me alone!"

"You won't be alone, darling. We have a hundred friends in Algiers. The doctor and the hospital are excellent."

Nicole picked up a feather duster and began moving around the room nervously, flicking it at picture frames, tidying up an overly tidy room. André stood in awkward silence.

"You want to leave me," she said.

"I think not."

"Then do something about this rotten job of yours. You said we have friends. All right, use them. Get yourself put into some place where we can have a few moments together. It's no sin in Algiers. Almost everyone hates Pierre La Croix for pushing them into a war against their will."

"As a matter of fact," André said in a resigned monotone, "I have already requested a transfer."

Nicole stopped her dusting. "I didn't know."

"I was refused. I asked to be sent to a fighting unit."

She seized a plate from the table. The lamb on the stove began to burn. She started to hurl the plate but let it slip from her hand and it fell to the floor and broke. "How long will you be gone, André?"

"I don't know. I'd better pack."

The de Havilland Dove of General Pierre La Croix slipped from the Maison Blanche Airport bucking headwinds. The coast of North Africa disappeared in the morning mist. General La Croix worked on a card table, thumbing through documents, sketching his forthcoming speech. Captain Robert Proust came down the aisle, stopped by the General's table, and spoke to him respectfully, giving the flight plan and progress. Pierre La Croix looked up for an instant and nodded without comment.

André went forward and sat in alongside Jacques Granville.

Jacques set his papers aside. "Fight with Nicole?"

"How do you know?"

"For an intelligence man you don't keep a very straight face. Besides, it figures, knowing you, knowing Nicole. There had to be an argument last night."

"What the hell, Jacques. She's pregnant and in a strange place. How can she be blamed?"

"Blamed? She should kiss your feet for the privilege of seeing you a few hours each night. We're in the middle of a war. How many millions of women have had their men taken away? She's entirely unreasonable."

"Somehow," André answered, "she does not associate herself with the war. When it's all over and we have some time to spend together, she'll change."

Jacques smiled and patted his friend's shoulder. "You are a perfect La Croix officer. Strange how a man can be so wise in so many areas, then carry with him such a blind spot."

"What blind spot?"

"The illusion that Nicole will change. And the further illusion that you yourself will change. Now all the hours you spend in your work are justified. It's war and you're a soldier. But you'll always spend those same hours later on, either out of choice or an inbred sense of duty."

An eruption of sizzling language was heard above the engines. General La Croix had obviously found something to cause him discomfort, and a half-dozen officers leaped to their feet and surrounded the General.

"Our leader calls," Jacques said. "Look, don't

worry about Nicole for now. She'll be in Algiers, fatter than ever, when we get back."

"No, she won't," André said, getting out of his seat to answer La Croix's summons. "She's left for Spain to rejoin her parents till the end of the war."

(10)

ALBERT HALL, LONDON
FEBRUARY, 1944

A HIGH-PITCHED MULTITUDE of French in exile filled every seat. Out in the street, thousands more jammed around loudspeakers. Inside the hall, red, white, and blue bunting knitted the balconies. On the rear of the stage stood an enormous Cross of Lorraine and the blazing words, FREE FRANCE. The gathered throng buzzed in nervous anticipation.

Now, a convoy of staff cars inched through the crowd. Inside Albert Hall they could hear the swelling roar outside and the audience came to its feet.

Pierre La Croix, who always aimed to make himself recognized, walked slowly, erect, a giant who hovered over his countrymen. He recognized the adulation by a papal-like wave of the hand. Behind him a bevy of Free French officers followed at a respectful distance.

By the time General La Croix had finished his slow, calculated trip into the hall, the crowd was hanging over the balcony rails and standing on their seats craning for a glance. He walked the center aisle slowly, allowing himself to be stopped by stretching hands, allowing the cheers to swell to a crescendo that trembled the hall.

On stage his military and political advisers and a gathering of French and foreign celebrities surrounded him as he ascended the stairs.

Silence fell.

There were speeches.

And then, the moment. In ringing oratory he was introduced and as he advanced to the rostrum they were all on their feet. The ovation went on as the great Pierre La Croix stared down on them and at last his awesome stature brought the crowd to silence.

André Devereaux watched La Croix's performance with a mixture of admiration and fear, for grave disenchantment had already begun within him. Yes, he knew that Pierre La Croix was France now and that without him the chances for self-determination and a return to greatness would be small. But in the end, France was France. It was the end that concerned André. The food of "glory" filled every fiber of Pierre La Croix.

"Sons and daughters of Mother France," La Croix began, "we are gathered here to proclaim to the world the mission of Free France and the mission of Pierre La Croix. La Croix," he cried, "has accepted the authority of France in the cause of national honor. He left the defeated motherland and climbed from the morass of defeat to the mountaintop. La Croix shall not come down until our beloved France is free!"

They were mesmerized by his phenomenal aura of authority. La Croix had them like a man practicing mass hypnosis. There was a scattering, like André Devereaux, who chilled at the sound of unvarnished demagoguery. What rattled from Pierre La Croix's throat were the words of a man who would be dictator.

"France has been mortified . . . debased . . .

schemed against . . . gone unrecognized . . . double-crossed by the very ones who claim to be our allies. But! So long as Pierre La Croix lives. So long as Pierre La Croix has assumed the burden of fallen France . . . we shall not succumb. That is my mission."

In the streets outside and over the clandestine radios in metropolitan France, millions more heard his words. In the name of national redemption it appeared they all stood ready to surrender to this single, fearless man.

"Who is La Croix? He is the man who struggles in the name of France tirelessly. He has unified Frenchmen outside of the defeated motherland. Now hear this clearly. No power on this earth will plot the fate of France behind her back. No power on this earth will make decisions involving the future of France without the consent of France! France will continue to be the mistress of her own destiny!"

People were coming to their feet once more.

"Long live France!"

"Long live La Croix!"

He ignored the emotional tide sweeping over the hall, accepting the adoration as normally and rightfully his. He calmly sipped from the water glass, then continued.

"I say to our most powerful ally, I deplore your ambition to rule the world after this war. I deplore your bad manners and gall and your greedy desires to impose your will on the ancient civilizations of Europe. Before this war is over the blood of Frenchmen in the forefront of battle will have established France's sovereign rights."

His voice dropped from its pitch to a trembling whisper. . . . "I weep for the men who die for France. But my heart also bursts with pride. And

I shall never be silent to men who plot against my fallen motherland."

There were tears and screaming and stomping and weeping! La Croix held out his hands for silence like a Christ demanding the waters to part.

"I open my arms to Admiral de St. Amertin! Despite the sin of Vichy, I forgive! But there is only one France! Free France! Join us!"

"To France!" he cried over the hysteria in Albert Hall. "We will free her! We will punish the traitors! And so help me God, we will resume our great and undeniable march to destiny!"

"La Croix!"

"La Croix!"

"La Croix!"

André Devereaux was dazed as a tremor of terror passed through him.

(11)

AFTER HIS DEVASTATING Albert Hall speech, Pierre La Croix and his staff buttoned up in their London headquarters at Carlton Garden to let the Anglo-Americans absorb and remember what he had said.

Two days later the Soviet Ambassador to England, Igor Luvetka, called for an appointment. He arrived at Carlton Garden with "Villard," a high-ranking member of the French Communist Party who had been brought into England. In addition, "Villard" was one of the chiefs of the FFI, the underground French Forces of the Interior. The Communist wing of FFI was large and powerful and in the forefront of resistance in metropolitan France.

Pierre La Croix summoned a few of his intimate staff, which included Robert Proust and André Devereaux, as he held court for Ambassador Luvetka and "Villard."

Niceties were exchanged. There were a few perfunctory questions about conditions in France and how the Resistance fared. Then the heart of the matter was reached.

"I have come from France," the clever and flamboyant "Villard" said, "with certain instructions and resolutions of the Central Committee of the Communist Party. I am also authorized to speak for all branches of the FFI. The matter concerns your struggle with Admiral de St. Amertin and the Anglo-Americans."

La Croix received the statement without expression and nodded for "Villard" to continue.

"Both the Communist Party and the FFI are prepared to declare the acceptance of your authority."

The meaning of "Villard's" words was electrifying. In an instant, Pierre La Croix could be given a tremendous new range of power, tipping the political scales. With the FFI preparing his way, the physical takeover of France could be planned. His staff looked to him expectantly. La Croix made no show of being touched or moved but continued to play the cool hand.

"I am certain you have terms to be considered for such recognition," he said.

It was the Russian, Luvetka, who spoke now. "Comrade Thorez and a number of French Communists were forced to flee to the Soviet Union because of political persecution before the war. We want them fully pardoned and returned to France with honor."

"For this backing," "Villard" continued, "we also expect Communist representation on any

316

national committees and that all French Communists in the Free French Forces will be treated with equality."

"Is that all, gentlemen?"

"Those are the general conditions. The details, numbers, and cooperation with the FFI can be worked out later."

"I'll give the matter full consideration. You will be contacted in due course before your return to France."

And with that, Ambassador Luvetka and "Villard" were dismissed. The half-dozen officers present came to their feet wordlessly. André looked to Robert Proust, who obviously did not like what he had heard but equally obviously was going to say nothing about it. The other men present also avoided André's eyes.

"I am afraid I am going to have to have words on this matter," André said, daring the General's wrath. Everyone froze.

"Speak up," La Croix commanded.

"Recognition by the Communists may buy an immediate objective, but to invite them as partners would be sowing the seeds of future grief."

"You are my intelligence adviser, Devereaux, not my political adviser."

"Then speaking from the intelligence standpoint," he persisted, "the General knows of Communist attempts to infiltrate our fighting forces solely for their own gains. As for the FFI, the Communists in it are so powerful that if we do not disarm them immediately after France is liberated I believe they will attempt a takeover. Sir, it is one thing to cooperate with the FFI as long as we fight a common enemy. But to allow Communists in our councils with access to our secrets is dangerous. They are not strong enough to do it alone so they are using Free France."

"Then we will use each other," La Croix answered.

The room now was ready for an explosion, but André still did not budge. " 'Villard' did not come to us as a Frenchman but in the company of and under the instructions of the Soviet Union."

"That's enough! The Russians have recognized La Croix!"

The next day Pierre La Croix sealed the bargain with "Villard," who then returned to France.

La Croix took to his London radio and gave a long heartwarming speech in praise of the Soviet ally, its historical associations with France, and he reaffirmed the alliance of the present and spoke of future alliances.

Within twenty-four hours, over the clandestine FFI radio came the broadcast that the French Communist Party and the FFI had accepted the authority of Fighting France.

For André this came as a terrible blow. To him it meant that La Croix could confuse his own ambitions with legitimate national goals.

After the political and military union had been achieved with the former Vichy garrisons, La Croix and de St. Amertin were placed as equals on the national committee. But Pierre La Croix chewed the Admiral up alive and finally forced him to resign.

With Admiral de St. Amertin out of the way, La Croix set up an office of Commissioners of the Republic. Thirty-five men were named who were to seize civil power in all the provinces after the liberation. Six of these commissioners were

Communists. Communists were to take over the public health authority and the social security.

Pierre La Croix had succeeded in outmaneuvering all who stood against him.

As the Allied armies moved on Paris, he badgered the high command to order a Free French division to enter first despite the possibility of baiting a battle which could destroy the city.

Moving in behind his troops, Pierre La Croix captured lightning in a bottle by playing one of the most emotion-filled moments in human history to his own ends.

The liberation of Paris was to become a stage for Pierre La Croix. Using his unlimited arrogance and flushed with a holy sense of calling, La Croix masterfully applied the *coup de grâce* on the divergent political forces of the underground.

By disdaining to meet the resistance leaders and officials first, he let it be known he did not accept their authority.

Instead, Pierre La Croix marched at the head of swarms of hysterical countrymen up the Champs Élysées to the Arc de Triomphe.

The "Marseillaise" was sung between choking tears of a million Parisians and La Croix was unmistakably proclaimed by the people. With "their mandate" and flanked by the arms of his forces, he then declared himself the President of France.

(12)

NICOLE'S PARENTS WERE KILLED in an automobile accident in Spain before the war ended. When the estate of Victor Thibaud went into probate, it was revealed that most of his holdings were speculative, and his wealth on paper. When it was all liquidated, there was but a small inheritance for Nicole.

She returned with Michele to France to join André in Montrichard as he plunged into the business of preserving the family fortunes.

The backlash of war had created a listless French people who had lost much of their pride and ambition. They were lethargic and exhausted by wars and defeats. The land was neglected and the machinery obsolete.

A small but elite Devereaux winery and some scattered resources proved solid, but many of the other Devereaux holdings had become liabilities. André and his father consolidated and reorganized as best they could and were able to retain the magnificent family home and enough income to support it.

But after his adventures during the war, Montrichard seemed a dull affair. Nonetheless André, as the heir and dutiful son, was determined to adjust and carry on.

Nicole was particularly unsuited for country life and after a time became vocal about her discontent, which increased as she became pregnant again. Petty squabbles came with the morning sickness, and soon there were full-dress arguments.

As if by prearranged fortune, Jacques Granville made a hearty and welcome appearance over a weekend with his new, second wife, heiress of a banking fortune. Jacques' first marriage, which he claimed really didn't count, had been in Algeria during the war. It was barely decently consummated between Jacques' liaison missions for General La Croix, and was dissolved along with other peace treaties of the times.

"André, damn it, you're rotting here," Jacques said when the two comrades were alone.

"Of course, you're right," André answered. "Strange, all during the war I dreamed of nothing but returning to Montrichard and the quiet life. But what's the use of lying to myself? Everything here has grown small. And what is more, Nicole hates it."

"Yes, we all enlarge our memory of home. Then when we return, it is so small."

"Anyhow," André said, "things are stabilized here. If this American Marshall Plan works, perhaps France will snap out of its funk. I want to start building again."

"For what?"

"Generations of Devereaux have always built in Montrichard . . . for the coming generations of Devereaux, I suppose."

"I know we worship tradition," Jacques said, "but hasn't the day really come that a Devereaux leaves home?"

"It's just not done," André answered.

"André, opportunity is calling . . . begging. Pierre La Croix has placed himself above partisan politics. He waits in the wings for the people to summon and, believe me, the way France continues to flounder, he will receive his summons. La Croix will lead an awakening. Those of us smart enough to be on the inside now and stay with him will be calling the shots later."

"You know, Jacques, I've always had misgivings about the General's personal ambitions."

"Reality, André, reality. No one but La Croix can pull France together."

André grunted. "Unfortunately, you are right."

"Then deal yourself in now. You're an intelligence man. The Secret Service is in a shambles

321

and will have to be rebuilt from the ground up. For the right kind of loyalty now, you can be one of the top people in France when the General takes over. What is more important is Nicole's happiness. You have a family now, and in this case she's right. She belongs in Paris and so do you."

"Jacques, if I ever go, it will be because I want to return to the service. I will not declare for La Croix."

"Then come now and make your mind up about the other later."

The elder Devereaux accepted the departure of his son with good grace.

André entered the Secret Service earmarked as one of its bright young leaders. Working in the reorganization, he helped section after section return to professional respectability in a few short months.

But then, true to the tradition of the French civil services, the ranks became cluttered with mediocrities, bureaucrats, and opportunists.

André detested the constant tug and pull of internal service politics which weakened the efficiency of the entire organization. He remained aloof from the cliques. Even Jacques was unable to get him to declare for that most powerful group, the military men inside SDECE loyal to Pierre La Croix.

Instead, André continued to fight as a purist, speaking up no matter who was offended. He became a bone in many throats. Far too skilled and valuable to dismiss, he was punished by banishment to the Far East in an attempt to do something about France's failing fortunes in Vietnam.

And so another farewell to Nicole, who returned to Montrichard in her seventh month of pregnancy to await the birth of their child.

From his base in Saigon, André was on a constant merry-go-round between Calcutta, Hanoi, Singapore, and other centers of Oriental activity.

It was soon apparent that Nicole would never be able to join him in Saigon. That part of the world was a cesspool of privation after the war, and his mission such that she would have had to be alone most of the time.

The handwriting was on the wall. A situation disastrous to France was shaping up in Vietnam, and his work was a total frustration. There was just so long that André could go it by himself.

The woman's name was Yvette Chang. She was a Eurasian of French and Chinese parentage, the third daughter of a wealthy Saigon merchant. Her beauty was exceptional. Yvette Chang was the one to break André's loneliness and ease the baffling disappointments of his mission.

Yvette Chang was also to become an innocent instrument in causing André an overflow of guilt. Just after he had come to know her as his woman, he received the cable from his father:

I AM SORRY TO INFORM YOU OF NICOLE'S MIS-CARRIAGE, YOUR SON WAS BORN DEAD. NICOLE RECOVERING.

And then, as suddenly as he had been banished, he was recalled to Paris.

(13)

"ANDRÉ," NICOLE CRIED, "you did not kill your son. You've got to stop grieving."

"He might have lived if I had been here. Now

323

we will never be able to have another one." He had taken the same sense of guilt his father took at the death of his mother.

"We have Michele and we have each other. And, for the first time, there is a chance to settle down. Jacques told me this new post of yours in America has every chance to be permanent. André, please, I'm all right now."

"I'll make it up to you, Nicole. I swear I'll make it up to you."

"Shhhh . . . there's nothing to make up. Only to begin anew, to really begin for the first time."

"Nicole. I know you know about her. That girl in Saigon. You have to believe that she meant nothing to me. I was sick and lonely. It was hell out there. I was . . . just very lonely."

"You are never to mention it again, André . . . never."

André's new mission was to establish himself in Washington in the French Embassy and help form an intelligence arm of the new NATO organization. Before he left France, Jacques called him to say that Pierre La Croix requested his presence at his country home.

The General still awaited the summons of his countrymen. Even now, as he wrote his memoirs of the war, his eyesight was failing. André was greeted with unusual hospitality, and he and La Croix settled before the fire of birch logs in the library.

"I asked you here today, Devereaux, because you have been chosen for a key mission. By the time you have established your office in Washington, France will no doubt have called upon me for leadership. You have never been among my close associates, yet I respect you as a Frenchman. It is well that you know the philosophical direction France must take in her return to greatness."

The General offered André a cognac and a cigar. He then squinted into the fireplace and spoke as though to himself. "Our foreign policy will be kept flexible. If we tie ourselves up with a Western bloc, we will be swamped and dominated by the Americans. We must always mask our preparations with a thick veil of deception. We must deliberately mislead the very men we intend to use, as we do now by joining NATO. Then . . . many treaties must be made to play one side against the other. You see, Devereaux, a man may have friendships, but a nation never."

He stopped and stared at André a long instant. "I see by that well-recognized expression of pain that you disagree with La Croix."

"Yes, sir, I have thoughts."

"They are?"

"General, I know what the Americans did to us. I know your feelings. For the most part they are justified. But America is a very young country, new on the international chessboard and, in our case, has made a bad mistake. Nonetheless, America has also inherited a world in ashes and despair. The only stabilizing force in the world today, the only thing that prevents collapse and chaos, is the power and the good will of the United States. Has America not rectified her wrongs to France through an unprecedented generosity that has allowed us to get up off our backs? General, I do not believe a smaller country such as ours can ever go it alone again. That is the one lesson I learned in Vietnam. We need the collective security of NATO."

Pierre La Croix was particularly indulgent that day. He even managed a small smile for André as he came from his seat and leaned on the marble mantle. "Well spoken, but you are naïve, Devereaux. For the fact is that one day there has to be great war between the Soviet Union and America. My mission is to see that France is not caught in the middle and destroyed. We will not go down in flames because of an alliance we cannot control. France shall disengage from NATO at a time of our choosing, when we have rebuilt our economy and military strength and covered ourselves with a cloak of treaties."

"General," André continued, "if you will look honestly and deeply, perhaps you will admit your feeling about America is one of extreme jealousy and hatred. It can be used by men who understand this. I beg of you, sir, don't let those around you distort and twist your feelings into a conspiracy against the democracies."

André had struck a nerve. Pierre La Croix's face grew taut with anger. "La Croix is not used!" the General said. "La Croix uses!"

There was no handshake as André rose. The General remained rigid, indicating a terse dismissal. André nodded and made for the door, then turned at the last instant.

"France needs order," André said. "Only you can give us that. Return us to stability and honor . . . and then . . ."

"And then what?" the General demanded.

"And then, sir, heed the words of General De Gaulle when he spoke of Marshal Pétain: 'Old age is a shipwreck.' "

A military revolt of the late fifties returned Pierre La Croix to power. Jacques Granville was one of the masterminds behind the plot. As his reward the multimarried, charming spendthrift

326

was appointed a deputy to the Vice Administrator. This powerful position in the executive put him in charge of much of La Croix's political empire within the government.

Of the three comrades, Robert Proust fared the worst. He had neither the ability nor ambition to remain at the top. Also enlisting in the rebuilding of SDECE, he settled as Chief of FFF, which dealt in the distasteful business of kidnapings and special underhanded operations. His slimy deputy, Ferdinand Fauchet, wielded enormous power as a colleague of the underworld. Robert Proust detested his job, but was a helpless plodder.

From the very beginning Devereaux won the respect of the Americans. At first he was aloof, but as he worked intimately with them in the building of ININ they gained his friendship. In the end, he became a devoted servant of NATO, even in the face of Pierre La Croix's unfolding policies.

As the courier jet approached the European continent, a bleary-eyed Marshall McKittrick yawned a good morning to André and stumbled to the men's room to tidy up.

Within a matter of hours, André would be facing President La Croix with news of the Soviet missiles in Cuba, but, even more importantly, with the letter from the American President on the Topaz network.

Topaz, the terrible price for the early alliances with the French Communists and the Soviet Union. Topaz, born of La Croix's blind spot, his extreme abhorrence of the Americans. Perhaps now there would be an end to the evil of Colonel Gabriel Brune, when and if he was bared as the master traitor, Columbine.

The "FASTEN SEAT BELT—NO SMOKING" sign

flashed on as the plane made its approach to Orly Field. The landing gear clumped down and locked into place. The plane slowed and lowered itself.

André Devereaux felt as though he were strangling.

PART V.

Columbine

(PROLOGUE)

THE PRESIDENT OPENED his official day posing for photographers in the garden with the regional winners of the National Spelling Bee. He was in a jovial mood, signing an Aid to Education Bill before the youngsters and passing out the pens as a souvenir.

Lowenstein came up from his basement office and went over the first draft of the pending speech to the nation on Cuba. They discussed revisions and made numerous marginal notes.

"Look up Wilson and Roosevelt's declaration-of-war speeches to the Congress and work up a draft . . . in case we need it," the President said.

There was a meeting with the space-program people. The President was concerned that defense of the gargantuan budget could be a campaign issue in the off-presidential-year elections the next month. The NASA head advised him that a twenty-odd orbit attempt would be made the following May.

Before noon the President's Executive Council came to order for its first of two daily meetings. For the most part the President listened to the reports and views, jotted notes and asked a few

331

questions, but mainly stayed out of the discussions.

Stu Taylor, Chief of the Latin-American desk, was next on the agenda. He advised the President that the delegates of the Organization of American States would be meeting simultaneously with the announcement of the quarantine ultimatum to the nation. Taylor felt certain the President would get near unanimous support from the OAS.

Throughout the previous night two American units, one armored and one infantry, broke camp in their Southwest and Far West bases. Flatcars at the sidings were loaded with tanks, artillery, and mobile equipment. The trains moved east. Long convoys of trucks filled with combat soldiers moved into military airfields to be airlifted to the East Coast.

Before lunch, the President and his children took a dip in the White House pool.

After lunch the President received the Indian Ambassador and agreed to push a surplus wheat shipment.

General St. James reported that all key officers of the general staff had cancelled any trips and remained on standby for "special budget planning meetings" at the Pentagon.

At Hampton Roads, Virginia, a squadron of destroyers passed the lightship, then sped south. Sealed orders were opened. They moved into blockade position across the Caribbean sea lanes to Cuba. Their ammunition was made ready for instant use.

In the late afternoon, McKittrick, the Press Secretary, and General St. James expressed concern over press inquiries on the troop movements into Florida.

They agreed with the President they should stick to the story of special maneuvers.

More photographic evidence was shown the President. Unusually heavy tonnage was strung out on the Atlantic heading for Cuba from Soviet bloc ports.

At five-thirty, the President was briefed in advance of his meeting with Vasili Leonov, the Soviet Foreign Minister. Leonov was due at the White House at six for an hour of semiformal discussions.

Leonov was one of the few surviving old hands in Soviet politics and by far the most knowledgeable on American affairs, having served as both ambassador and leader of the United Nations delegation.

The President greeted the Russian, twenty years his senior, with warmth. When they were seated comfortably the two men were left alone and conversed in English.

A small number of matters were touched upon and then the talk got around to the Berlin situation. Vasili Leonov assured the President that no pressure would be applied to Berlin until after the American elections the following month.

Each of them expressed views on Berlin long known to the other. The Soviets continued to press for an open-city status and considered the presence of Allied troops as an advance NATO base.

The President repeated the American position that the number of troops was symbolic and he could never abandon Berlin to an East German take-over.

Leonov hoped that a permanent accommodation could be worked out "before the East German regime was recognized by the Soviet Union," and suggested the possibility of a meeting with Khrushchev.

Since the harassment of Helsinki, the President thought that might be a good idea, and looked forward to a return bout.

The atmosphere was relaxed. They got around to talking about Cuba.

"You see, Mr. President," Leonov said, "so long as you openly support these refugee commandos, Castro feels there is the threat of another invasion, à la Bay of Pigs . . . but perhaps with greater American backing. Under the circumstances, we have to look favorably on Castro's requests for defensive weapons."

"But the number of Soviet military and technicians seems out of proportion to the situation."

"Speaking with utter frankness, Mr. President, Castro fears an American invasion. These defensive weapons are mainly to quell his fears. After all, what can little Cuba do against the United States?"

"I have talked this matter over with Khrushchev in Helsinki and I have given my word there will be no American invasion of Cuba. If we are to meet next year, this matter must be brought up again."

Leonov went on at great length to assure the President that the Russian intentions in Cuba were totally peaceful.

The meeting ended and Leonov returned to the Soviet Embassy for talks with his own people before a social evening with the American Secretary of State.

His prime mission was to find out what the Americans were going to do about Cuba. He spoke at great length with the Ambassador and the Resident. Washington seemed calm and normal.

The American troop movements? A little saber rattling, no more. With his years of shrewdness and wisdom Leonov was unable to detect American alarm or desire to action. If they did know of the missiles one had to conclude they did not want a confrontation with the Soviet Union.

The Russian Foreign Minister was a bit surprised. He likened the Americans and their President to their tradition of tall silent cowboys who, in times of stress, spoke little and made few threats but shot for the heart. He had argued this with Khrushchev but Khrushchev insisted the President could be bullied. Perhaps the new generation of Americans were not of the old staunch stuff.

Before leaving for his reception he cabled the waiting Kremlin.

TALKS TO CONTINUE WITH AMERICAN PRESIDENT IN THREE DAYS BUT EVERYTHING SEEMS NORMAL. EITHER THE AMERICANS ARE UNAWARE OR INTEND TO TAKE PASSIVE POSITION. ADVISE YOU TO GO FULL SPEED WITH CUBAN OPERATION.

After the second meeting of the day with the Executive Council, the President went into a midnight conference with Lowenstein on his speech and to go over the political situation in the coming election and what could be pushed through in Congress on the legislative program.

His last caller of the day came to his bedroom at one-thirty in the morning. He gave approval of a press release to give reason to him to cancel a speech outside of Washington: "The President has a slight cold and one degree of temperature. In light of the blustery weather, the White

335

House physician insists the President remain in Washington and cancel his Cleveland address."

Vasili Leonov was somewhat surprised when he read in the late Sunday papers that the President and his family had attended Mass just hours after he cancelled a campaign speech. Well, after all, he concluded, the President is a religious man and Americans like to know he is in church. A show of courage. The poor young man had to show his courage somehow.

(1)

OCTOBER, 1962

THE ENGINES OF THE jet whined to a halt, and a pair of automobiles raced over the apron as the ramp was rolled to the door. One was the Cadillac of the American Ambassador, Wilbur Davis, the other car a French government Citroën.

As the door of the plane swung open, André smiled and waved to Jacques Granville at the bottom of the stairs. Jacques was still handsome and devilish-looking, taking every advantage of the new gray hairs at his temples.

Greetings were exchanged. They assembled and knotted at the bottom of the stairs as a special customs officer passed their luggage through and a control man fixed their passports.

"President La Croix will receive you in two hours," Jacques said.

"Good. I need the time to brief the Ambassador."

"Then we'll meet at the Élysée Palace at ten."

The cars sped off toward Paris.

"What happy tidings do you bring?" Jacques asked.

"The Americans have full proof of Soviet offensive missiles in Cuba. They're going to announce a blockade."

"Oh, my Lord. Are they asking NATO involvement?"

"No, not yet."

"La Croix has a phobia about being dragged into some mess that isn't our business."

"Well, the Americans might have the same to say about the last two world wars . . . and being dragged in at Suez."

"André, as my oldest and dearest friend, don't go off on a tangent before La Croix. He's worse than ever on the matter."

"I never go off on pro-American tangents . . . unless it's in the interest of France."

A new dazzling white Paris burst before them. André mentioned that Paris was getting to look like Algiers and Casablanca. President La Croix had a mania for cleaning the centuries of dirt and grime from the buildings of Paris. The Parisians did not share this desire for whiteness but nonetheless found themselves sand-blasting and steaming under the threat of heavy fines. As usual, the President had his way.

They crossed to the Left Bank, stopping at André's apartment at 176 Rue de Rennes, where the ancient hydraulic elevator hoisted them with nauseating slowness.

The chauffeur set down André's bags and was ordered to wait downstairs.

There was an envelope in clear view.

PAPA!
Jacques Granville told me you were coming! He says it will be impossible to have any time alone for the first several days. There's a school holiday so I'm remaining in Montrichard with Mother.

Call me the instant you have a free moment and
I'll come right up to Paris.

François is coming back early next week. I'm
dying for you to meet him. Papa, I'm so glad you're
here. We have so much to talk over.

I love you, I love you.

MICHELE

"Have you met this young man?"

"François Picard? Yes, Michele dragged him
over for old Uncle Jacques' approval."

"Did he get it?"

"Bright enough. Works for Télévision Nationale, and I believe he does some sort of column
in one of the weeklies, but . . . well, no family
position to speak of, no money."

"Well, anything is better than Tucker Brown."

"Who?"

"Michele's last idiot."

André lifted his suitcase on the bed and unsnapped it. He was suddenly dead tired and filled
with a feeling of void.

"What's the matter, André?"

"I was hoping somehow . . . nothing."

"Nicole?"

"Yes."

"She was in Paris awhile, then just disappeared
to Montrichard, for some reason."

(2)

THE CARS BEARING the Americans and Granville
and Devereaux reached the Élysée Palace at almost the same instant. Imposing Republican
guards in uniforms of the Napoleonic era opened
the great iron-grille gates and they were passed
in. They drove on to the stone courtyard of the
edifice of splendor, a final extravagance of Louis

339

XV, purchased as a home for his mistress, Madame de Pompadour.

The President's ushers, wearing the chain of office, took them quickly past rooms filled with Louis XV objects, over the Aubusson rugs and Gobelin tapestries that rose clear to the thirty-foot ceilings.

The party was assembling in the outer office. André looked across the room to Colonel Gabriel Brune. A tall, thin man with gray eyes. André had always believed until now that the eyes veiled a dull bureaucrat. He walked to Brune and they shook hands coldly.

"How was the trip, Devereaux?"

"Fine."

After a long wordless stare, André turned and shook hands with a number of his friends. President La Croix's personal Chief of Staff came out and noted all were present, including a representative from the Sûreté whom André had sent for, then entered the inner office and returned in a moment. "The President is ready," he said.

Pierre La Croix rose majestically behind his massive gold ornate table, greeting the Americans with the thinnest possible warmth. To André Devereaux, whom he had not seen in over a year, there was a slight nod of the head.

Military and intelligence aides, the Director of the Presidential Executive, and Granville arranged themselves before him.

"Your President," La Croix said, "does me honor to send such a distinguished personage. I am certain the occasion is appropriate. But let's be clear on one point. Are you here to consult or inform?"

"To inform," Ambassador Davis answered.

340

"Then you are to be aware that La Croix and France favor making their own decisions."

"We are aware."

"You may proceed."

"We have complete evidence of the introduction of Soviet intermediate-range missiles in Cuba, and the President is going to announce a quarantine against further Soviet weapons," the Ambassador said.

"A blockade at sea?"

"A quarantine. Peaceful cargo will not be stopped."

Marshall McKittrick, speaking Yankee-accented French, gave a full briefing, explaining the photographs which he produced, the meanings of the other intelligence reports and the cause for the decision. Playing up to the President's vanity, McKittrick asked him to identify clusters of Russian fighter planes and missile towers, which he did, holding a magnifying glass over the photos.

"Of course," La Croix said, "it was the French Secret Service that identified these for you."

"The contribution of Monsieur Devereaux has been enormous," McKittrick agreed.

La Croix set the magnifying glass down, folded his hands and thought. Outside, through the four tall windows overlooking the garden they could see the Republican guards in their white leggings cross in patrol.

"Why do you believe the Soviets did this?" he asked.

"On the gamble they could get away with it," McKittrick answered. "They won't," he added.

Looking at the President, André remembered his earlier thoughts on a Russian-American confrontation. Had it come?

"Certainly a great power such as the United

341

States would not act without sufficient evidence," La Croix said. "Your President is using his national prerogative. You may tell him that France understands his position. Otherwise, until a request for committment is made by you, none will be made by us."

La Croix shoved the photographs and documents in the direction of Colonel Brune. "I want these studied and evaluated. Devereaux will remain in Paris to advise and assist. Granville, summon a Cabinet meeting for one hour from now. You gentlemen will attend, and until then no mention of this crisis will be made." He turned to the Americans. "Advice will be forthcoming on this matter," he said.

"The Ambassador will be at your service," McKittrick said. "I have to leave for London immediately to inform the Prime Minister."

"The British have not been informed?"

"Only the Ambassador in Washington."

La Croix digested this information with obvious skepticism, for he always looked for and suspected an Anglo-American plot.

"There is another matter," McKittrick said. "The President asked me to deliver this letter to you."

La Croix zipped open the envelope and adjusted his thick glasses. He finished the letter and folded it. "Have a safe journey to London," he said.

There was a shuffling of chairs as everyone came to his feet.

"Colonel Brune, you and Devereaux remain."

When the room was cleared, La Croix handed the letter to Colonel Brune. André watched his dull gray eyes for a telltale sign. The paper rattled a trifle in Brune's nervous hands. He looked up queerly from Devereaux to La Croix.

"Well?"

"I have no comment on this matter until I am further acquainted with the facts," Brune answered.

"How long have you known of this Topaz business, Devereaux?"

"It has been revealed just recently."

"Why weren't we informed at once?"

"I used my prerogative in that I believed it in the best interest not to sound a premature alarm."

"What is the source?"

"A Soviet defector named Boris Kuznetov. A very high-ranking officer in KGB in charge of the Anti-NATO Division."

"There is no Anti-NATO Division," Brune blurted.

"There is," André said. "The interrogation of this man has gone on for weeks. But only in the last several days did he tell us something of value."

"You've seen him, you talked to him?"

"Yes."

"What is your opinion?"

"I'll stake my professional reputation that Kuznetov is authentic and accurate, and that the Soviet Union has made the greatest intelligence coup of all time."

"You're always seeing Communists, Devereaux," the President said. "If this is true . . . if this is true . . . Brune, you will dispatch a team of investigators to Washington immediately. And I want the report personally," he emphasized by knocking his fist on the table.

"Yes, Monsieur le Président."

"I suggest," André said quickly, "that someone from the Sûreté go also."

"It's a matter for the SDECE alone," Colonel Brune answered quickly.

"I can vouch for the fact that much of the revelation concerns internal security," André retorted.

Brune shot a quick angry glance at André who had tricked him by having a member of the detested rival service present in order to cover himself.

"Devereaux's suggestion is in order," said La Croix. "Contact the Department for Internal Protection. Have Léon Roux send one of his people."

"Yes, Monsieur le Président," Brune said harshly.

An SDECE team flew out that night for Washington. Among their number was a stranger, Inspector Marcel Steinberger of Internal Protection of the Sûreté.

(3)

ANDRÉ AND MICHELE walked along the Boulevard St.-Germain toward the Café de Flore.

"I do hope you like François," Michele said.

"I'm certain to dislike him. It's a father's prerogative."

"I've never known a man like him."

"In all your twenty years."

"He's handsome and high-minded . . ."

"Oh, Lord, Michele, spare me."

The terrace of the Café de Flore held its usual complement of leftist journalists and students and crackpots tucked around marble-topped tables vociferously denouncing the world in general, America in particular.

André was waylaid greeting a half-dozen old

friends as Michele sought out her young man. Then he spotted Ferdinand Fauchet, the feared deputy of FFF. He was beefy and wore a bright scar over one eye, planted there by the knife of a pimp. Fauchet made for Devereaux.

"I heard you've been in Paris on the missile business," he said, raspy-voiced.

"Hello, Fauchet. Since when have you quit working in the sewers?"

Fauchet sucked in a breath and laughed and picked between his teeth with the nail of his little finger. "I have no affection for you, as you know, Devereaux. You have none for me. But as a colleague with many years in the service I'd like to give you some advice."

"Well?"

"Warn your daughter about the company she keeps. He's getting very noisy with his dirty journalism."

Fauchet passed on. André was stung by the words. He had read Picard in *Moniteur* with admiration. It was the kind of battle from which he never knew how to back away, but as for Michele . . .

She waved to him. André walked toward them, and after an introduction they took a booth inside and ordered Pernod. The drink offended André's Americanized taste, but the pleasures of bourbon had not yet reached the Left Bank of Paris.

Michele pressed François's hand. Both of them had a sad desperation about them. Lord, André thought, why do young lovers dote on misery? How nice to be an aging lover and when you walk into the room meet someone who is happy and loves in an uncomplicated way. Young people demand tragedy. He had had that with Nicole. Love for the young is a waste and a mess.

345

As Michele had promised, the boy was extremely intelligent, quite good-looking and enormously idealistic.

"I am a news editor and analyst on the First Channel."

"Yes, Michele told me."

"Monsieur Devereaux, I want to say candidly that I love your daughter very much."

"Yes, she informed me of that, too. Well, what do you intend to do about it?"

Michele and François looked at one another like pained puppies. "We will marry as soon as we can."

"Well, Picard, Michele has no doubt told you she and I are very close."

"She has."

"Then may I speak candidly?"

"Certainly."

"The bloom goes off the rose once you are stuffed together in one of Paris's magnificent one-room, fourth-floor, walk-up flats."

"Papa . . ."

"Michele is spoiled and lazy. She has no idea of how to manage money. So you ask her to wash your socks and underwear, prepare meals, keep house, be your lover, and also continue her studies."

"Papa, please . . ."

"And you, young man. What happens when your bachelor quarters are suddenly invaded by a permanent female hanging stockings, brassieres, and panties over the shower rail? A man changes with the burden of a wife. And then in a short time you will both see pimples on each other's backsides that you simply refuse to see now."

François shrugged. "Well, darling, you did tell

346

me he was this way. Are you telling me, Monsieur Devereaux, not to marry?"

"Of course not. Michele is happy studying at the Sorbonne. She has a lovely home and a good allowance. I suggest the two of you take an apartment together, not yours or hers but a neutral one belonging to both of you. Try it for six months, and if you still feel as you do now, then marry. Otherwise, part friends and no one is hurt."

"I knew you would suggest something like this," Michele said.

"Well, you're sleeping together now, aren't you?"

Their abashed silence was enough.

"And for God's sake, don't get pregnant," André said.

(4)

ROBERT PROUST'S APARTMENT on the Rue Poussin showed that it was the home of a moderately well-to-do bureaucrat. Proust had not fared so well personally. He was balding, dull, and tired.

André peered out of the window of Robert's study to the Bois de Boulogne, then let the drapes fall together and turned back to the room.

"I've been followed ever since I've returned to Paris. Is this the work of your office, Robert?"

Robert sighed. "Well, you know I haven't had a chance to see you once since you have been back. Otherwise, I would have told you."

"Who told you to put a tail on me?"

Robert balked. "The orders came from Colonel Brune personally."

"I saw Ferdinand Fauchet tonight."

"What the hell, André! Do you think I luxuriate

347

running this dirty division? My life has become ridden with people like Fauchet. Do you think I like it?"

"What's it all about? What did Colonel Brune say?"

"They say, all over the service, that you're in too thick with the Americans. That maybe . . ."

"Maybe I'm working for them?"

"Yes," Robert whispered. "Look, André, everything is crazy. Jacques gave me orders he claimed came from La Croix himself to put a tail on Colonel Brune. This Topaz business has the President in an absolute rage. If it turns out that one of the heads of the French Secret Service is a Soviet agent, we have the worst scandal on our hands since the war. Is it all true?"

"It's true."

"I know what's going to happen. Orders will come for liquidations. Ferdinand Fauchet will be a busy man. Christ, I hate this job," he whimpered, "but what can I do with all these years in the service? What kind of pension will I get? And if I leave on bad terms with La Croix, he will see to it that any decent job in France is closed to me."

There was no use in browbeating Robert Proust. He had had to be carried from the beginning. Now he wallowed in self-pity, terrified of the issues flaming around him.

"What about this boy Michele is going around with, this François Picard?"

Robert slipped into his deep chair and rubbed his eyes wearily. "I'd rather not . . ."

"Michele intends to marry him."

"There's a group of journalists, television writers, reporters, who are violently anti-La Croix.

348

They are getting too bold. We have orders from someone in the government to break them up."

"Break them up? My God, Robert, I know Pierre La Croix has established a personal regime in France, but destroying political opposition by the use of the Secret Service? Robert, we are still a democracy."

Robert Proust lifted his face and shook his head slowly. "No, André. Democracy in France is dead."

(5)

"DEMOCRACY IN FRANCE is dead," François Picard said heatedly. He paced before André, his black hair tumbling down his forehead, his speech filled with animation.

Michele was tucked up on the sofa watching with obvious admiration.

"In the past several months, Monsieur Devereaux, a half-dozen of my colleagues have been badly beaten. Two have totally disappeared. We know it's the work of Ferdinand Fauchet and your dear friend, Robert Proust."

"Well, what do you intend to do, François?"

"Keep on fighting. Michele has told me about you, how you crawled to Spain in order to fight for France. I love France the same way."

"I'm not telling you not to fight, but use your mind as well as your heart. There is a time and a place to make your move properly. You're far too headstrong. You're literally begging for a reprisal, and you'll get it, believe me."

"I've tried the soft way. It doesn't work. A year ago I was appointed to write the political reports on Channel One. But everything I wrote was censored and rewritten. The whole French Press

349

Agency is under orders to slant all news against the Americans. If the Americans put an astronaut in orbit, we are either to pass it by in a line or two or to make jokes about the difficulties. On the other hand, every achievement of the Soviet Union is to be inflated. Monsieur Devereaux, the Press Agency is crawling with Communists. They've got themselves in key spots. A few newspapers and magazines oppose La Croix, but Frenchmen do not read, they watch television. And the ambitious men around him are using his power to control the only television network. That's not all; they are infiltrating the police, which since the war have been totally under the Ministry of the Interior. So what are we to do? Wait for him to die?"

"And I suppose you're ready to die for your words," André said.

"Yes."

"You, Michele. Is that what you want? A dead husband?"

"I don't question François. He has to do his job as he sees it. I will never be like Mother. . . ."

André stared at her strangely.

"What is it, Papa?"

"All of a sudden, you are trying to be a woman."

(6)

THE AUTOMOBILE ROLLED out of SDECE headquarters down Avenue Gambetta and skidded slightly as it turned the rain slick street onto the Avenue de la République in a night race for the Élysée Palace. Charles Rochefort, a chief of the Secret Services, drove. Colonel Gabriel Brune at his side turned on the defroster to clear the windshield of their breath.

Once through the gates and in the Palace they doffed their rainwear and were taken to the personal apartment of President Pierre La Croix.

The President worked over his desk, framed in light from the fireplace.

Charles Rochefort was a run-of-the-mill political appointee, a figurehead under the domination of Colonel Brune. He spoke first to intone the necessary formalities. "We appreciate the appointment at this hour, Monsieur le Président, and regret the inconvenience to you, but this information on the Cuban missile situation should be brought to your immediate attention."

La Croix waved them to be seated opposite him, with the desk in between. Gabriel Brune opened his attaché case and withdrew a report marked "SECRET."

"Monsieur le Président," Brune said with a note of urgency in his voice, "we have uncovered a fantastic plot. It is our opinion that the entire missile crisis was a gigantic hoax dreamed up between the United States and the Soviet Union."

La Croix accepted the news with a deadpan expression as Colonel Brune's long fingers shuffled through the report to find a particular page. "After a thorough scrutiny, our scientific research committee is of the firm belief that from a technical aspect it was impossible to transport missiles of this nature." His finger ran down the page, then stopped. "For example, the electronic systems are so delicate they could not possibly have absorbed the shocks and vibrations of a long sea voyage. Further, here . . . hmmm . . . yes, the humidity and heat of Cuba would render the mechanism inoperable. There is much more, all conclusive scientific evidence to support this."

The slitted eyes of La Croix refused to give

indication of the quick mind working behind them. "What about the actual identification?" he asked.

"Photographs taken by U-2 airplanes are from extremely high altitudes. Our experts conclude these photographs are highly questionable. They may have been pictures of American sites, or clever fakes, or the old surface-to-air towers."

"But the missiles were also identified by personal observers."

"No one has actually seen one of these missiles, Monsieur le Président. What was seen were tire tracks, towers, trailers, tail fins. In every event the actual tube was covered by canvas. Even when the American planes photographed them they only showed canvas-covered tubes lashed to the decks of the ships. No one ever boarded to inspect. In our opinion, they could have been papier-mâché or some other material. The reason they were able to make such deep tire tracks, in our opinion, is that the undercarriages of the trailers were weighted."

"Would this not imply that Devereaux was consorting with the Americans?"

"It is our belief," Rochefort said, "that he was tricked, duped, and used."

La Croix's fingers twitched slightly, and for the first time he showed emotion with a slight reddening of his cheeks. "What is your theory on Devereaux?" he demanded.

"In the beginning," Brune said, "the Americans did not seek out Devereaux, although they relied on him heavily for information out of Cuba. Instead, they concocted and executed a brilliant plan with Devereaux as the foil. Why did the Cuban turncoat in the United Nations delegation in New York seek out the French? Because

352

he was on the American payroll and his orders were to plant fake papers among authentic ones and let the French steal them. Devereaux's own deputy in New York, Gustave Prévost, was suspicious of just this sort of thing and warned that we were being set up. But, nevertheless, Devereaux planned and executed an operation to steal copies of the Parra papers from the hotel in New York. Fakes had been planted among the real documents. The fakes aroused Devereaux's suspicions of missiles. He then took information to the Americans that the Americans had planted in the first place.

"Now Devereaux was obliged by his own doing to go down to Cuba, even though Ambassador D'Arcy objected. He saw what the Russians and Americans wanted him to see, no more, no less. No one, Monsieur le Président, can answer why the missiles were brought through Havana. Devereaux tells us it was a miscalculation on the width of the tunnel under the harbor. We say if they wanted secrecy they would have unloaded in a southern port. The so-called missiles were brought through Havana because they wished for Devereaux to discover them.

"Further," Brune argued, "the Russians knew why Devereaux was in Cuba. He was French Intelligence, sympathetic to the Americans as a matter of record. Is it believable they would have allowed him to leave Cuba with such information unless they planned for him to carry it out?

"Now, with Devereaux completely fooled, the Americans cleverly request him to come to France to authenticate this to us. As a trusted and reliable official, his word would carry enormous weight."

"I am certain that Devereaux does not endorse this report," La Croix said.

"Naturally not. No official of his caliber would ever admit to such a blunder. Nevertheless, not making accusations, we have been very skeptical about intelligence on Cuba for a long time."

"We may have been set up for months." Rochefort added.

"And you conclude there were never any offensive missiles in Cuba?"

"That is correct, Monsieur le Président."

"Thank you, gentlemen, good night," the President said tersely.

They stood, bowed slightly and backed to the door.

"By the way," La Croix called. "What further information do you have on the Topaz letter?"

"Our investigators are in Washington," Brune answered, "but I begin to suspect it may all be part of the same Soviet-American plot."

When they closed the door, Pierre La Croix put on his glasses and struggled through the report. He was not to be taken in so quickly. There was animosity between Brune and Devereaux. Perhaps Brune was trying to discredit Devereaux early in the game to blunt the scandal on Topaz. The President knew Devereaux would not be so easily fooled. He was a maverick, but he was a Frenchman.

Yet Devereaux could have been a victim to a master conspiracy. Brune's logic was sound. Furthermore, it smelled of the kind of shady American dealings France had suspected since World War II.

After the missile crisis simmered down, Washington and Moscow would establish a hot line. This direct, unusual communication would certainly be interpreted as an understanding between the Soviets and Americans about their respective spheres of domination, relegating France to secondary status.

Coincidentally with the missile crisis, both countries could increase their military expenditures. They would then be in a position to increase their domination over their allies.

By deliberately involving a French Intelligence officer of Devereaux's stature they could force France to follow American policy without protest or consultation.

And could he be sure the British were not plotting with the Americans to see France diminished?

France had been shut out of German-American talks. And now France would be totally bypassed by the Moscow-Washington hot line.

As a result of the "missile crisis," the Americans could assert an even fuller domination of NATO.

So the giant powers had played out a charade to thwart France of her true destiny as the leader of Europe.

But even if the SDECE report was wrong, the end result was the same. America would emerge more powerful than ever. In the mind of Pierre La Croix, it only furthered his obsession to break Anglo-American control of Europe.

(7)

COLONEL BRUNE PACED his high-ceilinged office in the converted barracks building on Boulevard Mortier that housed the SDECE. He stopped for a moment at the window and glared down on the courtyard, then returned to his desk.

Brune snatched up the weekly newspaper, *Moniteur*. It was filled with the usual anti-La

Croix tripe. But the column by François Picard was encircled in red.

> There is a strange smell on Boulevard Mortier. Rumors which will be confirmed soon reek of a scandal brewing inside the SDECE. It has long been known that the French Secret Service is rotted from within. So bad are its leaks that few of France's allies dare to share secrets with her anymore. But then, our President does not want allies. . . .

Brune flung the paper down angrily. Obviously the information had come to Picard from Devereaux in a play to discredit him. Since the Topaz letter from the American President he, Brune, a chief of the service, had been under watch like a common spy.

He sat down, looked at the column once more, then lifted his interoffice phone. "Send Ferdinand Fauchet to me right away," he said.

François and Michele slept tight in each other's arms. The phone rang. François yawned to wakefulness and groped for the instrument. "Hello," he said sleepily.

"Hello. I am calling for Monsieur Devereaux. He was working late and just left headquarters and said Michele might be with you."

"She's here. Do you wish to speak to her?"

"No. It is not necessary. Monsieur Devereaux asked me to phone and tell her to come home immediately."

"Is anything wrong?"

"He didn't say, but he did seem rather urgent."

"Yes, I'll have her come home."

Michele insisted François stay where he was,

that it was not necessary for him to drive her to the apartment. He gave in, and when they kissed good-bye it was past midnight.

Ferdinand Fauchet, parked across the street, watched her leave the building, get in Picard's car, and drive off. When she was out of sight, Fauchet nodded to four waiting thugs. They entered Picard's building.

François was about to turn off the light when the knock came at the door. He padded over to it unsuspectingly, certain that Michele had forgotten the car keys.

He opened the door. Two blows from black-jacks hit him at once in the mouth and on the temple.

(8)

VASILI LEONOV TIED on his falling pajama pants and examined himself in the bathroom mirror. He had a slight hangover from the night of partying. Americans were good sports. Leonov had enjoyed the give and take of ideological debate, the off-record inside jokes, and the lack of formality. Yes, Americans were extremely pleasant fellows.

Leonov opened the medicine cabinet and fished about for those wonderful American products. First a Bromo. He grimaced as he downed the fizzy stuff, smacked his lips together and reached for the aerosol spray can and lathered his face. A new stainless steel blade went into the razor. He scraped.

A knock on the door.

"Enter!"

Leonov's male secretary stopped opposite the toilet bowl and cleared his throat.

"Well?"

"Comrade Leonov, I have just received a telephone call from the White House. The President has cancelled his meeting with you today."

"Eh? What's this all about?"

"It has just been announced that he is going to speak on television today."

In the eternal gloom of the Soviet Embassy, Leonov, the Soviet Ambassador and Resident and a half-dozen of the top staff assembled before the television and watched with heart-pounding anticipation.

In the study of the American President, one of his female secretaries swiped at his unruly hair with a brush and comb an instant before the cameras focused.

"Ladies and gentlemen, the President of the United States."

"Good evening, my fellow citizens. The government, as promised, has maintained the closest surveillance of the Soviet military buildup on the island of Cuba. Within the past week, unmistakable evidence has established the fact that a series of offensive missile sites is now in preparation on that imprisoned island. The purpose of these bases can be none other than to provide a nuclear strike capability against the Western Hemisphere. . . .

". . . capable of striking Washington, D.C., the Panama Canal, Cape Canaveral, Mexico City. . . .

"Additional sites, not yet completed, appear to be designed for intermediate-range ballistic missiles. . . .

". . . and thus capable of striking most of the major cities in the Western Hemisphere.

". . . In addition, jet bombers, capable of

carrying nuclear weapons, are now being uncrated and assembled in Cuba, while the necessary air bases are being prepared. . . ."

Vasili Leonov grabbed the arms of his chair to hide his tremor. He dared not look right or left at his stunned and frightened colleagues. The American President now spoke with powerful righteousness, without threat. Yes, he was the silent cowboy who had been pushed too far and he was shooting for the heart. He continued on to denounce the Soviet Union's deliberate lies in the Cuban deception and he flung the gauntlet down by saying that American courage and commitments should never be doubted by friend or foe.

"All ships of any kind bound for Cuba from whatever nation or port will, if found to contain cargoes of offensive weapons, be turned back. . . .

". . . We are not at this time, however, denying the necessities of life as the Soviets attempted to do in their Berlin blockade of 1948.

". . . I call on Chairman Khrushchev to halt and eliminate this clandestine, reckless, and provocative threat to world peace. . . . I call upon him further to abandon this course of world domination. . . . He has an opportunity now to move the world back from the abyss of destruction. . . ."

In the Caribbean some two hundred warships of the United States Navy straddled the sea routes to Cuba as their patrol planes swept in search.

From underground bastions, maximum alerts were flashed to the far-flung American military bases.

B-47s with nuclear bombs dispersed from military airfields to civil airports to evade destruction in the event of a Soviet missile attack.

Fifteen dozen intercontinental ballistic missiles, enough to obliterate the cities and factories and military bases of the Soviet Union, were readied to fire from their silos.

Strategic Air Command put their B-52 bombers into an airborne alert. While part of them circled and waited for the order to strike, those on the ground were ready to take to the air and head for Soviet targets within fifteen minutes.

Divisions of Army and Marines were combat-ready and poised to swarm into Cuba by land, by air, and by sea.

Other fighter-bombers with close to a hundred percent destructive capability were straining to make a beeline to wipe out the Cuban missile sites.

This, the quickest, quietest, and most brilliant roundup of military power, had been accomplished without major detection. It was now in place and coiled to back up the words of the young man who now spoke to a startled world.

In the Soviet Embassy, they sat shaken and unmoving after the President had left the air. Even Vasili Leonov's years of studied poise abandoned him.

He knew he had made the ancient blunder. The bully's bluff had been called. Not only had the myth of the President's lack of courage been exploded but he had made a shrewd decision. He had taken his own strongest point, his navy, and pitted it against the Soviet Union's weakest point, their navy. He had skillfully chosen a battlefield to give him every advantage . . . a meeting on the high seas.

The Organization of American States unanimously and swiftly backed the American position.

In the United Nations, the outraged American Representative called the Soviet Union to task and demanded the dismantling of the Cuban bases.

And on the high seas, ships of the Soviet Union with their death cargoes inched toward Cuba for the confrontation with the United States Navy. And while the American people arose in anger, they and the entire human race wondered if they were living the last moments of its final folly.

(9)

ANDRÉ PARKED HIS car several blocks from the Place de la Madeleine and continued on foot in order to shake his followers. They were a clumsy pair and he was able to lose them quickly.

He entered the red velvet world of Lucas Carton's restaurant. Alex and a half-dozen members of the staff greeted him with great warmth for this was the restaurant of generations of Devereaux.

"How is your father?" Alex asked.

"I haven't had the opportunity to get to Montrichard this trip, but he's faring quite well."

"Please tell him I asked for him."

"Thank you."

Alex personally escorted André to one of the private dining salons on the second floor. In a moment a bottle of bourbon was produced and Alex went through the ritual of hand-crushing the ice with a small hammer for André's Manhattan while André studied the menu. He decided on Sole à la Carton, a specialty of the house.

"Madame Devereaux has arrived."

"Please show her up."

There was no embrace or touch or scarcely a

361

word as she was seated. She asked for a drink and lit up nervously. After the drink arrived they were closed in, and André asked that they not be disturbed until he rang for further service.

Nicole had that facility to always rise to a given situation with an appearance of loveliness. He commented on how beautiful she looked.

"Thank you."

"I haven't been able to answer your calls," André said, "for the usual reasons. I run out of hours in a day."

"I know you must be very busy during this crisis."

"Yes, Nicole. . . . I asked you to come to Paris because of Michele. She's taken the disappearance of François Picard extremely hard."

"Is there no word?"

"No. I can't even get information from Robert."

"What do you think?"

"I think he'll never return and we'll probably never learn what really happened to him."

"Oh Lord. . . ."

"I'm afraid it's what you call a clean job. They intended to make an example of him. Michele is going to have to go through a long and difficult period of adjustment. She'd better start now. Her place is with you. You can give her the time and the comfort she needs."

"She hasn't even answered my phone calls, André."

"Don't take that personally. She's pent it all up inside. Just before I came I talked to her, told her you were coming to take her to Montrichard. She finally opened up. She's crying it out now . . . and she said . . . she wants her mother very much."

"Poor baby. . . . André, let's go. . . ."

"There are some things in the world that are unforgivable," he said, "and one of them is to walk out on a plate of Sole à la Carton. Alex would be offended beyond repair. Seriously, let her have it out alone."

Nicole nodded that she understood. An awkward silence descended. André pressed the service bell. Nothing was said until the soup was tasted and complimented upon.

"What about us?" Nicole asked shakily.

"I don't think we should have a confrontation now. It's quite enough with the Russians and Americans about to meet in the Atlantic."

"I've had a long time to think things over," she said.

"Yes . . . I suppose there's a lot to say."

"When I first realized what kind of life I had condemned myself to I wanted to come back regardless of the past rights or wrongs. I was going to hang on to you at any price . . . under the guise of calling it love . . . under the excuse that you must accept a person you love with all her faults.

"When we married," she said, "we brought into the marriage the things which made us fall in love. We also brought in our childhood, our demons, our weaknesses. The things that can kill any marriage if they are allowed to flourish. A woman like me demands from her husband certain rights, certain recognitions, certain equalities. When a woman wins these . . . she's not a woman anymore.

"The man rarely has the woman he needs . . . but the one he gets. There are some who can't do it for their man. A rare few who can and will. But most . . . and these are the worst . . . are those who won't. We spend our energy in erect-

363

ing defenses . . . not daring to look into ourselves . . . but only to justify our ineptness.

"A marriage asks of a woman . . . skill, and just plain damned hard work. And we're too stupid and too lazy so we hide behind our defensive barriers and viciously repel what we believe to be attacks.

"If I had known I might have coped with the demon you brought into the marriage, your confusion over your mother. You tried to find mother's love from me . . . the love she denied you by death. And at the same time you tried to kill her through me.

"In my final act of desperation I tried to act out the fantasy that if I behaved like her, like two women, I would have a chance with you. I made myself believe it was something you always wanted me to do."

André's face became drawn. He knew that in her dark groping she had dared to open locked doors . . . her own . . . and his.

"From the beginning, André, you closed me out of a part of your life. You threw up a wall and said, 'I never forgave my mother for dying and leaving me alone, so I can never commit myself to any woman fully. Come close, but not too close. If you get too close, I'll reject you.' I lived in fear that you would find in some other woman what I was unable to provide you with. Much of what you call my possessiveness is just plain fear. And if I could not help you when you needed me, perhaps it was because you really didn't want that help. You were afraid of needing me too much and I might let you down . . . as your mother did."

"So . . . none of us is clean, right?" he asked.

"No, André, none of us is clean. I can't buy

back the mistakes . . . but by God, I'm going to know what I've done and I'm going to make a life, somehow or other. . . ."

Nicole sat on the edge of Michele's bed in a scene once played so very long ago and believed by both of them to be forgotten.

"Oh, Mamma . . . Mamma!"

"Shhh . . . I'm here now."

"I'm so ashamed I didn't talk to you when you called."

"You don't have to explain a thing, Michele," she said tucking the blankets firmly about her daughter and stroking her hair.

"Papa is trying to hide it from me . . . but I know. I'm never going to see François again."

"It's in God's hands now, darling. Michele . . ."

"What, Mamma?"

"In a strange sort of way, you are very lucky."

"I don't understand."

"Twenty years ago, if I had started giving your father what you gave to François from the beginning I wouldn't be alone in the darkness now."

"But you've given. . . ."

"Not really. Like most women I went into it asking, 'What's in it for me? What kind of life is he going to make for me?' I never really asked of myself, 'What can I do for him?'

"And so, we cook our meals because a meal has to be cooked. But we don't go into the kitchen filled with joy because what we are doing is going to bring happiness to our husbands. We cook to protect our position, for praise or just because it's our duty. And when we make love we do what is necessary and expected for our own selfish reasons. How many women make love to a man because of the joy it gives him? Yet only through

365

that joy can a woman really know what it is to be a woman. I've never known, Michele, because to be a woman is to give. And you've known that from the beginning."

Michele turned her head to the pillow.

"Don't cry and don't pity yourself. You didn't ask for an easy way when you set sail with a man like François."

"Mamma . . . is it too late for you and Papa?"

"Yes, I'm afraid so."

The girl's eyes fluttered, then closed from the sedative. Nicole leaned over and kissed her cheek. André was in the hallway and the bedroom door was open. She wondered if he had heard.

"We'll get her through this," Nicole said.

As André stared at his wife, that old feeling which had never entirely gone came back strongly. He wanted to reach out and touch the half dozen strands of gray hair at her temples. A short time ago she would have been worried sick about them. But now they seemed so in place and so charming. It was nice that Nicole was accepting her age gracefully and without panic and self-pity.

Yes, he wanted her but he knew that in the morning he would want Juanita de Córdoba more. So, he would have neither.

"Will you be leaving for Montrichard soon?"

"Tomorrow. I'll see that she gets to Paris when you have free time."

"Thank you, for everything." He turned for his study.

"Is there anything I can get you?" she asked.

"No." André entered his study, adjusted his glasses, and hunched over his papers. He looked up to her and they stared through the open door for a long time. She realized she had come to him too late and perhaps with too little. Her husband belonged to Juanita de Córdoba. Strangely, she felt no malice. But she also knew that there would never be another man for her but André Devereaux and she would wait.

(10)

As soon as Rico Parra's chauffeur drove the car into the grounds of Casa de Revolución to bring Juanita to his boss, she had an ominous feeling that something was wrong. But then, there was always something ugly about the place. They drove along a long palm-lined dirt road that hugged the Bahía del Sol. It was unusually quiet, devoid of the general activity of the guards and gardeners and men working on the pier. She got out of the car and looked around. Rico's speedboat bobbed at the anchor buoy. A gloomy overcast was moving in from the sea, dulling out the defeated sun. It would be a long, cold, morbid weekend.

The chauffeur followed her into the villa.

Juanita screamed as she saw Hernández, Rico's bodyguard, on his back staring up to her in death with blood still oozing from the bullet wounds in his fat stomach and chest.

The door slammed behind her and a pair of G-2 men seized her and another pair disarmed Rico's driver and held him at gunpoint.

The room was in a shambles!

Muñoz came from the bedroom with a wet rope whip in his hand. The room swayed around Juanita as the nightmarish scene closed in but she steadied herself quickly realizing what had taken place. She walked toward the bedroom. Muñoz stepped aside and ushered her in with a mock bow.

Rico was spread-eagled, lashed at the wrists

367

with leather thongs and tied to a pair of wooden ceiling beams. From the appearance of Muñoz's men, Rico had not been an easy customer to take alive.

Once they had gotten him strung up in the crucifix position he had still been able to get off a good kick that landed between Muñoz's legs. Then his feet were tied together and he was raised so that his toes barely touched the floor.

Even so, Muñoz got close enough to be spat on. A gag was shoved in Rico's mouth.

Muñoz had worked him over fearfully. The wet rope had ripped the flesh of his bared body. His face had been beaten to a grotesque distortion. One eye totally shut, the broken nose a lumpy discolored bruise, his lips like raw liver.

Juanita walked to the bathroom, soaked a couple of towels and wiped the blood from his face and compressed one behind his neck. Without seeking permission, she untied the gag from his mouth.

He spoke with semi-intelligibility through the swollen mouth. "Sure one hell of a way to end up. Funny part. Muñoz was my protégé when we were in the mountains. Always felt the bastard was a coward."

"I'll stay with you as long as they let me," she said.

"Huh . . . you know, Juanita . . . it wasn't that I ever expected you to fall in love. . . . I just wished that once or twice you really enjoyed it . . ."

"Rico . . ."

"Don't lie . . . don't lie. What a hell of a woman you are. When you make a bargain you go all the way. . . . Well . . . maybe you'll get together with the Frenchman in heaven."

"Enough!" Muñoz shouted. "Well, lovebirds, how do you like your honeymoon cottage now?" He advanced into the room, menacing them with the butt of the whip. "We all know now just how the Yankees found out about the missiles."

"For whatever it's worth, Rico Parra is innocent," Juanita said.

"For selling his country for a piece of ass!"

"Cuba should be proud of you, Señor Muñoz. Well, when is it my turn?"

Muñoz laughed softly. "Not just yet. You have too many friends around Cuba whose names we wish to know. Oh, perhaps you won't talk right away but after you watch what we do to Rico Parra now . . . tomorrow . . . the next day . . . your tongue will begin to loosen. It happens that way when the mind goes."

Juanita was lashed to a bulky chest of drawers so she was directly opposite Rico fifteen feet away. She neither flinched nor closed her eyes. Muñoz circled the hanging target, threw his whip away. "Why don't you spit?" he taunted.

Muñoz brought the heel of his boot up and jammed it between Rico's legs. Rico's body shuddered and he moaned softly and swayed from his crucifixion.

And then Rico smiled. "You hit like a woman, Muñoz."

Muñoz was infuriated. He kicked Rico again and again but Rico refused to cry out his agony. And then he vomited and Muñoz had his victory.

Muñoz's eyes rolled insanely and the sweat poured over him as he pounded the defenseless bloated face until his knuckles began to shred and swell. And, as a blessed darkness fell over Rico, Muñoz continued to pound the half-dead

369

man until he fell exhausted against him. Even some of his bloodthirsty colleagues were forced to look away. One came over and pulled him off.

Muñoz staggered to Juanita and ripped the clothing from the upper part of her body then unflicked a gleaming razor-sharp switchblade knife. "For you, Little Dove," he gasped, "some very special art work. Those breasts of yours won't look so beautiful when I finish carving them up. . . . Put the lovers in their bridal bed."

Rico was cut down. He and Juanita were tied together from neck to ankle back to back and thrown on the bed and in a moment the sheets were blood-soaked.

As soon as he arrived at G-2 Headquarters at the Green House on Avenida Quinta, Muñoz showered and changed clothing but all of the stench and blood could never be washed away.

The Soviet Resident, Oleg Gorgoni, waited anxiously in his office. "I have just received urgent instructions from Moscow that you are not to harm Juanita de Córdoba. She is to be turned over to us."

"I also have instructions," Muñoz said. "No."

"Don't play with me, Muñoz."

"Who plays? I said no."

"I said it was urgent!"

"So you did."

"You are on dangerous ground. Juanita de Córdoba is to be kept alive for reasons important to the Soviet Union."

"She is to be taken care of for reasons important to Cuba."

"You are angering the Soviet Union!"

"Isn't that just too bad," Muñoz answered. "Maybe you think you can bully us because we are small. Maybe it might work with Cuba because you're too yellow to bully the Yankees!"

Gorgoni turned ashen as Muñoz stormed to his feet and snatched the morning paper from his desk and thrust it under the Russian's nose.

"The Americans tell you to get the hell out of Cuba and what do you answer? Your great and courageous chairman engages in writing love letters to a doddering, inept British philosopher and cries and weeps and moans about the Yankee piracy and tells us all . . . let's sit down and talk . . . brotherhood . . . peace for mankind." He flung the paper away. "Where is all the goddam missile power you've been threatening to use on the Yankees? You're yellow . . . liars!"

"Enough! Enough! Enough!"

"Yellow!"

"I demand Juanita de Córdoba."

"Demand your ass off. You see, my brave señor comrade resident, we are telling you we run Cuba and we warn you to start showing some spine."

(11)

LONDON . . . THE PRESIDENT answered the telegram from the aged British philosopher with the terse comment . . . "I think your attention might well be directed to the burglars rather than to those who caught the burglars."

KEY WEST . . . low-level Navy P8U reconnaissance planes have now positively identified twenty-four Soviet bloc ships steaming toward Cuba and are keeping them under tight surveillance. All sources say that the confrontation at sea must take place within the next few days. . . .

WASHINGTON . . . The President has ignored

Walter Lippmann's column which pleads for ne‐
gotiation, as well as brushing aside U Thant's
United Nations appeal that both sides stop their
collision course. In the face of swelling world
criticism of the brazen American position, the
President sent a telegram to each of the OAS
members, with the exception of abstaining Uru‐
guay, which read in part: "By your swift and
decisive action we have shown the world and
particularly the Soviet Union we stand united in
our determination to defend the integrity of the
hemisphere. . . ."

In Moscow, the Soviet Premier in another of
those paradoxes belied logic by summoning Pom‐
eroy Bidwell, a visiting American industrialist, to
the Kremlin. Bidwell was seated opposite a man
who appeared on the brink of total exhaustion.
The Soviet Premier was well aware that the begin‐
ning of the end of his reign of power might be
taking place and that his bully tactics would never
again effectively cow America.

Arguing with Bidwell as though he were an
official representative of the United States instead
of a visiting fireman, the Premier tried to con‐
vince him the weapons in Cuba were truly defen‐
sive. He debated in semantics using verbal gym‐
nastics. Pomeroy Bidwell was not at all convinced
and cited Sweden's weaponry and proximity to
the Soviet Union as an example.

The Russian tried to appeal his case as he had
to the pacifist British philosopher. When unsuc‐
cessful, he launched a series of threats and
swore that if the Americans boarded a single Rus‐
sian ship his submarines would sink the American
fleet.

And suddenly, the Soviet leader complained in

almost a whimper. "How can I negotiate with a man who is younger than my son?"

Pomeroy Bidwell rushed to the American Embassy to arrange transportation to Washington. The Ambassador closeted him in.

"How did it go, Pomeroy?"

"Well, Mr. Ambassador, we were just sitting there, eyeball to eyeball . . . and I could swear I saw the other guy blink."

(12)

ANDRÉ'S DOORBELL RANG as he took breakfast. It was an ININ colleague from the American Embassy.

"Got a cable for you. It just cleared the code room."

"Thanks for bringing it, Ted."

I AM EN ROUTE TO PARIS FOR TWO WEEKS OF NATO BUSINESS AND WILL BE LANDING AT ORLY SIX O'CLOCK PAN-AM THIS EVENING. I HAVE BEEN ABLE TO OPEN A NEW SOURCE OF INFORMATION INSIDE CUBA OF PARTICULAR INTEREST TO YOU. PLEASE MEET ME IF YOU CAN. (SIGNED) MICHAEL NORDSTROM

André's assistant sped toward Orly Field to meet Nordstrom. He sat beside the driver reading through the stack of the day's newspapers.

Much of the attention was focused on a parade and rally in Havana. Castro had called in units of militia and army from all over Cuba and demonstrated his Soviet-made armor, artillery, and aircraft.

After the parade there was a rally in the square under the statue of the liberator, Martí. Castro launched into the kind of harangue now familiar to the entire world. As his breast-beating rage heightened he vowed that Cuba would not abide by any unilateral agreement reached by the Soviets and Americans without his approval. He vowed, further, to defend the country to the last man. He repeated the demand that the Americans leave the Guantánamo Base.

The most violent part of the speech was directed against the "treachery" of the Organization of American States and he swore to inflame revolution throughout Latin America.

"Even now!" Castro cried, "our beloved *compadre* and the most trusted lieutenant of the revolution, Rico Parra, is on a secret mission somewhere in the Caribbean."

Parra's absence, already speculated upon by the journalists present, further brought their attention to the conspicuous absence of one of Cuba's leading figures. "Also missing from the demonstration was an intimate of Rico Parra, Juanita de Córdoba, known throughout Cuba as 'The Little Dove.' "

Michael Nordstrom cleared Customs. "Let's get in to Paris," he said grimly to André.

"No," André answered firmly. "I want to know it now. I borrowed an office here."

Mike procrastinated. He seemed trapped and unwilling . . . a man who had rehearsed a speech during his flight over and over.

"I know the worst has happened," André said abruptly.

"Yes."

"I could almost hear her cry out to me two nights ago in some kind of terrible agony. I haven't slept much since I returned from Cuba.

374

I didn't at all last night. It was as though I knew your message was coming and I had to wait up for it."

"All right," Nordstrom said. "Let's get it over with for God's sake."

Mike sat on the edge of the desk in a small office gesturing with his hand, rubbing his face and sighing over and over again. André closed the door, shutting out the hollow echoes bouncing off the marble floors and the whine of the jets. He settled in the only extra chair and waited for Mike.

"You know the Casa de Revolución?" Nordstrom asked.

"Yes. On the Bahía del Sol. It once belonged to the De Fuentes family. You remember Pedro de Fuentes. He was one of the best ballplayers who ever came out of Cuba. He was the one who first interested me. Anyhow, Rico Parra took the villa away from the family."

"André," Mike sputtered, "you don't know how rough the rest of this is going to be."

"Damn it, Mike. I know Juanita and Parra were together there and they weren't playing Chinese checkers. Now, let's hear it."

"Muñoz got orders to do away with Parra for complicity in allowing you to escape Cuba. Further orders, to make Juanita de Córdoba talk. You know Muñoz. Nothing clean and merciful about that butcher. The Casa was turned into a prison with two prisoners, Juanita and Parra."

Mike related just what had taken place. André hovered close to collapse until Mike's words became unreal . . . dreamlike.

"One of the G-2 men by the name of Jesús Zapata became revolted by Muñoz's brutality. He searched around Havana for a contact on our side. Zapata felt the story had to be known. Do you know Karel Vasek?"

"Heard the name . . . I don't remember . . ."

"Vasek is a Czech engineer. Been in Cuba over a year in charge of a bridge-building program. He started working with British Intelligence six months ago. Vasek and Zapata set up their future meeting places.

"Parra was a tough cookie," Nordstrom continued. "His brains were so scrambled from the beating he reverted to idiocy. In the end he never knew what was happening. Juanita was half-crazy from being forced to watch the atrocities on Parra. I don't have to spell out what Muñoz did to him."

"No . . ."

"With Rico dead, Muñoz was going to start on Juanita. With a knife. Zapata came into Havana desperate. Vasek gave him a cyanide capsule. He was able to slip it to her. It was the only merciful thing to do. Before Muñoz could lay a finger on her, she died instantly and peacefully."

"Thank God for that. . . ."

"André, are you going to be all right?"

"Yes . . . I . . . I am. You see, Mike, if that beautiful woman's life meant anything to this world I have to fight on to the end."

"André, what can I do?"

"Just leave me alone for a while."

(13)

ANDRÉ WAS THE LAST to enter the big conference room on the first floor of SDECE headquarters. The assemblage appeared to him like a gang of eager alley cats around the long table covered with billiard-green felt cloth. The omnipresent portrait of Pierre La Croix looked down on them like a stern father.

At the head of the table was Charles Rochefort, the witless bureaucrat of medium weight but of great wealth and power inherited from his family.

Along the left side of the table sat the five-man SDECE team which had investigated the Topaz affair. Their head was one Daniel DuBay, an excellent intelligence man of long standing, but one who was more preoccupied with never getting caught on the wrong side of the political fence.

Immediately to Rochefort's right sat Colonel Gabriel Brune, there to give dominating counsel. This morning he owned a slight smirk as he nodded grayly to André and sucked on a long cigarette held by nicotine-stained fingers.

Next to André's chair was his only possible ally, Léon Roux, Chief of Internal Protection of the Sûreté. Roux introduced André to Inspector Marcel Steinberger, who had been Sûreté's man on the team.

Colonel Brune nodded to Daniel DuBay, who stood. He was a short, plump person with a great gold watch chain spanning his girth. He opened a loose-leaf notebook, fitted his glasses on the end of his nose and tucked a thumb into his vest like a lawyer preparing a court argument.

"We have returned from Washington, these gentlemen and Inspector Steinberger of the Sûreté, after having studied the interrogation records, tapes, and other evidence supplied by the American division of ININ. We have also held visits with one who is referred to as Boris Kuznetov."

"And you have had the opportunity to evaluate your findings for a report and recommendation?" Rochefort asked.

"We have."

"You may continue."

"Monsieur DuBay," Colonel Brune interrupted. "All of us present are familiar with the case. We would like at this time to have a summary of your conclusions."

"Yes . . . very well." DuBay gloried in the spotlight. "At the same time the United States and the Soviet Union concocted the Cuban missile hoax, they meticulously plotted a second part of the scheme for the purpose of discrediting the French Secret Service."

There was no reaction from André or Roux. Steinberger played with a nail file dreamily.

"Boris Kuznetov, or whoever he really is, has proved out to be an excellent KGB officer and probably as brilliant a memory artist as we are ever apt to encounter. Kuznetov was assigned by KGB, with American cooperation, to act out a defection to the United States."

DuBay flipped the page, puckered his lips and studied the faces around the table, only avoiding the eyes of André Devereaux. He bent, picked up his place in the notes and straightened up again.

"Kuznetov was sent to Scandinavia, to Copenhagen, fully groomed by the Soviet side as to his past and past functions. In Copenhagen he obviously held tens of dozens of meetings in a secret place where he was further coached by American ININ people. It is our feeling that he was schooled by the very same people who pretended to be his interrogators later on, namely, Dr. Billings, W. Smith, Jaffe, and Kramer. So that when they met again in Washington both sides had thoroughly rehearsed all the questions and answers previously.

"Kuznetov was given a schooling in depth in

certain NATO matters, supplied with certain NATO documents to memorize, and was instructed on the workings, divisions, and directors of the French Secret Service. With this intensive training done, probably over a period of six or eight months, the United States and the Soviet Union played out a defection.

"It is beyond belief, is it not, that a KGB officer could escape from a Western country *with* his wife and daughter unless both sides were party to the escape?

"Now in America, Kuznetov shows he is just as capable an actor as he is a memory expert. According to a prearranged time schedule, he plays out the game. At first he doesn't talk, then he talks a little, then he goes into great shows of fear. In the meantime, his innocent wife and daughter have terrible family quarrels with him.

"Then, somewhere along the line he asks to see a diplomat. But a *certain* diplomat. A French diplomat. Monsieur Devereaux, to be specific. The bait is swallowed. Over a period of time, Devereaux is lured in and becomes convinced of Kuznetov's authenticity. *But* Kuznetov also convinces him not to report all this to Paris . . . not, of course, until they are ready to spring the trap.

"Nothing is left to chance, up to and including a fake heart attack. With his knowledge and permission, Kuznetov is given drugs to make it appear he is on the verge of death. The real sorrow of his unwitting wife and daughter adds to the appearance of legitimacy, and all this draws in Devereaux more and more.

"Devereuax returns from Cuba, fulfilling the first part of the scheme by handing over information designed to drag France along behind America into the fake missile crisis. Now, phase

379

two of the plot unfolds: the so-called confession of Boris Kuznetov.

"Topaz, Disinformation, a nonexistent Anti-NATO Division of KGB, are all myths dreamed up by the Russians and Americans. Is it not strange, strange indeed, that the chief of an Anti-NATO Division cannot name a single agent in this so-called Topaz network? The final icing on the cake: The President of the United States personally becomes party to this scheme by challenging the honor of the French Secret Service.

"What better way is there for the Americans to increase their control of Europe than by creating a scandal to destroy the present organization of SDECE . . . and perhaps then clutter it up with new people . . . perhaps of Devereaux's leanings? And what more clever way could this be done than by using a high-ranking French Intelligence man, André Devereaux, to deliver the message to the President of France and vouch for its authenticity?

"Our report to President La Croix will be that there is no Topaz network and that Boris Kuznetov is nothing more than a brilliant fake."

DuBay snapped the book shut, mopped a wet brow and sat down.

The gray eyes of Colonel Gabriel Brune hung hard on André Devereaux. "Do you have anything to say, Monsieur Devereaux?"

"Yes, I must be a very stupid person."

"Is that all?"

"If I have any cards to play," André said without emotion, "I prefer not to play them at this table."

Brune's forefinger hit the table like a woodpecker. "I don't like threats. Speak up now or the report stands."

"A moment please," Léon Roux said from the other side of the table. His little eyes twinkled more than usual. "The Department of Internal Protection of Sûreté intends to file a separate report on the Topaz investigation. It is the expressed opinion of Inspector Steinberger that there exists a Topaz network, that Disinformation has been used against the French and that, indeed, someone quite close to the President is a Communist agent."

"I am suggesting," Colonel Brune said with a heightening pitch to his voice, "that the Sûreté is doing this to embarrass a sister service. This investigation team stands five to one. Certainly President La Croix will recognize your position as a petty interservice quarrel."

Roux was unimpressed with Brune's anger.

"Perhaps," he said, "the good Colonel will explain something to me?"

"Just what do you have in mind?"

"Yesterday, Henri Jarré, of NATO, was arrested in the act of transferring secret NATO documents to a member of the Soviet Embassy. En route to prison, he was extremely talkative."

Roux deliberately stopped his explosive announcement to luxuriate in the stupefaction he had wrought on the room. Pixielike, he looked to the portrait of La Croix at the end of the room. "Inspector Steinberger," he said slyly, "you were a member of the arresting team, were you not?"

"Yes."

"Did you accompany Henri Jarré to La Santé Prison?"

"I did."

"Did he talk . . . say something about himself?"

"Yes."

"Specifically, what did he call himself?"

"He called himself Topaz No. 2."

(14)

"GET OVER HERE right away!"

There could be no mistaking the urgency in Léon Roux's voice in his middle-of-the-night summons. André groggily fought into a pair of slacks, a sport shirt and overcoat.

He sped toward Montparnasse through a sleeping Paris, knowing in his heart that the worst had happened. Inspector Marcel Steinberger, also haphazardly dressed, awaited him at the main entrance of La Santé Prison. They walked briskly across the courtyard, past the cell blocks, until a barred gate blocked their way. Steinberger rattled it to arouse a drowsy jailor.

Their leather heels clicked in unison as they continued down a long dim corridor. Léon Roux waited and led them into a small, foul-smelling, concrete-walled room holding a line of slabs.

Roux pulled the sheet back, revealing a waxen, hate-filled face, that of Henri Jarré, now permanently etched in death.

"When? How?"

"He was found an hour ago," Steinberger said and pointed to the red indentation about the neck of the corpse, "hanging in his cell."

"Suicide?"

"We don't know yet, but in either event he'll have no more to say."

"His confession?"

"It was verbal. Nothing is in writing."

Roux put the sheet back over Jarré's face. "I'm sorry, Devereaux," Roux said, "I'm really very sorry. I'll have to stay around to hold the press off. Steinberger, see Devereaux out, will you?"

Their breath frosted in the chill air as they retraced their steps over the courtyard to the street. André leaned against the car and sighed wearily.

"Don't let this beat you," the Inspector said.

"The enemy forces have us routed, Inspector. You saw Léon Roux now. He's had a loss of heart."

"The Chief is a practical police officer. I'm impractical and I want Columbine flushed out as much as you do. Roux will tell you how dogged I am. I have access to all the records and files of the Department. You keep quiet, lay low, and give me guidance. I'll do the rest. Tomorrow we'll set up a way of contacting each other."

"Why are you really doing this?"

"I owe you a great favor."

"Me? But I've just met you."

"We met before, a long time ago. I have a sister who lives in Israel. She and I are all that remain of our family. I was able to get her out of France before the Gestapo picked me up. You see . . . you took us over the River Cher twenty years ago when we were children."

(15)

ANDRÉ WAS SUMMONED to the office of Charles Rochefort. A strange mixture of persons had gathered. There was the ever-present Colonel Gabriel Brune. There were Robert Proust and the sinister Ferdinand Fauchet, and Jacques Granville was present.

Jacques spoke. "The President asked me to come here today to advise you of his decision on the Topaz matter. He has been fully briefed and the SDECE report has been accepted. The President sees no reason to investigate the Secret Services, and is further advising that he gives full confidence to the present leadership."

"Then, of course, gentlemen," André answered, "you will have my resignation before the end of the day."

"I spoke at great length with the President," Jacques said, "and was able to convince him you were the victim of a master plot and should not be discredited. There's too much good work in the past and too good an organization built. Of course, you have all the best contacts. The President has agreed that you should return to your post in Washington."

André knew the price that was about to be named. The victorious Colonel Brune smiled. "All things considered, you are very fortunate."

"Everything exactly the same?" André asked.

"Well, almost," Brune said. "A slight expansion of your operation. You'll be given additional personnel and funds, of course."

"Actually," Robert Proust said, "it will be a small, highly secret subsection under my department that will be administered by Monsieur Fauchet. It will be known under the code name of Section P."

"I hate to disappoint you, gentlemen, but the Americans already know of the intentions of Section P. The information was revealed by the nonexistent Boris Kuznetov."

"We believe," Brune said, "the Americans got wind of Section P through other sources. In order to prove Kuznetov's authenticity they instructed him to reveal it to you."

"You see," Granville said, "you have the confidence of the Americans. If we were to send a

384

new man in your place, he would come under complete suspicion and any and all chance for intelligence cooperation would disappear. But . . . if you return to America and they know you know of Section P, then you will be able to convince them in time that we've abandoned the idea."

André came out of his chair slowly and thoughtfully. "Just what is it you want to know?"

"Through French exchange scientists working in America we should be able to get a complete wrap-up on American military installations, location of Minutemen, and other ICBM rocket sites, location of missile fabrication plants, location of atomic stockpiles, organization of coastal defenses."

"And you have no fear of this information getting back to Moscow?"

"Of course not," Rochefort said indignantly. "The plan to discredit us has failed. The SDECE has a clean bill of health."

"But it's immoral to commit this kind of espionage on an ally," André said.

"We're not monks in a monastery," Brune said, "and intelligence work is not a morality play."

"In the end, André," his friend Jacques said, speaking in most familiar terms, "you are a Frenchman, and you must act in the national interest even though you personally disagree."

André looked from one to the other. His old friend Robert with downcast eyes, and Jacques, a debonair politician. Rochefort, born with the silver spoon, but was he quite so innocent of it all? Colonel Gabriel Brune, who had rotted the service. And the trigger man, Ferdinand Fauchet. How far did Fauchet's personal little empire reach?

And suddenly it all became quite clear. The riddle of Topaz was solved. Columbine, the master spy, sat before him. He knew the answer and in that instant he had made his decision.

(16)

THE MAGNIFICENT MULTIBALCONIED library of the Peabody Institute in Baltimore made a perfect setting for small concerts.

This night, the seats were filled with students, parents, and teachers for an introduction recital of a number of the new scholarship winners.

Midway through the affair, Dr. Schoeberlein, Dean of Students, came on to the stage. "I wish to announce a change in the program," he said. "Unfortunately, Mr. Richard Holtz, who was to play next, has come down with the virus. Substituting in his absence I should like to introduce a brand new student of extreme promise, Miss Anita Dahlander."

A slim, poised and extremely lovely young lady once known as Tamara Kuznetov came to center stage, rested her hand on the piano, and spoke in a sure voice with only the faintest trace of accent.

"For my first number," she said, "I should like to play a short composition of my own which I call, 'An American Dream.' "

As the library become hushed save for the melody of Tamara's piano, Boris Kuznetov took his wife's hand. . . . "We did the right thing," he said. "I'm so glad they let me come from the hospital tonight . . . we did the right thing."

When the concert was over, Anita Dahlander and her parents accepted congratulations at a tea.

"You can be mighty proud of that girl," Dr. Schoeberlein said.

"Yes, we are," Boris answered.

"Where do you folk call home?"

"California. I'm recuperating from an illness but we will be heading west soon."

"Great country. I'll bet you're anxious to get back."

"Yes. It is always wonderful to go home."

"Oh, by the way," Dr. Schoeberlein said, "did you hear the late news?"

"No, what?"

"The United States has stopped and boarded a Russian ship."

(17)

ANDRÉ WALKED ENDLESSLY and aimlessly about Paris by night, a stooped and semitragic figure.

At three in the morning he found himself standing before the door of Michael Nordstrom's apartment on Rue de la Fontaine. Mike locked the door behind them and stretched to wakefulness. André looked out of the window to the street where a pair of men shifted about in the cold just beyond the light of the lamp post.

"My honor guard," André said. "They walk a hundred paces behind me at all times. Do you have a drink?"

Nordstrom tugged at the ice cube tray in the kitchenette while André raided the liquor cabinet. He spun the tinkling cubes, staring into the glass. "La Croix is going to reject the Topaz letter."

"It's not possible!"

"Anything is possible at the Élysée Palace these days." André took a healthy belt. "It's the same kind of position they set up on the Cuban missile business."

"I can't comprehend that a man of La Croix's mind would believe this."

"Pierre La Croix believes what is convenient for him to believe. He'll take whatever position is necessary to protect his personal power."

"And there's going to be no investigation of your service?"

"No. The whole thing is whitewashed. La Croix is not going to risk an open scandal that would discredit his Secret Service. Nor would he allow it to be proved that someone near him is a Soviet agent. It would make him look like a fool and weaken his grip on the throat of the country."

In sudden anger, Michael Nordstrom's large fist cracked the cabinet top. "What the hell's the matter with France! The worst of it is you people allow these slime pots into office!"

André glared at Nordstrom with contempt. "You're shouting," he said.

"I'm sick of this whole goddamned French treachery!"

"Are you?"

"Yes, I am, André. Sick of the insults our citizens receive in your streets. Sick of the attempts to break us financially. Sick of French ingratitude. Sick of the fifteen billion dollars we poured down a sewer pulling this place together. And I'll tell you what else makes me sick. I'm sick that eighty-five thousand American boys sleep in graves in France . . . fighting for what . . . so you can crap on us?"

"There are half a million Frenchmen buried in Verdun," André said, "and in that battle we probably lost more than America has in all her wars combined. When you speak of debts, you owe us more than you can ever repay, for France has taken the blows and been destroyed, and because we have perished you have flourished. Well, in the next war, all the casualties and all the ruin may be on your sacred soil."

"Well, we hope to God we don't have to come to France for help."

"The way you helped us? France, your oldest ally, lay bleeding and what did you do? You recognized the traitors of Vichy. We pleaded for arms and you turned your backs. You plotted to reduce us to obscurity. And you plotted to occupy us as though we were a defeated enemy. And after the war you sat and applauded in silence while Frenchmen died in Vietnam and Algeria. And now you try to dictate to France her life and death. . . . Yes, Pierre La Croix may be guilty of making peace with the Communists, but here is a fact you can carry to your grave: If America had backed Free France, we would have never dealt with the Communists. You are a sanctimonious hypocrite."

André heaved a stifled gasp as his glass fell to the floor. He clutched his deadened left arm as he sunk to his knees and fished desperately for the pills.

Mike quickly stretched him on the floor, got a pill into him, loosened his tie and then phoned for the doctor. Tears streamed down Nordstrom's cheeks as he looked down at his friend.

In a few moments the attack had waned and André's eyes fluttered open. "I'm sorry, Mike. I'm so sorry we've all come to this."

18

MIKE NORDSTROM STARED listlessly at the stack of paper work on his desk. He was not in the mood to tackle it. He walked to the window and leaned against the frame looking out to the always splendid view down the Avenue Foch. From his Paris office he could get a glimpse of the Place de l'Étoile and the Arc de Triomphe. He turned as his secretary entered.

"Mr. McKittrick is on his way up."

"Send him right in."

Michael returned to his desk and sorted out a number of documents that McKittrick was to take back to the States with him.

The President's assistant entered, and they went through the papers together before locking them into his attaché case.

"How much longer are you going to be in Paris, Mike?"

"Few weeks anyhow. I've got a meeting with the Scandinavian people next Wednesday. Give Liz a ring when you get back to Washington and tell her I wasn't able to find the material she wanted. If she'll send me another sample, I'll see what I can do. My boy Jim has a birthday coming up. Have my secretary get him a left-hand fielder's glove, Ted Williams model."

"Right." McKittrick looked at his watch. "My car should be here in a few minutes."

They fenced in silence for a few moments. "Hell, you may as well say it," Nordstrom said.

"I've got the official word from La Croix. They're ignoring the entire Topaz affair. What's next, Mike?"

"Damned if I know. But NATO is going to be

in big danger soon. Marsh, there can only be one leader of the free world, can't there? We've done a pretty good job, haven't we?"

"We've done a lot better than when the French were running the show, and we've done it for a lot more decent reasons."

"The boss of this planet is seldom appreciated," Mike said, "by those he has replaced in the job."

"Mike," McKittrick said haltingly, "there's a base I have to touch. I know how fond you are of Devereaux. We all are. He's top-drawer. But he's in big trouble."

"What are you trying to tell me?"

"If Devereaux comes to you for help, you are under orders not to help him. He's been written off. And we've got to keep on doing business with France."

"You know, I remember the first time I saw Boris Kuznetov. A scared little guy in a hotel room in Copenhagen. He said something then I'll never forget. He said, 'It makes no difference if you are Russian or American. Our profession is cruel, yet . . . they cannot take from us all that is human. Humans, in the end, are compassionate. Someday you may need a friend. Someday a friend will need you.'"

"Mike, I'm just delivering the message."

"I got the goddamned message," Nordstrom snapped.

The secretary entered. "Your car is waiting, Mr. McKittrick."

"So long, Marsh. Have a good flight back."

As McKittrick left, he knew that if Devereaux sought help, there was a good chance Mike Nordstrom would disobey his orders.

19

AT TEN O'CLOCK SHARP at night, André left the Café des Deux Magots as had been prearranged by the telephone conversation.

He drove across the Seine by the Pont d'Austerlitz with an eye on the rear mirror. His tails were still behind him as he continued up Rue de Rivoli, so he circled the great Place de la Concorde and doubled back into the Place Vendôme and at last lost them.

He drove on to the greenery of the Bois de Boulogne and slowed and drifted back and forth near the Pavillon d'Armenonville. During his third pass, headlights of another car, which had pulled off in the bushes, blinked off and on. André turned off the road and parked near the second car.

Robert Proust waited nervously, perspiring even in the cold. They watched the area silently for several moments to assure that all was clear.

"Well, Robert, we've come a long way to have to make a secret rendezvous."

"It's not very advantageous to be your friend these days," Robert answered. "Well, I came anyhow. André, you know how closely you're being watched. Every move, every call. Even if you return to your post in Washington, one of the new people will have orders to watch you."

"What are you trying to tell me?"

"I'm trying to talk you out of your damn madness. The service knows I would never personally carry out an order against you, but in your case there are standing orders that Fauchet has received from Colonel Brune personally."

"Yes, good old Ferdinand. He'd like nothing

better than to pull the trigger on me himself. Or does he use a strangling wire these days?"

"You have one advantage now . . . your years in the service and many friends. They won't play with you now because it would wreck the morale of the SDECE. But when the time comes, Fauchet will do a clean job. He knows his work."

André laughed, ignoring the warning. "Do you have the same private postbox at the Rue des Capucines Station?"

"Yes."

"Good. I've found what I was looking for. In a day or two there will be a letter. It will have my resignation and reveal an interesting name. Through your own ingenious resources you must see to it that it gets directly into the hands of President La Croix. There will be an extra copy in a separate envelope for your own information."

"André, for God's sake, don't go through with this."

"It's not for God's sake, it's for France's sake. Will you get my letter into the hands of the President?"

"Yes, I promise."

"Now, what about Michele? Did you see her in Montrichard?"

"Yes. She's headed to the Spanish frontier. More than likely she's made it over to Spain by now. She'll be waiting at the town you said. From there, you've got your fifty-fifty chance to make the break for Mexico or South America. You know those places better than anyone."

"Good. Well, at least Michele didn't have to walk over the mountains as we did, eh, Robert?"

"You mean as I was carried. It's hard for a squalid lump like me to understand, but I guess I always knew you wouldn't back down."

"Don't berate yourself, Robert. You've been a loyal friend."

"André . . ."

"Yes?"

"Nicole went to Spain also. When I saw her she said, 'I beg André not to turn me away.' "

"Nicole? Well, we started in Spain. But can two people so scarred by each other's wounds really start over?"

"Somehow, it might work."

"Does she know about Juanita?"

"Yes. She said you'll need her more than ever now."

"Robert. I won't delude myself into believing a miracle is about to take place. She may think she found answers in the quiet of her room. It is something else to come out into the world and put those answers to work. When the pressure comes, all of us revert to what we are. People rarely change, except to go downhill."

"Then, you are going to turn her away?"

"Nicole and I still have a power to reach each other, to hurt each other and to thrill each other. In the end the things we have may have to be enough. I won't know until I see her again . . . or if I ever will."

André shook Robert's hand and gave him a "chin up" smack on the shoulder, got into his car, backed out and drove away. Robert Proust watched him disappear knowing he would never see him again.

(20)

JACQUES GRANVILLE'S COUNTRY estate in Normandy consisted of thirty-six rooms showing exquisite taste and set in a private forest and hunting grounds. Paulette received a raised eyebrow from her husband to indicate he wished to chat alone with André. She retreated from the paneled study.

Jacques made to a portable bar near his desk and produced a bottle of bourbon. "How's that?"

"You remember my weakness," André said.

They saluted with raised glasses. "When do you return to Washington?" Jacques asked.

"I expect to be traveling very soon."

"I'm glad we were able to have this weekend together. You know I moved heaven and earth to open up the New Zealand Embassy post for you. I was simply overruled. Everyone thinks you're too valuable in Washington. Christ, André, I can still get the post if you'll consider it and back me."

"You've had my answer on that. I'm not going to New Zealand."

"I'm only trying to help you," Jacques said. "I know what an ordeal these past weeks have been and how hurt you are. But you've got to look at the broad concept, the big canvas. Pierre La Croix is right. At least for France he's right. We're not the kind of people to be dominated or even led by outsiders. I have no vendetta against the Americans and I can't share all this violent anti-American opinion but we have the right to make our own mistakes. Now with this new section on scientific intelligence, try to send back some good information."

"I'll try my best, as always."

"And ease up. You'll have an expanded staff. Give them more of the work load. With Cuba off limits for you, you are in a position to take life easier."

"I suppose I am tired."

"Queer breed, you intelligence people. I often wondered why you and Robert stayed in this business after the war."

"For Robert, it was a way to make a living. Most of the people in most of the secret services are simply decent civil servants."

"But you, André, you puzzle me. You could have had the whole world."

"But I have had the world I really wanted. I've worked with the kind of men and women more beautiful as humans, more courageous, more idealistic, than any others on earth. Only someone with a deep and mystic love for country can serve that way, in silence."

"Yes," Jacques said, "but what about the others? The scoundrels, the cutthroats, the double-dealers."

"I've lived with the scum of the earth, too. Traitors always fascinate me. I've never stopped wondering how a man is able to turn against his country."

André set his drink down, clasped his hands behind him and stared past the brocaded drapes to a stand of birch trees in winter bareness. "Some men like Boris Kuznetov cross over out of fear or horrible disenchantment. A Henri Jarré is so consumed with hatred it was no crime in his eyes to spy on NATO because he honestly felt it was in the interest of his country, or rather what he thought France's interest should be. There are dedicated Communists about us who spy because they believe in Communism, just as we have those who spy for democracy. There are others who feel that Russia is going to win out over the West in the end and they want to get on the right side. There are the little fish caught in the wrong bed or with their hands in the cash till and laid open to blackmail."

"Well . . . no matter. André, the main reason I wanted to see you is to urge you to put this Topaz affair to rest. Frankly, I don't know if Topaz is real or not at this point, but I do know there's no way you can win. You've hit a blank wall. Let me and the rest of us who are alerted take care of Colonel Brune in our own good time."

"Brune? I made a mistake about him," André said.

"What do you mean?"

"I made him much bigger than he is. All he really is is a bureaucrat fighting for his life and afraid of his own mediocrity. He's played the anti-American, anti-Devereaux game with slanted and distorted reports because he thought it would please La Croix and because he was otherwise advised to do so. But the worst that Brune can be charged with is being a rotten administrator, of playing politics to hang on to his office and of allowing the service to deteriorate. But a Soviet agent? No. Brune is not guilty. When faced with the Topaz scandal he was absolutely forced to discredit me or be drummed out of office in disgrace."

André turned from the window past Jacques' magnificent collection of Dumas, Voltaire, Hugo.

"A man like Colonel Brune is easy to manipulate. Like a puppet he has been manipulated by a clever, vicious devil."

André leaned against the thick Renaissance table. "Too bad you haven't gotten a good look at America, Jacques."

"You know how it is. My visits are short and official."

"Shame. America is a country of unbelievable

397

varieties of physical beauty. I never cease to marvel. Four time zones in one country. Imagine. God-made vistas, man-made miracles. Total splendor. I think I like Colorado best . . . yes, I like it best. Great wild mountains. Not with manicured villages like below the Alps but wild and rugged terrain and weathered old ruins of mining towns. Rushing streams filled with trout. In the early summer the high country around Aspen, the valleys and fields, are a veritable carpet of wild flowers."

"Good Lord, André. What brought on all this nostalgia?"

"The wild flowers."

Jacques showed a hint of a smile. He set his drink down and sat behind his desk. "Tell me about the wild flowers."

"Certainly you should know the state flower of Colorado. You have the same name . . . Columbine."

As perspiration popped out on Granville's lip, he inched the top drawer of his desk open. "You are being highly entertaining," he said.

"We were talking about traitors," André continued. "Worse than the whores, the pimps, the paid stranglers. The infinite scum, the most vile being is the man who betrays his country for money."

Granville's fingers felt around the drawer and stopped on the cold metal of his pistol. His hand wrapped around it slowly.

"Jacques, you look dumbstruck. Let's see how it all went. During the war you made a number of liaison missions to Moscow for the Free French. The Russians sized you up as a charming young reprobate who would remain close to La Croix and they knew that someday he would rule

France. So you were approached and eighteen years ago your grooming started. Once in, one does not get out. That's a long time for any man to lead a double life. But, even considering the normal graft of your office, the wealth of two of your ex-wives, and your own inheritance, it was not enough to keep up your style of living . . . and you do have style, Jacques.

"What an astonishing rapport you have with the Swiss banks in Geneva," André continued. "Blank numbered accounts XXF 12908 and BFI 2202 at the Bank de Groff alone hold over forty thousand American dollars. And the money flows in almost on demand to one C. S. Bouchard. Well, Monsieur Bouchard, alias Columbine, alias Jacques Granville, it's not small business with you, but then why should it be when the Soviet Union has one of its agents briefing Disinformation to our half-blind President?

"I've seen them come and go, but by God, Jacques, you are the shrewdest son of a bitch of them all. You used everyone. You used the President of France to peddle your filth. You stole the fortunes of two women. You used Colonel Brune and twisted things around so that he carried on the dirty work of Disinformation on the pretense you were being his friend and saving his job. You used me. And you even used my wife to get information on Kuznetov's whereabouts. Too bad, Jacques, his escape is a clean job."

Granville had worked around to the study door, locked it quickly and turned, leveling a small Beretta pistol on André. "We'd better talk," Granville growled.

"It's your turn, Jacques, and put that pistol away. You look silly."

Jacques continued to keep it aimed. André

walked to him. Granville trembled. His hand became slippery wet. André took it from him as though it was an unwanted toy, removed the bullet clip and flipped it on the desk.

"You never did have the strength to pull your own trigger. But before you turn your hatchet men loose, I didn't walk in here as a target and I'm not walking out that way. Several journalist friends have been given sealed envelopes containing my letter of resignation and further information on your bank accounts. The envelopes which name you as Columbine will be opened in the event of my death or disappearance."

"If that letter is printed you won't live twenty-four hours."

"No, no, no, Jacques. I'm not going to publish it now. I still desire to live, very much. As long as I keep the envelopes sealed, then you'll see to it I get out of France. But for now, even Jacques Granville cannot survive my murder without signing his own death warrant. We are in a position to serve each other mutually. Do you follow me?"

"Within hours," Jacques cried, "all trace of the bank accounts will disappear. In a year . . . two . . . three . . . we will build a case against you that you were a drunk, a thief, a malcontent . . . that you were a Soviet agent trying to save his own neck. Issues will be so confused your precious letter will have no value. And then . . . you'll be hunted down like an animal to your dying day."

"Jacques, I know a writer. A novelist. American, no less. He has an extremely faithful international audience, despite some of the critics' complaints over his syntax. I personally would have preferred someone with a bit more literary flair . . . like Hemingway or Faulkner, but no matter. I sent for him when I realized how it would be necessary for

me to destroy you. He's working on the story now
. . . all of it. We have even given it a name . . .
Topaz, what else. So no matter what happens to
me, and that's not important, the world will be
alerted when Pierre La Croix dies to stop you and
your pack of jackals from devouring France."

André brushed Jacques away from the door
and turned the key.

Jacques was seized with desperation. "André!
There's another way! Come in with us! Stop your
madness! Stop this insane martyrdom! Don't condemn yourself to this kind of life! What you don't
realize, what you don't really understand, is what
money really means. There's no end to it. Millions
upon millions of francs. And power. Power beyond
conception. The power of France. Name anything
. . . anything at all. The moment we are rid of
La Croix you can have the SDECE. Even a ministry . . ."

"Good Lord, Jacques, now what would I do
with all that power and all that money?"

Jacques grabbed his arm. "You're not even
human! Be man enough to be outraged about
me and your wife!"

"Outraged? A little. Hurt? A great deal. A man?
I first became a man the day I learned about my
wife and I knew I had the compassion to forgive
her. I was going to make a dramatic exit by spitting in your face but it's a waste of good spittle."

André walked out.

(21)

ROBERT PROUST retrieved the letters from his
private post box at the Capucines Station and
rushed back to the privacy of his apartment. Two
letters—one to the President, the other a copy

addressed to him. His fingers tore at the envelope of the copy clumsily, and he unfolded it with a shaking hand and read:

October 30, 1963
Le Président de la République
Élysée Palace
Paris, France
My Dear Monsieur le Président,
   As of this date I resign my mission.
   However, I resign in protest. I do not defect to any enemy or ally. I resign as a Frenchman. I remain a Frenchman with the right to return and to serve honorably as soon as I am able.
   I accuse you of refusal to answer to the charges of infiltration of the French Government by a Soviet Union espionage ring known by the code name of Topaz.
   I suggest that you, personally, have been the subject of Soviet Disinformation supplied to you by Topaz No. 1. His code name is Columbine and he is your Executive Aide, Jacques Granville.
   I deplore the return to an archaic foreign policy that has led to the destruction of France twice in this century.
   I condemn your scheme to abandon NATO and the combined security of the Western world.
   I will not, in all conscience, serve France under your orders to commit espionage against the United States of America.
   I warn you and the world of the monstrous plot to create anarchy and deliver France to a Communist conspiracy after your death.
   I love France as you claim to love France, and I say you have betrayed France to further your personal ambitions.
   Long live France!

                                        André Devereaux

(22)

Pierre La Croix arranged himself before his desk as his late and highly personal mail and messages were set in place for him to read before retiring. He sipped the coffee beside him and went into an exaggerated reading posture to get his eyes close to the paper.

The third envelope in the stack was unmarked except for his name. He turned it over, back and front, then put the silver letter opener into the fold and ripped the envelope open. He looked puzzled an instant at the handwritten letter, for his orders were to have all written material typed and in capitals for easier reading.

It was the resignation of André Devereaux.

When he was finished, his hand slowly pulled off the thick glasses. A terrible cold sweat swept over him as he grunted aloud, "Devereaux!" Almost the last of those who dared stand up to him. Damn Devereaux!

How long ago had the young man sat unflinching before him? His words . . . now they taunted. . . . "If you will look honestly and deeply, perhaps you will admit your feeling about America is one of extreme jealousy and hatred. It can be used by men who understand this. *I beg of you, don't let those around you distort and twist your feelings into a conspiracy against the democracies.*"

Pierre La Croix's fist cracked the desk. "La Croix is not used! La Croix uses! Damned old fool," he uttered harshly to himself.

But all that really mattered to him now was to protect his place in history. Damned if he would go out in disgrace, in scandal, a laughingstock. A pawn used, as he had played others for pawns all his life. No, he would not go out like that. Not after what he had done for France. No, not after he had returned France to greatness. No stupid little affair would dethrone him. France would never know.

The letter in the great ashtray blackened

around the edges and curled and blazed. As he watched it disintegrate, the terrible words ran over and over. . . . Old age is a shipwreck . . . old age is a shipwreck . . . old age is a shipwreck. . . .

(23)

IT WAS A pleasant spring day. That certain magic of Paris and the Champs Élysées had Michael Nordstrom all but tranquilized. From his table at a sidewalk café he could observe in depth the march of slender and shapely legs, poodles, spike heels, and wiggling backsides. He finished his glass of wine and turned to Per Nosdahl, his Norwegian ININ counterpart.

"I keep telling old Liz I'll bring her to Paris some spring. You know, Per, strictly a vacation, no business . . . whatever the hell a vacation happens to be."

The restaurant's captain approached. "Mr. Nordstrom?"

"Yes?"

"Telephone for you, sir."

"Be right back," he said, folding his napkin and following the captain into the building. Inside, the orchestra played "Paris in the Spring" for the lingering luncheon diners.

The captain pointed to a phone booth across the lobby.

"Thanks," he said and closed the door behind him. "Nordstrom."

"Do you know who this is?" the muffled voice of André Devereaux asked.

"Yes, I know."

"I may need help."

"I will if I can. . . . I don't know."

404

"I'll be at the Louvre, looking at the statue of the Winged Victory. That may be our only victory . . . en route to heaven."

"I'll be there."

Mike hung up and moved his large frame quickly to the outdoor tables. "I've got to go," he apologized to Per Nosdahl. "I've got to say goodbye to an old friend."

"Is your old friend in trouble?" Per Nosdahl asked.

"Yes, I'm afraid so."

"Are you going to be able to help him?"

"I swear . . . I just don't know."

"Please give him my heartfelt wishes," Per Nosdahl said.

"Yes, I'll do that."

Michael Nordstrom went to the curb and hailed a taxi.

The driver dropped the flag, fell into the stream of traffic, and glanced in his rearview mirror.

"You are an American?" he asked.

"Yes."

"Congratulations."

"For what?"

"Just this minute I heard the news. The Russians have surrendered. They are going to take the missiles out of Cuba. . . . Eh, you are tough guys, like cowboys."

"Sometimes."

"Where to, Monsieur?"

"The Louvre."

ABOUT THE AUTHOR

LEON URIS, born in Baltimore in 1924, left high school to join the Marine Corps. In 1950, Esquire magazine bought an article from him—and it encouraged him to begin work on a novel. The result was his acclaimed bestseller *Battle Cry*. *The Angry Hills*, a novel set in war-time Greece, was his second book. As a screen writer and then newspaper correspondent, he became interested in the dramatic events surrounding the rebirth of the state of Israel. This interest led to *Exodus*, his monumental success which has been read by millions of people. From one of the episodes in *Exodus* came *Mila 18*, the story of the heroic uprising of Jewish fighters in the Warsaw Ghetto. *Exodus Revisited*, a work of nonfiction, presents the author's feeling for the land and the people of Israel. Mr. Uris is also the author of *Armageddon, Topaz, QB VII, Trinity* and (with his wife, Jill) *Ireland: A Terrible Beauty*—all sensational bestsellers.

At present, Leon and Jill Uris live in Aspen, Colorado.